HE GATHERED HER IN HIS ARMS

Richard forgot all his vows not to touch her. And with his first caress Heather's pulse quickened, and she gave herself up to the fierce emotions raging through her, answering his kisses ardently, trembling as his lips traced a path of fire across her eager flesh. . . .

"Love me, Richard," she cried, her body responding with a will of its own. And then there was only ecstasy, deep currents flooding her, drowning her in a sea of desire. . . .

FLAME OF DESIRE

SIGNET  ONYX

JOURNEY TO ROMANCE

(0451)

☐ **MIDNIGHT STAR by Catherine Coulter.** British heiress Chauncey FitzHugh had come to San Francisco to ruin Delaney as he had financially ruined her father back in 1850. She had plotted to reject his fiery advances, but even as her mind commanded resistance, her desire exploded. She pulled him to her . . . tenderly whispering the name of this man she had sworn to hate. . . . (142977—$3.95)

☐ **THE REBEL AND THE ROSE by Joan Wolf.** The handsome Virginian made Lady Barbara Carr shiver with fear and desire. He was her new husband, a stranger, wed to her so his wealth could pay her father's debts. And Alan Maxwell had never wanted any woman the way he wanted this delicate English lady. . . . (145372—$3.95)

☐ **FIRES OF DESTINY by Linda Barlow.** He wanted her desperately—Alexandra could feel it with every sweet, slow, deepening kiss. That was why Roger Trevor, Protestant heir to the Baron of Chilton, had met her at the ancient cottage . . . why she, a Catholic woman on her way to Mary Tudor's court, had stayed after he warned her to run from him, after he told her he could never marry her. . . . (400011—$3.95)

☐ **FLAME OF DESIRE by Katherine Vickery.** The sheltered daughter of London's richest silk merchant, Heather Bowen had known such fierce desire only in her dreams until she met the dark, handsome Richard Morgan. Through the storms of a land divided by war, Heather burned hungrily for him, and Richard reached out with all his masculine power to claim her. . . . (400070—$3.95)

Prices slightly higher in Canada.

Buy them at your local bookstore or use this convenient coupon for ordering.

NEW AMERICAN LIBRARY,
P.O. Box 999, Bergenfield, New Jersey 07621

Please send me the books I have checked above. I am enclosing $________ (please add $1.00 to this order to cover postage and handling). Send check or money order—no cash or C.O.D.'s. Prices and numbers are subject to change without notice.

Name____________________________________

Address____________________________________

City______________State______________Zip Code__________

Allow 4-6 weeks for delivery.
This offer is subject to withdrawal without notice.

Flame of Desire

Katherine Vickery

AN ONYX BOOK
NEW AMERICAN LIBRARY

This book is dedicated to my mother, Marcia Hockett, who so diligently aided me in the research for this work and encouraged me in this endeavor.

A special thank-you to my family, who have been very supportive, and to my editor, Hilary Ross, for her encouragement and guidance.

NAL BOOKS ARE AVAILABLE AT QUANTITY DISCOUNTS WHEN USED TO PROMOTE PRODUCTS OR SERVICES. FOR INFORMATION PLEASE WRITE TO PREMIUM MARKETING DIVISION, NEW AMERICAN LIBRARY, 1633 BROADWAY, NEW YORK, NEW YORK 10019.

Copyright © 1986 by Kathryn Lynn Kramer

All rights reserved

Onyx is a trademark of New American Library.

SIGNET, SIGNET CLASSIC, MENTOR, ONYX, PLUME, MERIDIAN AND NAL BOOKS are published by New American Library, 1633 Broadway, New York, New York 10019

First Printing, September 1986

1 2 3 4 5 6 7 8 9

PRINTED IN THE UNITED STATES OF AMERICA

Doubt thou the stars are fire;
  Doubt that the sun doth move;
Doubt truth to be a liar;
  But never doubt I love.

—Shakespeare, *Hamlet,* II, 2

Author's Note

Under the Tudor reign the changes in England were drastic: socially, politically, and theologically. The Rome-dominated Middle Ages gave way to a new era of national expansion and sovereignty.

During the reign of Henry VIII the Catholic Church was crippled, then abolished as the absolute power of the Church was replaced by the absolute power of the King. With the seizure of church property, including almshouses, aid to the poor was abolished. At the same time, the decline of the feudal system and feudal lord gave way to the world of the merchant and the growth of industry and commerce. People flooded into towns to seek employment, thus expanding cities beyond their medieval walls. It was a time of the rise of the middle class and redistribution of wealth. Merchants and others of the middle class could now buy offices once held by nobles and in turn were resented deeply by the nobility. If money is the root of all evil, surely that evil had changed hands.

Edward VI had the potential to be a great king, but tragically he died at the age of fifteen after a brief reign. During his rule he was victimized by his guardians in their struggle for power and wealth. During Edward VI's short reign, however, the English church developed its strong Protestant roots, roots so strong that no subsequent reverse action was able to dislodge them.

Not a desire to return to Catholicism but the sense of justice to see the rightful Tudor heir succeed to the throne inspired the people of England to support Mary Tudor and resist Northumberland. But to Mary's mind, it was a sign the English people wanted to return to the old faith, a faith that she had suffered for and thus felt it her sacred mission to restore.

In the New World Spanish explorers had discovered new avenues of wealth which poured gold into Spain. England wanted her share and greatly feared this powerful Catholic empire and the threat that arose with the marriage of its Queen Mary to Philip of Spain. That Mary was half-Spanish (her mother being Catherine of Aragon, her grandparents Queen Isabella and King Ferdinand) added to their fears, thus turning the tide from support of Mary to feelings against her.

Mary has been greatly maligned in being called "Bloody Mary." Her conduct in the early months of her reign shows more lenience and tolerance than other rulers of her time, but she was transformed, by adversity and threats to her sovereignty and life, into one of the most hated of English queens, alienating England from Rome as surely as had her father. She burned more men and women for their opinions and beliefs than any contemporary monarchs, including Spain's during the Inquisition. At her death England accepted eagerly the new faith which she had tried so hard to destroy. Her half-sister, Elizabeth, learned from Mary's mistakes and became the beloved Queen Elizabeth under whose influence the "Golden Age of England" flourished.

My story is political rather than theological, as two lovers—he of the nobility and she a merchant's daughter—are swept up into the tumult of the times, fighting the raging flames of hatred which threaten their desire.

I

The Maiden and the Rebel

London

Maidens' hearts are always soft:
Would that men's were truer!
—William C. Bryant, song

1

THE SLENDER TAPERS flickered in the wisp of the breezes which swept through the palace from the open windows, casting eerie shadows against the walls of the great hall. In the bedchamber all was silent. No one breathed a word as the white-haired court physician bent over the frail, pathetically thin body of the suffering boy-king, Edward.

Richard Morgan could hear his own heart thundering in the noiseless room as his eyes stared at the face of this king, this clever and beloved boy who might very well have been a great king. Henry VIII's long-awaited son had become king at the age of nine, a king of personal charm and great intellect, the hope of a nation in the throes of great change. Richard had been his friend and confidant, in spite of their differences, and the king had trusted him and looked upon him as the elder brother he had never had. Now the king was dying—of this Richard Morgan was certain, and there was nothing he could do to ease the boy's pain.

"You should have called me sooner," Richard could hear the physician saying. He watched as the doctor drew a sandglass from his bag with which to take the young king's pulse.

Damn Northumberland! he thought, looking in the duke's direction, wondering if the rumors were true that Northumberland, that ambitious upstart, had poisoned the boy. Was it the concoctions of the old woman the duke had brought in to cure the king that were finally taking his life? He would never know. He and many others could only wonder.

Rising to his feet, the physician opened his mouth and Richard knew before that wise man spoke what words he would utter. "The king is dead!"

"Lord have mercy upon his soul," Richard whispered, crossing himself despite Northumberland's frown. Looking at the discolored skin, at the pain-twisted face of Edward, he felt unmanly tears sting his eyes at the memory of the suffering the poor young man had borne these last months. "At last, my poor king, it is done."

Turning his head, Richard looked again at Northumberland, wondering how long it would be before he made his grab for the throne. Would he at least give Edward a proper burial?

As if sensing Richard Morgan's thoughts, the Duke of Northumberland turned his cold beady eyes upon him, staring at him as if to warn him to hold his tongue.

"I do not want one word of what has happened here tonight to leave this room," his raspy voice whispered. "Silence is my order and I will have none disobey."

Never one to be intimidated by this swaggering reptile, Richard Morgan spoke out at once. "The Princess Mary must be told about this immediately!"

"No!" Northumberland was to have none of this. He had fought too hard to see his dreams realized to have them spoiled now. Rising from his chair next to the sickbed, he stood before his antagonist. "It is not Mary's business to know as of yet."

Anger coiled in Richard's stomach. He started to speak again, to tell this viper what he thought of him, but thought better of it. A show of temper now would do Mary no good. In his heart he knew what was afoot. Northumberland had married the Lady Jane Grey to his son at the end of May in secret and had cajoled the dying king to draw up his will naming her as his heir. That the old king, Henry, had declared both of his daughters illegitimate, at one time or another, to suit his own interests, made it possible for such a thing to happen. Richard cursed the name of Henry for doing such a thing.

A roar of thunder ripped through the silence of the room, causing all within to shudder. A streak of light flared into the death chamber, casting a glow on the paintings hung upon the walls. It was as if for a moment they came to life to issue their judgment.

" 'Tis just a storm," Northumberland said all too quickly, as if for just a moment he feared otherwise. He moved to the window to look upon the dark gray of the fading day, already making his plans.

"What are we to do? What are we to do?" piped up a short, balding man standing beside Northumberland. Before he would answer, Northumberland motioned for the other onlookers to leave the room. Moving into the shadows, Richard attuned his ears to the answer.

"Why summon our dear departed sovereign's sweet sisters." Northumberland answered with a smile. Looking about the room to make certain that all had left and feeling himself to be safe, he voiced his plan. "We will bid them come to London to see their brother ere he dies." His laughter sounded menacing and Richard could have no doubt as to what was planned. A trap. He must warn Mary Tudor. He must. A sense of justice overcame him, a desire to see the rightful Tudor heir succeed to the throne. Mary.

Hurrying out of the room, away from the hall, down the steps of the palace, Richard glanced behind him. He was being followed. Undoubtedly the duke would take no chance of his plans being spoiled. It would be prison or worse were Richard to be caught. He winced as a thunderclap illuminated his fleeing form.

"There he is. After him!" The voices echoed in his ears as he fled from the danger which stalked him, searching desperately for a place to hide.

* * *

Rain pelted through the open window as Heather Bowen reached out to close the shutters of her bedchamber window. Such a storm! It seemed to rend the very heavens. Brushing several strands of her damp dark red hair from her eyes, she stepped back from the window as a sudden streak of lightning shot through the sky like a flame. What was it about storms that so unnerved her? Ever since she was a child they had frightened her. Was it because they seemed to be a portent of misfortune? Perhaps.

Drops of rain glistened on her thick lashes and brows and she reached up to wipe them away. "Poor Mother and Father, to be caught in this." They were across town visiting her father's sister and she worried lest they be caught in the fury raging outside. If only there were something she could do. But there was not. She would just have to wait until they returned and hope that the dampness would not cause them to take a chill.

As she walked across the room, away from the storm's fury, her eyes caught her image in the small silver mirror upon the wall. Brushing her long hair in an effort to dry its tangled curls, she wondered where she had come by this color, a dark red, almost mahogany. Not from her mother, nor from her father. And the eyes. Gray, not the blue or brown of her parents. Her face shape, however, was like her mother's—oval with a slight widow's peak at the forehead; and the nose, straight but with a slight tilt at the tip which gave her a haughty look. She smiled at her image, showing her straight white teeth.

"Well, at least I can say that I am no foundling." She laughed, for the features of Blythe were clearly reflected for all to see.

A boom of thunder caused her to shudder and she thought how much she hated storms. She sat upon the large canopied bed, and her hand brushed the soft fur of Saffron, her tabby cat. They would comfort each other as this tempest raged about them. The animal purred loudly as she stroked it, and for a moment both cat and young woman were content.

"Sometimes I think you are my best friend, Saffron," she said wistfully. Her father was always busy with his books and her mother occupied with the household. They had little time for her.

Another clap of thunder sounded through the night and Heather reached out for her cat as it jumped from the bed. It was not the storm, however, that had caused the sudden movement, but a mouse. A small brown mouse had caught the animal's eye. Darting to and fro, it managed to escape the claws of its pursuer, finding safety in a large hole in the wall. For several minutes the cat held vigil, green eyes watching intently for the mouse to leave its sanctuary.

"Not quite fast enough, Saffron. You let that one get away. Perhaps I feed you too much. Soon you will be as fat as Father."

A noise from the stairway, in the direction of her father's storehouse, seemed to startle the cat, and Heather watched as the animal bounded down the stairs to investigate just as another loud noise sounded from below.

Thinking that the wind had blown open one of the shutters in the storeroom, Heather ran down the stairs in her bare feet to investigate. In the dark she stubbed her toe more than once, uttering a curse beneath her breath that would have caused her father to severely rebuke her.

At last reaching the first floor, which housed her merchant father's storehouse and counting room, she found and closed the open window, latching it securely. Walking about the room filled with bolts and bolts of her father's finest cloth, she let her hands caress the smooth brocades and silks to ensure that the blowing rain had done no serious damage. Her father was one of London's wealthiest merchants and a man respected in the city. He would be greatly distressed if his merchandise were ruined.

A sudden noise behind her caused Heather to start, and for just a moment she felt frightened. "Who is there?" she demanded, only to be met with silence. The soft brush of fur against her leg caused her to laugh at her fear. "Saffron, what are you up to now, you silly cat?" It was only the cat!

Another noise, the sound of someone bumping into a chair, told her that she was not alone. A chill of fear swept over her, but before she could react, Heather found herself held captive by large arms which encircled her waist. She opened her mouth to scream, but before she could make a sound, a large hand clamped over her mouth, nearly smothering her.

2

HEATHER STRUGGLED IN the grasp of her captor. This was no dream, but a nightmare. She was in danger and there was no one to help her. The silence of the room was shattered by her throaty moans, which issued forth despite the hand over her mouth.

"M-m-m-m-m-m-m-m!"

"Be quiet! I mean you no harm," said a husky male voice. The musky masculine scent of him teased her nostrils as he held her tight.

In answer to his words Heather fought to free her arms, outraged to be held captive. She wanted to lash out at her tormentor as Saffron might do, but she was no match for the strength of the arms which held her.

"You're a lively one," the voice said softly, holding her all the more firmly. "Hold still. I won't hurt you. I just want to take care that you don't give me away."

Heather ignored his words, struggling until she was exhausted. Whoever this man was, he certainly seemed to be a strong brute. She could feel the muscles of his body through the thin linen of her gown as he held her close against him. Her full, firm breasts were crushed against his hard chest. It was shocking to feel a man's body like this, every inch of their bodies caressing so intimately. Struggling against the overwhelming masculinity of him, she at last grew quiet and he relaxed his hold.

"I'm going to take my hand from your mouth, but I warn you: if you scream . . ." He pulled his hand away and although she yearned to call for help, she remained quiet. There was no reason to cause herself injury. His speech was that of a well-bred man without any trace of accent. Certainly then he was no thief or ruffian from the street. Perhaps if she did as this man told her, he would leave her alone.

"Ah, that's a good girl."

Heather had the urge to utter a curse at this man who dared to take such liberties with her person, but she wisely held back from the temptation. Instead she asked, "Who are you?"

Laughter was her answer, a low rumbling sound like the thunder that brought forth the rain. How she wished that there was some sort of light so that she could get a look at this lout.

Again she asked, "Who are you?"

"You're a bold one, lass."

"Why are you in my father's storeroom?" She judged this man to be very tall from the way he held her, and thus she directed her voice upward. "Are you here to *steal* from us?"

She regretted her words as she felt the arms which held her tighten in anger. "No, I have never stolen anything in my life!" The words were said with a gruff tone which was almost a growl.

"Then why . . . ?" Immediately she knew the answer. This man was running away from someone, hiding here in the darkened storeroom. He must have slipped through the open window to seek refuge among the wool and silks. From whom was he running, and why?

"I'd like to answer your question. However, at this moment I have other things more pressing to consider." The husky voice of the man sounded tired, depressed, as if somehow he wanted to forget something which saddened him. She could feel the rise and fall of his chest, the warmth of his breath as he sighed, and she tried again to separate her body from this heated pressure which made it nearly impossible to think clearly.

"Let me go," she implored. "I won't run away."

He seemed to hesitate as if weighing whether or

not she could be trusted. "Do you swear by all that's holy that you will not scream or try to leave this room or do anything to put me in danger?"

"I so swear," she answered, anxious to be away fron this hard male body whose nearness was causing her senses to act so traitorously. Was it fear which was making her heart pound so violently? Or was it something else?

He let her go, his hand gently brushing the tips of her breasts as he did so. Was it by accident that he touched her with such familiarity? She decided that it was.

"Is there an oil lamp down here?" the husky voice asked. "I'm tired of this darkness."

"Yes, it's suspended from the west wall by a chain." Somehow she would feel much safer in the light, and in truth her curiosity was piqued to see this man.

Heather could hear the sound of his footsteps as he walked in that direction, and wondered if she should flee, run for the door and shout for help. She decided against such a move for she had given her word and somehow she sensed that this man would not harm her. He had said as much and would surely have done so by now were that his intent.

"Why, I nearly feel sorry for him," she whispered. "He, a fugitive!"

The scratching of flint against iron told her that the man was starting a fire. Soon the room was aglow with light from the oil lamp and Heather's eyes squinted at the glare.

"You're beautiful. I had no idea," came the voice she was becoming accustomed to. Heather looked up through her long dark lashes at the imposing figure who spoke.

The man was tall and lean, but well-muscled with a strength about him that was almost overpowering. This man was no thief. He walked toward her with a swagger which told her that he was used to being in a position of leadership. His hair was a midnight black, his face half-hidden by a mustache and short clipped beard, yet she could see that it was a handsome face with a strong jaw and chiseled nose.

"What is your name?" he asked of her, looking at her with piercing blue eyes, eyes fringed by dark lashes which surprisingly did not make him look the least bit feminine despite their length.

She met his gaze for a long moment, unable to look away. "Heather. My name is Heather," she murmured as if in a trance.

He startled her with a smile. "Heather. It suits you. Like the heather which grows on the hill, you are lovely." And indeed he thought her to be so as his eyes appraised her. She had felt so soft in his arms. He should have left this place before now, as soon as he deemed it safe beyond the door, and yet he had not. Why? Because somehow he had wanted to get a look at the woman with the soft curves and the pleasing voice. He was not disappointed; indeed his vision of what she would look like paled beside her beauty.

His eyes looked into hers. What color were her eyes? Gray, blue, green? They seemed to take on a different hue each time he looked into their depths. And her hair. The red tresses tumbled to her waist. Never had he seen such a shade, the color of the finest wine.

Heather fought to regain her composure and regarded him coolly, choosing to ignore his compliments. "I have told you my name, sir. What is your name?"

He shook his head. "It would not do to tell you. I'm sorry. I wish that things were different."

Her eyes swept over him, taking in his manner of dress. Surely no pauper or vagabond, this one. Dressed in plum-colored velvet doublet, parchment-yellow jerkin, gold-colored trunk hose, plum hose, brown leather belt and shoes, his fingers bedecked with rings, he was hardly dressed like a man on the run.

"If you cannot tell me who you are, at least tell me what it is you are running from," she insisted.

"Enemies of England," he answered, clenching his jaw in anger. "From him who would cast aside our rightful queen."

"Queen?" Heather was confused. There was no queen. Edward was not married, and his mother had died at his birth. Whom, then, did this man speak of?

"Mary Tudor." Gently he touched her arm. "The king is dead. He died an hour ago. The Duke of Northumberland seeks to place the Lady Jane Grey, his daughter-in-law, upon the throne to feed his own ambitions." Somehow he wanted to confide all to this lovely young woman who stood before him, but instead he stopped his prattle.

Heather shook her head in dismay. The king dead? It was hard to believe, yet it had been rumored that he was gravely ill, perhaps dying, several months ago. Edward had been held up at a window of the palace so that the crowds outside could see him, to know that he lived. The pale, skinny boy had hardly inspired the Londoners with confidence. But now he *was* dead, or so this man said.

"I don't believe you." Why had she not heard the bells, the mourning bells tolling the news? No, it wasn't true. "How dare you break into my father's home, hold me captive, and then expect me to believe such an outlandish story. Lady Jane Grey as queen. Absurd!"

"And yet I fear that it is true!"

Her eyes flashed with her ire. "Do you think me a fool? How would you know these secrets that no one else seems to know?"

"I was at the palace tonight when the king died. Believe me when I tell you what Northumberland plans. He is as sly as a weasel, as treacherous as a snake, and as ruthless as a vulture."

She looked at him with scrutiny. He had managed to put up a persuasive argument, yet the magnitude of the treachery Northumberland planned stunned her. What if he spoke the truth?

A loud banging at the door caused both Heather

and the man to cease their musing. Heather looked toward the portal with apprehension, knowing full well that it could mean this man's death were she to betray him. He no doubt would be in danger of losing his head to the executioner's ax were she to act rashly. She had the sudden urge to help him. Why? Why would she want to help a fugitive? She could not understand her feelings as she called out, "Coming."

What if he were a traitor, a rebel? What if he were lying to her? She should not shield him, screamed her brain; she could not betray him, whispered her heart.

Richard Morgan watched her walk to the door, knowing full well that he was at her mercy. In her white gown she looked like an angel, gliding gracefully toward his enemies. He ducked back into the shadows, wondering what his fate would be this night.

"Yes?" Heather whispered as she answered the door. She feared that her legs would give way beneath her, that her eyes would tell of her nervousness, her voice sounded choked with her emotions.

"Sorry to bother you, miss," an old man said curtly, looking past the door as if to examine each nook and cranny. "We're looking for a rebel, an enemy of the king. Nearly had him in our clutches, but the clever bastard escaped. Have you seen any men pass this way tonight?"

"No!" She did not falter for one moment in her answer. She fought to maintain every inch of her self-control so as not to give herself away, betray the tumult within her breast.

"Are you certain? We saw him headed this way." The man at the door looked back at his companions as if wondering if they should search this place.

"My dear sir, believe me when I tell you that I have not! My father, Thomas Bowen, gave me the strictest orders to keep this door locked and bolted during his absence and I am ever the dutiful daughter. With the exception of yourselves, I have seen no men here tonight. I fear you will have to look for your rebel elsewhere." She had lied for a stranger.

The old man took a step forward and for a moment Heather feared that he would search her father's house. In answer to the man's movement she closed the door, leaving it open only the span of a man's hand. "Please, sir. I am alone here. It would not be right . . ."

With a shrug the old man turned to walk away, satisfied that she spoke the truth. Why would she lie? Closing and bolting the door, Heather fought to calm her trembling. What would have been her punishment to be caught harboring an enemy of the Duke of Northumberland? She reached up to touch her neck, remembering those who had lost their heads in the past. She breathed a sigh and turned toward the dark-haired stranger, whose eyes were raking over her.

Richard Morgan feasted his eyes upon her for several moments. "Heather, how can I ever thank you? You have saved me from imprisonment or worse." He drew her to him, looking again at the lovely face before him. Her skin, he noticed, was unmarked by the freckles that usually accompanied hair of a dark red color. Were any eyes so large, any mouth so tempting?

Before Heather could make a sound, could answer his words of gratitude, his mouth claimed hers in a gentle kiss, yet a kiss that devastated her senses, engulfed her in a whirlpool of fiery sensations. Hadn't she wanted this to happen when first she had looked upon him? Yes, she thought, aware of her body now as she had never been before. Though her logic told her that she should pull away, she somehow found herself reaching up slim arms to draw him closer, wanting to savor this tender assault. A groan was her answer as his mouth plundered hers with lips which seemed to brand her very soul. In all her dreams she had never thought a kiss could be so overpowering, yet so gentle, igniting a fire in her blood.

His lips parted hers, searching out the honey of

her mouth. The passion of their kiss, the fierce hunger he felt at her nearness, shook Richard. He had kissed fair maidens before, but never had a kiss excited him so. His arms tightened around her, his mouth sensuously explored the inner warmth of her lips, his fingers stroked the softness of her neck and shoulders. How he wished that he could stay with her this night. It was as if she made him forget who he was, the danger he faced, all that he must do. How could he leave her now?

I must! he thought, before this spark between us flames too high. Reluctantly he pulled away from her, longing for the touch of her as soon as she had left his arms.

His sudden withdrawal startled Heather. Coming back to her senses, she stiffened, regretting having let this bold man be so familiar. What was wrong with her? She had always managed to keep the local swains at arm's length. That she wanted him to kiss her again, hold her again, mortified her and so she hid behind a veil of false anger.

"You are overbold, sir!" She backed away from him but he caught up with her in three swift strides.

"Nay, do not flee from me, Heather. I apologize for my actions, but truly you have touched my heart."

She did not answer him but he could see by the look in her eyes that she was not really angry. Lord, she was beautiful. He ached to hold her, make love to her, but she deserved much more than one night of passion. This was no tavern trollop, but a woman of breeding.

I would give all my worldly possessions to stay, he thought. But he knew that he could not. There was danger if he did not warn Mary in time. Tempted by her full pouting mouth, her tender curves, he quickly walked to the door before he succumbed to his desires. He had not the *right* to claim her.

Looking out into the night, he could see no sign of those who stalked him. His pursuers had quickly vanished into the night. It appeared to be safe out on the cobbled streets of the city. Seeing that it was still stormy, he sought his cloak.

Turning to look at Heather one more time, he whispered, "Good-bye. Such a lonely word."

"Good-bye?" she repeated, raising a trembling hand to her mouth. She wanted to take back her harsh words, to ask him to stay, if only for a moment longer, but instead she remained silent, watching as he stepped out into the dark and rain as suddenly as he had come into her life. Would she ever forget him? She knew that she would not. Closing the door, she knew that somehow she would never quite be the same again.

Running to the courtyard, Richard Morgan quickly untethered a stallion, not knowing or caring to whom the animal belonged. Mounting the horse, he spurred the beast onward, away from the dangers of London.

3

SITTING BEFORE THE fire, clad in her chemise, a blanket pulled close around her to ward off the chill, Heather stared out the window watching as the rain splattered against the sill. She shivered, but not from the cold, nor from fear; instead another emotion rocked her body as she remembered what had taken place between the stranger and herself. Touching her fingers to her lips, she remembered the kiss and gently licked her lips as if to taste again of its sweetness.

"I know not even his name," she murmured, hungry for knowledge of him. Meeting him had made her clearly realize just how monotonous her life was. She had known before that there must be more to life than ledgers, cooking pots, and stitchery, but his entrance into her life had emphasized how dreary her existence was. He was handsome, so handsome.

"Listen to me. I sound like some infatuated fledgling schoolgirl," she chided, straightening upright in her chair. She was hardly that at nineteen. Since girlhood she had been older than her years, thrust early into the world of finance and markets; but in matters of the heart, perhaps she was untried. Her father seemed loath to part with her, no doubt fearing that he would have to hire someone else to do the bookkeeping and chores. Many local merchants had asked for her hand but he would not consider them rich enough to suit him and sent them on their way. Thus it was that Heather was considered a "spinster," albeit a comely one.

Leaning back in the chair again, wrapping her

arms around her knees, Heather curled up in a ball and closed her eyes as if to envision again the face of the man she had met tonight. Lost in the haze of her dreams, she was lulled to sleep by the beat of the rain on the roof.

A loud pounding woke her with a start. It was her father's voice that she heard yelling in anger at the top of his lungs. Casting the blanket aside, she ran down the stairs to open the thick wooden door. The force of the wind slammed the door against the wall and Heather stared into the frowning face of her portly father.

"God's blood, girl, what took you so long?"

"I'm sorry, Father." The mist of the rain caressed her face, cooling her flaming cheeks.

"Now, Thomas. Heather was probably asleep. Don't be so harsh with her." The voice was that of Heather's mother, a woman with gray hair and a figure now plump in her fortieth year.

Husband and wife stepped into the large hall, soaking the floor as the rain dripped from their sodden garments. Still in her fog of dreams, Heather stood watching as the drops mingled to form a large puddle.

"What addles your brain, daughter? Get something to clean this mess up." Stamping his feet, her father sought to wipe the mud from his shoes. "Soaked to the skin, I am, and this my finest gown." His hands brushed at the velvet and fur as if to undo what had been done.

Heather sought several large towels from the kitchen and bent down to mop up the mess on the floor, knowing well how quickly her father's anger could be fanned. When that was done she stood up and reached to take her father's fur-trimmed outer gown and soft-crowned black velvet cap with its upturned brim. Being a merchant eager to display his wealth, he wore a floor-length gown that was quite bulky to manage.

"Don't drag it on the floor, girl."

Finding the nearest peg, Heather sought to hang

the garment carefully, but she had no doubt that it was damaged beyond repair. Velvet could be ruined and matted by moisture. Her mother stepped up beside her, hanging her hooded cloak next to the gown. Her eyes were soft and gentle, blue eyes which seemed to hold a sadness that Heather had never been able to understand.

"Your father nearly got trampled by some horsemen chasing a fugitive. That is why he is so out of sorts, dear. Don't let his gruff manner upset you." Blythe Bowen smiled her sad smile.

Heather's heart lurched in her breast. "They didn't catch him, did they?" she asked all too quickly before measuring her words. The thought of the rebel being killed was disturbing.

Her father grunted in anger. "I daresay not. At least not then. Bumbling fools, I say. Northumberland should have their heads." He headed up the stairs and for the solar, that living and dining room combined, where the family spent many hours. Heather and Blythe Bowen followed close behind.

"Ah . . . warmth at last." Rubbing his hands before the fire, Thomas Bowen at last smiled.

This time Heather weighed her words. "Have you heard any news about the king?"

He looked at her with surprise, rubbing his rather large nose. "No. Should I have?"

Heather averted her eyes. "I heard that he . . . that he was very ill." Again the fear nagged at her brain that perhaps the dark-haired rebel had lied to her. "Perhaps even dead."

"Dead!" her father thundered. "Where would you hear such a churlish lie as that?" His ruddy complexion took on an even redder glow.

Heather did not answer. What could she say? Could she tell her parents that she had heard the words from a man who held her captive, a man in danger of losing his life, a man she had helped escape?

Why has the word of the king's death not been heard by now? she wondered. Surely it should have been shouted from the rooftops. Had the dark-haired man tricked her so that she would not denounce him, playing on her sympathy with his charms? Was he even now laughing at the ploy, at the simple merchant's daughter who had fallen so easily for his words?

Thomas Bowen answered his own question for her. "Jabbering servants. Always letting their tongues rattle in their heads." He raised one eyebrow and grimaced. "God help us if Edward were to die. Mary Tudor, indeed. A Catholic upon the throne again would put this land to ruin."

Seeking to soothe her husband's ill temper, Blythe Bowen stepped forward with her cool and gentle hands to stroke his graying hair, what there was left of it. Thomas Bowen was bald on top, though hardly anyone but family and servants were aware of that fact as he usually covered his shiny dome with a hat.

"Don't fret so, Thomas, everything will be all right," Blythe Bowen's voice crooned.

Heather thought that they made an odd pair, her mother taller than her father and slimmer by comparison to his considerable bulk. She looked at her mother and could nearly imagine what a beauty she must have been once. Now her face seemed to be lined with sadness, a touch of melancholy. Why? She seemed to be devoted to Thomas Bowen, but Heather could not help wondering if she loved him. Thomas Bowen could often be a difficult man, as Heather well knew.

As a child Heather had tried hard to please him, only to fall victim to his seeming resentment of her. Were she to speak her mind he would call her defiant and disrespectful. Chiding her for her temper, her only fault, he more often than not sought to break her spirit. Now as a woman she fought against her bitterness toward him, being always the dutiful daughter despite his constant demands and miserly ways. He was her father and she longed to be able to love him. If only he showed her more affection. She bowed her head meekly to him as a good obedient daughter was expected to do even when he treated her harshly, but all the while her eyes blazed in secret anger.

People made the comment that they did not know where Heather came by her good looks, certainly not from Thomas, and more than one guest in the house had laughingly quipped that Heather's gentle manner was obviously not patterned after Thomas' temperament. Was it that she was so unlike him that he begrudged her?

"Are you hungry, Thomas?" It was Heather's mother who spoke. It was quiet in the household, the two servants already abed.

"Famished. My sister is such a stingy hostess. One helping is not enough for me."

Heather helped her mother assemble some of the leftovers from the noon meal—cheese, bread, meat—then watched as Thomas Bowen ate the food greedily, licking his fingers when he was through. Leaning back in his chair, he smiled in contentment. Gone now was the lion and in its place was the lamb. His thoughts seemed far away as he gazed into space, finally saying, "All in all it has been a good year. Northumberland is an able protector, not like that fool Somerset. We are well rid of him, king's uncle or not. Too soft on the poor he was, and look what it brought us. Ket's rebellion. No, we are better off with Northumberland. Henry himself would be pleased by the strength of his administration."

Heather remembered the words the rebel had spoken, that the Duke of Northumberland was ambitious, that he planned to place his daughter-in-law, Lady Jane Grey, on the throne, and wondered at the truth of those words. She knew nothing about politics but sensed something sinister about the duke despite the fact that he had frequent business dealings with her father.

Could the Duke of Northumberland actually think to usurp the throne? Nearly all England took Mary's accession as inevitable and just. Would he dare to be so bold? Yes. Had he not seen to the execution of the king's own uncle, Edward Seymour, the Duke of

Somerset, grabbing more and more power until he was virtually all but the king now? From the talk that Heather had heard on the streets of London, the people hated Northumberland. No administration had ever been so loathed. Was it possible that he would seek to hide the news of the king's death?

Hoping to hear at least some of what was happening at the palace, she listened intently to her parents' conversation as she cleared the table, only to be disappointed as the tide of the talking turned to domestic matters.

"Thomas, a new carpet would make the house so much warmer," Blythe Bowen was saying, as if his better mood would loosen his purse. "Would you ask Jonathan if we could make arrangements with him to purchase one for us on his next trip?"

With his elbows firmly planted on the table, Thomas Bowen curled his lips up in a sneer as he looked daggers at his wife. "Good heavens, woman, I have just purchased three hundred acres of land and now must have it fenced to keep the sheep from wandering. That is an investment to put shillings in my pocket, not take them out. First things first, I always say."

Heather saw the look of disappointment in her mother's eyes but was not surprised by the old miser's answer. It was not that they did not have luxuries in their home, but that most of them were to make her father's life more comfortable or to impress his associates with his wealth. Sooner or later her mother would get her carpet, for Thomas Bowen was not one to be outdone and carpets were beginning to be seen in a few homes throughout the city.

"As you say, Thomas." As always, Blythe Bowen gave in to her husband without an argument.

Why does she not speak up to him? Heather wondered in frustration. Just once she would have liked to see her mother show more spirit. Wanting to be alone with her thoughts, Heather took her leave of her parents and climbed the stairs to her bedroom.

She would never be so docile with a man; this she vowed.

Padding on bare feet to the window to look out upon the night, to that cobbled street the dark-haired man had ridden down, she seemed to see his face before her. Closing the shutters tightly for the night, she walked to the fire and leaned her head back, trying to quench the flame in her blood that the memory of him sparked tonight. His hot, soft, exploring mouth and husky voice now tormented her with a yearning she could not quite understand. She imagined strong arms holding her, caressing her. She had never thought much about lovemaking before, but her curiosity was piqued by the encounter with the stranger.

Snuffing the candles, she slowly removed her chemise and undergarments, hanging up the clothes on the horizontal pole above the head of her bed. Standing beside the bed with her hair swirling about her shoulders, she ignored the chill of the night and let her long tresses tickle her back as she swayed from side to side.

The tolling of a bell startled her out of her reverie, the midnight bell. The spell was broken and for a moment Heather felt wicked to have been thinking in such a way about a man she scarcely knew. Getting under the covers, she pulled them up to her chin to bring warmth to her chilled body. She tried hard to push all thoughts of the man from her mind but could not, no matter how hard she tried. Tossing and turning on the straw-filled mattress, she had only her memories to comfort her, her memories and Saffron, who curled up at the foot of the bed.

Breathing softly, closing her eyes, Heather said a silent prayer for his safety and wished with all her heart that they would meet again.

4

RICHARD MORGAN RODE at a furious pace toward Hunsdon. The wind howled about him; the rain soaked him to the skin as he shivered against the chill and gathered his cloak about him in a futile effort to keep dry. He would not be daunted in his mission despite the misery, he vowed. His only concern was that he get to the Princess Mary before Northumberland or his cronies did.

"Mary," he whispered, his voice lost in the wind. "My queen." He knew well the dangers which lurked behind the bushes. Outlaws roamed the countryside, ambushing unwary travelers. And what of Northumberland? Was he even now following Richard?

More than once he looked behind him, watching for any sign that his enemy was following, and thought with relief that it did not appear that he was being pursued. At least for the time being.

At last the rain stopped as the fading sun tried desperately to come from behind the thick clouds and give to the earth its warmth. The condition of the road was deplorable, little more than bridle paths linking one village with another, and he soon decided that perhaps it would be safer and more comfortable to his aching backside to travel across the fields instead of the muddy road.

The night seemed to fly by as he galloped north, pushing at a furious pace. When he could stand no more, when his body was exhausted beyond endurance, he pulled at the reins to urge the horse to a halt. In the shelter of an old gnarled tree he gathered together twigs and leaves to make a soggy bed for himself. His eyes burned and throbbed from lack of sleep, yet sleep was long in coming to him, his mind instead haunted by the memory of a sweet smile, of hair the color of red wine, of skin as soft as velvet. The young woman came vividly to his mind and he thought of how lovely she had been. If only they had met under different circumstances, perhaps . . . But no, he had to forget her! There was no future for them despite the hunger he had felt when he held her in his arms.

Forget her? It was easier to say the words than to do the deed. "Sweet Heather," he whispered, aching to hold her in his arms again but sufficing himself with his warm woolen cloak. Dreaming of her, he drifted into a deep slumber.

The sound of cruel laughter awakened Richard from his sleep. Opening his eyes with a start, he found himself being surveyed by a grinning bearded man he knew all too well.

"Hugh Seton!"

The stocky brown-haired man took a step forward, hands placed upon his thick tree-trunk thighs, his cold brown eyes squinting against the light of the sun.

"Yes, it is I. Did you think none would stop you from your traitorous journey?"

Richard's eyes blazed as he sat up. He would not be called a traitor by this man or any other. " 'Tis you who are traitor, not I." He reached for his sword but he was not fast enough. The pressure of his enemy's blade pricked his shoulder.

"Move one inch and you are dead!" With a grace which belied his girth, Hugh Seton kicked Richard's weapon aside as if it were merely a twig. His eyes took on a wicked glint. "You don't know how long I have wanted to kill you! And now I can do so and be well rewarded."

Richard's eyes met his adversary's and he could see the hatred and jealousy blazing forth. If he did not want to breathe his last this day, he had to make good his escape.

"Rewarded by Northumberland?"

In reply the stocky man nodded his head, pressing the sword he held in hand so hard against Richard's arm that it drew blood. "I wonder how your head will look atop London Bridge." His mouth curled in a sneer.

Richard's eyes darted from the weapon which threatened him, to the sword which lay upon the ground, his sword. Was there any way to retrieve that blessed weapon without causing his death? Could he take this boasting braggart by surprise?

Seeing the direction of his glance, Hugh Seton once again gave vent to his mirth, a cruel, wicked sound more animal than human. "Oh, I think not, my friend. One false move from you will find this sword pierced through your heart."

Richard refused to cower before this man, this bully. He could not forget that it was by this man's lies that his uncle had been executed for treason. And all for what? Power. Such a fleeting treasure in these times.

"You are going to kill me anyway. Why not do it now?" He steeled himself for the thrust, his eyes blazing his hatred.

The other man shrugged. "I wait for Northumberland. He is due to meet with me before the sun is high in the sky. I want him to witness my act."

Hugh Seton's answer gave Richard Morgan new hope. He was not to meet his maker immediately. Taking a deep breath, he leaned away from the tip of the sword.

"Well, if you are not going to murder me, I daresay I'll return to my nap." He looked at his captor defiantly and was even so bold as to flash him a grin. "Please awaken me when our *guest* arrives." Closing his eyes, he feigned sleep as if finally giving in to his fate, as if resigned to death, perhaps even scoffing at the idea.

"I'll wipe that smile off your face when Northumberland joins us," was the reply. Richard could see his enemy's face turn red with rage as it had so many times when they were at each other's throats.

"We'll see," he said beneath his breath. Controlling his breathing, ignoring the pounding of his heart, Richard reached his left hand behind his back ever so slowly, clawing frantically at the earth, clutching up the precious substance. Opening one eye, he watched the short, stocky figure pacing the ground before him, his hand still clutching the executioner's sword. Moving with the rapidity of a striking snake, Richard flung the fistful of mud into the face of his hated captor, rolling away from the strike of the sword thrust blindly into the soft soil just inches away from Richard's head.

"Missed me, Seton!" he taunted.

"Damn you!" Hugh Seton swore violently as he wiped his brocaded sleeve across his eyes in an effort to regain his sight. Richard had just enough time to reach for and grip the hard hilt of his sword before the larger man struck out again. The blow was parried just in time.

"I have always been more than a match for you, Seton," he chided.

A cry of anger was his answer as the man lunged again, but as before, found his thrust parried. The sound of sword on sword rent the air as the two fought a furious battle, a test of strength and of skill.

Again and again Hugh Seton lunged, his anger at having been thwarted making him careless. Reacting to the warning of his senses, his sword arm swinging forward, Richard blocked each thrust, at last knocking his enemy's sword to the ground. The tables had turned quickly. Now it was Richard Morgan who held a sword at Seton's heart.

"Go ahead and kill me."

"I ought to kill you, Seton, but you are not worth endangering my soul. I think in time your own ambition will cause your death." Disarming his enemy, he stood before him, searching his face for any sign of his father in the man who claimed to be his bastard half-brother. He saw none, yet could not draw this man's blood. What if there was truth in his claim?

Reading his mind, Hugh Seton sneered. "You will not kill me, though you would do well to do so for I swear that someday I will cause you such pain that you will remember this day and wish you had drawn my blood." He wanted to say more but the sound of horses' hooves in the distance drew his attention. His small piggish eyes glanced in the direction whence they came. A smile touched his lips and Richard cringed in revulsion at this man who had taunted him since childhood. Although he did not want to shed his blood, he could not stand here and chatter while Northumberland even now rode toward them. He had to act, and act quickly, and thus, raising his sword, he aimed a blow with the side of the blade, rendering his enemy unconscious.

"I hope that I am not foolish in sparing you, Seton," Richard Morgan said between clenched teeth, bending over the still form. He had an overpowering urge to finish the job, to revenge his uncle and his father, but he instead held back. Murder was not in his blood. He would not stoop to Seton's level. Instead he mounted his horse to begin again his journey.

Richard rode at a furious pace now, threatened by the fact that Northumberland would by now have found his henchman Seton and would be following close behind. Only once did he stop, and then only briefly to quench his thirst.

Near the end of the day he entered a part of the land far different from that which he had traveled before. Gone now were the gently rolling hills, the wide meadows and moors; now steep rocky hills loomed in his path, bordered by swiftly rushing streams. The terrain slowed his pace and he fought his way over the stones and rocks. At last when he reached the top of the hill he shifted on his horse to look around.

"Northumberland!" he whispered, his voice hardly more than a croak. Frustration and alarm knifed through him like the sharpest dagger as he saw the approaching horsemen descending upon him. In their somber clothes of black and brown they looked like insects creeping over the hill. There were too many to fight; he had to escape.

Across the rocky hillside his horse galloped, toward the forest. Its leafy branches beckoned him like the arms of a lover as he fled his enemy.

5

RICHARD BENT CLOSE to the churning muscles of his horse as if to become one with the animal. He sought a firm grip on the reins as he guided the horse onward. His death sentence. That was what it would mean if he were caught. He could see the last rays of the sun fading behind the hilltops and knew the light would soon be extinguished, adding further safety. This gave him hope as he urged the stallion onward. He would beat Northumberland yet!

The sound of horses' hooves coming closer and closer echoed in his ears. He was drenched in perspiration from the strain and exertion of his ride, his heart was beating like a drum in his chest, yet he smiled, knowing that each moment he was getting closer to the forest. Once there he could seek the shelter of its dense foliage, double back, make a large circle, and emerge from the trees to take a different path to Hunsdon.

Feeling the pulsating rhythm of the horse's flanks beneath the high leather of his boots, he at last reached the foliage. Reining in his mount he hid behind a tall, stout tree, scarcely daring to breathe. From his position he could see the shadows of the men on horseback as they rode past him. He could hear their shouts, the plop of their horses' hooves, could nearly smell the sweat of man and beast as they passed him.

Ride, ride, you bastards! he thought. *For your journey will be all in vain.*

Only when he was certain that they were gone did

he come forth from his concealment to ride in the opposite direction. He knew a shortcut to Hunsdon, a dangerous one to be sure, but he had to take the chance. He had to reach Mary before Northumberland did, before the queen fell into the duke's clutches.

Using only one hand on the reins, clutching his sword in the other, Richard Morgan rode through the wilder nooks in the forest, that area where robbers and thieves were known to hide. His fancy velvet and brocade clothing would surely invite ambush, he thought, but he had to take the chance. Strangely enough, no such attack took place, although he could sense that he was being watched from behind many a tree. It came to mind that perhaps those who had admired his uncle, mourned his death, would leave the nephew alone to complete his journey. Right he was in his supposition, for he reached his destination safely, though not as quickly as he would have liked.

Dismounting his horse, Richard appraised his appearance. He was covered from head to foot with the dust of the road, hardly a fitting figure to stand before the queen, and yet, it could not be helped. Time was of the essence.

Taking the steps of the rambling brick manor two at a time, he found his way blocked by two men-at-arms, their scowls telling him that they thought him a vagabond.

"I must see Princess Mary at once!" he ordered, ignoring their appraising looks upon his person.

"She is preparing herself for a long journey," came the answer. "She has no time for the likes of you."

So, thought Richard, Northumberland has already sent a message to her bidding her to come to London. He could imagine what the fate of the princess, now the queen, would be if she did as she were told.

"She must not go!" he shouted, taking a step forward. Strong arms pushed him back.

"You hardly look the sort to tell a princess what to do," one of the guards growled. "Now, be gone." He gave Richard a push which sent him sprawling.

"No!" he shouted, standing up again and moving

forward. "Tell her Richard Morgan is here and must speak with her."

Laughter was his answer and he cursed these buffoons beneath his breath. All the danger he had faced would be for naught if they kept him from seeing Mary.

"Your heads will roll if you do not at least tell her that I am here," Richard barked. His voice was so forceful, so commanding that the men-at-arms stopped their chuckling and stared at him.

At last one of the guards spoke. "I'll go to her but it will be *your* head if she is angered by the interruption." He was gone but a short while and when he returned he nodded his head at his companion. "She says to let him in."

Richard pushed his way through the door and stood in the hall to await his queen. His eyes roamed over his surroundings, taking in the silken hangings drawn back from the latticed windows, the murals, paintings, and tapestries. A fire was burning in the great hearth and Richard welcomed the warmth. The night was growing chilly. The enticing aroma of cooking food made his mouth water. He had not eaten all day.

"Richard," he heard a deep, slightly masculine woman's voice say. "It has been so long."

He turned and watched as she entered the room. Dressed in blue brocade and velvet, her full skirts over the stiff farthingale rustling as she walked, the princess greeted him with an outstretched hand in welcome. Her usually tight lips were drawn in a half-smile.

"How glad I am to see you, though I fear that I cannot prolong the visit. Edward is sick and has sent for me. Perhaps my brother and I can finally lay to rest the bitterness between us and heal old wounds."

Richard quickly bent his knee to kneel before her, only to hear her voice plead with him to rise. His eyes gazed upon her and he was filled with pity for this poor woman who had suffered so much because of the follies and vanities of her father. Had she ever tasted of happiness? He doubted it. She was barely two when her father took to mistresses and neglected his grieving wife, eight when he had asked for an annulment of his marriage to marry the ill-fated Anne Boleyn, fifteen when forced to go into exile, and still a young girl when declared a bastard and shorn of her title of princess so that the king could declare the child of his union with Anne Boleyn his heir. Was it any wonder that she resented her half-sister the Princess Elizabeth?

"I have some sad news for you," he whispered.

Her pale face seemed to grow even paler. "Tell me quickly."

"Edward is dead. He died last night. Northumberland plans a trap." He hated to bring her more grief, but she had to be told quickly.

"Dead!" She touched her throat as if afraid that she could not breathe. The lines around her eyes and mouth seemed to grow deeper, and though she was but thirty-seven she looked to be a much older woman. She fought back her tears and held her head up proudly with the regal bearing of her rank.

Richard again bowed before her. "Your Majesty." He could hear her ragged breathing as she fought for control, and he feared for a moment that she would faint. But she was a strong woman despite her thin and frail body. "We must leave here at once. Northumberland and his men are close behind me, no doubt hoping to intercept you upon the road to London."

"Northumberland!"

"I overheard him talking. Edward's death has been kept secret until he can see to his plans. We cannot tarry. We must go. Now."

Her eyes looked upon him, eyes filled with trust. She did not doubt for a moment the truth of his words. "Let us go then."

Gathering up what personal belongings she might need, Richard helped her prepare for the journey she must make, all the while shouting his orders to her staff and servants. Only when they had left the great hall, were safely hidden in the shadows of the trees, did he speak to her again.

"You will be safe at Kenninghall Palace in Norfolk, my queen."

"Yes, I will be safe there, at least for a time. By then I will know exactly what Northumberland has planned, or will with your help." Her eyes looked into his and he remembered the young woman she had once been before the cruelty of others and illness had stolen the bloom of her gentle beauty.

"I will do whatever you command me," he answered, wishing that he could ease her pain.

"My brother always trusted you, despite the fact that you did not hold the same religious views. I will do the same, for I remember well how you pleaded with him on my behalf to allow me to continue with my Mass." Forgetting for a moment her demeanor as queen, she reached for his hand, holding it only briefly before she let it go. "Go back to London," she whispered.

"Back to London? But I must see you safely to Norfolk."

She shook her head. "I will be quite safe with my men-at-arms to protect me. I need someone I trust to keep an eye on Northumberland for me. I know that you will be in great danger, but nonetheless I ask this of you."

Richard Morgan hesitated, feeling a strong sense of protectiveness toward the woman standing before him. So much was at stake, least of all his safety.

Sensing his feelings, Mary said. "I will send you a message from Kenninghall Palace. Ere two nights have passed I will have made my decision. Your messenger will be at the Cap and Crown."

"The Cap and Crown." He knew well that tavern. Many a stratagem had been hatched there. "How will I know him?"

"He will wear both a red and a white feather in his cap, for the blend of the roses that are Tudor." He stood looking at her, wondering what it was she planned. "Go. Now." She started to say more, instead turned her back upon him. As she walked away he felt a lump in his throat to think of all she must now face, she who wanted only to love and be loved and to say her rosary.

"God speed you, my queen," he whispered.

He hurried to seek out the queen's groom to procure a horse for his ride back to London. The stallion he had ridden to Hunsdon deserved a long rest. At last mounting a brown mare, he sought to retrace his path.

6

THROUGH THE SMALL window of her father's counting room, Heather could hear the sounds of London: the clatter of the carts, the barking of the hounds, the din of the pedestrians as they wound their way past the shops, the voices of the peddlers hustling their wares, and loudest of all the pealing bells announcing a new sovereign. The entire country was in a state of shock. King Edward was dead and Lady Jane Grey Dudley had been proclaimed Queen of England.

"So the rebel told me true," Heather said softly, absentmindedly tapping the quill she held in her hand against her fingers. She had doubted him, had felt herself the fool, when two days had come and gone and still no word had been heard about the fate of the king. But then London had been rocked by the news that the king was dead.

"Edward," she murmured, remembering the red-haired young king. In his feathered hat and ermine-collared robe he had looked so young at his coronation. He had been but nine years old, his gentle face so like his mother Jane Seymour's. So opposite from his father had he been that it had been said that an ogre had been buried to make way for a saint.

Heather looked across the room to where her father sat at his calculating board, that table marked out with horizontal lines on which bone counters were manipulated. He was busy at his work, adding up the pounds of profit he had made the past few days on his wool and furs. He had been frightened at the news of the king's death; certain that now his money would be in jeopardy, but had sighed with relief to hear that instead of the king's sister Mary it would be the king's cousin who would wear the crown. Always before her father had been concerned for only one thing—money—though now something else was taking up a great deal of his time. Several times now she had seen Thomas Bowen sneaking out at all hours of the night as if fearful of being seen. Whom was he meeting, and why?

"Heather, fetch me my strongbox!" Thomas Bowen pursed his lips together as soon as the words were out, in the expression Heather knew all too well. The profit was not as great as he had thought.

Picking up the bound iron box, fastened with a large iron lock, Heather was surprised by the weight of the coins within. It was twice as heavy as it had been this time last night. Had she then misunderstood her father's sour look?

"Ah, that's a good girl." With stubby, clumsy fingers he unfastened the lock, hesitating slightly before opening the lid a crack. He seemed loath to let Heather see inside, and this puzzled her, for since there was no son to work her father's trade, Heather had helped Thomas run his business and more often than not had kept her father's books.

I must be wrong, she thought, taking a step forward with the intent of tallying up the amounts contained within the box. Thomas Bowen seemed to draw back from her.

"Why don't you go outside, Heather? A breath of fresh air would do you good. Your cheeks are pale." His smile was insincere, more of a grimace. "How will I ever be able to find a husband for you if you don't get some color in that pretty face of yours?"

Heather stood looking at him in confusion. Always before he had wanted her help in counting the coins. Why now would he want to do it alone?

"Well, don't stand there." His tone was one of irritation.

Shrugging her shoulders in indifference, she left

the room. "I care not what the strongbox contains," she said beneath her breath.

Walking through the workroom, she eyed the piles of silks, wool, brocades, and furs, wishing for a new dress, yet knowing well that her father would be hard pressed to part with any of his precious materials. Stepping outside, she squinted at the glare which met her eyes. The light had been poor in the counting room and now the sun nearly blinded her.

"Apples! Ripe red apples," trilled a voice from the cobbled street.

"Mussels. Cockles. Oysters," cried a male voice.

"Coo, try me fine tarts," yelled an old woman.

The air smelled of fish, spices, and musty decay. The breeze tugged at her long unbound mahogany-colored hair as Heather walked along the street, carefully avoiding the open gutters and the slop pails being emptied overhead. The gabled roofs of the houses, the church spires, and the turreted towers rose from the mists of the chimney smoke and Heather's eyes took in the familiar sight. London. Her home. Was there any other place quite like it?

Everywhere there were street peddlers and vendors. London had always been a marketplace before anything else.

An onion seller stepped in front of her carrying his pole across his shoulders. At each end were tied white and red onions. "Buy me four ropes of hard onions!" he called out, looking at Heather and cocking his brow as if to ask if she wanted some. She shook her head no.

There were stalls of fresh vegetables and fish—indeed you could find almost any wares on the street.

"Any knives or scissors to grind? Bring them here, my pretty, and I'll make them like new," a tall scissors sharpener implored her as she walked past his large-wheeled grinding machine. His little white dog ran toward her wagging his tail, and she bent down to give him a pat on his furry head. The animal sniffed at the hem of her gown and Heather laughed.

"You smell my cat, don't you, dog?"

"Knives? Scissors? I will make them good again," the scissors sharpener said, no doubt encouraged by her stopping.

"Perhaps later. I don't have them with me right now," Heather answered, walking away.

Strolling musicians wound through the crowd with their lutes and harps, strumming as they wandered about. One looked at Heather and gave her a bold wink, singing a song about a red-haired maiden. Smiling at him, but averting her eyes, she threw him a coin and went on her way.

"Violets."

Turning around, Heather found herself looking into the large eyes of a ragged little girl. The child's frail body and pale face spoke of deprivation, the unfortunate plight of the needy in the city. Sympathy swept over Heather.

"Please, mum. Buy me violets."

Pulling three angels out of her apron pocket and placing the coins into the hand of the street urchin, Heather gestured that she wanted one of the bouquets.

"Thankee, mum," mumbled the child, biting one coin to make certain that it was real. Thrusting two bunches of the lavender flowers into Heather's hands instead of one, the child scurried off as if fearful lest the coins be reclaimed.

Heather felt pity for the poor child tug at her heart. It didn't seem fair that some should have so much and others so little. Was it really, as her father had said, "God's will"? She sincerely doubted it. More likely it was greed of the few which had caused such misery.

Henry VIII had swept away the almshouses, hospitals had been abandoned, priories, monasteries, and convents torn down and the bricks carried away to build houses for rich nobles. Now there was nowhere for the sick and famished to go, yet nothing was being done. To add to the misery, the currency had been debased and prices had soared. Was it any wonder that many of the poor had turned to a life of crime?

"Would that I could help them," she murmured, but knew in her heart that there was little she could do. There were so many poor. What would be their fate with Northumberland in power? He was known for squeezing the poor of their life's blood and had put to death Edward Seymour, the only friend in power who had shown them any sympathy.

Heather continued along her way, feeling the rough stones beneath her slippers. She passed the colorful wooden signs which marked each shop: a unicorn for the goldsmith, the head of a horse for a harness maker, three round pills for the apothecary, a white arm with stripes of red for the surgeon-barber. Standing in the doorway in his checkered apron, the barber raised his hand in greeting to Heather. She was well-respected in the area, being one who bought their wares.

Next to the barber was the baker's shop, where an apprentice was removing loaves of bread from the oven with a long-handled wooden shovel. The whispers of the housewives standing in a circle around the baker came to Heather's ears.

"Who *is* this Jane Grey Dudley that she call herself our queen?"

"A half-cousin of Edward's, the granddaughter of Henry's sister."

"Ha, she is no queen. Mary is our rightful ruler. She is her father's true daughter and the king's sister."

"Mary is a papist. It will be much better with one of our own for queen. She is virtuous and learned, this Jane, though just a chit of sixteen."

"Mary is just as virtuous and learned and she is of royal blood on both sides. Her mother was a Spanish princess."

"Poor Mary. She has suffered so these many years. Would that she were to be our ruler. Perhaps she would govern us with gentleness. I fear this Jane and her father-in-law, Northumberland."

Heather heard many rumors, that Jane was reluctant, had fainted, had protested that she was unfit for the perilous honor forced upon her, that she had accepted only after her relatives had pleaded with her, telling her their lives would be forfeit were she to refuse.

Heather felt pity for this young woman, only a couple of years younger than she. Perhaps the crown would prove a heavy burden for one so young. And Northumberland, what would he do now?

Northumberland. She could not think of him without being reminded of her father. Although she had tried to put it from her mind, Heather was bothered by her father's actions, his reluctance to let her see inside the moneybox. Had it anything to do with the meeting of the Privy Council, that meeting that Northumberland himself had called? Her father was one of its newest members.

She thought: I wish that my father would stay far away from the duke. Was the duke perhaps bribing her father? Heather decided that it could not be true. Thomas was miserly, but he had so far proven to be an honest man.

Perhaps instead he feared that I would ask for a new dress if I were to see the abundance of coins within the moneybox, she reasoned. Looking down at the plain linen gown she wore, a simple frock of brown with long sleeves, at the plain apron covering it, she thought how well she fit in with the surroundings. She could nearly be mistaken for a servant or a simple housewife.

Adroitly dodging a foul-smelling drunk, Heather was shocked to realize that she had come farther than usual, no doubt lost to her thoughts. The area was a haunt for sailors and the like, a dingy narrow street where taverns dotted the landscape. Although unfamiliar with the area, she had no fear for it was still daylight and honest men were still at their work. Besides, Heather had lived in London all her life and was no country miss. Keeping her wits about her, she merely turned around in her tracks with the intent to retrace her steps and return to her father's counting room. It was then that she saw him. There could be no mistake. How could she forget that swagger, those shoulders—wide and strong—that raven-black hair and beard?

"The rebel!" she breathed, breaking into a run, intent upon catching him. She could see that he was headed for one of the largest taverns, the Cap and Crown by name, and wondered at his haste. With strides nearly twice her own he seemed to be increasing the distance between them. She wanted to call out to him but wisely held back, instead picking up her skirts to hurry along. There was so much she had to ask him, to tell him.

A figure stepped out of the shadows before her, blocking her view of him for just a moment, and she swore an oath beneath her breath. A rickety hay wagon rumbling down the street stopped Heather for several moments while she stood watching in helpless frustration. She would never catch up with him now. He would be gone from her sight in just a moment. Gone, and she would never even know his name.

"But no, he's stopping." She could see him in deep conversation with another man, a man with a red and a white feather in his hat, a man who held out a piece of paper toward him. Heather closed the distance between them, watching as the man, who seemed to be some sort of messenger, walked away to vanish out of sight.

The rebel stood reading the paper intently, oblivious of the world around him, and Heather wondered what could be written upon it to so transfix his eyes.

Coming close to him, Heather opened her mouth to speak, but instead gasped. A man in the shadows, the one who had been walking in front of her, held a knife in his fist, a knife poised to strike the dark-haired rebel. Springing forward, he lashed out at his quarry, just as Heather screamed.

Richard Morgan heard the piercing scream, turning slightly to see from whence it came, just as he felt the slicing pain of the blade. Like flames of white fire, driving the breath from his lungs, the agony came as he fell to the ground to lie gasping on the hard cobblestones of the road. He struggled to get up, clutching his letter to his chest.

He felt a hot flood of warmth wet his hand and fought to keep it from the paper that he held. Was it his imagination that he saw the face before him that had haunted his nights, saw the auburn tresses blowing near his cheek, felt a soft hand touch his face? Opening his mouth to speak, he reached out his hand to touch her, groaning as he did so, "Heather."

7

HEATHER HOVERED OVER the wounded man, trying frantically to stanch the bleeding with the torn cloth of her chemise. The blood appeared to come from his shoulder wound and she knew instinctively that her cries had saved his life. The knife had been aimed to strike at the heart but had missed its target.

Watching him writhe in pain, Heather felt his suffering as if it were her flesh which had been pierced. A tremor of apprehension ran through her, a deep fear that he would not survive. The possibility struck her like a physical blow.

Despite his agony he clutched tightly to a letter, his face nearly as pale as that piece of paper. Pulling it from his hands despite his protests, Heather stuffed it into her bodice where it would be safe. If it was so precious to him, then how could it be less so to her?

"I'm going to help you. Lie back and be quiet." Her words had a calming effect on him and he closed his eyes.

Looking about her at the people walking by, she sought to find someone to aid her, gesturing to them, crying out, but there was no one who would help. London was a city filled with crime and misery, and the horde of persons within had long ago learned to ignore any pleas for assistance. There were too many thieves who used such methods to filch one's purse. Thus they passed her by, ignoring the man whose life's blood was oozing onto the ground.

Taking off one of her stockings, Heather tied it firmly around the wound, knowing full well that whether he lived or died was up to her now. The stocking slowed the spill of blood and for the first time she felt a faint ray of hope.

"I have to find someone to help me," she murmured, and remembered at once the surgeon-barber with his checkered apron and kind smile. He was often called upon to pull teeth and perform minor surgery. It would be difficult to get the man there, but she must. Although petite, about five-feet-two, she was determined she would manage the task. She had to. Some way.

"I'm going to help you stand," she said, struggling with his muscular form. Tugging, pulling, careful of his wound, she managed to get him to his feet. For just a moment his eyes flickered, he moaned, and Heather pleaded with him to put one foot in front of the other, to walk with her despite his pain.

It was two blocks to the barber's shop, yet it seemed a mile as she staggered toward it. More than one sailor called out to her, pleading with her to leave her drunk companion and come instead with him, yet none offered to help her, hurrying off at once at the sight of the red seeping from the wound.

"Cowards! Blackguards!" Heather sobbed, seeing the worst of men's nature. Exhausted, trembling, she nonetheless managed to find the strength and courage to at last reach the barber's door. "Help me! Please help me!"

About the town shutters were rattling shut. The bells warned of day's end, that time when thieves would come from hiding to replace the honest folk upon the streets. Dusk would soon be sending its gray shroud to clothe the earth.

Finding the barber's shutters and door locked for the night, Heather panicked. All that struggle for nothing.

"No. He can't die. I won't let him die."

Gently laying the rebel upon the hard ground, Heather beat upon the strong wood of the barber's door until her hands were bruised. She would not give up. At last the door was opened. "Help me!" she sobbed.

Seeing the face of the young woman he recognized, the barber replaced his surly frown with a look of concern. "What be wrong, miss?"

"He's been stabbed. We must stop the bleeding." Heather motioned toward the form of the wounded man.

With a strength which belied his skinny form, the barber picked up the rebel and carried him inside his sparsely furnished shop, depositing him on a large wooden bench upon which his customers waited to be served. Heather bent down beside where the wounded man lay, reaching out to take hold of his wrist. The faint beat of his pulse reassured her that he still lived and she nearly sobbed out loud with relief.

Muttering beneath his breath, the barber examined the wound, dabbing at the sticky red wetness with a cloth he held in his hands.

"This one be lucky. It could 'ave been 'is 'eart." He pinched the folds of the wound together tightly, stopping for a moment the flow of blood. "Fetch me a needle, miss."

Heather looked at him in bewilderment, not knowing where to look, nor what he would want with such a thing.

"In that pewter jar," he instructed with a nod of his head.

Heather watched in fascination as he took the needle from her hand, threaded it, and set about stitching the wound as if it were a piece of her father's finest cloth. Sprinkling a white powder atop the wound, he stood back to appraise his work. At her look of inquiry he muttered, "Alum. I use it for nicks and cuts when I give a shave."

"Will he live?" Her voice was scarcely more than a whisper.

" 'E's strong. 'E'll recover in time, unless 'ooever stabbed 'im comes back to finish the job." The answer struck fear to her heart, as she was aware of how vulnerable he was at this moment. He could not be turned back out upon the street. What could be done with the wounded man? She would have to leave him here.

It was as if the barber read her mind. He shook his head in denial. " 'E can't stay 'ere. I got me family to think of. I don't want violence to touch 'em!"

"But where . . . ?" She knew the answer as soon as the words left her mouth. "Can he be moved?"

"Aye, though I think it would be well to find a quiet place where 'e can gain back 'is strength. 'Oo is 'e?"

"I don't know his name. I only saw him once before today," she answered. Hearing the wounded man's moan of pain, she bent over him, smoothing back the hair from his face and whispering to him gently. His eyes remained closed. He was nearly unconscious, but Heather now had the hope that he would recover.

The barber's eyes met Heather's, seeing the tender look for the injured man clearly written there. "Don't know 'is name and yet you 'elped 'im." He smiled. "Me mother told me once that if one saves a life, from that moment on 'is fate was entwined with that of 'im 'oo he saved." Heather felt a flush color her cheeks, knowing at that moment that what this man's mother said was true.

Heather closed her eyes, thinking of what she could do, where she could take the rebel. The only place that would be safe, where she could care for him, was her father's house. But surely she could not be so daring!

" 'E can't stay 'ere!" the barber repeated, misunderstanding her frown.

The stables. She could hide him in her father's stables. Thomas Bowen would never deign to go there. It was beneath his dignity. And Harold, that kind old man, would help her. Wasn't he always pilfering food to give to the needy with her help? She would go back to her house, get Harold to help her, and then return with a wagon to bring the wounded rebel back with her.

"I will take him with me, but I must go back home first and get a wagon. He's been moved around enough today and I don't think he has the strength to walk a long distance." She turned to leave but the barber reached out to touch her arm.

"No! Take 'im with you now. 'Ow can I know that you will return for 'im?"

She looked at him and her eyes held the truth of her words. "I'll come back. On that you have my word."

"Aye, I believe you. Methinks 'e be a lucky gent to 'ave so fine a lady care for 'im." He opened the door for her and Heather stepped out into the gray of the London dusk.

It was a far different London which now met her eyes, a world of thieves and beggars and women of questionable morals. She averted her eyes as a girl younger than herself openly solicited upon the streets, and narrowly escaped the clutching hands of a bedraggled fat man who mistakenly took Heather to be a woman of the night. Clutching her few coins tightly in her fist to keep them from a pickpocket's grasp, she fled the nightmare of the night, her long red hair blowing in wild array about her shoulders as she ran.

Arriving home, she was pale and trembling, her heart beating like a timpani. Never had her house looked so dear to her eyes, never had she so welcomed the flood of light which came from the windows. Grasping the knob, she was relieved to find it open, not yet locked for the night. With a wrench she opened it, only to find her father's corpulent frame blocking her entrance.

"Where in God's name have you been, girl?" he asked in anger. "Your mother has been sick with worry and I have had to tally up my profits all alone!"

She felt a flood of resentment arise like a tide, but fought against it. He was within his rights in being angry with her. "I'm sorry, Father." Taking a deep breath, she fought to regain her composure. How she wished that she could tell him the truth of what had happened and know that he would understand. Instead she said, "I stopped at the cobbler's. My shoes are nearly worn through."

He sniffed in disdain. "Another pair? You will soon impoverish me. Only last year you had a new pair made." He led her inside, closing the door tightly behind her. In the light his eyes were drawn to the bloodstains on her gown. Noticing the direction of his glance, Heather sought for an explanation.

"I stopped by the butcher's, Father." She nervously brushed at her gown. "He was slaughtering a pig and I fear that I got some of the blood on my dress."

He grunted. "Well, be more careful in the future. Cloth is expensive, as you well know." Giving her a little push, he said, "Hurry with you now. Your mother and Tabitha are already preparing the evening meal." He grinned at her. "You know how much I like *your* plum pudding. Along with you, now."

Hurrying up the stairs, Heather thought wildly of a way to escape, to find Harold and bring the wounded rebel to safety. For the moment there was no way. She would have to be patient and wait until the time came.

8

THE FLICKERING FLAMES of the oil lamp illuminated the pale face of the man lying on the rough bed of linen and straw in the stable loft. Heather gently wiped the perspiration from his face. He was weak from loss of blood and had lapsed into unconsciousness from time to time, but he was alive and for this she gave thanks to God. Surely it had been divine intervention which had caused her to cross the rebel's path just in time.

Heather had removed his shirt, doublet, and jerkin in order to tend his wound, and now she let her eyes roam over what she could see of his body. His skin was several shades darker than hers, with a swarthy, natural tan. His arms and chest were well-muscled and she remembered their strength when he had held her that night they met. A tuft of black hair covered his broad chest and trailed in a thin straight line down to his navel. Not having viewed an unclothed male torso before, she nonetheless knew him to be powerfully masculine. Just looking at him was strangely exciting.

As if sensing her searching eyes, the man stirred in his sleep, a soft groan escaping from his mouth.

"You are safe now. There is none here who will harm you. Rest," she whispered. His pain tugged at her heart. In his defenseless slumber he brought out all the protective instincts within her and she vowed to do everything in her power to see that he would be safe. Reaching for a linen sheet, she pulled it over his half-nude form.

"How is he, mum?" The voice was Harold's. Harold Perriwincle. How could she ever thank him for his help tonight? It had been quite a struggle to place the wounded man's unconscious form in her father's wagon, but Harold, whom Heather affectionately called Perri, had been more than up to the task as usual. Despite his advanced years he was still a strong man.

Heather turned around to look into the kind brown eyes of the faithful servant. "He's in a deep slumber from the sleeping draft the barber gave him, but so far there is no sign of a fever." Now that the danger of his bleeding to death had passed, it was the worry of a fever which haunted Heather, for it was this that had taken many a man to the next world.

" 'Tis a pity we have no camomile or nettle," the servant answered. He had fought in many a war as a young man, being as it were an adventurer, and knew all about wounds and the like.

"I cannot chance going into the kitchen now. The door is most likely locked for the night. I will stay here with him, and with the first cock crow will go inside to gather all I need."

He grinned his toothless smile at her. " 'Twould perhaps do him good to have a swig of ale. Nothing like strong drink to heal a man right proper. Take me bloody oath on that."

Heather smiled at the man, knowing full well that he too wanted a sip of the brew. It was the least she could do to thank him for the help he had given tonight. If her father ever found out that the servant had gone off into the night with his wagon to aid an injured man of unknown name, it would mean instant dismissal. Jobs were scarce even for those of younger years. But then Perri had always been one to use his wits, and the chance of her father coming out to the stable was slim.

"I'll see what I can do," she promised. Again the old man smiled, and then took his leave of her to sleep in his own small quarters adjacent to the stables.

"If you need me, mum, just call," he flung over his shoulder.

Heather realized how tired she was. Tonight had been a harrowing experience that she would not soon forget. For a time she had thought never to have the stranger safe within her father's stables, as one problem after another had arisen to keep her from sneaking out of the house.

First she had the food to prepare, the cleaning, mincing, blanching, and parboiling of vegetables; then she had to crush herbs in the mortar and do the other tasks which a servant would normally do. Since her father was so miserly there was only Tabitha to aid them; thus both Blythe and Heather had to take on such chores every night in order to see that the meal was prepared. Tonight each hour had dragged by with the speed of a snail while Heather had worried that the barber would grow tired of waiting and put the wounded man outside his door. Was it any wonder that she could not eat a bite when finally supper was on the table? Her mother and Tabitha had both anxiously watched her, fearful that she was ill.

Only when the house had made ready for bedtime did she dare think of carrying out the plan to return to the barber's shop. Her father had taken an unusual interest in her health, lingering by the door and asking questions. Only when he himself had finally sneaked out into the night had Heather been able to run quickly from the house to rouse Harold Perriwincle.

With each squeak of the wagon wheel she had feared they would be caught, but at long last they had arrived at the barber's door, and banging upon that portal, had been let inside to regain their precious cargo. Now the wounded man was safely ensconced in the stable behind her father's house, hidden away from the danger which threatened him.

Suddenly remembering the letter, she reached in her bodice and pulled the missive out, curious as to its contents. The paper was of the finest quality, the writing of a bold lettering.

"It is from Mary Tudor!" she exclaimed in a soundless whisper. So he had not lied about his desire to aid the rightful queen. She would not call him a rebel again, for surely there had never been a truer subject of the crown. In the dim light she anxiously skimmed the words written. It was a letter to the council ordering them to acknowledge Mary Tudor as rightful queen and promising them forgiveness if they would do so promptly. Now she knew why the wounded man had cried out over and over for the letter.

Finding a safe hiding place for the queen's missive, a spot that only she knew behind a loose board, Heather returned to the side of the bed to look at the man who had nearly given his life for this precious piece of paper. No wonder he had been stabbed. The assailant undoubtedly knew about the message. And what of Northumberland? What was his part in all of this? Had it been by his orders that this man had nearly been killed? She wondered what her father would do if he knew that they harbored an enemy of the duke. For that matter, what would become of them all if it were known?

"I care not. I will not betray him," she vowed fiercely. She knew nothing about this man, not even his name. Why then would she put herself so in danger?

Touching his face with her hand, she knew the reason. This man had stolen her heart as surely as the Duke of Northumberland had stolen the crown.

"Sleep," she whispered to him. "I will find out who you are on the morrow and see to your letter."

The light from the oil lamp sputtered, then died as Heather removed her bloodstained apron. Clad in her loose-fitting chemise, she paced the floor until exhaustion overcame her, the excitement of the day taking its toll.

Lying down next to the wounded man, Heather sought her own slumber, feeling serene in the comfort of the warmth of his male body. Despite the circumstances, the danger and his condition, she felt giddy at his closeness, in much the same manner as when she had partaken of too much wine at her cousin's wedding. She drifted off to sleep with the rebel's head on her shoulder, his arms and legs entwined with her own.

Richard Morgan was lost to his haze of dreams, frantic visions which tortured him as he twisted and turned in the throes of sleep. Edlyn. He could see her face before him. No. He did not want her. Tricked. Tricked by his own mother for gold.

"No. How could you? You knew all along. Edlyn. I am bound now. No happiness for me." He reached out his hand, grasping, groping like a drowning man, wanting to escape, to get away from this madness. "Edlyn."

His loud mumbling woke Heather. Fearing that his thrashing about would do injury to his wound, she sought to quiet him, putting her hands on the center of his chest to hold him down. What had the barber given him to make him act in such a manner?

In the haze of his dreams Richard Morgan felt the hands upon his chest and tried desperately to escape them. It was as if he were walking down a long tunnel, moving toward a garden, but someone was holding him back, trying to keep him from his destination. He saw the face looming in his path, blocking his way.

"Seton! Hugh Seton. You devil. Get out of my way. Let me go," he murmured, reaching out to clutch at the villain's throat. Destroy him. He had to destroy him just as Seton had tried so hard to destroy the Morgan family. He reached up to squeeze the neck of that leering face which mocked him.

Heather fought wildly against the strength of the hands which held her. His fevered energy was nearly more than she could manage as she sought to tear his fingers from her slender neck. He was choking her; she couldn't breathe. He envisioned her as some devious enemy.

She tried to call out for Harold, for her beloved Perri, but no sound escaped her lips until at last she managed to gasp, "It's Heather. Heather."

As if he recognized her name, his hold upon her loosened. Heather's heart was still pounding wildly in her breast as she sought to calm her trembling. A nightmare had caused his violence and she wondered what demon he had been grappling with.

"It's only a dream," she said softly, reaching out to touch his brow. There was no sign of a fever. The barber's potion then? Her words soothed him, for he quieted.

"Heather." He was calling out to her, yet she could see in the dim moonlight that his eyes remained closed. He was still in that state of consciousness halfway between reality and dreams.

Fearing that his thrashing about had reopened his wound, she gently examined it with her fingers. At her touch he stiffened and issued forth a moan, but the wound was dry. The barber's stitches had held tight.

"Heather. So lovely." She felt the warm, soft touch of his fingers upon her breast, sending a shiver of desire coursing through her blood. His hand cupped the tender flesh, caressing the peak through the thin material of her chemise with infinite tenderness. She moved her hand with the intent to remove the fingers, but the sensation was so stirring that she somehow could not bear to do so. She rationalized that he did not know what he was doing, that she must not wake him.

His exploring hand moved lower, sliding over her small waist to rest on the full curve of her hip. She had never known that a man's caress could cause such a spark, a fire in the blood. The shock of pleasure took her breath away and she shivered, or was it the night air which caused her to tremble so? Seeking his warmth, she nestled close to his body once again. His warmth enveloped her and she raised her hand to touch his face. Somehow she had the feeling that she was dreaming too. If that was true, then she never wanted to awaken.

Richard Morgan held the vision of loveliness tightly in his arms. He had dreamed about her so many times, and now she was with him. He brushed his lips over her cheek, tracing the curves of her ear with his tongue, smelling the soft spice scent of her hair. He moved his mouth to her lips and gently kissed her, rolling with her to one side to draw her against him possessively, enraptured by the embrace. A violent storm of feeling shot through him, pushing away the clouds of haze from his mind, but it was not passion which shook him, but pain. It shot through him and he groaned.

"Your wound!" Heather was mortified as the spell was broken and reality flooded over her. She had forgotten all in the wonder of his arms, and now she had caused him pain.

"Wound?" He tried to get up but instead lay back down.

"Be careful!" she cautioned, touching his shoulder with gentle hands.

"The letter. Where is it?" he mumbled.

"I have it. All is well," she assured him; her eyes moving to that hidden alcove where it rested securely.

Again he tried to get up, but was overcome by his weakness and in despair lay once again back down upon the hard straw bed. "Must get it to council. Mary." His eyes closed tightly as he relaxed against her, all strength completely drained. "Don't leave me."

"I won't leave you," she promised. "I'll stay right here by your side." She lay back down beside him, her hair spread out like a satin cloak over them both. He slept now as peacefully as a babe, and she too closed her eyes to return to that blissful mist of slumber.

9

HEATHER AWOKE AS the first pale pink streaks of the dawn's light filtered through the tiny windows of the stable. She opened her eyes slowly, expecting full well to be within the familiar confines of her bedchamber, but instead saw before her stark brown wooden walls. Her heart quickened as she stiffened, eyes opening wide to take in her surroundings. She could hear the steady breathing of the man who lay beside her and she turned her head in that direction to stare into his sleeping face.

"I was not dreaming," she breathed, assailed by the memory of being held close in this man's arms, of the hard planes of his chest teasing her breasts, his strong thighs touching hers. Flushing, she turned away, only to return her gaze to him.

His face was etched with pain, yet still such a handsome face. His dark eyelashes cast a shadow on his cheekbones, and his full lips were parted as he drew in a shallow breath. She was tempted to reach out and touch that soft mouth which had tasted of hers with such passion, but she did not.

"There is such a strength about him, even in his wounded state," she whispered. This time she could not resist the urge to caress him, and let her fingers touch the prickle of his beard. He stirred in his sleep and Heather, not wishing to awaken him, molded her body once again to his.

The heat of his body was arousing as they lay curled up together, his uninjured arm flung across her stomach, his leg resting between hers in a position of intimacy. They seemed to fit together with perfect unity as if made each for the other. She spread her hand over his chest and felt the light furring of hair there, heard the beat of his heart, and closed her eyes in contentment.

The sound of neighing horses, chirping birds, and Harold Perriwincle's hammering awoke Heather anew. Easing herself onto her elbow, slowly as not to waken the man beside her, she let her eyes drift down his body. The wound did not appear to be infected, nor was there any sign of bleeding. Her gaze moved lower, lingering on his chest and hips in a manner unmaidenly and quite bold. Having slept alone all her life, she now wondered what it would be like to awaken to this man beside her, his arms about her possessively, his hands tangled in the long strands of her hair, for all the mornings of her life.

"Am I still dreaming?" A husky voice startled her and she looked up to find the penetrating blue depths of his eyes staring at her. He shook his head in confusion.

Heather flushed as she wondered if he remembered what had passed between them, or had nearly done so, in the night, but the look in his eyes told her that he did not. He would no doubt think it all a dream.

"You've been wounded," she said stiffly, reaching for her soiled gown to cover her scantily clothed body.

"How in hell . . . ?" he swore beneath his breath. His jaw tightened in anger as the memory of the deed came back to him.

Slipping her full-skirted dress over her head, Heather quickly related all that she had seen and of how she had tended him and brought him safely to her father's premises. All the while she kept her eyes cast down, fearing that he would read in them the emotions she was feeling at being so near to him.

"And so you saved my life yet again," he whispered. Lifting himself in an effort to sit up, he was engulfed in a wave of dizziness and sank back down in despair. "I am as weak as a kitten."

"You will gain back your strength. I know of healing herbs that will soon have you back on your feet. Trust me."

"Aye, I trust you," he breathed. She looked at him and saw in his eyes the depth of emotion that was overwhelming and spoke more clearly than words could ever have done.

He inhaled deeply of the morning air in an effort to clear his head of its whirling, then said, "The letter. Let me see the letter."

Heather withdrew the precious paper from hiding and handed it to him. "Poor Mary," she said softly. "I fear that it is too late for her to claim her rightful legacy."

He shook his head in denial. "No. It cannot be too late! I will not let it be. With every breath left in my body I will fight Northumberland." He paused to catch his breath. "When the council sees this letter, knows that Mary has the courage and tenacious strength to fight for what is rightly hers, they will support her." His voice was a croak, a whisper as he fought against the fatigue which threatened to engulf him.

Heather could sense his frustration at being struck down at a time when he so needed to be strong, yet she knew that were he to attempt to complete his mission it could mean his death. He would be no match for his enemies in his weakened state. Thus she said, "You cannot think to go to the council."

In answer he gathered all his energy to sit up, his long legs dangling over the makeshift bed, his hand reaching out to steady himself on the thick wooden beam of the low-ceilinged room. On shaky legs he sought to stand, to walk, only to sink in desperation to the straw-covered wooden floor.

Heather was at his side in an instant, offering her arms to him, pulling him to his feet, then pushing him back gently onto the hard bed.

"Damn! Damn!" he groaned. "How can I ever

forgive myself for failing my queen in her hour of need?" His face was a mask of defeat and sorrow.

"Don't say such things," she cried. "'Twas not your fault to be set upon and wounded."

"I should have been more careful." In his weakness he leaned against her, his breath stirring her hair. "Now all is lost."

Heather could hear a voice answering him. Was that her voice speaking with such intensity? "All is not lost. I will deliver the letter to the council!"

"You?" His eyes swept over her. "No! There is too much danger. How could a woman, a delicate woman, manage such a task? You have not the strength to force your way into that council chamber."

"Perhaps not the strength, but instead the cunning and courage that will be needed." If he deemed Mary Tudor a heroine, she would prove herself to be one as well. "Do not underestimate the power of a woman." Just because women could not sit on councils or in courts, did not have voice in government, did not mean they were without their influence, albeit a more subtle one than brute force.

"But if you were to be caught . . ."

"That, sir, I will not allow to happen." With that she lifted her chin defiantly. "If you can fight for Mary's cause, then so can I."

"Well-spoken," he answered, his eyes smoldering with suppressed passion. "You are a brave woman as well as a beautiful one." He could see that her mind was made up and he admired her tenacity, yet he feared for her safety. What if he were to lose her, never to see her again? He had no choice but to let her go, but if anything happened to her, could he forgive himself?

As if reading his mind, she whispered, "I'll think of a plan. All will be well." The tolling of the morning bell made her stiffen. She had to return to the house before she was missed and someone came looking for her. "I must go."

"Wait!" He could not let her leave now, not now before he knew what she was going to do.

"I'll be back." She crossed the small room, but at the doorway turned back. "Your name. I don't even . . ."

"Richard," he answered. "Richard Morgan."

"Richard," she murmured, liking the name. She started to say more but at that moment Harold Perriwincle bounded through the door, nearly knocking her over.

"Your father, mum. He is already up and about. You must hurry." Seeing the direction of her eyes, he added, "I'll be right here with him. If he needs anything I'll see to it." And she knew that he would.

Hurrying across the courtyard, she paused to glance back once or twice before making her way toward the four-story wooden house. Opening the back entrance, with its steep stairs that led all the way up to the floor attic and the servants' quarters, she picked up her skirts, taking the stairs two at a time. No doubt her father would be in the solar awaiting his breakfast, his ledgers held tightly in his hands. If God was with her she would not yet have been missed and could slip inside her bedchamber to change her clothing before her mother called upon her to help with the morning chores. So thinking, Heather made her way to her room.

She had barely had time to change into a fresh chemise when a light tapping at the door and a soft voice announced that her mother awaited her.

"Heather. Heather, are you all right?" Blythe Bowen called.

Heather opened the door to allow her mother entrance. "I'm fine, Mother," she said softly, running her fingers through the tangles of her auburn tresses. "I guess I just overslept."

"I'm glad that you are better this morning. I was so worried last night when you didn't eat." She reached out to cup Heather's face in her hand, looking deep within her daughter's eyes. "Your face. It is quite flushed. Are you certain that you are feeling well?"

Heather felt a wave of affection for this plump

and pretty woman who always showed her such love. "Yes. I was just tired, that's all. Pray do not worry."

Stepping toward the small table with the washbasin perched on top, she splashed her face with cold water. With so much excitement, it was no wonder that her face was flushed. For a moment she was tempted to tell her mother all that had happened, but knowing how protective Blythe always was, thought better of it. She would tell her later, after the mission had been accomplished.

Blythe Bowen stood wringing her hands as she always did when something troubled her. She eyed her daughter with dismay, not certain what it was that troubled her but knowing well that something was on Heather's mind. She could read her as surely as Heather could read her husband's journals.

"Heather . . ." she began, but the words were lost to her and she merely said, "come help me make up the beds as soon as you are dressed." The beds were so wide, nearly seven feet in width, that it took two to manage the task or one person using a long stick to reach across the vast breadth.

Heather watched her mother leave, then donned a linen gown, one which was well worn and would not be spoiled with dirt and grease from the morning's chores. She had best be about her duties quickly, for there was much to be done yet before she could see about Richard Morgan's letter.

"Richard Morgan." The name sounded well upon her lips. It was a fine name, one that suited him. She smiled as she thought about the way in which they had met. Had he claimed her heart even then? she asked herself, and knew the answer to be yes. He had brought excitement to her life, and love, something she had not experienced much of in recent years. No more would she be the merchant's daughter, spending her days in boredom among her father's weights and measures. She had tasted of passion and adventure. And who knew what might happen? Perhaps when Richard Morgan left he would take her with him. This she knew was her fondest hope.

10

THE GREAT TOWER of London rose to the sky like a giant man-at-arms guarding the city, and Heather could not suppress a shudder as she saw it looming in the distance. It was there that she was destined to go, and she could only pray that she would return from there as well.

Richard Morgan's words rang in her ears, his warning to her ere they parted. "Do not be caught with the letter upon your person. It could well mean your death if it is discovered."

He had tried again to dissuade her from taking the letter to the council, but Heather had been stubborn and his arguments were defeated. Her words had been spirited then, but now as she walked along, shards of fear pricked at her heart.

"The Tower. The White Tower," she whispered, remembering well the stories she had heard about it in her childhood. Not only was the council there, but many a prisoner as well. Indeed, Sir Thomas More, Anne Boleyn, and the two young sons of Edward IV had languished there before their deaths; Henry VI had been murdered in the Tower, and how many royal corpses lay within the cemetery next to the Tower? Was it any wonder that she felt apprehensive just looking in that direction? That Northumberland, his family, and his supporters were housed in the Tower only added to her peril.

It was a bold plan that she had devised. One without disguise or need for arms. She would merely go to the Tower as herself, the merchant's daughter.

Heather had attired herself in one of her better gowns for the journey, for it would not do to look the pauper. Her cornflower-blue dress with bell-shaped sleeves was a copy of those worn by ladies of the court, the full skirt worn over the stiff Spanish farthingale, so in vogue. Over the gown was worn a partlet, a yoke with a V neck and standing collar, tied under the armpits with tape. The full high collar of her chemise peeked from beneath. She thought with a smile that she rather resembled a walking dinner bell.

Reaching up, she touched her hair to make certain that it was still tidy. Parted in the center and rolled back over a pad, the red tresses were covered by a French hood secured with ribbons tied under her chin. She was well pleased with her efforts and laughed as two young apprentices nearly collided with each other while looking in her direction.

Walking down the cobbled streets, that twisting and turning path through the city, Heather looked up at the tall plaster-and-timber "magpie"-styled houses, so like her father's. The two- and three-story buildings leaned forward and looked as if they could nearly touch their neighbors on the other side of the narrow gray-cobbled street. Her father had wanted to go his neighbors one better, and so his abode had been structured with four stories.

Ah, Father, she thought. Safe at home napping. At least she would not have to worry about him this day. It had been her fear to suffer his ire upon reaching the council, but apparently he had not been summoned this time.

Heather passed several cathedrals along the route, boarded up long ago before she was born. The stained glass of the windows was now shattered, replaced by tattered waxed paper. Her mother had often related to her stories of their beauty, much to her father's annoyance. He had scowled at Blythe and chastised her "papist" sympathies, cautioning her about such talk in a time dangerous for Catholics.

Now it was Cramer's *Book of Common Prayer* which

was read so fervently in the whitewashed churches. No more the Latin Masses, which Edward had considered blasphemous idolatry.

The clamor of church bells rang out the noon hour as Heather continued on her way, at last reaching the Thames, that most practical and popular of waterways which divided London into northern and southern halves. Dotted with boats and barges which looked like leaves floating toward the shore, its waters sparkled in the midday sun and looked deceptively inviting. Crossing the river, adorned with its three-story buildings on either side, was London Bridge.

Heather tried to elbow her way through the crowd which was forming, adding to the confusion of the carts and wagons in the street. She had no need to ask what was going on; the crowd was very vocal in its protestations. Lady Jane Grey had been brought down by water to the Tower and received there as queen amidst great ceremony this very day.

"I still can't believe it!" cried an old man standing next to Heather. "Mary is the true heir to the throne." As quickly as his words were out, a black-garbed man moved in the old man's direction and she feared for his life. Instead he was given a sound boxing to his ears.

" 'Tis not Jane who rules, but Northumberland. God will punish him for his deeds, I say!" The woman's voice was no more than a whisper, yet it had fallen upon the wrong ears.

"You'll suffer for your words!" cried out a man clothed in black hat and padded doublet. Grabbing the woman by the shoulder, he proceeded to drag her away.

Several more shocked protests were suppressed by force and thus the city people quieted their opinions, afraid to voice them openly. Even a fool could see that Northumberland had peppered the crowd with his supporters, who loudly "hurrahed" Queen Jane while their cohorts silenced any protests. The crowd dispersed, overcome by fear, but from the looks upon their faces it was obvious that they were against Queen Jane, no matter that they were forced to keep silent. If they had loathed Northumberland before, they clearly did so more now than in the past. Had he then won a victory this day? Heather wondered.

The travesty of the situation swept over her like a wave. If she had not been a staunch supporter of Mary's claim before, she was now. Patting her bosom, where nested that precious letter, she smiled.

"Perhaps you have not won after all, my Lord Northumberland," she whispered. Over and over again in her mind she thought of what she must do. That Jane was in London, in the Tower, would make it all the easier.

Stephen Vickery. The name was implanted in her mind as she said it over and over. It was to him that she must slip the letter, for Richard Morgan knew well that he could be trusted.

So preoccupied with her thoughts was she that Heather did not see the shadow which fell across her path. Only when she felt the touch of a hand upon her shoulder did she glance up. Before her stood a large, stocky, brown-haired man with small eyes which seemed to undress her as they looked upon her.

"Are you lost, fair lady?" he asked with a grin.

"No!" she said quickly, feeling a fierce revulsion for him and not knowing why. There was something sinister about him despite his smile.

"Well, then, allow me to accompany you to wherever you are going." He took her arm before she could protest. "My name is Seton. Hugh Seton."

Heather could not recall why, but somehow she had the feeling that she had heard that name before. Whoever he was, she had to get rid of him.

"I can find my own way," she said coldly, trying to shrug off his hands. Instead he gripped her more firmly.

"No, I insist. It is not safe for a lady to be upon the streets alone. One is never certain what sort of rabble can be met upon the road." He eyed her up and down, taking in every inch of her person, including her full breasts. His penetrating gaze made Heather fear for a moment that he could see the letter, but he said only, "Blue becomes you." His full lips turned up in another smile and she felt like a lamb about to be devoured by a wolf. She was more determined than ever to rid herself immediately of his company.

"This is my favorite gown," she mumbled, her eyes darting to and fro for means of an escape. This man made her flesh crawl. Fearing that he might guess her destination, she stopped in her tracks.

"Your favorite gown. Then it will be mine also." He sounded as if he had put some claim upon her, and Heather fought against her anger, instinctively knowing that a show of temper would do her no good with this man.

Thinking at last of a way to rid herself of his company, she said, "My fan. I left it at the cobbler's." Bowing her head, she took leave of him, walking in the opposite direction, but she had not taken more than three steps when she felt his hand on her arm again. The man was worse than a leech.

"What is your name?" he demanded loudly, causing all about them to stare. "I have told you mine."

"Jane," Heather answered quickly, that name coming to her lips. "Jane Dawson."

"Jane, like our queen. The name suits you well. Let us hope that you are not as virtuous and pious as is that royal personage." He leered down at her, his hand slipping about her waist with a familiarity which left no doubt as to his intentions. His eyes seemed to seek out a dark corner and every fiber of Heather's body was aware of danger.

"I am just as virtuous, sir," she retorted, turning her head away in time to escape his mouth as it sought her own. Yanking free of him with a violence which took him off guard, Heather fled down the rough-stoned road, dodging the people milling about. She put as great a distance between them as she could manage. From time to time she tripped over her long skirts and cursed the farthingale which hindered her flight. Stumbling over a loose cobblestone, she was hurled to the ground by the force of her haste and looked behind her, fearful that now her pursuer would catch up with her. Instead she was relieved to see that she had lost him.

"That overbold buffoon!" she swore, panting hard to catch her breath and reaching her hand into her bodice to make certain the letter was still safely nestled there. "If our paths never cross again in this lifetime, I will have no regrets." She felt as if his very touch had soiled her, and shuddered again.

Picking herself up and dusting off the dirt from her dress, she once again headed for the Tower, keeping careful watch lest she again suffer the company of the man named Hugh Seton.

At last, after hiring a boatman to paddle her up the Thames, Heather found herself before the water gate at the Tower of London and eyed that formidable portal with awe. Her heart lurched in her breast at the thought of what she was about to do, but it was too late to turn back now.

After announcing herself to the guard and pulling the samples of cloth from the folds of her sleeve, she stepped out of the barge and upon the first stone step which led up to the Tower. Hearing the gate click shut, she swallowed hard. Now was not the time to become queasy.

Taking a step forward, nearly slipping on the wet stone step, she asked the guard to lead her to the council chambers. The red-clothed man-at-arms looked at her with suspicion, his black bushy brows furled in annoyance.

"I've not seen you before," he snarled. "What is your business?" He stepped in front of Heather to block her way.

"I am here on the *queen's* business," Heather answered, speaking the truth. She neglected to mention which queen.

"The queen, eh?"

"Yes, the queen." Head held up, shoulders thrust back, she took on a regal stance as he looked her up and down. "I have samples of cloth for her coronation gown." She held the pieces of cloth before her for his inspection.

"Come this way, then."

Up and up the gray stone stairs she climbed, following close behind the guard. The steps were steep and she stopped once or twice to catch her breath. At last they were in front of the thick wooden portal which housed the council. Lifting the bar from the door, he opened the portals wide. Inside was a throng of men talking excitedly as they stood in a semicircle about a diminutive girl in brocades and furs, Lady Jane Grey, who was now the Queen of England.

"I cannot try on the crown until the coronation. It is a sacred thing and cannot be handled lightly," she was saying in a high voice which sounded like a child's.

"She is taking this business of being queen far more seriously than Northumberland foresaw," chuckled a man near Heather.

"Aye, it appears he may have his hands full in managing this monarch," answered another.

Heather looked upon the queen and was surprised at how small she was, even more so than Heather. She had not expected the queen to be in the council chambers, instead had supposed her to be in her own quarters and had therefore thought to be able to carry out her plan before the queen could be summoned. The temptation to turn around and leave before anyone noticed her teased Heather, but taking a deep breath she resolved herself to carry on what had been started.

"And as to my husband being called 'king,' such a thing cannot be allowed. He is not of the blood royal," the queen continued, adamant in her anger.

"The queen is a stubborn one." The voice was that of Northumberland and Heather trembled in spite of her resolve. He looked in her direction as if angered by the intrusion, and she held her breath, awaiting his ire. Instead he turned back to the queen. "Is there nothing I can say to change your mind and make you see that for the good of England we need a king as well as a queen?"

Queen Jane stamped her foot in outrage. "No! My husband will be named as duke." She turned her back upon him, talking to her ladies-in-waiting, who looked like brightly colored flowers in their full-skirted gowns.

Infuriated by her snub, the duke strode from the room in anger, thus saving the day for Heather, who feared confronting him. Breathing a sigh of relief, she sought out Lord Stephen Vickery, remembering the description Richard had given to her. She found him standing across the room, his hand fondling his red-gold beard in agitation. Starting over in his direction, Heather was stopped in her tracks by a short bulbous-nosed man who grabbed her none too gently by the elbow.

"Are you the merchant's daughter? The one who claims to have been sent for?" he asked gruffly.

"Yes. My father is Thomas Bowen. I have swatches of his finest cloth with me for the queen to view." Heather's hands trembled and she fought to remain calm.

His eyes squinted as he looked at her. "Well, there is some mistake. You were not sent for. We are in the midst of an important meeting here and you are not welcome this day."

Heather forced a smile. "I'm afraid it is you who are mistaken, sir. If you will only ask the queen herself, I'm certain that she will tell you." Would her boldness be her undoing? She would have to take the chance.

He faltered for a moment, the bluff nearly working, but then said, much to her chagrin, "I will ask her. If you are telling me false, you will be punished, that I can tell you for certain." He made his way toward the freckle-faced queen, giving Heather the precious moment she needed to seek out Stephen Vickery. Taking the man's arm, she drew him toward the shadows.

"I have something for you. Something of greatest importance from Richard Morgan," she whispered.

"From Richard?"

"A letter from Queen Mary herself." Pulling the paper discreetly from her bodice, she slipped it into his doublet. Seeing the man with the bulbous nose returning and fearing that he might suspect what was going on, she urgently whispered to Stephen Vickery, "Kiss me, act the lover."

Stunned, Stephen Vickery nonetheless complied, gathering her close in his arms and molding his tight lips to hers. When he drew away Heather turned to find the man behind them standing with his hairy hands upon his hips, livid with fury.

"So this is what this intrusion is all about! Lord Vickery, you must keep your womanizing beyond these walls." He took a step forward as if to cause more trouble as Heather stepped between the two men.

"I'm sorry, it's just that I had to see him," she sobbed dramatically, wondering all the while what punishment her father would dole out when he heard *this* story.

The bulbous-nosed man snorted in disdain, giving Heather a push toward the entrance. "The queen said that she did not send for you." At his motion several guards armed with pikestaffs took a step forward. Heather's heart nearly stopped beating. There was no use in running; she was trapped and could only suffer her punishment with grace. Turning toward the queen, she curtsied low as if to tell her that her fate was in her hands. It was then their eyes met as Heather pleaded silently.

"No!" It was the voice of Queen Jane, who motioned for Heather's tormentor to come to her. Heather could see them talking and could only wonder what was going to happen next. At last the guard walked back to give sentence. The look of annoyance on his face gave Heather hope.

"Queen Jane is a kindhearted woman and has requested that you not be punished. She will keep the swatches which you have brought, for I daresay being a woman she fancies a new gown." He took the materials from Heather's shaking fingers, then pushed her beyond the doorway, saying, "Now, be gone with you and thank your lucky stars that you have been shown mercy. Were it up to me I would have you flogged for such a deception." With that said, he banged the portals shut.

Heather's heart nearly burst, and her hands trembled like the leaves in an autumn wind. She took a deep breath. The letter had been delivered. She had done it. Closing her eyes, she fought to regain her composure. Now it was up to Stephen Vickery to aid the queen and get the letter into the right hands.

"Come with me!" It was the guard returning, a scowl on his face. No doubt he had heard that she had come uninvited.

Walking down the stairs, Heather felt an overpowering sense of relief, despite the feel of the guard's hand in the small of her back, pushing her along. She could return to Richard Morgan and pridefully relate to him the experiences of this important mission she had taken upon herself.

It is done, she thought to herself, and I had a part in it. Stepping into the boat which would take her up the Thames, she somehow felt that all would be well.

11

RICHARD MORGAN TOSSED and turned upon his straw bed, besieged by worry. How could he have allowed her to go on such a hazardous mission? He should have insisted that someone else be sent. What if she were caught? What if Seton or Northumberland held her captive at this very moment? He knew what treachery they were capable of.

"Where is she? What is taking her so long?" His voice was a mournful cry. His jaw was clenched as he thought about what had befallen *him*. No doubt it was Seton's work. The bastard! Had it not been for Heather, lovely red-haired Heather, he would be dead, a victim of an assassin's blade. Instead of thanking her, he had sent her into danger.

"Heather," he whispered. The name came forth like a benediction. She was everything he could want in a woman, beautiful, brave, kind, loving. Even with the danger and excitement of riding to Hunsdon, he had not been able to put her out of his mind.

He glanced up at the rough wooden ceiling with its thatched roof and envisioned her face before his eyes, the slight slant to her brows, her full mouth, the gleaming white teeth, those fascinating eyes which seemed to change color with her moods. And her hair, that mahogany-rich glory which glistened like flames in the sunlight. She had felt so right in his arms. What a mockery it was that he could not claim her.

"If I were any kind of man I would leave here as soon as I can and never see her again," he groaned.

He was not free. Not free to offer her that which she so rightly deserved. But how could he do what was right when with every ounce of his being he wanted to taste of her honey, feel her body entwined with his, plunge deep within her softness?

"No! I cannot even think such thoughts." He sat up so quickly that his head seemed to spin in a whirl of dizziness. His strength still had not come back despite the young woman's ministrations of prickly ash, nettle, and shepherd's purse. If he were to leave he could not go far in his condition; thus he lay back down.

Closing his eyes, he was assailed by memories of days gone by. He thought about his brother Roderick, that holy monk who so closely resembled him. No twin could have looked more like him than his younger brother. He hoped for Roderick's sake that he was happy in his calling and had no regrets.

"No regrets," he whispered. Richard had so many. He had trusted those to whom he should have given none, and the thought was like a pain in his heart. If one could not trust one's own mother, then whom could one trust? And yet she had been the one to enslave him in this hopeless bondage, this farce called matrimony. He had believed her, let her arrange the proxy ceremony, not knowing that he was soon to be tied to a woman with a child's mind. Insane. That was what Edlyn was, and well his mother had known it at the time, yet her greed at the thought of latching on to the poor young woman's fortune had been more temptation than she could resist, and so Richard had found himself married to the poor pitiful creature.

I may as well have taken religious vows, he thought angrily, for my body has been forced to be as celibate as has Roderick's own. What a cruel jest life had played upon him.

And now to find the woman he had dreamed about, only to have to turn away from her. If only he had not crawled through her father's window that night, had not waited to light the lamp, had not gazed upon her beauty, had not kissed her, perhaps then he would not be suffering this agony which was far more painful than his wound. That she seemed to feel the same about him was added torture. He had seen the spark of love in her eyes. How could he extinguish it without breaking her heart and his as well?

Hearing the loud tread of footsteps, he turned his eyes toward the door. "How you be feeling?" The man named Harold Perriwincle stood in the room. He had tended Richard faithfully and for this, the dark-haired man was grateful.

"I fear I won't be dancing any jigs for a while," Richard answered, "but I do feel better than I did last night."

The old man's eyes were kind as he smiled his toothless grin. "Bloody shame it is, you being wounded and all. London is going to ruin, I say. Too many people. Not like the old days." He seemed to lapse into memories of days gone by. "Too much violence."

"Times are changing. With the enclosure of lands by the wool merchants, I fear there are many who would soon starve if they did not flock into the cities. We cannot begrudge them, my friend."

"No, I suppose not," the old man answered. "Still, it breaks me heart to think of what is happening. Bloody shame. Bloody shame." He reached into a large box nearby and came up with a bottle. "Got a surprise for you. This will heal you right proper. 'Tis a present from Mistress Heather."

"A bottle of ale. You sly devil, you." At the sight of it Richard's throat felt dry. Heather had given him many potions of drink, but he knew well that this would heal him more readily. He eagerly accepted the gift, somehow wanting to feel the oblivion this brew could render.

Perriwincle poured the drink into two mugs and offered one to the man who lay before him. He liked this man. This was the kind of man he had fought with in the old days. A man of honesty and courage. Just the right man for Mistress Bowen. It would be good to see her married off and far away from that pinch-penny father of hers. But what if this man already had a wife? That would be the rub. Clearing his throat, crossing his fingers, he asked, "Is there a loving wife at home who will be worrying her head about you?"

Richard took a swig of the drink, feeling the molten fire trickle down his throat. "A *loving* wife? No," he said in bitterness. He drained the mug in an instant and held out the cup for another mugful.

Perriwincle smiled. So this Richard Morgan was free. Cocking his eyebrows, he resolved to do everything in his power to see the two of them thrown together.

"Has she returned yet?" Richard asked, feeling the warmth of the ale course through his blood. His face was ravaged by worry, which did not go unnoticed by Harold Perriwincle. He smiled in approval. He was not wrong, then; this man did have an eye for the mistress and perhaps cared a mite more than even he knew.

"Don't you worry about Mistress Heather. She is more than a beautiful face. I don't know where she went off to, but I know for certain that she will be back soon. You have my bloody word on that."

Richard Morgan tried to stand up. He had to go after her. He had to make certain that she was all right. His knees buckled under him and he cursed aloud in his defeat.

Harold Perriwincle was beside him in an instant. "I don't think you be going anywhere." He helped his patient to sit back upon the rough, hard bed. "Tell you what. If the mistress still be gone at the tolling of the last bell, I'll go out in the wagon. On that you have my bloody word."

His promise soothed Richard Morgan, who leaned back upon the bed. Usually ale gave him stamina, but tonight it seemed to loll him to sleep. Closing his eyes, he soon was snoring, much to Perriwincle's amusement. Tiptoeing out of the stable loft, the old man closed the door.

* * *

Heather opened the creaky wooden door and stood looking down at the man on the bed. Her gaze wandered over him, capturing the memory of his muscular strength nestling close in her arms. A feeling of anticipation overcame her, a pleasant vision of years together that they would share. She felt that her life was just now beginning, that she had never lived before her encounter with him.

"Heather?" Richard's eyes opened as if aware of her scrutiny. "You're back!" His joy at seeing her was plain upon his face, and she smiled.

"Of course I'm back. Did you think otherwise?" Heather was in a teasing mood. The success of the afternoon had gone to her head like Richard's mug of ale.

"Then it is done. The letter is in Lord Vickery's hands?"

"It is done," she whispered, relating to him quickly all about her entry into the Tower, Northumberland's anger with the new queen, how she had quickly sought out Lord Stephen Vickery, the kiss, her own fright when she thought she would be punished for being caught in a lie of having been summoned by the queen.

All the while she spoke, he looked at her. Surely dressed in that blue gown, the French hood perched atop her dark red hair, she looked as regal as any lady of the court. Lord, what a beauty! He could nearly imagine in his mind's eye the scene she related to him, could see the proud tilt of her chin as she stepped forward. He had never seen her dressed like this before. Always it had been the shapeless dresses and gowns she wore, or her loose chemise, but now he could fully appreciate her loveliness, could see the outline of her tantalizing breasts. Round, high, firm, they seemed to invite his touch. Her waist was so small, he could well imagine that he could easily span it with his hands. He found himself wanting to see the rest of her, to strip away those full skirts and view what lay beneath. The hot ache of desire sparked within him and it was all he could do to fight the urge to reach out for her. Tearing his gaze from her, he sought to control his baser urge.

"And so all went as planned," he said. "Not only do I thank you, but Mary Tudor will do so as well." He sat up quickly, too quickly. Reaching up a hand to his head, he fought off the dizziness which consumed him.

Heather was beside him in an instant, offering her arms to steady him, assailing him with the beguiling scent of roses which came from her hair. Her hands reached out to touch him, to caress him, and that touch was his undoing.

"God's blood. What are you doing to me?" His fingers closed around hers, all reason and caution gone from his mind. "Are you a witch, to so cast a spell upon me?" His eyes seemed to devour her, hypnotize her.

As she stared into his eyes, Heather's heart began to hammer at the glitter of desire she read there. She found herself remembering the firm gentleness and pressure of those warm lips against her own. Without any awareness of what she was doing, she leaned toward him, the soft material of her gown tightening across her breasts as she did so, making him aware of their tempting allure.

With a groan he dropped her hand and reached for the soft swell of her breast, caressing it with gentle, exploring fingers.

"I've wanted to touch you like that for so long. Since first I saw you."

Heather shivered with pleasure, remembering another time he had touched her breasts, that time that he did not remember. "And I to have you touch me."

They moved together into an embrace as he kissed her, her mouth opening under the pressure of his as the kiss deepened in intensity. The kiss had the taste of ale and was just as intoxicating as she was caught up in the tide of their passion.

He pulled her with him to the hard bed, ignoring the pain that blazed in his shoulder. For a man once so close to death, desire had given him sudden strength. He was completely ruled by his emotions, as all his resolve, his vow not to touch her, was swept away in the tide of his passion. All thought of Edlyn and his married state was gone from his mind. He only knew that Heather was beside him and that he wanted her as he had never wanted any other woman. She was lovely and tempting and warm. Since that first night in her father's storehouse he had wanted her.

He clasped her in his arms, and they lay side by side, he tugging at the hem of her gown and cursing the stiff farthingale, she hurrying to remove it and toss it aside. His muscles strained against the softness of her curves as they continued to drink of each other's kisses. Heather gave herself up to him, feeling as dizzy as Richard Morgan had only a moment before.

"Heather. Lovely, lovely Heather," he breathed. His fingers parted the neck of her gown and he reached inside her bodice to feel the warmth of her, stroking and teasing the peaks of her breasts until she moaned low and whispered his name just as he had whispered hers. She yielded to his hands, those hands that searched out the secrets of her woman's body .

Richard Morgan was on fire. Sliding his hand up the smooth velvet of her thigh, muffling her moan of protest with his lips, he reveled in her softness, seeking the petals of her womanhood.

Heather stiffened slightly, unprepared for the touch of his fingers upon her legs, that part of a woman that must never be seen. Despite her desire, she began to struggle against his questing fingers, looking at him with questioning eyes.

Richard Morgan stared into those eyes, green eyes now, filled with a vulnerability that caused him shame. Muttering a curse beneath his breath, he pulled away from her, embarrassed at how quickly he had lost all self-control. At the realization of what had nearly happened, he felt self-disgust. She had saved his neck when Northumberland's cronies were after him, had saved him from an untimely death, had nursed him, had even taken on his duty to bring forth Mary's letter, and he had come close to repaying her by stealing her virtue with nary a second thought. If she had been a tavern wench, one used to men before, it would have been a different story, but well he knew her to be an untried maiden. Her reaction to his bold touch was confirmation of his premise.

Heather saw the dark look which swept over his face and wondered at the cause. Did he think her the wanton? Was he disgusted by her lack of constraint? What had she done to cause such a sour look?

The silence grew between them as each was tortured by doubts and shame. It was a long while before she could bring herself to look at him, and her voice was barely a whisper as she asked, "Are you in pain?"

"No," he answered, all too quickly, looking at her then turning away again. She was meant to wed a handsome young man who would cherish her and bring forth many children from their union. He could not offer marriage. His love would only bring her shame.

"Richard . . ." she called out, but he did not look at her. She reached out to him but he recoiled at her touch, knowing well that he could easily be again consumed by her nearness. Turning his back upon her, he lay upon his hard bed and closed his eyes. It was as if happiness beckoned to him, only to taunt him all the while.

"Richard . . ." she whispered again. His eyes met hers for only a moment, then quickly glanced away again. She wanted to ask him what was wrong, why he had pulled away from her, but the words stuck in her throat.

At last she said, "You are tired, so I will leave you for now. If you want me or need anything, Perriwincle will be nearby." Her eyes swept over him as she donned her farthingale.

He didn't answer. All his strength and passion

seemed to have drained out of him with the realization that she could never be his.

Heather fought against the pain his rejection aroused in her as she stood up and walked toward the door. She wanted him to call her back, ask her to stay, but he did not and she realized that she had best hurry into the house. Surely her father would already be angered by her long absence, and perhaps her mother as well. Casting a glance at the figure on the straw bed, she hastened away.

12

SITTING AMID THE stack of ledgers and logs, Heather felt like a condemned prisoner. How could she concentrate upon sums and numbers when every fiber of her being longed to be with Richard Morgan? Closing her eyes, she remembered every word they had exchanged, every gesture, the way he had kissed and caressed her. Why had he suddenly changed toward her? What had she done to make him suddenly stiffen and draw away from her? Was it because he had been in pain?

Over and over again in her mind she sought out every detail, finding herself blameless of anything that might have angered or offended him. Had she been too free with her affections? Did he find her shameless to so abandon herself to their passion? Or was she just being too sensitive and foolish?

And there was another matter which plagued her mind. What would happen when her father learned of her bold entry to the Tower? That he would be livid with anger, she was certain. What if her impetuous actions brought forth punishment upon her father's household? What if Stephen Vickery were found out and under torture told all, implicating her in the delivery of the letter? At the thought her hands shook so violently that she dropped the quill from her fingers.

"Heather!" Coming up behind her, Thomas Bowen nearly shattered any shred of composure that Heather could maintain.

Turning to look at him, her gray eyes wide, she

saw him reading a letter and she thought at once that the time had come when she would be forced to answer for her deeds.

"Yes, Father. What is it?" she managed to ask.

His round red face broke into a broad smile. "A miracle, daughter, that's what. Didn't I always say that there would come a time when I would be rewarded for my labors?" He thrust the paper in front of her eyes, tapping it with his stubby fingers. "See this! An order for cloth from our new queen herself. Imagine that."

Heather took the letter from her father's hands, scanning it quickly. She wanted to laugh aloud, to tell him that he had her to thank for his good fortune, but she held her tongue, fearful that to do so would raise too many questions. There was still Richard Morgan to think of. Although under her watchful eye and tender care he was regaining his strength, she still could not risk his being discovered hidden away in the stable.

"Of course they would want the queen dressed in the finest cloth. Everyone in London knows that Thomas Bowen's cloth is the finest for miles around." His chest was puffed out in pride, reminding Heather of a peacock, proud and strutting. She smiled to herself, thankful for his good fortune. His jovial mood would definitely make it more pleasant around the house.

"Yes, Father. Everyone knows that you are London's leading merchant," she said, rising to her feet. She had to go to Richard, to see that he was all right. Perriwincle had promised to watch over him, but it wasn't the same as her being there to see for herself that he was well. And besides, after last night there was so much she needed to say to him, to ask him.

"Sit down, girl!" His voice thundered in her ears. "If I am to be the queen's own merchant, there is much that needs to bc donc."

"But . . ." It was useless to argue. With a sigh of disappointment Heather returned to the task at hand, her eyes barely seeing what was written on the paper, her ears scarcely hearing her father's voice calling out his sums. Only Tabitha's entrance a half-hour later pardoned her.

"Master Bowen," the flaxen-haired servant girl began, shyly lowering her eyes as she always did when talking to the head of the household. She was tall and thin, her actions more those of someone small and petite, making her appear awkward as she bowed.

Thomas Bowen grunted in answer, but when she did not speak, turned around to look upon her with eyes blazing. "Well, speak up. If you are going to interrupt me, be about your business and be quick about it!"

The girl's square jaw tightened, her face reddened, and as always, Heather's heart went out to this timid young woman who was certainly no match for her father's temperament.

"His . . . his grace. The . . . the Duke of Northumberland." She stood wringing her hands in nervous agitation.

"Yes?"

"He . . . he's here!"

Thomas stood up, scattering the ledgers to and fro. "He's here? Why didn't you say so sooner? You silly chit." He gestured wildly to Heather. "Set the table. Fetch our best wine! Put out the silverware. God's blood, how I wish I'd had some warning."

Heather could find no words to answer her father; her voice was choked with fear. Northumberland! Richard's enemy was hers now too. What was he doing here? That he would find Richard was her greatest fear.

Thomas Bowen's face was bright with anger. "Well, go on, daughter! Away with you." He looked at Tabitha, who stood rooted to the spot. "You too, girl. Am I surrounded by idiots?"

With Tabitha close behind her, Heather did as she was bid, running up the stairs so fast that she was panting to catch her breath. She had to get word to Perriwincle so that just in case there was any danger, he could hide Richard. Feeling like a cornered rabbit, she sought a means of escape, to flee out to the stables for only a moment, but her father's corpulent form blocked the doorway as he supervised the proceedings. She could hear his booming voice ordering Blythe Bowen to greet their guests.

"Tabitha . . ." she began, as they both spread the cloth upon the trestle table in the solar.

Tabitha looked up at her mistress, her bright blue eyes mirroring her adoration for the young woman with the dark red hair and lovely face. How she had always longed to be even half as pretty, instead of being so very, very plain.

"Yes, Heather?"

Heather's answer was silence as her father's eyes turned upon her. Filling the goblets with wine, setting the table with knives, forks, and spoons, and putting the two-handled bowls upon the table in case the duke decided to sup with them, she thought frantically about what she must do. It was time that she told Tabitha of her secret, of Richard Morgan. She felt instinctively that the servant girl could be trusted, and unlike Blythe, would not fret about the consequences of what she had done. She needed a friend right now, and Richard needed help. As they readied the napkins, basins, and pitchers, she quickly related her story to Tabitha in a voice which was hardly more than a whisper, just in case the wrong ears were attuned to the conversation.

Tabitha's eyes shone with excitement, her thin lips stretched in a smile. "And he's here, in the stables?" she asked in amazement, full of admiration for such an act of courage. That she was now to be part of this daring event filled her with pride. "Is he terribly handsome?"

Heather's face answered the question, shining with the radiance of those who love. She wanted to say more but the untimely entrance of the duke and his cohorts silenced her tongue.

"And if you would care to sup with us . . ." Heather's father was saying.

Feeling the sensation of eyes staring at her, Heather

turned around, only to be met by small beady eyes which sent a shiver of revulsion pulsing through her.

"Why, by my faith, if it isn't Mistress Dawson. Jane Dawson," rasped a voice she had thought never to hear again. It was the same man who had tried to be so familiar with her on her way to the Tower.

"I'm sorry," she whispered, feigning ignorance of his identity. Perhaps if she pretended not to know him, he would think her not to be the woman he had met.

He tried to smile but managed only a grimace. "Seton. Hugh Seton. And I see that you are not Mistress Dawson at all, but the merchant's daughter." He cocked an eyebrow at her. "Why did you lie?"

She looked him directly in the eye, not wavering in her answer. "Because you were overbold and I had no intention of succumbing to your advances. In short, I had no desire to see you again."

He threw back his head and laughed at her answer, but the sound was more menacing than cheerful. "I see you are not afraid to speak your mind." His eyes raked over her, smoldering with desire. Even in her shapeless frock she was a pretty sight. "You need taming, wench, and I am the man to do it."

"I doubt that, sir," she answered, turning her back upon him to attend to the guests. How she managed to pour the wine without spilling it, she would never know.

"And Mary has had the gall to proclaim herself queen," she heard Northumberland saying. "And the northern nobles, traitors that they are, are flocking to her support. Even now it is said that they are marching upon the capital. It looks like there will be battle after all. I must raise my own troops and count on you for support."

"You have it," Thomas Bowen answered loudly.

"Ah, if only I knew how Mary's letter had been smuggled to the council. Therein lies my trouble. Traitorous bastard. Whoever did the deed will surely rot in hell for his papist sympathies. Though I have no doubt that Richard Morgan is at the bottom of it."

At the mention of Richard's name, Heather nearly dropped the wine cask. She must warn him that Northumberland was here. He must stay hidden. If anyone were to go into the loft . . .

The Duke of Northumberland's voice lowered and Heather strained her ears to hear. "Perhaps I need send my brother to Calais and Guines to seek for Henry II's support. Gold and jewels should prompt him to invade England, eh? I doubt that he would like to see a half-Spanish queen."

Why, that traitor! Heather thought. She could see her father's body stiffen as he caught her looking his way, no doubt intent upon keeping his own treacherous deeds secret. Now she knew beyond a reasonable doubt the reason for the great weight of the money-box. Her father, she knew, would just as easily change sides were Mary to appear the victor, at least if there was a profit for him in doing so.

Thomas Bowen was animated in his discussion with the duke, but Heather could not hear what they were saying because of Hugh Seton's prattle. He hovered about her, laughing and chattering in his attempt to gain her affection, and had it not been for the presence of her mother, she would have felt frightened by his advances, for the man did not know enough to keep his hands to himself, seeking a pat here and there when no one else was looking. She longed to pour some wine upon his person to so cool his ardor, but dared not. Her only respite from his unwelcome attentions came when the duke motioned him to his side.

"We must be on our way. Thomas, here, has some fine horses that could be put to our use. Come, let us view them."

Heather's heart pounded so violently at the duke's words that she thought surely all in the room could hear it. She looked over at Tabitha, their eyes meeting and joining in silent conversation. Warn him! Like a will-o'-the-wisp Tabitha vanished from the room and Heather sought to distract her guests as they turned to leave.

"Gentlemen, another glass of wine? It will be a long dry journey." Hugh Seton stepped forward, his arm encircling her waist as he held forth his cup.

"We have not time!" the Duke of Northumberland grumbled, motioning the stocky man forward. His eyes touched upon Heather as if trying to place where he had seen her before, outside this household, and she quickly turned her back as if intent upon flirting with her bold departing guest, who smiled broadly at her sudden attentions. Running his fingers over the bare skin of her shoulder, he grinned.

"We will finish this another time," he rasped, pulling away regretfully to tag along behind his departing leader. Heather sought for a way to detain them, but could not, for her father's piercing eyes were upon her and she knew that to act unseemly would only endanger Richard Morgan all the more. She could only watch as the party of men took their leave, and say a silent prayer that the man she loved would be safe from their prying eyes and ears.

13

RICHARD MORGAN STARED up at the pale frightened face of the girl hovering above him, wondering if he dared trust this stranger. "Who are you?"

"Tabitha. We have no time to talk—the duke is here."

"Northumberland?"

"Yes. And a man named Seton." She tugged at his sleeve to hurry him.

"If I have jeopardized Heather in any way by being here, I will never forgive myself," he whispered beneath his breath. Something was afoot, he knew it. But what? Why were the duke and his cohorts here? Was Heather in any danger? "Northumberland! Seton! Bigod, is this the truth?"

"Yes. Please, hurry. They are coming this way." The emotion in her eyes and voice urged him to do as she said.

"If Seton lays one hand upon Heather, I swear I will kill him!" he swore. Leaning upon this tall, thin girl who sought to help him, he managed to hide himself behind a large haystack across the room just as Perriwincle bounded in, oblivious of the danger threatening. At sight of the empty cot, he became frantic.

"Where . . . ?" he breathed, only to be silenced by Tabitha's finger held to his trembling lips. From down below they could hear the din of horses and men, and peeking over the edge of the loft, it was possible for them to see the blacks and browns of those who wore the duke's livery.

"Andalusian, did you say, Thomas?"

"All three, your Grace."

"Fine. I will take them with me. And, Thomas . . ."

"Yes, your Grace."

"I will be very generous, as I have been before. I will leave it to you to gather together my supporters among the bankers and merchants of the city."

From his hiding place Richard Morgan seethed with anger. To be so close to these treacherous snakes, yet to be as weak as a kitten, was nearly more than he could bear. If only he could procure a sword, he would gladly sacrifice his own life to rid England of the duke's foul existence.

"We meet at Bury."

"Yes, your Grace."

"Bury!" Richard whispered. Taking a step closer to hear more, he tripped over a bucket, clumsy in his excitement.

"What was that?" Seton's loathsome voice.

"Who is up there, Thomas? I cannot take the risk of anyone spying upon me and letting their tongues rattle on. Come, let us see."

The haystack was not large enough to fully hide Richard Morgan. He was trapped. The sound of stumbling feet sounded from below as the party of men climbed up the steps to the loft. He would have to prepare himself to face his fate like a man.

"Bloody damn!" It was Perriwincle who swore, thinking quickly to save the situation. "Always was clumsy." He leaned over the loft, grinning toothlessly at Thomas. "Sorry, sir. Seems I've dented your new bucket."

Looking up and seeing Perriwincle from his perch in the loft, Thomas Bowen stamped his foot in anger. "Perriwincle! I should have known it was you." He motioned to the men to come back down. "It's just my stablehand."

The duke paused for a moment on the top rung of the ladder steps. "Are you certain?"

"Yes. The old man works out here, though I have a suspicion that he does more napping than working. No doubt that was what he was doing just now and I caught him. Ha!"

Mumbling beneath his breath, the Duke of Northumberland climbed back down the ladder steps, and Thomas, anxious to placate him, waved excitedly at Perriwincle.

"Get down here, Harold, and help the duke! Don't dawdle there looking like a frightened nanny goat."

"Yes, sir." Perriwincle was down the ladder before the merchant could say another word.

Richard Morgan strained to hear what was going on, but only the sound of the horses' thrashing hooves, Perriwincle's cursing, and the grumbling of the men anxious to be upon their way could be heard; then there was silence, startling in contrast to the noise before. Richard Morgan could hear his own breathing, as loud to him now as the roar of the wind, yet he kept his hiding place until Tabitha and Harold Perriwincle came to help him back.

"May God curse that man!" he rasped in anger. "Northumberland is the worst catastrophe to overtake our land since the war between the houses of Lancaster and York."

"Aye," Perriwincle hastily agreed. "How I would like to go to our rightful queen and fight by her side. God bless her! Oh to have me youth again. She'll need every man." He looked at Richard Morgan and felt pity for the poor man, to be so laid up when he was sorely needed. "I know just how you feel, honest I do."

"Yes, I think you do." He sat down upon the edge of the cot, feeling defeated and drained of all his strength. He was not a man used to being idle, particularly when he was so needed. Covering his face with his hands he fought with difficulty against the rising tide of his emotions.

"Richard!" At the sight of him, his shoulders hunched over, his face buried in his hands, Heather forgot about the presence of her two servants and ran to his side, gathering him in her arms as if he were a small child. "Are you all right?"

His blue eyes touched upon her and there was such love written there that Harold Perriwincle smiled. Yes, these two belonged together, of that there was no doubt.

Burying his face in the warm softness of her breasts, Richard held her close. Her near proximity made him forget all else, only an exhilarating happiness engulfing him. He wanted to touch her, to explore every curve, to find the fullness of her lips and caress them with his own.

"I was so worried. I thought for a certainty that you would be discovered." Heather longed to ease away the lines of strain about his mouth, to soothe his troubled brow. Reaching out her hand, she ran her fingers through the thick dark hair, knowing that if he had been killed by Northumberland she would not have wished to survive. How was it possible to fall in love so quickly, to find that another being had become your sun and moon?

"She needs me. My queen needs me and I am about as useless as a gelded stallion," he murmured hoarsely. "Northumberland might just as well have killed me."

Tears sprang to her eyes and she blinked them away. "Had he done so, I too would have died." She could feel him relax in the shelter of her arms, could hear the steady rhythm of his breathing. Heedless of the onlookers, she whispered what was in her heart. "I love you, Richard."

He stiffened in her arms as she spoke the words. His jaw tightened. She had said it. Love. God, how he loved her too, but he would not say the words, he could not. She was all trusting innocence and he the biggest bastard in the world if he took advantage of that fact. He broke free of her arms, and his manner was now cool aloofness. "Don't love me."

She was shattered, longing to hear him say the same words to her. She wanted to feel his arms around her again, hear him utter the words "Be mine, go away with me, be my wife." Did he have no feelings for her at all? Oh, yes. Gratitude. She had saved his life and knew him to be grateful for that, but she wanted more from him.

"I'm . . . I'm sorry," she stammered, and Perriwincle, viewing the scene, looked upon his mistress with sympathy. It was not easy to open your heart to someone only to be rejected. He was confused. What on earth was wrong with this Richard Morgan? He would soon have back his strength and be gone, and there would be little chance for the flower of love to blossom, unless he, Perriwincle, took a hand in the matter.

At the pain written upon her face, Richard Morgan cringed. Why didn't I just slap her and get it over with? he thought. Could he have wounded her more deeply if he had?

He wanted to tell her that he loved her too, but he held himself in restraint, saying only, "You have nothing to be sorry for. You are brave and beautiful and I owe you my life."

Heather averted her eyes so that he could not see how deeply he had hurt her. She could not force him to feel what he did not feel, but she had thought . . .

"Mary has proclaimed herself queen. There will be warfare. We can only hope that she will be victorious." Heather's voice was just as cool and aloof as Richard's as she fought to maintain her dignity.

"She will win. Mary will win," Tabitha exclaimed, coming up behind Heather. "Right has to overpower wrong, and she will have God on her side."

"Aye, that she will," Perriwincle heartily agreed.

Heather relayed to Richard what little she had been able to overhear and he merely nodded in silence until she mentioned the duke's plan to seek the aid of the King of France.

"He would bribe Henry II to invade England? Even Satan himself could not be so evil. When the council gets wind of this, they will surely hasten to Mary's cause, Catholic or Reformist." His eyes searched the face of Harold Perriwincle, whom he had come to trust. "Will you deliver a letter for me?"

Heather stepped forward but he vehemently shook

his head. He would not let her place herself in danger yet again.

"I'll do whatever you ask of me," Perriwincle proclaimed, adding, "I cut quite a dapper figure in me day, I did."

Richard Morgan smiled. "I don't doubt it, my friend."

Heather sent Tabitha for paper and a quill, fearing that if she were the one to go it would be nearly impossible to return to the stable. Thomas Bowen would be searching for her even at this moment. Although he never told her so, Heather knew that without her skill with numbers her father would never have been as successful at his profits.

Tabitha was flushed when she returned, but smiling. "Here you are, sir." Thrusting the articles into Richard's hands she curtsied, her eyes never leaving his face. Would she ever find someone this handsome to love? No. No one would look upon her with favor with her plain face and common heritage. Another woman would have been jealous of her mistress, for despite Richard Morgan's words Tabitha knew in her heart that he loved Heather Bowen; it was written on his face whenever he looked her way. Yet Tabitha was happy for Heather. There was not one jealous bone in her entire body for any other person.

Richard hastily scrawled his message, then thrust the missive into the old man's hands. "Give this to Sir Nicholas Throckmorton. With Northumberland upon the road there should be little danger. I have no doubt that our kind duke has more important things upon his mind at the moment." He reached out and patted the old man on the shoulder. "But take care lest you end up like me, a pincushion."

Perriwincle roared with laughter. "I will take care."

Leaning back upon his pillows, Richard Morgan closed his eyes, fatigue overcoming him at last. Heather looked down at his face as she left the room, and only when she was alone did she succumb to her tears. She was unprepared for this pain his words had caused her. Nothing she had read or done could have prepared her for this violent desire, this longing to follow him to the end of the world if he would beckon her. She wanted to know everything about him, to tread in his footsteps, know all the people he loved, watch over him, melt her own body into his being.

"But he does not love me." Her words were mournful, echoing her sadness. She had thought that loving him as much as she did, he would have to love her back, had thought that he did by the way he had kissed her and caressed her. Why, then, had he told her not to love him? The answer was brutal: because he did not love her and didn't want her to suffer an unrequited love. In his own way he was being kind to her. But it was too late. She was hopelessly in love, caught up in a windmill of desire where she could only wait and dare to dream that he could one day love her too.

14

LOOKING VERY MUCH like a caged bear as he paced back and forth over the straw-strewn floor of his stable room, Richard Morgan waited eagerly for Perriwincle's return. It had been two days now since Northumberland's visit to the Bowen residence and Richard was feeling his strength slowly seeping back into his limbs. Soon he would be gone from here, a fact which caused him more pain than elation. He would be gone, never again to see the lovely face, the wide gray eyes of Heather.

She had still tended him faithfully, even after his plea with her not to love him, but she had been distant, the ache in her heart all too plain upon her face. He had wanted to take back his words, to tell her that he loved her, that his fondest wish was that she love him too, but each time he started to say the words the flashing dark eyes of his wife, of Edlyn, came before his eyes like a wall between them. He would never be free of Edlyn. Never. Her father was the most powerful man in the land next to the duke. With the resurgence of the Catholic faith in England, which would surely follow Mary's ascent to the throne, he would be doubly trapped. There would be no divorce. He should have sought his freedom long before now, while Edward and his Reformists were on the throne. It was too late now.

"No!" It is not too late. Kicking at a small pile of straw, he vented his temper. What kind of a coward was he to give in to his fate so easily? If he really loved Heather Bowen, and he did, he would move heaven and earth to be with her.

He should tell her the truth of his feelings before he left, open up his heart as she had opened up her arms to him. She was a kind and loving woman. She would understand and perhaps wait until he was free, if he became free. Ah, there was the rub. Could he ask her to wait faithfully while he tried to escape from his loveless marriage, growing older and older in a tangled web of passion and desire? Could he do to her what his father had done to Hugh Seton's mother? If indeed it had been as Hugh Seton had claimed, that he was Morgan's father's bastard son.

"I will plant no bastards in her shapely belly!" he vowed. He would not seek her love until he *was* free, risking instead that she would be there if and whenever he was able to claim her. And yet . . . It would be the bravest, most noble thing he had ever done. Much too easy would be the desire to give in to his temptations and claim her, brand her his own. "I must be away from here while I still have strength of will to do what is right for *her*."

The mask of pure torture which was branded upon Richard's face was not lost upon Harold Perriwincle as he entered the room. He knew the reason. Hadn't he once been in love?

"He loves her, he does, and for some reason he's holding it all back," he whispered to himself. He could not have mistaken the looks which flashed between his mistress and this man. He was old, perhaps a fool at times, but he was not blind. "And soon he will be gone and that sweet kind lady condemned to a life of pleasing her father." He had to do something, and soon.

He reasoned that if only they would taste freely of the love that they felt for each other all would be well. Perhaps if he had claimed Elizabeth so many years ago he would not now be a lonely old man. Love. That was what was important in life. Alas, he had learned all too late. But it was not too late for

Heather. And what could be the consequence if he helped the lovers along, if he played cupid?

"Why, Richard Morgan will take her away with him, he will." What could possibly go wrong? If they were caught, Heather's father would demand that Richard Morgan marry his daughter. Either as mistress or wife Heather would be happy and far away from the beady watchful eyes of Thomas Bowen.

"Aha. Red sage and summer savory!" he said aloud, startling Richard, who thought himself the only one in the room.

"Perriwincle!" he said, turning. "You nearly caused me to have a heart attack," Richard said with a sad smile.

"Sorry, sir," the old man said with apology. "That certainly would not do." He took off his old hat and flung it into a pile of hay.

"Well . . . ?"

"The whole country is divided, it is. Even families have different loyalties, but if you ask me, I think Mary's support is growing every day."

"And the council. Have you heard anything?"

Perriwincle shook his head sadly. "No. Bloody cowards they are, if they don't do something soon." He wiped his grimy sleeve across his brow. "But I can tell you this, I can. The people are for Mary. The swaggering braggart has vowed to bring in the Lady Mary captive or dead, like the rebel she is, but it will be his head, I wager, that will be adorning traitor's gate. When he passed through London there were people gathered, all right, but watching the soldiers go, these folks were sullen and silent. Not one said 'Godspeed.' "

"And with Northumberland busy fighting, the council will most certainly be swayed. Vickery and Throckmorton will most ably persuade them to do what is right. And when the council knows that every day people of all sorts are going over to our queen's side, our victory will be assured."

"Aye, that it will, sir." The old man could read well

the thoughts in the younger man's mind. "And you will be leaving us, sir. Soon?"

"First thing tomorrow morning. I must go to Mary's side. I am strong enough now to carry a sword, and would do so even if I had to crawl."

"How I wish I could go with you." Harold Perriwincle stared off into space as if remembering another place, another time. Had the years really passed by so quickly? For several moments he was silent, then turned toward Richard with a wide, toothless grin. "I have something that will make you stronger. Herbs that I got from an old Gypsy woman during the war. She gave me the secret, that she did, and I would like to share it with you. It will be my toast to your good fortune and to your happiness."

"Herbs?"

"Aye. Red sage and summer savory." He chuckled deep in his throat, and turning, set about to prepare the concoction. It was said that the potion heightened only desires already in the heart. He would see, he would see.

15

HEATHER SAT THROUGH the evening meal with her eyes downcast, hardly tasting the food which passed between her lips. He would be leaving soon and there was nothing she could say or do to stop him. How would he ever know how much sunshine he had brought into her life?

"Heather, dear, pass the salt to your father. He has asked for it three times." Blythe Bowen's voice was filled with concern. She wondered at the sadness she saw in her daughter's eyes. Was Heather really so unhappy?

"I'm sorry, Father," Heather answered, passing the large chunk of bread, scooped deeply in the middle, containing salt. Usually a man who came to anger easily, her father was unusually subdued tonight, and what's more, it seemed that his loyalty to Northumberland was waning. He did not talk of the duke in such glowing terms tonight, nor of Mary in such a derogatory way, and in fact had not said much all day.

"It doesn't matter," he answered bleakly. "My appetite has left me." Wiping his mouth on the tablecloth, which trailed onto the floor and served as a communal napkin, he rose to his feet to return to his counting room.

"What on earth is going on?" Heather heard her mother say. "Thomas is not himself these days. He has me worried."

"No doubt Mary is gaining ground. Father has

come too far to change sides now," Heather answered listlessly.

"Yes, I suppose he has. If only he had not involved himself in these political matters. It can be dangerous."

Blythe Bowen knew her daughter very well. She could see a change in Heather, could see how she seemed to hurry through her chores as if she had an appointment to keep. How many times had she seen her rush out of the house on some pretext or other? More than worry about Thomas plagued her. Beckoning to Tabitha to take a seat at the table, she resolved to watch her daughter more closely in the coming days.

Tabitha munched on a hard piece of bread, talking with her mouth full, much to Blythe Bowen's annoyance. Casting the servant a reproving glance, she left the solar to go to her husband's side.

Unlike Blythe Bowen, Tabitha knew very well what was troubling Heather. Reaching out, she covered Heather's hand with her own in a gesture of friendship.

"He loves you. I know that he does. No man could look at a woman the way he does you and not feel some deep emotion for her," she whispered.

"It is only gratitude."

"No! He is grateful to Perri too, but he doesn't look at him with smoldering eyes."

Heather sighed. How she wished Tabitha was right. It was true that she had seen Richard's eyes upon her, that steady gaze which made her overly conscious of her appearance. She had begun fussing about her dressing each morning, had concentrated upon walking with a more graceful air.

"Well, it doesn't matter," she lied, gathering together some sliced meat, cheese, bread, and vegetables for his dinner. If only she had the courage to ask him to take her with him. Would he? she wondered.

Taking the stairs two at a time, she pondered the matter, knowing that the answer would most likely be no. He would go straightaway to Mary's side to fight. There would be no place for a woman by his side. But later, when this was all over and Mary secure on her throne, what then?

Stepping outside, she breathed deeply of the fresh air, of the smell of flowers, hay, and earth. All her senses assailed her. She felt the tingling of the cool night air on her skin, listened to the sounds of the owls and the crickets, looked up at the sky. It was a brilliant dark blue summer sky filled with thousands of bright pulsating stars and a golden moon, a lovers' moon, which looked like a coin balancing in the sky.

A soft meow blended with the other night sounds and Heather looked down to see Saffron winding around her legs, begging to be stroked. "I have neglected you something awful, haven't I?" she said by way of apology, reaching down to run her fingers through the soft fur of the cat. "Had it not been for you, Saffron, I might never have met him. Don't be jealous, my pet." Saffron opened his jaws as if to answer, but just yawned and stretched himself languorously in the moonlight. Laughing, Heather continued to the stables, climbed the steps of the ladder, and stepped inside the small room.

Richard Morgan was not asleep. He stood looking out one of the small slits in the wall at those same stars which Heather had gazed at only moments before. Hearing her footsteps, he turned to look at her. Lord, she was lovely in the moonlight. Like some pagan goddess, her red hair billowed around her shoulders. Looking at her caused a gnawing ache in his groin, that same ache which had kept him from sleeping. He felt a fire consuming him, desire pounding in his blood.

"I brought you your supper," Heather whispered, taking a step toward him.

Richard Morgan licked his lips, wondering again at the strange taste of the brew the old man Perriwincle had offered to him. What *was* it the old man had given him to drink? "I'm not hungry," he answered, knowing that it was not true. He was a starving man, driven on by his hunger, only *she* was the connoisseur's delight, a feast of beauty which tempted him beyond his endurance.

"I'll put the food on the floor," Heather said softly, ignorant of his torment. He seemed so remote, so faraway tonight. What was he thinking?

He didn't say a word, merely looked at her, at the way her gown clung to the tantalizing curves and planes of her body. His blood surged wildly through his veins. Desire rose up to choke him and he felt as if he were drowning in the gray pools of her eyes. As if in a trance, he closed the distance between them, standing only inches away from her, breathing in the fragrance of her hair.

"You smell of roses," he breathed, reaching out to stroke her shoulders lightly. She answered with a deep throaty purr, like Saffron's when he was content, she thought. Just being with him made her happy. How soothing his nearness always was.

He could no longer master his longing for her, the most powerful desire he had ever experienced. It was as if he were no longer in complete control of himself, as if another force urged him on.

"Dear God in Heaven, I can't help myself!" he groaned, trembling as if possessed. Gathering her into his arms, he ignored the thoughts and vows not to touch her.

Heather's pulse quickened at the passion which burned in his eyes. Closing her arms around his neck, she offered her lips to him, wanting him to kiss her. His mouth descended upon hers, kissing her like a man with a deep thirst to assuage, drinking in the honey of her lips. He babbled words of love, reaching for her, stroking her. It all seemed so unreal, as if he moved in a dream—a sleepwalker.

Picking her up in his arms, he carried her to the straw mattress and she offered no resistance as her dreams seemed destined to come true.

Wrapped in each other's arms, they kissed, his mouth moving upon hers, pressing her lips apart, hers responding, exploring gently the sweet firmness of his. She gave herself up to the fierce emotions which raced through her, answering his kisses ardently, as if to memorize the feel of each one for those moments when they would not be together.

"Heather!" he groaned, his mouth roaming freely, stopping briefly at the hollow of her throat, lingering there, then moving slowly downward to the skin of her bare shoulder. A fire in the blood, that's what he felt at this moment. A raging inferno.

Heather could feel the pulsating hardness of his manhood through the thin cotton of her gown and wanted desperately to be naked against him, to feel the warmth and power of him. She wore no farthingale this time to hinder him in his quest.

"I tried to stay away from you," he murmured, fumbling with the fastenings of her gown, seeking to free the encumbrance of the rough cotton cloth. He ached with a pulsating desire, an all-encompassing need to be one with her.

Freeing the soft mounds of her breasts, reaching out to touch their softness, his fingers brought forth a tingling pleasure. "Richard," she moaned, winding her arms around him.

He knew that he should pull away from her but he could not. Never had it been so impossible to control his desires. What was happening to him?

"I can't stop myself," he breathed. His lips caught hers, molding his mouth to hers as his fingers slid down the front of her gown, to her stomach, to explore the softness there.

Heather was lost in the flush of sensations which swept over her. Holding him tightly against her, she felt wanton, aware of her body as she had never been before.

His mouth flamed on hers, plundering the softness. Like a bolt of lightning, passion passed between them.

Her breasts ached for his touch again. Sensing her feelings, he reached up to touch the swollen peaks again and smiled as she sighed with satisfaction.

"You are beautiful," he whispered. "I love to touch you."

"And I to feel you touch me." She could feel his hot breath stir the veil of her hair, could feel the brush of his lips against her temple. He sought to remove her garments, aided by her own hands. She was beautiful as she lay there before him, her body illuminated by the soft moonlight. His pulse began to pound as his eyes took in her long legs, the slim waist, the firm, rose-tipped breasts. Her body was perfection, but then, he had known that it would be. Admiring her body, running his fingers over her soft skin with adoration, he whispered words of love to her. Tracing a path of fire, his lips moved across her stomach and she trembled at his expert caresses.

Flinging aside his doublet, his shirt, his hose, nearly tearing them in his frenzy, he flamed with desire as their bodies touched. Heather was hypnotized by the masculine beauty of him. The rippling muscles of his arms and chest beckoned her touch as she reached out to him, caressing him as he had done to her. Passion exploded between them with a wild oblivion. Richard molded her against him, the fire released in him finding its match in her own passions, her own desire. She melted with his every touch, tangling her fingers in his thick black hair as he slid his fingers down to explore the center of her being.

"Love me, Richard," she cried, her body responding with a will of its own, writhing as his fingers touched the opening petals of her womanhood. She had no fear, though she was a virgin and had heard that the first time brought forth pain. He would be gentle with her—this she sensed.

The probing length of his manhood slipped hotly between her thighs, and he came to her with a slow but strong thrust, entering her softness as their bodies met in that most intimate of embraces.

"Your body is a vessel of sweetness," he breathed, only to hear her cry out softly at the pain as his throbbing, thrusting manhood broke the membrane of her maidenhead. "No more hurt. No more. Only pleasure from now on, I promise you."

Burying his length deeply within her, he let her

adjust to this sudden invasion of her softness. She found he spoke the truth: there was no more hurt, only ecstasy, like the currents of the deep sea as his body drew hers. She was consumed by his warmth, his hardness. Tightening her thighs around his waist, she arched up to him, wanting him to move within her. He did so, slowly at first, then with a sensual urgency. His lovemaking was like nothing she could ever have imagined, filling her, flooding her, nearly drowning her in ecstasy. She was sailing upon a sea of desire, plunging down, down, down into an abyss, aching with the pleasure of their love. Clinging to him, she called out his name.

Richard gazed down upon her face, gently brushing back the tangled red hair from her eyes. From this moment on she was his. He would never share her with anyone. She would be his wife in fact if not in name.

"Sleep now," he whispered, still holding her close. With a sigh she snuggled up against him, burying her face in the warmth of his chest, breathing in the manly scent of him. She didn't want to sleep, not now; she wanted to savor this moment of joy, but as he caressed her back, tracing his fingers along her spine, she drifted off.

16

Richard awoke to the sound of the first cock's crow to find Heather cradled in his arms. Her thick lashes fanned out over her pale cheeks and her mane of dark red hair was spread like a cloak over his chest and shoulders. As he looked at her he felt an aching tenderness. She looked much younger, snuggling up against him in her sleep. The passion they had shared passed before his eyes and he felt a tightening inside, an inward anger at himself that he could have so easily forgotten his vow not to claim her, and yet, were he to live forever, chastised and imprisoned away from her, he would remember last night.

"I love you, Heather. May God forgive me."

As if hearing his words in her sleep, she shivered and he gathered her into his arms, the heat of his body warming hers. He stroked her hair and closed his eyes, remembering. Never had he realized that love could be like this, such shattering ecstasy as to be almost pain. Were anything to happen to her, were anyone to harm her . . . It was a thought he dared not even imagine.

If only he could protect her from the world, this world which could often be cruel. What would happen to her now, now that he had sparked this all-consuming flame, this sea of desire? How could he leave now?

He felt her stir and looked down into her eyes. Last night in her passion they had appeared green; this morning they were blue. Ah, such marvelous eyes.

"Richard," she breathed, reaching up to touch his cheek as if to confirm that he was real and not some fabrication of her dreams.

"Forgive me," he whispered.

"There is nothing to forgive."

He cupped her face with his hand, bending his lips to kiss her soft open lips. Like a flower opening to sunshine, she moved her mouth upon his, feeling again the wondrous enchantment of the night before.

Richard's hand reached out to caress her, sliding his fingers over the soft mounds of her breasts. How could he fight these feelings he had for her? Her body, pressed against his, drove him beyond all thought, all reasoning. Even the commotion in the courtyard could not shatter this rapture. He shuddered, burying his face in the silk cloud of her hair.

They did not hear the sound of footsteps as Blythe Bowen, broom in hand, chased the straggly hound which had dared to chase after her Heather's cat. Saffron, judging the loft to be a safe place, sought refuge there, with Heather's mother following close behind, curious at the voices she heard coming from that direction. Nor did they see the tormented face of the woman watching them. Only a whispered "Dear Lord!" brought them back to reality.

"Mother!" Heather was horrified as she saw the figure of Blythe in the open doorway, a broom held upward in her hands. Reaching for her chemise, Heather sought to cover her nakedness. What had seemed so right, so wondrous, now seemed somehow shameful.

Blythe Bowen could not answer her daughter's cry; instead she stood staring, openmouthed, her eyes filled with tears.

Richard Morgan fumbled with his clothing, standing before Heather to shield her. "It is not what you think, madam," he said, looking Blythe Bowen squarely in the eyes. "She is not to blame in this. I am the guilty party. I took advantage of her innocence. Do not seek to punish her. Punish me instead."

"No!" Heather would not allow him to take the blame. "I wanted him to make love to me."

Blythe Bowen succumbed to her anguish, tears rolling down her cheeks, her face contorted in her sorrow. It was as if she could see another man standing there, another woman. Herself. So many years ago. Was her daughter to suffer the same fate? Tears were shed for her own shattered dreams as well as for her daughter's honor.

Heather donned her chemise and gown and stood beside her mother, reaching out her hand to touch Blythe Bowen's arm. "Don't weep, Mother. I cannot bear to see you cry."

The tears melted from Blythe Bowen's eyes to be replaced by flashing fire. "You!" she rasped at Richard Morgan, pointing her broom at him as if to strike him down. "That I should live to see . . ."

Taking a step forward, Richard sought to calm her. "Please, let me explain."

"Explain. What can you say? Will you marry my daughter?" Her look was one of pure hatred. "No. I do not hear you hurry to seek for her hand. You are alike, you men. Every one of you!"

Heather stepped between them, tears marring *her* face now. What had been so beautiful was now ruined beyond repair. "Mother, please. You do not understand!"

"Understand! It is you who do not understand." She had been betrayed by one such as this man, left with child and broken promises. "If he values his life he will leave this instant."

Hurrying to put on his doublet and lace his codpiece, Richard stood his ground. Only a coward would leave Heather now, and he was no coward. Reaching out quickly, like a striking serpent, he grasped the handle of the broom, disarming the woman before she did any harm.

"Madam, hear me out!"

"You have nothing to say that I want to hear. You have taken my daughter's virtue, that is all too plain to see. Nothing you can say to me can change that fact, nor give her back her maidenhead." She stood wringing her hands, her emotions swaying from anger to despair. What would Thomas say? What would he do?

"Heather saved my life. If not for her I would be with God and his angels at this moment. . . ."

"And you repaid her by stealing that which is a woman's most precious possession. You are beneath contempt!" As he tried desperately to explain to her his love for her daughter, Blythe Bowen steadfastly covered her ears with her hands, blocking out all sound. Thinking that she was doing what was best for Heather, she demanded that he leave the premises immediately.

"Mother. No. Please. I love him," Heather pleaded, going down on bended knee. She couldn't let things between them end this way. She might never see him again.

"If he does not leave this instant I will hasten the blue-clothed beadles to arrest him. It is a crime to trespass." As if making good on her threat, she turned her back upon him and walked to the doorway.

"Arrest him?" Heather's fear for the man she loved was all-consuming. If he were caught by Northumberland now it would surely mean his life. He had to go away before her mother's anger brought forth tragedy. It was as if the quiet, demure woman had turned into another person, fighting like a lioness for her cub.

"Heather." Richard's voice was hardly more than a whisper.

Touching him gently on the shoulder, she pleaded with him, "Go. I will speak with her, calm her. I could not live with myself if you were to come to harm."

He started to protest, to tell her again that he would not leave her, but the sound of footsteps, voices sounding closer and closer, changed his mind. Putting his fingers to his lips, throwing Heather a kiss, he started for the door, taking Heather's heart with him.

17

IT TOOK LONGER to calm Blythe Bowen than Heather could have ever imagined. It was as if a demon had been unleashed, yet much as Heather had feared that her mother would relate the story to Thomas Bowen, strangely enough Blythe remained silent about her daughter's lover. Perhaps, Heather reasoned, it was because he was already openly distraught with worry that the council would decide in favor of Mary. It seemed that when he talked he did so of this subject and nothing else, hardly touching his breakfast, pacing the floor until Heather was certain he would wear it through. All the while he muttered, "I am finished, I am undone!"

Now, standing in the hot midday sun, Heather helped her mother and Tabitha with the laundry, putting the shirts, gowns, tablecloths, and bed linens in the large wooden trough to soak in the mixture of wood ashes and caustic soda. It was the one household chore Heather loathed, for the mixture chapped her hands until they bled and the pounding of the dampened cloth was a tedious chore. Still, she knew that it had to be done.

All the while they worked, Tabitha chattered on merrily, unaware of the morning's trauma, while Heather and her mother remained silent, each in a world of her own.

"Where is Richard now?" Heather whispered to herself, closing her eyes briefly to envision his face. Was he even now riding north to join Mary? Was he safe? Her mind was filled with unanswered questions, worry, and turmoil. Lifting up one of the wooden buckets, she walked to the well as if in a daze, remembering Richard's touch, his kiss. What would have happened if her mother had not come upon the scene?

"Poor Mother," she sighed, remembering the expression etched upon the poor woman's face at viewing her daughter entwined with her lover's body. Heather looked at her mother, bending over the trough, pounding one of the linens with a fury as if envisioning it to be Richard Morgan himself. Heather had to convince her of his gentleness, his kindness. She could not have the two people she loved most in the world so at odds.

Drawing water from the well, filling the bucket, Heather reached in her hands, splashing some of the cool water on her sun-parched face, fearful of a sunburn. It felt refreshing, soothing her skin as if by magic.

As if to atone for his part in her troubles, Saffron perched gracefully atop the stones of the well, purring contentedly, then quenching his thirst with the water in the bucket.

"Ah, Saffron! It is easy for you to be content, but my whole world has come tumbling about me."

The cat's green eyes stared into hers, blinking his "cat kiss" in her direction. Had she not known better she would have sworn he was trying to answer her.

"If only that dog had not chased you, if only you had not run to the loft to seek your safety with Mother close behind. But then, it does no good to lament."

Sighing, she returned to the laundry, emptying the dirty water, pouring fresh rinse water upon the cloth within the trough, then putting the cloth to dry in the sun.

Blythe was now at work upon the furs and woolens, beating, shaking, and scrutinizing them with her keen eyes. The furs which had hardened from the dampness of the rains were sprinkled with wine and flour, then allowed to dry, rubbed back to their original softness. Those which needed a more thorough cleaning would be cleaned with a special fluid made of wine, lye, fuller's earth, and verjuice, made from the juice of green grapes. As she worked, Blythe Bowen would now and again look askance at her daughter, but as before, spoke not a word.

"What ails your mother?" Tabitha asked at last, noticing the strain and not being able to stand it much longer.

Heather blushed to the roots of her hair. "Sh-she . . . came upon Richard and me . . ."

Tabitha smiled. "He was kissing you. I knew that he was smitten. But tell me, how would such a thing truly upset your mother? There are few merchants' daughters who have not disobeyed the rules of conduct to taste of a kiss."

Only a husband was supposed to kiss a woman; it was an unwritten law, along with many others that bespoke of how a young woman of middle class should act.

"I fear there was more than a kiss!" Heather turned her face away. "I fear you will think me brazen to speak so, but I love him, Tabitha. I felt no shame in what we did."

Heather wondered why she was baring her soul to this young woman and decided that it was because she knew somehow that Tabitha would understand.

"More than a kiss? Is it possible . . . ?" Her blue eyes widened as the truth dawned upon her. "Oh no! Mistress Bowen. And to be caught . . ."

Heather sought to silence the servant girl, whose voice caused Madam Bowen to turn in that direction, but before anyone could say another word, Perriwincle's shouting drew all ears and eyes.

"'Tis a mutiny, it is. A mutiny," he shouted, running about on his short, skinny legs, arms waving wildly in the air.

"A what?" Blythe Bowen asked, leaving her woolens and furs to come upon the old man.

"It's true. A body of ships sent to cut off one of the lines of Mary's retreat has mutinied in Mary's favor. Bloody well time, I'd say. And at Bury it's said the soldiers told Northumberland they will not take one more step against their lawful sovereign."

"God be praised," Tabitha breathed, only to put her fingers to her lips as she was given a scowl from Blythe Bowen.

"We must be careful, Tabitha," Blythe said softly but firmly. "We must not talk freely, even among ourselves. Heaven knows what is going to happen."

But Heather could not keep silent. She was excited at the news of the success of that mission in which she herself had taken a part. Perhaps now Richard would return to her all the sooner. Perhaps once Northumberland realized how hopeless his cause was he would cease the fighting. Richard would be safe!

"Oh, Perri, how wonderful it is," she said, smiling.

At her enthusiasm the old man continued, "Me friend Egbert has a cousin up Norfolk way. He said that all those who came to uphold Mary's cause asked no pay. Even brought their own supplies, they did, and offered their personal fortunes to finance the campaign. Rallied to her support, they did, every last man, he said."

"Hush, Perriwincle," Blythe Bowen scolded, but Heather could see by the gleam in her mother's eye that Blythe too was in favor of Mary's cause. She seemed to be smiling, and as she walked back to the laundry her step seemed lighter, as if the worries of the morning had faded a bit from her mind.

Perriwincle took Heather aside. It was as if they shared a special secret. "Egbert says that Mary has already been proclaimed Queen of Norwich and has set up her standard at Framlingham Castle."

"Northumberland has lost."

"Aye. 'Tis only a matter of time. Serves him right, it does. He is a cruel and wicked man. He burned and pillaged as he went, and met with nothing but opposition at every turn. The people know their rightful queen, I say."

Nor was it only the North that was faithful to Mary. London was in a furious turmoil, with the bells pealing for Queen Jane one moment, then Queen Mary the next.

"Where will it all end?" Thomas Bowen asked woefully that evening at dinner. "What is the world coming to? Queen Jane has the favor of the bishops of London. Who can argue that? Who can say that Northumberland has not been an able administrator? Who?" He was met by silence.

When at long last the hectic day was over, a day which had brought anger, excitement, love, and triumph, after the household was abed, Blythe at last sought out her daughter. Opening the door of Heather's room, she came swiftly to her daughter's side, joining her as she looked out the window.

"Do you hope to see him, this young man of yours?" she asked softly.

"Yes," Heather answered, turning slowly to face her mother, searching the woman's face for the love she had once seen there. Did her mother still love her?

"Oh, Heather, what can I do to save you? How can I bear it if you suffer all the pain I had to bear?" Taking her daughter in her arms, she stroked her hair gently, remembering all the times she had comforted her like this, remembering the baby, the child, the young girl, now the woman. She wanted so much for this child. The world. There was so much she had to make up for. Was it too much to ask God that all the heartache that she had borne would be spared this beloved child?

"I love him, Mother. I do not need to be saved from anything save the loneliness I suffer when he is not with me. He does not bring me pain, only joy." They held each other tight, mother and daughter, at last walking over toward the bed to sit upon it side by side.

"Do you want to tell me about him? How did you meet? What is his name?" Blythe whispered. If Heather loved him so much, then she would try to find it in her heart to feel the same about this man.

Heather smiled. "Where can I begin? His name is

Richard Morgan. The night that you and Father were at his sister's I found him hiding in the storerooms, running from Northumberland's wrath, and then again on the streets of London. He had been wounded. Again, by Northumberland's treachery." The story poured forth and the two women talked long into the night.

As Heather talked, her mother envisioned Rodrigo de Vega whispering beautiful words and promises. She had been just about Heather's age, filled with the beauty of love and the dreams of the young.

"Do you love Father?" Heather asked suddenly. Somehow the look on her mother's face made her wonder.

"Love? What is love? He has been kind to me. He has taken care of me and of you." She wanted to tell Heather so many things, but now was not the time.

"But there is so much more, Mother," Heather whispered.

Her answer was a sad smile. "I know. I know. I too once had the notion that life is a fairy tale with happy endings." She walked toward the door as if the thought of opening her heart any further was just too painful.

"Will you tell Father?" Heather asked.

"No. I will keep your secret." Heather watched as her mother left the room. She did not hear her whisper, "And mine as well."

18

IT WAS A devilishly hot July night, a night filled with riotous shouting and laughter as bonfires blazed far and wide. Even at this late hour the people of London were celebrating with wild rejoicing as bells chimed throughout the city.

"Long live Queen Mary! God bless our good queen. Long may she reign."

Heather leaned out from her bedroom window, much too excited by the day's events to sleep. How could one slumber after the events that had occurred this day? Mary Tudor had been proclaimed queen in London, casting aside once and for all the pretender Lady Jane Grey and her father-in-law, Northumberland.

During the last few days Perriwincle had kept Heather well informed as to the fury of the storm that was taking place in the government. He would keep his eyes and ears open as he drove about the city, picking up bits and pieces of gossip and some information at first hand.

On the eighteenth he had been told some enlightening news, that Northumberland was sending out urgent messages demanding reinforcements, but that the councillors were turning to Mary.

"Every lock, stock, and barrel of 'em, I say," he had said with a laugh. "They're meeting tonight at the Thames-side Palace of Baynard Castle. Richard will be home in no time," he had added, flashing his toothless smile.

"So the councillors soon turn tail when they see

that the country is not behind them," Heather had exclaimed.

The afternoon of the following day there had been more news. Perriwincle had stood before her as she dried herbs in the sun, talking so fast that she could hardly understand him. "Lord Arundel gave an impassioned speech saying the crown is due to Mary." He chuckled. "The same Arundel who only a few days ago offered to spend his blood at Northumberland's feet. This bloody well assures Mary the crown."

It seemed that all England had now turned against the duke; even his loyal friends and followers said the crown was rightfully Mary's. Heather had watched from her window as the royal herald, bedecked in the lilies and leopards of England, had ridden up and down the street proclaiming the news to all of London that the council had proclaimed Mary the rightful ruler. The order had gone out for Northumberland's arrest. There would be no more fighting. The nine-day reign of Queen Jane was over. The diminutive red-haired lady was now confined to the Tower and Heather wondered how soon it would be before Northumberland and Hugh Seton joined her.

"All has been set to rights now," Heather murmured, brushing several strands of her dark red hair from her eyes. And yet she could not help but remember the kindness of the young queen that day at the Tower. How could Heather be indifferent to the fate of the young woman who had been reluctant to take the crown, that young woman whose eyes had met hers and softened, sparing Heather any punishment for her deception? Lady Jane had been but a pawn in the game of ambition, and this made her fate all the more pitiable.

From below the third-story window where Heather stood watching the rejoicing, several young men among the crowd waved up at her, some even throwing their caps up in the air.

"Come down and join us, fair lady," said one of the bolder of the men. As if to further entice her, he flung up a handful of gold "angels." Heather watched as those coins fell to the ground, only to be snatched up by the paupers dressed in their tattered garments.

"No, I cannot!" she called down. She was answered by loud pleadings from below and hastily stepped away from the window lest she be tempted. Thomas Bowen had given strict orders that neither Blythe nor Heather join the "rabble" in this revelry.

"Look at them. Look at them." Heather turned to find her father standing behind her, the one man who did not feel elation at Mary's victory. He had tried his best to hide his resentment, but only a fool would not see that his heart was not in the festivities.

"They are ready to give Mary their love, loyalty, and even their lives," Heather answered. She wondered how many people knew of her father's dealings with the man who had sought to be the ruler of England—Hugh Seton and Northumberland himself of course, but who else? Would her father be punished or forgiven? Even though Thomas Bowen was not always kind to her, she still did not want to see him suffer in any way.

As if reading her mind, he said softly, "Aye, their lives. I pray to God that I will not forfeit mine."

Heather hastened to his side, laying a gentle hand upon his arm. "I've heard that Mary is most forgiving. All will be well, Father."

He pulled away from her, fighting to gain control of himself and the terrible fear which threatened to turn him into a trembling mass of flesh. "Nary a one has bought my cloth these last few days. They know. They know. No doubt they saw me with Northumberland. Oh, curse the day I first set eyes upon him. I will be undone. Undone. My fortune will dissolve away like moistened salt. I cannot stand the thought of being poor." He walked to the window and looked down at the street. "That traitor. That churlish traitor, Northumberland. How he fooled me. I am a loyal Londoner, a loyal subject. I witnessed the coronation of Edward, of Henry, and served them well."

As a cheer rose again, a hailing of Mary, he quickly leaned out the window and joined his voice to the din. "God save the queen. God save Queen Mary!"

"All will be well, Father. You will see," Heather said softly. If the situation had not been so dangerous, she might have been amused. How easily for some men to change their loyalties, as easily as a snake shed its skin.

He turned to her, his eyes haunted. "Yes. It will. It will. No one will know. Why, even now Northumberland and Seton might be prisoners in the Tower, but perhaps they will not tell. If they do, I will refute their story. I will. I have always been loyal to Mary. You know. You will tell them."

Heather sighed. "Yes, Mother and I will be behind you in this. Now, get some sleep." Leading him over to the door, she opened it and Saffron bounded inside.

"That cat!" her father said sourly. "He is the cause of my troubles. Witches and cats. Bad luck!"

Heather could not contain her anger. "It was not Saffron who brought this upon you, but yourself. Your greed." She waited for his anger, but he merely looked at her, then left, closing the door behind him. Heather stood watching the door, wondering if the elation she felt at Mary's victory would be bittersweet.

Lying down upon the bed, she closed her eyes in an effort to forget her father's actions and words, tossing and turning on the straw-filled mattress. It was impossible. Thoughts swirled through her brain; the noise, the heat of the night, and her own anxieties made slumber out of the question. All she got for her efforts was frustration.

"'Tis not possible to sleep!" she cried at last, bounding from the bed to return to the window. The crowd below was celebrating, setting up tables as they picnicked beneath her window and danced in the streets to many a fine tune. At last Heather found her own feet tapping in time to the rhythm of timpani, recorder, fiddle, and lute as she wished for a moment to join them. Already there were songs abounding about the valor of Queen Mary, jovial songs and those of a more serious air.

One such song caused her anger, for it credited Sir Nicholas Throckmorton with being the one to warn Mary of Northumberland's intent, when Heather knew very well that it had been Richard Morgan who had ridden the night of the king's death to warn the queen.

"Richard," she murmured, hugging her arms around her body. When would she see him again? "Soon," she whispered, saying a silent prayer that he would return for her.

19

RICHARD MORGAN'S EVERY muscle ached as he arrived at the rickety back door of the small village inn. He would not have stopped at all except that he was not as strong as he needed to be for such a journey.

As he reached out to open the door, he noticed a proclamation nailed upon it which read: "Jane Grey Dudley, Queen of England." Yanking the missive from the door, he angrily tore it to shreds as self-incrimination surged through him. "Things might have been different if I had not suffered my wound and had fought beside my queen. What if I am not in time and Northumberland is victorious?" he mumbled half-aloud.

At the sound of the creaking wooden door he looked up into the face of the tavern keeper, a man of enormous girth with a thick black beard and a patch over one eye.

"Do you have a room?" Richard asked, letting the shards of the proclamation filter through his fingers like the snows of winter.

"A room? Ale, a hot bath, the round curves of a woman, and a much-needed rest, eh? In that order, I would wager," the tavern keeper replied with a smile which changed his image into that of a jovial jester. He opened the door wide and motioned for Richard to follow him.

The murky wooden dwelling smelled of sweat, grease, smoke from the kitchen stove, and stale wine and ale. A young boy led him to a seat at a corner table and while Richard waited to be served his eyes scanned his surroundings. The south wall was stacked with large barrels which looked as if they would topple over at any moment. The plaster was chipped, the hard planked floor covered with dirt, but he was glad to be at rest for at least a little while. Perhaps if he supped and tasted a mug of ale he would find sleep a welcome companion.

He closed his eyes, and the memory of Heather's lovely face drifted before him. Guilt that he had left her tore at his heart, although she had told him to do so, thinking of him all the while. Was her mother even now angry with her? If only he had been able to bring her with him, but it was folly even to think of such a thing. War and battlefields were no place for a young woman.

"As soon as I can, I will go back," he vowed silently. She was as precious to him now as a rare and beautiful jewel, indeed more so.

"What will ye have, me lord?" asked a shrill voice, bringing him out of his reverie.

"Fish, a loaf of bread, and ale," he answered, looking up to find himself the object of severe scrutiny. The woman made it very clear that she had more than serving food on her mind. She leaned over, affording him a look at her pair of enormous breasts which seemed about ready to tumble out of their binding at any moment. Thinking of Heather's delicately shaped breasts, so soft and alluring, he knew it would be a sacrilege to even cast his eyes in any other woman's direction and so he made his lack of interest for the woman plain to see. She stalked away in silence, at last bringing him his food and casting him a sullen look.

As Richard ate he wondered if these people around him were on Mary's side. Would they give him shelter, hide him if the duke won the battle? He tried to remember just how much farther it was to Framlingham Castle and decided that it was half a day's ride. Before the sun rose in the east he would set out again.

"Fifteen miles from the coast," he mumbled to himself. The castle was situated in a position so that if, heaven forbid, Mary were to lose, escape would be near at hand. "Escape?" The word sounded bitter upon his tongue. He would not leave England without Heather. No, he could not. Life without her by his side was unthinkable to him now.

Scanning the crowd, Richard saw among the dun- and brown-clothed villagers a fisherman or two, carrying with them the rewards of their patience, perchance selling a few of the fish to the tavern keeper or trading them for an ale. He listened to their talk about ships and nets and the open sea, wondering at the freedom their words portrayed. Perhaps one day he and Heather could find such freedom, a life together without the worries of warfare and politics.

"Together." He liked the word. Taking a drink of his ale, he let his mind wander with dreams and visions. Even the loud crash of the door being thrown open hardly unnerved him. Was he growing careless? Had love made him daring and frivolous?

As if to heed his own warning, in an effort to take precautions lest this intruder be one of Northumberland's kind, Richard shrank back into the shadows, watching as all eyes turned toward the new arrival.

"Did you hear? Did you hear?" the man shouted, grabbing hastily for a goblet of wine. "London's proclaimed Mary as queen. The council has spoken the word. Northumberland is even now being hunted down for the dog that he is!"

The onlookers gave a gasp in unison; then choruses of chattering broke forth as everyone vented their questions and opinions.

"So, there will be no fight!" grumbled a man at the front door. "I had thought to serve Mary."

"Northumberland declared a traitor. 'Tis a just proclamation," snorted another. "His ambition was as a wart on the nose of England."

"Ah, Mary has suffered," said a tavern maid. "My mother told me that even when the queen's mother, Catherine of Aragon, was dying, Mary was forbidden to go to her. Surely then she will show her people mercy, knowing well what injustice is."

"Aye. I do not have much love for her papist leanings, but I do honor my queen. It is only right that the real Tudor heir be upon the throne."

Richard could sit silent no longer. Rising to his feet, he sought out the new guest. "How long?" he asked, grabbing the man by the arm. "How long has it been since Mary was proclaimed queen?"

"Two days," the red-bearded man replied.

"Two days?" Richard repeated. Had he known of this turn of events, he would have stayed by Heather's side. Even now the urge to retrace his path, to go once again to London, overtook him. But he had traveled so far already. He was nearly to Framlingham. Wouldn't it be better to keep on with his journey? The queen would have need of him still, and what of Northumberland and Hugh Seton? They were still roaming about, a danger to everyone as long as they were free. Grabbing his cloak, he strode to the door, pushing aside the horde of yeomen, sailors, fishermen, and villagers who stood about.

"You! Where are you going?" shouted out the tavern keeper. "What about your room? Do you intend to come back?"

Richard tossed his head and grinned. "No. Give it to one of these fine people. I am off to see my queen." Feeling as if the weight of the world had been lifted from his shoulders, he sought out his horse from the stablehand and began the ride to Framlingham upon the rocky road.

The rough pink stones of the castle walls loomed in the distance against the purple haze of the dawn as Richard Morgan rode forth to Framlingham Castle. The stones of the walls formed a circle, looking strangely from the distance like the ringed stones of Stonehenge, that mystical druid sanctuary from years gone by.

Approaching the castle, he could hear even at this hour the riotous rejoicing. He smiled, knowing well how pious Mary was and how she abhorred such outpouring of emotions. But even Mary, even the queen, would have little control over such an enthusiastic crowd.

The hooves of his horse clattered loudly against the stones of the outer courtyard, blending with the buzzing voices of those who celebrated their well-earned victory.

Dismounting from his horse, giving the animal up to the hands of a groom, he sought out the queen, finding her where he expected her to be, in the chapel. When at last she was finished with her prayers, she rose from her knees and turned in his direction, a smile lighting up her face as she saw him.

"Richard!" Her pale face flushed with color, her pinched features softened.

Kneeling at her feet, he kissed the cross she held in her hands, offering her his allegiance. She bade him rise and listened intently as his story poured forth, of all that had happened, of his brush with death, of the beautiful young woman who had saved him, taking on his mission of delivery of Mary's letter to the council. He humbly begged her forgiveness that he had not been at her side when she had need of him.

"You are here now," she answered gently. "How glad I am to see you. It is only fitting that you be with me to celebrate this victory. God was with me—how could I have ever doubted that he would be? May he forgive me. My people have proven to me that they long to return to the old ways, the true religion." Her eyes gleamed with a fervor he had seen before.

"Well-spoken," came a voice from the shadows. The queen beckoned the man into the light, and Richard, turning his eyes in that direction, gasped in surprise, for standing in front of him was none other than Hugh Seton.

20

"WHAT IS HE doing here? Arrest him. He is one of Northumberland's men." Richard Morgan reached for his sword, feeling outraged to see the leering face of his adversary. The gall of the man was unbelievable. Only Mary's intervention prevented him from pointing his sword at the traitor's throat.

"No! Richard. He is no more Northumberland's man, he is my loyal servant. A miracle has been wrought."

Richard laughed bitterly. "Your loyal servant indeed. I would say that like the turncoat he is, he fled to your banner to save his hide. Let me run him through like the *dog* that he is."

The leer that Hugh Seton gave him was one of pure hatred, but he managed a smile for Mary's benefit, his face a mask of noble subservience. "Calm yourself, brother. I can well understand your feelings. It no doubt is difficult for you to believe my newfound loyalty. God works in mysterious ways."

"Leave God out of this. He would not bother with the likes of you!" Indignity oozed forth from Richard's every pore.

"Richard, I command you to hold your tongue." Mary's voice was sharp and angry. "Let him speak his mind."

Hugh Seton smiled at the queen, bending his head in a noble salute. "Do not be angry with him. It is difficult for me to believe the wonder of it all." He turned to Richard with an expression of the cat who swallowed the sparrow. "It was as if God himself spoke to me, told me to honor my lawful ruler." The sun shone through the colored glass of the windows of the chapel, casting dancing beams of light upon the face of the man who now spoke with fervor. "Paul on the road to Damascus was blessed, and like Paul, God made me see the error of my ways and led me back to the truth."

"The truth!" Richard's face twitched in agitation. It was not that he did not believe in miracles, only that he could never be fooled by one such as Hugh Seton. The man was playing upon Mary's religious zest, upon her basic goodness and trusting nature. Knowing how much she longed to bring the country back to Catholicism, Hugh Seton had found the way to her heart.

Hugh Seton looked demonic to Richard, with his face cast in a swirl of colors from the mosaic window, but Mary did not seem to notice. "We must bring England back to the true faith."

"Yes!" Mary cried, looking upward, raising her eyes as if to look God in the face. "My brother was young. A mere child. He was influenced by those whose minds were corrupt with sin and greed. My father broke away from the Church of Rome in order to commit a dastardly sin, to marry *that* woman. I can only pray for his soul that God in his mercy will forgive him."

Richard too was a loyal Catholic, had suffered his share of persecution by the staunch Calvinists who had taken the young King Edward into their power. He had been forced to hear Mass in secret after it was said to be blasphemous idolatry and forbidden, had shed tears at the desecration of the monasteries, the destruction of the churches and holy statues, he had wept at the misery that his fellowman had wrought upon each other in the name of God. But fear now overcame him as he looked at the faces of the queen and the burly, self-seeking man who thought to gain his power by playing upon her heart's desire. When would the day come when a man could worship God according to his own conscience? If

Mary now sought to force her own beliefs upon others, there would be more suffering, more tragedy. This he knew in his heart, but for the moment he had to keep silent. He would talk to the queen when they were alone.

Sensing his mood, Mary sought to bring peace between the two men. Taking Richard's right hand and Seton's left, placing the two together in a gesture that seemed nearly ceremonial in magnitude, she spoke softly. "We are all on God's side. You must from henceforth work together. That is my command. When we ride into London you will both be with me!"

Richard Morgan felt as if he were in a trap, as if a net were slowly closing over his head. He remembered Hugh Seton's words to him that day when he had failed to kill him. Seton had said, "I swear that someday I will cause you such pain that you will remember this day and wish you had drawn my blood."

This dastardly scoundrel had wormed his way into Mary's confidence and for now there was nothing Richard could do about it.

21

IT WAS A glorious August day, the sky unfolding above London like a blue canopy, the golden sunshine radiating a glow which bathed the city in its warmth. It seemed that even the weather welcomed the queen.

The narrow cobbled streets were blanketed with flowers—posies, violets, and roses of both white and red. Flowers even floated down the open gutters, their perfume mingling with the smells of the city: smoke, decaying refuse, and a salty breeze. From far and wide through every part of London the bells pealed a joyous clamor. The people were greeting their queen and heralding her reign.

Heather had joined the throng of people lining the streets, listening eagerly to everything that was being said, looking intently for any sign of Richard. It had been over two weeks since he had left her. She had heard nary a word from him, and this silence had left her pale and nervous for fear that something fatal had befallen him, a state which had not gone unnoticed by her mother.

"Please, God, please let him be safe. I pray that no injury has come to him." She felt an elbow poke her in the side and looked to see the baker's wife pushing through the crowd. With a murmured apology the heavyset woman was soon buried in the crowd which seemed to be a human carpet, shoulder to shoulder. There were those standing upon someone else's shoulders, people leaned from windows, climbed poles, did everything possible in order to afford themselves a better view. Even her father was hanging out his bedroom window, praising the queen. Now an avid supporter of Mary, it was hard to remember that he had once been against this "papist."

A horn sounded and all heads turned, jostling and shoving each other in eagerness to get a look at this queen who had won the throne against all odds, without foreign intervention or the spilling of her subjects' blood.

The staccato banging of the drums was echoed by the beating of Heather's heart as she looked upon the great procession that was approaching. The Earl of Arundel rode in a place of honor beside Mary, and behind her . . . behind her . . .

"Richard!" He looked magnificent in his black velvet garments, hose, doublet, and leather boots. A breeze was blowing his black cloak about his shoulders and he appeared to Heather's eyes to be of royal blood himself. Pushing through the crowd, she sought to get a closer look, stepping on dozens of feet as she managed to move a few feet from where she had stood.

"Mary. Mary. Mary," the crowd intoned, chanting as she turned to look upon them. The cry of "God save the queen" became a roar.

Heather hardly noticed the purple and violet velvet which adorned her monarch; her eyes were too full of the man she loved. He was even more handsome than she remembered, and she flushed at the memory of his naked body pressed against her own.

"Richard," she said again, willing him to look at her. He did, his eyes sparkling as he smiled. He mouthed the words "I love you" and tipped his hat to her as the procession rode by. There were other eyes which turned upon her, and Heather gave a gasp of surprise to see Hugh Seton riding beside him. She could not believe her eyes. How had he escaped his rightful punishment to now share a place of honor in Mary's procession?

Heather followed the riders as if in a trance, only to be pushed back by one of the soldiers. She had to see Richard, had to talk with him. How could he not remember that Seton was his enemy?

The bells, the trumpets, and the pounding drums hurt her ears, and the shouts of the people nearly deafened her as she ran past the sea of faces. The Tower, the procession was headed for the Tower. That would be her destination too. She was glad now that her father had been generous in granting her the cloth for a new dress, for she could hardly go to the Tower in her old homespun. The dress she wore was a copy of those of the ladies of the court, a lemon-yellow linen, with overgown held up by fastenings and belts, a starched headdress adorning her mahogany tresses.

Making her way over the Tower Bridge, she heard the many whispers, saying that the queen intended to reside in state in the Tower, and wondered if it would be Richard's home now too. The hope that he would be near her was close to her heart.

It was easier this time to get inside the Tower. There were no red-clothed guards to block her entry, no soldiers to tell her to go away. With such a large throng it was merely a matter of flowing with the tide as they pushed through the door. Mary had given instructions that none of her "people" were to be manhandled. Once inside, however, it was a different story, for the guards were thick and numerous, holding the crowd at bay. Still it was possible to see the proceedings, and Heather's eyes were riveted upon the figure clothed in black, standing tall and proud beside the woman who now ruled England.

Four prisoners knelt before Mary, but neither Lady Jane Grey nor Northumberland was among them; instead it was whispered that these four were captives from the past—the Duke of Norfolk, now an old man who had been put in the Tower by Henry VIII to await his death, Gardiner, a Catholic bishop also a prisoner of Mary's father, the Duchess of Somerset, the duke's haughty widow, and a young graceful, handsome blond man who was said to be one of the Plantagenets.

"Why, its Edward Courtenay, great-grandson of Edward IV," whispered an old man standing next to Heather. "Poor lad. He was thrown into prison during the reign of King Henry just because of his royal blood."

"Ha, there be a likely husband for our dear queen," cooed a blacksmith's gray-haired wife. "With him in her bed she would soon produce an heir for England, he being so fair and all."

A hushed din of whispers echoed her hopes. Above all, this man was an Englishman, soothing the fears of a foreign husband for the queen.

Heather saw Mary motion for the prisoners to rise from their knees and felt tears sting her eyes. How terrible to be held captive, caged like a wild beast, and all because of the most trivial reasons at times. Henry VIII had been a tyrant in that respect, jailing even those whose only crime was to be of blood more royal than his own.

"People of England," Mary cried out in a deep mannish voice, "I thank you all, my loyal subjects. God has answered our prayers." Her voice broke and Heather could see that the queen was deeply moved by the sight of all those who showed her homage. At last regaining her composure, she motioned toward the four. "These are my prisoners, and as such I offer them their freedom. From this day forward let them see no more iron bars before them. Go. Bring England back to its former glory."

The cry of "Long live the queen" surged and echoed like a roll of thumder, and Heather felt a shiver jolt through her. Richard's queen, her queen—the future seemed assured to be a bright one, one devoid of the cruelty of Northumberland and his cronies.

Heather waited as the festivities continued, her eyes watching Richard's every move, every gesture, until at last the ceremony was at an end. She watched as he took his leave of the queen, walking in the direction of Tower Green, and Heather made her way toward him.

When she at last came to him, he stood near the

green beside an ancient scaffold where many had met their deaths in the past. He was deep in thought and at first she hated to disturb him, but the longing in her heart to be near overcame her caution.

"Richard." Her voice was barely more than a whisper, yet he heard her. She could see the worry etched deep in his face as he turned to her, and she wondered at the cause.

Running into the circle of his arms, she was engulfed within the cloak of passion his nearness brought forth. Her lips found his, her body arching against him as he crushed her into his arms, kissing her hungrily, fiercely.

"Dear Lord, how I longed for you and now you are with me," he murmured between kisses. Her weeks of worry dissolved at his touch. She belonged in his arms.

Richard's mouth left hers to travel to her temple, brushing aside the silky strands of her hair with his lips, breathing in the fragrant rose scent of her that had haunted his nights.

"Your mother, did she harm you?" he asked in a whisper.

"No, she would never do that. At last she quieted down and we talked. She knows that I love you, and though she worries for my happiness, I think she understands. I think perhaps she loved once, though not my father."

"I felt like a cur to leave you."

"You had to leave."

"Heather, oh, Heather!" His fingers touched her breast, sending a spark of desire through her. "How I wish that we were somewhere alone, away from the threat of peering eyes and rattling tongues. I want you so."

From inside the Tower they could hear the sound of laughter and revelry, voices raised in praise and in song, yet there were only the two of them on the earth as they gazed into each other's eyes. Heather was mesmerized by her happiness, afraid to move for fear that this moment would dissolve as so many dreams had done these past few days. Would she awaken to find it morning again and be alone? Alone without him?

Richard looked deep into her eyes. She loved and trusted him. He had to tell her the truth. Now. "Heather," he whispered. "There is something I must tell you . . ."

"Hush," she breathed. "Let us not spoil this moment." Reaching out to touch his mouth with her fingers, she was filled with the sweetness of the moment. He was hers again, no matter for how brief a time. Forgotten now was all else but their love. They were unaware of the eyes which watched them. Cunning eyes.

"So, I find the way to wound you, Morgan," the man said between clenched teeth, watching the lovers in their embrace. He had noticed the way Richard's eyes had sought out a figure in the crowd. That was why when he saw him push through the throng he followed him, intent on finding a way to compromise his hated half-brother. Now he was not disappointed. "Such a lovely creature. It will be my pleasure to use her to torture you." From the doorway he laughed, a sound which drifted on the wind to Heather's ears.

"Someone is watching us," she said, breaking away from Richard's arms. She had been so happy to see him, longed so much for his touch that she had forgotten all about propriety.

"Who is there?" Richard asked, irritated at the intrusion. He had thought that the crowd would be too enthralled with the proceedings inside to gawk at him. Obviously he was wrong, and he cursed himself for being careless. He did not want Heather to become an object of gossip. Standing in front of her in an attempt to hide her identity, he whispered, "Go, but meet me tomorrow at the barber's shop, in the courtyard behind. There is much that I must tell you, but for now I must get back before the queen is angered by my absence."

Heather left him with reluctance, longing for his

arms the moment she had left them. "At noon in the courtyard," she said, taking to her heels, running from him while she had the strength of mind to do so. Only the knowledge that she would see him upon the morrow gave her the will and heart to abandon him now.

Watching her go, Richard was filled with a great tenderness. She was everything he had ever wanted in a woman, and more. Beauty, grace, a kind heart, and courage—all were of abundant supply in this red-haired maiden named Heather Bowen. If only she could be his wife.

"I must tell her. She must know about Edlyn. It is not right to keep such a secret from her. Tomorrow, when we meet in the courtyard, I will explain all, and if she then still wants me, I will make her mine again." The thought of making love to her stirred his blood, and taking a deep breath of the summer air, he sought to quench his ardor.

Looking about, he saw no sign that anyone was nearby; indeed whoever had made the noise had vanished without a trace, and he began to wonder if it had been only their imagination or some grisly ghost of the past who had stirred the air.

"Tomorrow." Putting all caution behind him, looking over his shoulder just once, Richard Morgan left the Tower Green.

22

"TABITHA, WHAT AILS me? My hands are shaking so violently that I can scarce hold my brush!" Heather exclaimed as she stood before the tiny mirror in her bedchamber.

"It is called love," Tabitha answered with a laugh, taking the brush from Heather's hands to run its bristles through the mass of red tangles, fashioning them in soft waves on either side of her head, the back hair hanging freely to touch below Heather's waist.

"Yes, love." The thought of meeting Richard had caused Heather anxiety as well as pleasure, tossing and turning in a sleepless night as so many unanswered questions plagued her. What was it he had to tell her? He had sounded so stern that for just a moment she had thought he had bad news, and yet the way he had kissed her, held her . . . Was that not the way of a man who cherishes his lover? "But what has he to tell me?"

"You will soon know," Tabitha said softly, putting down the brush. Heather turned to look at the servant girl, who was quickly becoming her friend. Tabitha was at least a head taller than Heather, a large woman by the day's standards, yet there was an attractiveness about her height, which sadly the young woman was not aware of.

"You are right, Tabitha, I will soon know. Though I am nervous just the same." There was a long pause, a silence between them as each woman succumbed to her own thoughts. The fear nagged at Heather that her father would in some way hinder her meeting with Richard. At first edgy and in constant fear of being thrown into the Tower, Thomas was quickly coming back to his old self, especially since Mary was showing mercy for most of those who had tried to keep her from her throne. Mercy for all but Northumberland and six others who had been condemned to die. It was said that the queen wanted to pardon even Northumberland, but that Simon Renard, now her imperial ambassador, had persuaded her otherwise. And Jane—poor Lady Jane was to be kept confined within the Tower grounds.

Tabitha seemed to sense Heather's fears. "If your father tries to detain you, I will lend a hand. There will be some way to smuggle you out of here, even if under his very nose." As much as Tabitha feared Thomas Bowen, she was determined to see Heather happy with the man she loved.

"Without Richard I am but half-alive," Heather whispered. But much to her good fortune, no such problem arose. When it came time for her to leave, Thomas was nowhere in sight and Blythe Bowen was too preoccupied in her housecleaning to notice her daughter's departure. Dressed in the same blue gown and farthingale that she had worn to take Mary's letter to the Tower, Heather now made her way to her lover.

Richard Morgan stood alone, half-hidden by the foliage which encircled the courtyard of the barber's shop. His back was turned to Heather and he seemed to be deep in thought as she approached. Although the sun shone overhead, he had a cloak flung about his shoulders and a hat upon his head.

"Richard?"

He did not turn around. Heather crept closer, wondering what there was about him that did not seem quite right. Only when she was right behind him did the truth dawn on her. It was not Richard. This man was too stocky, too short. He whirled around, reaching out his strong arms to pull her toward him, and it was then that her worst fears were realized.

"Hugh Seton!" Terrified, she struggled, but he was much too strong. "Let me go!" Her eyes searched frantically for Richard.

"He will be a little late. The queen, at my suggestion, detained him." He laughed while dragging her along with him as he walked to the shelter of a row of hedges. His voice became gruff and sinister as he spoke to her. "Keep your silence or you will be the worse for it. There is something that I wish to say to you, and it will be spoken if I have to sit on you to make you listen."

Heather's hair, pulled free of its confinement, blew in wild disarray about her shoulders, and her blue gown had snagged and torn from the scuffle. As she looked at the man, her breasts heaved in anger. "I do not know what you could possibly have to say to me. You are a beast to so treat a lady." She turned to leave, but he made good his threat, pushing her to the ground and straddling her so that she could not get up. Fear that he would ravish her overcame her and she squirmed and sought to cry out. As his hand clamped over her mouth, she thought about that time when Richard had held her captive. Even then *he* had been gentle, not brutal like this man.

"I said you were going to listen, and listen you will, woman!" His eyes raked over her with the leer she knew only too well. "You think I'm going to force myself on you, don't you? Well, still your fears, at least this time, although I am tempted to sample the fare that you have no doubt given freely to him." Pressing himself closer against her, he intimately writhed his body upon hers. Heather shut her eyes in terror, but he moved away and only laughed at her expression of abhorrence, taking his hand away from her mouth for just a moment.

"Please!"

"I told you I am not going to take you, I haven't the time, but sooner or later you will taste of me. I'm going to be your husband, Mistress Bowen."

"Never!" she spat.

"Never is a long time." Seeming amused by her answers, he left her mouth free. "I know some things about your father that the queen would be all too happy to learn. She has shown tolerance to some, but with the right word spoken here or there, she could very well change her mind. My influence is great with her majesty."

"You are a traitor! I know that you were on Northumberland's side. You cannot implicate my father without endangering yourself as well."

He rolled to one side of her, reaching out to hold her wrists securely in his big pawlike hands. "The queen knows well that I was Northumberland's man but that a miracle came upon me so that I took up her banner instead."

Heather looked about wildly for any sign of help. Where was the barber? Could he not see from his window what ill fate had befallen her? No, this big beast had made certain that they were well out of sight.

"A miracle!" she scoffed. Laughter was her answer.

"I have no doubt that your father will see the advantage of such a match as ours. Marriages joining prosperous burgher families and nobility are common enough. I am in great need of money. It will be a fair enough exchange, your father's money for my title."

"You have no title."

"Ah, but I will. I will."

Heather sought to remember what Richard had told her of this man, but could not recall his words. There had been so much excitement, so much happening. All she knew was that he was Richard's enemy. His words seemed to have some threat attached to them, and she suddenly feared that he sought in some way to harm the man she loved.

"I will never marry you. I love another," she said defiantly. If he was Richard's enemy, then he was hers also.

His face turned red with rage. "You whore! You

think that he will marry you. I tell you he will not. He cannot!"

His words made her tremble. Did he know of whom she spoke? How could he? His next words answered her question.

"I saw you with him, with Richard Morgan, my half-brother."

"Half-brother!" she gasped.

"I am the bastard son of Richard's father and a blacksmith's daughter. Humble beginnings, but then, so had Thomas Cromwell, and he became Henry VIII's chief minister. I will one day have what is rightfully mine, but I fear that you will never have what you so long for. A man can hardly have two wives."

"Two wives?" Her voice trembled, as her mind refused to accept the possibility that he meant Richard.

He let her go, knowing full well that she would not seek to run from him now.

"Two wives," he repeated, taking satisfaction in the look of shock which passed over her face. "He cannot marry you. My dear half-brother is already married. He has been happily wed for two years to a dark-eyed, dark-haired woman of nobility. Edlyn is her name. She is his *wife*. Do you hear me? Richard Morgan is a married man."

"Married! No! No!" It was as if a knife tore at her heart. "You are lying. Lying!" Slowly she got to her feet, staring at the ground, wanting to run but feeling as if she could not move a muscle.

"Ask him yourself if you do not believe me, or better yet, ask the queen. She knows well of the Lady Morgan." He bowed mockingly, taking his leave of her. "I will leave you to think heartily upon my proposal of marriage."

She hardly knew that he had left; she was only aware of the stabbing ache within her heart, of the numbness she felt, the utter sense of loss. Of course she would ask Richard if Hugh Seton's words were true, but a voice inside her whispered that they were. Why would the man lie when such a thing could so easily be found out? What would Hugh Seton gain by telling her a falsehood?

"No," she whispered. "Let it not be true." Sobs racked her body as she gave vent to her sorrow.

23

RICHARD THOUGHT THAT she looked like a painting by Hans Holbein the Younger as she stood there, still and silent. A beauty, that's what she was. Lord, how he loved her. Would he ever find the words to let her know how much?

"Heather." In two strides he was beside her. "Forgive me for being late. The queen had matters of state to discuss with me. There was no way that I could tell her no." He reached out to take her in his arms but she was cold and unresponsive. "Are you ill? Heather, what is it?"

Heather tried to speak but her words were choked and she feared that she would collapse in a heap at his feet. Only with the greatest effort was she able to maintain her dignity, saying at last, "Tell me that it isn't true."

Their gazes locked in silence for the length of a heartbeat. "Tell you that what isn't true?"

The ache in Heather's throat threatened to choke her, yet she managed the words: "Are you . . . are you . . . married?"

His eyes answered for him, a spasm of pain that flitted briefly across his face. "Heather . . ."

She stiffened as she heard him speak her name. Was this the man who had held her, loved her? Now he seemed to be a stranger, one who had taken her love knowing well that he was not free.

"It is true. I can see the answer written on your face!" A soft groan of despair tore from her throat.

He tried to take her in his arms but she flung

herself free of his embrace. She felt used, dirtied. Together they had committed adultery, a grievous sin, and all the while she had been so naive, loving him, dreaming of the day when they would be together. But that day would never come. He belonged to another, Edlyn.

"It is not what you think, Heather. Let me explain." Again he tried to gather her into his arms, but she would have none of his tenderness.

"Leave me alone. Don't touch me." Tears spilled down her flushed face as the pain for the loss of her heart's desires swept through her.

"I tried to stay away from you. I tried. I told you not to love me. My intentions were honorable, I swear to you, but that night . . . It was as if a dam burst. All my love for you spilled forth and I could no longer hold back all that I felt for you. I had no control. But God forgive me, I will never regret that night."

Blinking back her tears, she looked into his face. Every fiber of her being cried out that she loved him, would always love him. But his mistress she would never be! He belonged to another, to a wife, to Edlyn. His possessions, his name, his body, his lovemaking, all belonged to another woman. Wife. The word seemed to scream in her ears.

His eyes burned like blue flames. "I love you. Nothing else matters to me. Not my life, not my honor. I love you. I never meant to hurt you."

"You did not tell me. Omission is the same as a lie."

He looked as if she had struck him. "I asked you here *today* to tell you, before the spark of love between us flamed again. My marriage is—"

"To be your mistress. You thought I would consent to be your mistress. How wrong you were. I never want to see you again." Her features appeared to be carved in stone, except for the trickle of moisture from her eyes.

"Listen to me. My marriage is a sham, a deception of all that is—"

She did not stay to listen, knowing well that if she looked once more into his eyes she would be lost, would crumble into a thousand pieces, like the Humpty Dumpty of her childhood nursery rhyme. Taking to her heels, she fled down the rough cobblestones of the street, stopping only when she reached the safety of her father's doorway. There, leaning against the thick wood of that portal, she gave vent to the flood of grief for a dream shattered beyond repair, a dream which had been as beautiful as a rainbow, but was now only a storm.

"Oh, how can I forget him? How will I ever be able to wipe him from my heart, my mind?" How long she huddled against the door crying, she did not know. She only knew that suddenly a soft hand was stroking her hair, that a gentle voice was urging her to stop her sobbing. Looking up, she saw her mother's face, the blue eyes filled with sorrow and pain. Together they walked the steep stairs to Heather's bedroom, where Blythe Bowen undressed her daughter and put her to bed as she had when Heather had been a child. When at last Heather's tears were spent, the weeping only a memory, she sat down upon her daughter's bed.

"I wish I were dead!" Heather said bitterly, turning her face away from her mother.

"Hush. Don't ever say such a thing. Life is precious, a gift from God. No man is worth such sorrow. No man."

"How did you know? How could you sense the cause of my grief?" Heather felt like a little girl again, coming to her mother with a scraped knee, a bee sting, a broken toy.

"Because I too have been wounded by love's arrows." At this moment Richard Morgan and Rodrigo de Vega blended into one in Blythe Bowen's mind. Closing her eyes, she could remember the way her own lover had held her in his arms, whispering beautiful phrases in his own language, promising to return to her. She had been just about Heather's age when he had swept her off her feet and into the bedchamber, only to leave her with a child. He had never returned, leaving her to face her shame alone. If not for Thomas . . .

"You do not love Father?"

"I have grown to respect him. He has provided for us, Heather. We are not without food or a roof over our heads."

"Who was he, this man you loved?"

"An explorer. A Spanish explorer." Looking at Heather was like looking into his eyes, gray just like hers, the hair the same mahogany color.

"Was he married?" Saying the word again, remembering, brought forth a new wave of tears, and as Blythe Bowen watched her daughter cry, anger for the man named Richard Morgan boiled forth like a caldron.

"Hush. Don't cry, my darling. You will forget him." Yet she knew that Heather would not. Had she in all these years ever forgotten Rodrigo? No. How many times had she imagined that it was his arms that held her, his mouth that kissed her?

From outside the window Heather could hear Richard calling her name, demanding that she come down and hear him out. What could he say to her that he hadn't said already?

"I will soon chase him away!" Blythe hissed, clenching her hands tightly at her sides. Heather thought about that time in the stables when her mother had come at Richard with a broom, and in spite of her heartache she laughed. How could she have ever thought of her mother as meek and shy? If only Thomas Bowen would feel her sting upon occasion.

In a moment Blythe was back. "He will not leave. Not even your father could convince him to go. The man says that he must talk with you, that if need be he will stay outside your window all through the night. Hasn't he done enough damage? Already he has broken your heart."

"He can never be mine, Mama. Never. And yet I fear that were I to see him now, were he to crook his little finger, I would run to him, share the scraps of affection he could give me." As if in an effort to hide from the temptation, Heather pulled the blanket up around her neck, pulling herself into a tight ball, wishing that she could vanish. Her head ached, her throat felt dry, every nerve in her body quivered. It was as if she suffered a wound that would not heal, could never heal. She wanted to run, but there was nowhere that she could go. How could one run away from her own heart?

Outside the window Richard paced up and down the gray stone street. He had caught a tiger by the tail and he could not let it go. The tiger named love.

"Heather. Please listen to me. Forgive me. I did not mean to hurt you." If only he could tell her all about Edlyn, about his betrayal at the hands of his mother, at least she would forgive him. "I must tell her the whole story."

But as long as he waited, hoping for at least a glimpse of Heather, he was to be disappointed. When at last darkness shrouded the sky, he left.

24

THE NEXT FEW weeks passed by in a haze of unhappiness for Heather. Uneventful days in her own life which were only highlighted by the events taking place throughout the realm. At last poor Edward VI was buried now that the threat of rebellion was over. At first Mary intended to give her brother a Catholic funeral but at last conceded to bury Edward as he had lived, a Reformist.

Thomas Bowen had ranted and raved. "It's been twenty years since England broke from Rome! Twenty years. A whole generation has grown up in the Reformed Church and has sought the tutelage of Cranmer's *Book of Common Prayer.* That woman will be the ruination of us all."

"That woman is our queen," Heather had reminded him. Her words silenced his tirade and she suspected that his anger was in reality due to the fact that another merchant had been chosen to clothe the queen and her dead brother for the funeral.

Six days later the queen issued an official declaration that she would not "compel or constrain consciences" in the matter of religious belief, thus setting Thomas Bowen's mind at ease upon the matter of religion.

As for Richard Morgan, he did not give up his hope that Heather would hear him out. Each morning he would stand outside the door, waiting, watching for any sign of her, but each day she disappointed him and there came a time at last when he appeared at the door no longer.

Having grown used to seeing him below her window, Heather was devastated when his daily vigil ended. Just seeing him had been a torment, but a bittersweet travail. His walk, that so-familiar swagger, had been dear to her, watching from the window. The sound of his voice had melted her heart, and time after time she had been tempted to go to him, to tell him that she would be his mistress, that she didn't care if he was married, she only wanted to be with him. But the certainty that she would be hurt ail the more were she to see him, touch him, kept her from running down the stairs to be at his side.

Only one thing eased her mind. Hugh Seton had not come to call upon her father, and she breathed easier, hoping that his had been an idle threat. She would never marry him. Better to die a spinster than to spend her days with a cruel, bestial man.

Sitting in front of the fire with Tabitha at her side, Heather had resigned herself to her unmarried state and the way of life that she had grown used to over the years. If she was not happy, well, she was not truly unhappy, except for the times when the memory of Richard Morgan tugged at her heart.

"It will be a fine tapestry," Tabitha said softly, taking a look at Heather's stitchery. "I have always loved unicorns. Do you think perchance they really existed?"

Heather smiled, knowing quite well that Tabitha was trying valiantly to cheer her out of her troubles. "I like to think that they did." She wondered sadly if love would ever stir her heart again. Tabitha had been such a rock for her to lean on the past few days, listening patiently to Heather's mournful words. What would she have done without the servant girl? she wondered. Settling back in her chair, picking up the needle again, she set about her stitching. It took patience to work on a tapestry. One stitch at a time until finally each stitch blended into a work of astounding beauty. Perhaps one's life was like that.

One stitch at a time, one day at a time. The thought cheered her.

A knock sounded at the door, causing Heather to prick her finger. "So much for philosophic musing."

"I'll get it," Tabitha announced, rising from her wooden chair. She was not quick enough. Thomas Bowen had already answered the door, hopeful of a new customer at hand. He returned, his face as pale as his undyed wool. In his hand he held up a letter, vibrating in his fingers like a banner in the breeze.

"A . . . a . . . missive . . . from the queen," he stuttered, fearing the worst. Heather pitied him. Would he never get over his fear that the queen would seek retribution for his past deeds?

Putting aside her sewing, she walked over to take the paper from his hands. The queen's seal was emblazoned upon it, leaving no doubt that it was indeed from her. Tearing it open, scanning the words written there, remembering another time, another letter, Heather could hardly believe her eyes.

"It's to me!" She read the words again, thinking surely she must have read them wrong. "I've been summoned to court. I'm to be a lady-in-waiting. Me, a commoner."

"Let me see that!" Thomas Bowen yanked it violently out of her hands. "As a reward for your help? What, dare I ask, did *you* do?" He seemed angered by her good fortune, well aware that he would not be able to keep her from going. Was he wondering who would now do the work and keep the ledgers?

"I played but a tiny part in helping her, Father. I merely delivered a message for her."

"A message?" He rubbed his finger across the bridge of his large nose, squinting at her as if to see into her mind. "It seems a large endowment for such a minor accomplishment." He paced the floor, tugging nervously at the sleeves of his gown. "Who will help me with my books? I will have to train an apprentice. It will cost me money."

"A lady-in-waiting!" piped up Tabitha, beaming with pride. "Such an honor."

Thomas Bowen cleared his throat, eyeing Heather up and down. "An honor. Yes. Yes." He smiled suddenly, showing his uneven teeth. "You must do all you can to see that the queen and her court purchase their cloth from me. Just think, the queen's own merchant." He now walked about like a strutting rooster, as if he and not Heather had been the one called to court. All the while his eyes darted back and forth as if counting unseen coins.

"It is an honor, but I can't go." The thought of seeing Richard Morgan day after day frightened her. Besides, how would she ever fit in with those of the nobility? She would be out of place, like a duck in a henhouse. Even her clothes would cause amusement. She had only three good dresses to her name.

"Can't go? Don't be silly, girl. Of course you will go. Do you think to disobey the queen?"

"I have nothing to wear, Father."

His eyes widened at her answer as the truth of her words dawned upon him. He flushed a bright red as guilt for his miserly ways pricked him. He took a deep breath and then exhaled it, saying quickly, "I will see that you are well attired. A merchant's daughter must not be wanting." Taking her hand, he led her toward the storeroom, parading her past the bolts and bolts of cloth which had so pleased her eyes. Never had she thought to have a gown made from any such material. Silks, brocades, velvets, satins, and the finest furs.

"Father . . . I . . ." In spite of the gratitude she felt at his offer, she still hesitated to go. She was not prepared for life at court, to see Richard Morgan again, to spar with the likes of Hugh Seton. She was but a humble merchant's daughter.

"You will go. I will hear no more complaints." For one who had at first abhorred the idea, Thomas Bowen was now set upon it. What a feather in his cap it would be. His daughter, lady-in-waiting to the queen. He would be the talk of all London. He.

Thomas Bowen. Perhaps at last the red-haired child of his wife's would be of value to him. Smiling, he reached down to unroll a bolt of emerald-green satin.

25

HEATHER KNEW THE moment she arrived at court that if she lived to be a hundred years old she would never forget the sights and sounds which awaited her. Her sheltered world had never prepared her for the splendor of Greenwich.

Thomas Bowen himself escorted her to the palace, and as they crested the hill and saw the magnificent walls and grounds, Heather blinked her eyes, expecting full well to have the sight disappear, thinking it at first to be a figment of her imagination. The outer walls seemed to rise up to the sky and rather resembled an old castle. Sumptuous gardens surrounded the towering structure filled with sculptured yews and fruit trees. The hedges around the gardens were carefully trimmed with a gateway cut from the foliage itself. There were several ponds filled with ducks, geese, and swans, and as she dismounted from her horse Heather paused to listen to the gabbling and quacking sound and to smell the perfume of the flowers which were in full bloom, their brilliant colors blinding to the eye.

She longed to walk in the garden, to touch the petals of the flowers which beckoned her, but her father was eager to go inside, being thirsty from the journey and desirous of a mug of ale.

"Come, come, girl," he scolded. "Don't dawdle." Taking her arm, he led her up to the double door and she felt her knees go weak beneath her, sought to still the trembling of her hands.

The scarlet-liveried yeoman of the guard stepped

aside to open the portal and Heather found herself looking into the midst of opulent splendor which even her dreams could not have prepared her for.

"Don't just stand there with your mouth open, girl," Thomas Bowen said between clenched teeth. "You will make us out to be country bumpkins. Move."

Stepping inside the crowded anteroom, she looked about her, careful to keep from "dawdling," as her father put it. The walls were of dark wood paneling covered with murals and richly worked tapestries. At either end of the room were tall windows draped with lustrous brocade curtains. Raising her eyes to the ceiling, she could see the swirls and ornately carved designs of the pictures painted there. How many months had it taken the artist to work this magic?

Walking into the banqueting hall, she could see the rows and rows of royal portraits which adorned the walls. King Henry VIII, Jane Seymour, the poor ill-fated Edward VI, and the queen herself. Grouped around the fireplace were chairs and stools covered in the finest brocade. A long table of solid mahogany, carved with designs along the edge, spread nearly the entire length of the marble floor, a floor which shone with such a bright polish that she could see her image reflected there.

"As always, you are beautiful." The voice was that of someone she knew all too well. Richard Morgan. Whirling to face him, she was achingly aware of his nearness and fought to maintain her composure.

"Thank you. My father has been most generous in outfitting me," she managed to say. Looking around for Thomas Bowen, she sought a hasty escape from this man who made her feel weak with longing. Her father was not to offer her refuge; instead he had quickly found his longed-for refreshment and was now drinking his fill.

"Your father has richly attired you, but even dressed in a flour sack you would far outshine the other women here. I have missed you." There was something in his voice which deeply touched her, a sadness, a longing.

"Richard . . ."

He took her arm, sending forth a spark at his touch which she remembered so well. It made her forget all else but the compelling need to be in his arms again. They walked farther into the hall, seeking a corner of the room for a small bit of privacy.

"Why wouldn't you see me? I waited by your front door every morning, wishing, praying, that you would but give me one smile. Were you trying to break my heart or your own?" His dark-fringed blue eyes shone with a fire which was a mixture of annoyance and desire.

"I couldn't . . ." She looked away from him, not wishing to lay bare her very soul to him. How could she tell him of all those nights she had lain awake imagining him in the arms of his dark-haired wife, giving another woman the ecstasy of his love?

Richard's pulse beat in his temples at her nearness, remembering the sight of her lying naked in his arms. His body remembered the heat and warmth of her, the softness. He wanted to tell her again that he loved her, but said only, "At least here you will not be able to run from me." His voice was defiant.

Heather's heart ached with a mixture of love and anger. "You had the queen send for me. It was you!"

"Aye, it was me. There is much I have to say to you, and this time you will listen."

They were interrupted by a tall, graceful young man with the straight nose, blond hair, and classically handsome features which marked him one of the Plantagenet family. Edward Courtenay. "Who is this lovely creature, Richard? I don't believe I have met her."

Richard's blood boiled with anger and jealousy. Courtenay was a known womanizer, a worthless rake who, though seeking the hand of the queen, did not think it amiss to chase after every lovely woman he set eyes upon. Heather would not fall prey to him, not while Richard breathed the air of life.

"She has already been claimed."

The angelically handsome man cocked an eyebrow at him. "You? Why, my dear sir, I thought I had heard that you were married to Sir Renfred's daughter. Don't you think you are being a bit greedy?"

"And aren't you being a bit too persistent for one who is seeking the queen's hand?" Richard retorted, glaring at his would-be rival in agitation. They stood nose to nose like two roosters at a cockfight as Heather broke free of the two men, leaving them alone to argue over her. She sought out her father, who was busily engaged in conversation with a velvet-clad noble. She heard the man grumble that it was not as it had been in Northumberland's rule. "No more games of chance. Flirtations are frowned upon, talk of politics forbidden. This queen is a pious one and as such she expects those about her to be pious also," the man said, looking at Heather as if to give her proper warning.

"My daughter will be a pillar of piety," Thomas Bowen answered, giving Heather a look which told her that he expected her to be just that. Beckoning to Perriwincle, who had driven the wagon filled with Heather's belongings and who had only now arrived, he seemed content.

Perriwincle looked a sight in his hose and doublet and trunk hose. More comfortable by far in his dun-colored tunic and breeches, he grinned sheepishly at Heather. Thomas Bowen had been of a mind to make a good impression upon the court, even to the humiliation of his stablehand, who looked like a jester in his brightly hued garments.

"I feel like a bloody fool," he whispered to Heather, causing her to giggle. Handing over her trunks to one of the servants of the household, he held out his large callused hand to her, grasping hers in a tight embrace. "Take care of yourself, Mistress Heather. You deserve every happiness." His eyes traveled to where Richard Morgan stood.

Heather's eyes misted with tears. "I'll miss you, Perri," she whispered. "I will miss you most of all."

She watched as the old man left, following her father. She was all alone, alone with people she did not even know. Except for Richard. And yet she suddenly wondered if she really knew him at all. She had the feeling that there was another side to this man she had come to love, an unknown side. How long could she fight the feelings that she had for him? Certainly she was no match for him. Looking about her, at the surroundings of his life-style, she felt suddenly lost.

26

STANDING BEFORE THE large circular mirror, Heather studied herself, wanting desperately to please the queen. She fretted over her appearance, fearing that the gowns that had been designed for her were too gaudy. The queen was said to prefer more somber colors, yet everything that Heather had brought with her was colorful and low of décolletage. The gown she wore now was perhaps the most demure of the dresses. Of gold and pink shot silk it was square cut in the neck, affording more expanse of neck and shoulders than Heather would have liked. The bodice was open an inch or two at the bust, ornamented in coral-red embroidered silk, the sleeves puffed and petal-shaped with hand ruffs. Pearls were sewn the length of the sleeves and around the hem of the gown. Thomas Bowen had spared no expense, as if making up for the years of pinching his pennies. A Spanish farthingale cinched in Heather's already small waist and caused the skirt to flare out from the hips like a bell. An overskirt of the same coral-red silk dipped all the way to the ground, slashed in front to show the skirt of the inner garment. A French hood of gold, decorated with pearls, adorned her head.

After Perriwincle and her father left, Heather had been shown to her bedchamber, a large room on the second floor hung with tapestries and murals much the same as were in the hall below, and it was here that she had changed from her traveling clothes to the dress she now wore.

"I wish I were at home with Mother, Tabitha,

Perri, and Father," she whispered to the image in the mirror. She felt out of place, even in this room which was to be hers. It was a mammoth room compared to the one at home, with a large bed in the corner, curtained, with linen hangings that could be pulled back in daytime and closed at night for privacy and protection from drafts. Seeing the small carpet reminded Heather of how much her mother had wanted one for the solar at home. With the money her father had spent on her gowns, he could have bought her mother a dozen carpets, but she knew that her mother did not begrudge her, for Blythe Bowen had hovered over her daughter, seeing to every little detail of the dresses, smiling with pride that her daughter would live at court.

The one thing about the bedchamber Heather had loved at first sight was the large curtained window. It offered her a delightful view of the garden, which she now looked upon, wishing at the moment that she were among its flowers.

"Shame, shame, shame. Mustn't keep the queen waiting." The voice startled Heather. "I didn't mean to frighten you. Being held in the Tower for so many years took a toll on my manners. Let me apologize." The tall blond-haired man bowed.

"Edward Courtenay!"

"At your service." He smiled. "You have no idea what a stiff bribe I had to pay to learn exactly where your bedchamber is. But let us hurry. The queen would certainly frown to learn that I had been so bold." His manner was so friendly that Heather felt relaxed and suddenly at ease.

"The queen, what is she like?" she asked him as they descended the wide stairs.

"A bit of a bore, if you ask me. I much prefer her younger sister." As they entered the hall, he became suddenly silent.

The room was bathed in firelight and candleglow, which cast large shadows of those assembled upon the wall. Strolling musicians idled about with lute and harp in hand, singing slow, stately songs. There were dozens of servants in attendance, cup bearers, bread carvers, and the like. The aroma of roasting meat permeated the air and Heather realized just how famished she was. She started to follow Edward Courtenay to the long center table, but a short, stout page detained her.

"The queen would like to see you," he said, leading her to another, smaller room where a woman in gold brocade and black velvet awaited.

Heather curtsied, bowing her head.

"Rise, my dear. I would look at you," a low masculine voice said. "So you are the one who marched right into the Tower with my letter in hand. I would have thought you to be taller."

Looking into the face of the queen, Heather was surprised to see the lines there. Tiny wrinkles at the eyes and upon the forehead made the queen look older than her years. Her reddish hair was streaked with gray and she was thinner than Heather had imagined her to be, giving her a rather frail appearance.

"I did what had to be done, your Majesty," Heather replied.

The queen stared at Heather, squinting in the light, and Heather realized that the woman's eyesight was poor. "Ah, but you are pretty. No wonder my dear friend Richard appears to be so smitten. I hope that you are virtuous as well." The words seemed to have a hidden meaning, a warning, and Heather thought the queen might be reminding her in gentle tones that Richard Morgan was married. Blushing, trying hard to forget the night spent in Richard's arms, Heather nodded.

"Good. Good. My household will be a strict one. We will arise early to attend Mass in the chapel, then we will have our breakfast. You will help me to dress and go about a few routine tasks." She stood up, looking at Heather out of the corner of her eye. "Can you read?"

"Yes. Both English and Spanish."

The queen seemed delighted. "Then you will read

to me. That will be your most important duty. Do not tell anyone, but I can read only if the page is held very close. It is a cause of embarrassment to me, but you will aid me, will you not?"

"Yes, your Majesty." The queen smiled at her answer. She seemed to like Heather.

Gesturing to the page, the queen demanded her "special treat," which was brought before her on a silver tray. "Try some," she said to Heather, taking several herself. "It is cherries dipped in wine. When I was a child I always delighted in them. My father always spoiled me. He loved me then." Her voice was low and tinged with sadness as she remembered another time.

Tasting one of the cherries, Heather found them to be delicious and reached for another one. There was something about the queen which touched her heart, the need to love and be loved, a loneliness which even a crown could not soothe. Even after the queen had dismissed her to take her place at the table, Heather was haunted by the sadness in Mary's eyes. Did she long for a man to love? Did she ache for the arms of a husband to hold her? Rich or poor, peasant or king, surely all people hungered for the same things. Were they really so different, then?

"Ah, there you are. I was watching for you. I was afraid she might have had you clapped in irons for jealousy of your beauty." Edward Courtenay took a seat next to Heather.

"She was very kind." Sensing that someone was watching her, she looked toward the head of the table to see Richard's eyes smoldering as he looked in her direction. Her heart began hammering painfully in her breast, and she could not say another word, could only stare at him mutely as he regarded her with his blazing blue eyes.

Looking at her, Richard was starved for more than food. She was beautiful in the candlelight, flawless and glowing, her red hair shining fire. The outline of her breasts, where the silk clung to her body, made him long to reach out and touch her soft beauty. Hers were the only arms he wanted around him, hers the only mouth he wanted to kiss. She was the only woman he would ever love, and if not for his mother's treachery he could have claimed her as his bride.

"Damn!" he said beneath his breath, only to find the queen looking at him with a scathing expression. Quickly he turned away, but not before he noticed Edward Courtenay by her side. Impotent fury filled him, jealousy. The man had no right. But he was free. Free. While I am tied, he thought, wondering at the wisdom of bringing Heather to court. Had he been a fool to do so? He was frantic, could hardly eat a bite. He had to make her listen to him, to love him again.

But what can I offer her? He had sought to annul his marriage with Edlyn, but Mary had been adamant, no doubt remembering the way her own mother had been set aside. She had merely said a prayer for Edlyn, that God would show his mercy.

"It is plain to see that you are not hungry, Richard. Is the roast swan too tough, the beef overdone?"

The queen. He had forgotten the queen, who now appraised him with her knowing eyes. Reaching for his goblet, he raised it to his lips.

"I am thirsty," he answered.

All sorts of exotic dishes were placed before him—in truth the table bulged with the large platters of venison, duckling, swan, pig, and pastries of every kind—but although he tried his best, he could not eat a bite. All he could do was look across the table at the beauty of the woman he loved, watching as another man laughed with her, touched her hand, passed the cup for her lips to relish, cast his eyes upon her. He was helpless, with nothing to soothe him but the silver chalice which flowed with the sweet magic of wine and forgetfulness.

When the dishes were cleared away, the tumblers, acrobats, and musicians competing with each other for the attention of the guests, Richard sought to go to her side, but was blocked by the figure of the queen, who seemed to read his mind. If she were jealous of the attentions this Edward Courtenay showed another, this man who had been whispered to be a possible consort, she did not show it, and he suspected that she had no intention of marrying the man at all. Unlike Heather, pure, innocent Heather, Mary knew what Courtenay was. A wastrel.

From across the room Heather looked wistfully at Richard. Not even the gaudily clad acrobats balanced upon their poles could cheer her. She felt Edward Courtenay's arm encircle her waist and nearly cried aloud with her desire to have Richard's placed there instead. She could sense that the attentions of the man at her side were causing him pain and loathed the thought of doing so.

"You look sad," she heard Courtenay's voice say. "Someone as lovely as you should always be laughing." Taking her hand as the dancing notes of harp, lute, viol, and timpani echoed through the hall, he led her in a round dance, twisting and whirling through the intricate maze of steps until they were out of breath and dizzy.

"I believe this dance is mine." Stepping between the dancers, Richard led her onto the floor for a stately pavan. "I have to talk to you," he whispered, his voice soft as velvet, stirring a chord within her like a harpist's touch.

"Shhh. The queen is watching," she breathed. She could smell the wine upon his breath, could see him weaving upon his feet. Was she the cause of his state?

"I don't care. God's blood, you are lovely."

Taking her hands in his, he kissed them, letting his lips brush her fingers as lightly as the wings of a butterfly. Just this gesture set Heather's senses spinning. She wanted him with a passion that was like a fever in the blood, but the fear that all about them would know of her desires, and the remembrance of his married state, caused her to pull away as the music changed tempo.

"She is mine again!" Courtenay stated with a laugh, pulling her in his direction.

Richard found himself feeling a fierce impulse to tear her out of the other man's arms, and he reached out for her. He was no longer able to watch her beside Edward Courtenay.

"Leave me, Richard," Heather chided, fighting to remember that he could never be hers.

Richard's eyes turned hard at her rebuke as he lashed out in anger. "Take her and be damned!" Turning away, he stalked off, leaving the hall, and Heather was helpless to do anything but watch him go.

27

RICHARD MORGAN SOUGHT the quiet of the garden to soothe his jealous anger. He had never felt this emotion before, and its effect was therefore all the more devastating. He felt impotent with his misery, helpless to stop the pain that seeing Heather with the Plantagenet Courtenay had brought to him. He had come close not only to making a fool of himself before the entire court but also to causing Mary's censure and anger. Never having loved, the queen would hardly understand the torture he was going through.

"How could I have nearly lost control of my emotions that way?" he asked himself bitterly. Courtenay was not his enemy. If he was a rather self-centered, immoral young man, he had always been polite and friendly toward Richard, yet tonight Richard had come perilously close to actually harming him, and would have if he had been so bold as to touch her with any more familiarity than he had displayed.

Idly he walked about the garden. Like a man chased by the very devil, he paced about, trying with difficulty to wipe away the memory of Heather. The image of her lying in his arms came back to him, her red hair spread about her slim body like a cloak. She had been all loving softness. How could he ever forget that night in the stable?

How long he walked about the yew trees, he did not know; he only knew that he could not sleep without seeing her. Reaching forth his hands, he ignored the prick of thorns to pluck several of the roses which grew in fragrant abundance. They seemed the perfect gift for her.

"I would pick all the roses in the world and throw them at her feet if she would but love me again as she did before," he murmured beneath his breath.

"Do you pick them for *her*?" The woman's voice was low and seductive as she asked the question. It was a voice he knew well. Catherine Todd.

Turning, he saw her standing a few steps away from him, her green eyes looking very much like a cat's. He didn't deem it wise to offer her an answer.

She moved with feline grace toward him. "Oh, Dickon, darling. I can read you like a book."

Dickon. He hadn't been called that for years. The name brought back bitter memories of his childhood.

With a swish of her skirts she stood before him, pouting petulantly. "I do believe you were so busy looking at her that you scarce noticed my arrival at all."

"I'm sorry, Catherine." His voice held the tone of a father's with an errant child. Catherine Todd was spoiled, used to being the center of attention. How could he have so easily forgotten?

"Are you?" Reaching up her hand, she traced the hard-muscled lines of his chest. "Well, you should be. All the while I was traveling here, I thought of nothing but you, of seeing you again."

His fingers caught her wrist, pushing her probing fingers away. "Don't do this, Catherine. What was between us was over long ago. Five years ago."

She raised her haughty head, her eyes blazed anger, but she controlled herself well, tossing her well-coiffed black hair. "Not for me it isn't. Never for me."

He shook his head, not believing her words for a moment. He had not been her first lover, nor her last. Catherine Todd had a voracious appetite for men, and when she was widowed it had not taken her long to seek others to take her husband's place in bed. How could he help but compare her to Heather and find Catherine wanting? Heather was all that Catherine was not. There was more to a woman than beauty.

Walking in and out between the yew trees, Catherine cast him a furtive glance. "Will you not even give to me some shred of affection? One rose?"

He shook his head, and she offered him a dark look. As if to taunt him, she reached out her hand to pick a rose for herself, crying out as a thorn pricked her finger. To seek revenge for her injury, to vent her frustration at being denied, she tore the rosebud from the stem to crush it with her shoe upon the ground.

"I much prefer violets anyway."

Richard's blood ran cold as he witnessed her temper tantrum. How could he ever have desired her? Had she not testified against his uncle, he might never have witnessed firsthand her heartlessness and treachery.

As if sensing his appraisal of her, she smiled, asking suddenly, "Is she your mistress, this merchant's daughter?"

"Hold your tongue!" he thundered, his expression a grimace of warning.

"Ah, just as I feared. Well, 'twill be no secret, not if you look at her again as you did tonight. Half the court was buzzing about it." Her smile was full of venom.

"She is not my mistress, though if she were, it is none of your concern."

Cocking her head to one side, she looked up at him. "If she is not, it is because she has learned of your marriage, is that not so?"

He forgot about the roses in his hands as he clenched his fists in anger, only to suffer the flowers' barbs. "She knows about the marriage. It will do you no good to work your evil with a rattling tongue. I would have told her, had she not found out already. I am ever the honest man."

"Or the fool, Dickon." She shrugged her shoulders. "Ah, well. That is your concern." Walking around him slowly, sensuously, stalking him as a cat does its prey, she whispered in parting, "Remember that my arms are warm and soft to soothe you. Think of me when you sleep in your lonely bed tonight. I would not shun you because of a wife." With that said she was gone, vanishing into the trees like a night bird.

Richard pondered her words. Had he been a fool? Too much the gentleman? No. Love was based on honesty and trust. To betray either would be to destroy whatever chance there was for happiness.

Leaving the garden, making his way toward the door, Richard was again filled with a longing to see Heather. To tell her of his love, seek her promise to wait for him until he could be free of his marital chains.

Climbing the stairs, he stood before her door, only to hide in the shadows like a thief in the night as he heard laughter and the sound of approaching footsteps. He knew instinctively that it was Heather—she was not alone. The fact that Edward Courtenay was escorting her to her bedchamber flamed Richard's jealousy anew.

"No, I'm sorry," Heather was saying, "I cannot go for a walk in the garden with you, Edward. It is late. I must be abed."

"At least leave me with a kiss." The sound of rustling cloth told Richard that the man was gathering her into his arms.

"No. No, please."

"I will not take no for an answer."

Richard advanced out of the shadows. "I will see that you do."

"Ah, my lady's watchdog." Edward Courtenay flashed a toothy smile, throwing up his hands in the air in defeat. "For the moment I yield." With a jaunty walk he departed, leaving Heather and Richard alone.

"We have to talk." Richard moved toward her, fighting against the longing to take her in his arms. He held out the roses to her, the red and pink roses. "These are for you." He took a step toward her, still unsteady on his feet from the wine he had partaken of at dinner. Instinctively she stepped away.

He stepped toward her again as she stared at him mutely, mesmerized by the potency of his gaze. Taking the roses from his hands, she admired their beauty, touched by his gift, but wary of his intentions.

"It is late," she breathed. Her voice was tinged with sadness. She loved him. She wished that she could say that she did not, but she could not do so.

"I know it is late, but you must hear me out." He reached out for her and she was unable to pull away. His arm encircled her waist, and he spoke her name.

They did not hear the footsteps behind them until it was too late. "A midnight tryst?" A young red-haired page stood behind them, his eyes urging them to caution.

"I brought a gift of roses to the queen's new lady-in-waiting, nothing more." Richard swore beneath his breath at the interruption, wishing again that he had not been so determined to bring Heather to Greenwich.

The young page looked as if he did not believe him, making no comment, but asking of Heather, "Are you Heather Bowen?"

"Yes." She eyed the boy cautiously.

"The queen has need of you. There are some letters that she would read before she retires for the night. Come this way." With a look of regret, Heather followed after the boy, clutching the roses to her breast as they walked.

Richard watched as she quickly made her escape to the queen's chambers, and clenched his fists in frustration. She had eluded him this time, but he was determined to settle once and for all this ill feeling between them.

Unaware of Richard's resolve, of the torment her rejection of him was causing, Heather read to the queen. She had a longing to be home again. Perhaps there she could forget Richard. She knew how loath Thomas Bowen would be to part with the pennies to hire another to take her place.

"Poor Tabitha. She will have to do my share of work as well as her own. She will be old before her time."

"What did you say, my dear?" the queen asked. Heather liked her, sensing that Mary was a forgiving soul. She was by far the most pious ruler England had seen, maintaining a constant observance of her devotions.

"I'm sorry. I was just thinking about home," Heather whispered quickly, bending to the task of reading a letter from the Lady Jane Grey. In the letter she begged forgiveness.

"I cannot and will not execute my little cousin Jane," Mary was saying now, "no matter what Simon Renard tells me." Heather had learned that Simon was the diplomat from the court of Charles V. This Holy Roman Emperor was also Charles I of Spain, Mary's cousin, whose influence was growing greater day by day. "Why, I remember her from babyhood, adorned in her swaddling. We exchanged Christmas presents, she and I."

Remembering Jane's kindness to her, Heather said a silent prayer of thanks, then reached for another letter. "The Lady Elizabeth has written to you, your Majesty," she said, opening the letter.

"What does she want?" Mary snapped in answer. If she was fond of Jane Grey, the feeling did not extend to Mary's half-sister. Seeing Heather's wounded expression, Mary softened her tone. "I'm sorry, I did not mean to sound unkind.'

"Shall I read it, your Majesty?" Heather asked, unsure of how to soothe the ruffled royal feathers.

"Yes." It was a plea for friendship between them, a flowery letter full of praise for her "noble sister." Mary listened as Heather read, but her expression spoke of her true feelings. Heather could see that though Mary tried to keep the bitterness at bay, her dislike ran very deep.

"God knows I try to remember that she is my sister," the queen whispered, reaching up to pass her hand before her eyes. Heather had heard it said that

Mary suffered from migraine headaches. "But how can I forget that *her* mother replaced my own as queen or that the *concubine,* Anne, had me called bastard when it was her own child of a bigamous union that was truly illegitimate? Elizabeth!"

Heather soothed the queen with gentle words of understanding, remembering the stories she had heard from her mother regarding Anne Boleyn, yet Elizabeth could not be blamed for what her mother had done. Elizabeth had been but a mere babe.

Heather knew that Simon Renard fanned the flames of resentment between the two, speaking of the queen's sister as dangerous and crying for her imprisonment. He spoke of Elizabeth's power of enchantment, but Heather suspected that it was just that the princess was pretty and had an air about her that drew people to her.

Renard. From what Heather had heard whispered last night at dinner, nearly everyone at court was ill-at-ease about the power this new ambassador was gaining. That he was foreign caused ire, and the fear that Mary would heed his advice and marry a foreign husband seemed to cause the others at court to be wary of this Spaniard. No one wanted England to be brought under the domination of another country.

"You are deep in thought, my child," Heather heard the queen say, and looking up, found herself the object of scrutiny. "Let us hope that your thoughts are not of Richard."

"Richard?" Heather was flustered, averting her gaze from those searching eyes. "No . . . no . . . I . . . I—"

"I hope that I need not remind you that he is married. I will have no infidelity at my court. Let us hope that you are not of the ilk of Catherine Todd."

"Catherine Todd?"

The queen waved her hand in annoyance. "Enough said. Now leave me. I am overly tired and seek the blessed peacefulness of slumber."

Heather took her leave of the queen, pondering her words, the name Catherine Todd branded on her mind.

28

THE SUN HAD not yet appeared upon the horizon when Heather heard the clang of a bell through the haze of her deep sleep, a bell bidding all to arise for the morning Mass. Thrusting aside the curtains of her bed, she shivered in the slight chill of the damp early-morning air and hurried to start a fire in the small fireplace in the room. Going to the window, she could see that it was raining, a light mist only, but the moisture seemed to put an emerald-green hue upon the world beyond the walls of the palace.

A second bell sounded as she washed her face and hands with water poured from a pitcher into a small china basin. Her eyes were drawn to the roses in their glass vase nearby, and she thought again of Richard. His eyes had been gentle as he had looked at her, and she had wanted him to put his arms around her. Was she still clinging to her dream that one day they would be together? Yes. She wondered what he wanted to tell her, and realized that he had not had a chance to explain. Yet what could he say? How could he change the truth?

Hastening to dress, she nonetheless took special care with her person, choosing a gown of white velvet with red-and-gold brocade underskirt and fur-trimmed sleeves. Combing her hair, she plaited it into two thick braids which she wore in coils on either side of her head.

The same page who had interrupted her meeting

with Richard the night before was there to greet her outside the door, urging her to hurry.

"The queen is already rising from her bed," he admonished, opening the large paneled doors for Heather's entry.

All the ladies-in-waiting gathered around as the queen was dressed, twittering excitedly as each went about her duties. Mary at last silenced them with a harsh word, wanting to keep her mind upon celestial matters and not on the court's latest tattlings. Heather was quickly growing fond of Mary, despite her strict discipline. She seemed to be honest, and unlike Northumberland, seemed to have a care for the poor of her land.

As if sensing Heather's goodwill, the queen gave to her the honor of putting the crucifix, fastened by a long chain to the queen's belt, upon Mary's royal person.

When the queen was dressed, all the women curtsied, bowing low before her. She bid them rise, saying, "We must hurry to Mass to show our Lord that we are eager to offer him our most humble prayers."

Heather noticed how often the queen spoke of "we." We must do this, we must do that. Often she used the term "we" when talking about herself. It was a curious thing.

Surrounded by other ladies-in-waiting and an assembly of officials and dignitaries, Heather followed Mary toward the chapel.

"Ah, the merchant's daughter." The words were said as if in insult, and Heather turned to find an extremely beautiful dark-haired woman beside her. At the thought that this might be Richard's wife, her heart stopped, but it was green eyes, not dark, that regarded her. Hugh Seton had told her that Edlyn Morgan had dark eyes.

The woman forced a smile. "At last we meet. I have heard *much* about you." Her eyes scrutinized Heather's apparel. "Ah, white, the color of purity. You and the queen will get on well together."

Heather was taken aback by the woman's forward manner. "I beg your pardon?"

"It is said that Mary is a virgin, and I do not doubt it. Were she not, she would most likely not have such a sour disposition nor spend so much time upon her knees. A lover would do her a world of good," she said softly, looking at Heather as if wondering the state of Heather's virtue. Heather found herself blushing profusely.

They continued down the long corridor, Heather maintaining a careful silence, unnerved by the woman beside her. Who was she? Why did she keep staring at her? Reaching the chapel, she put great distance between herself and the dark-haired beauty, kneeling behind the queen as the Mass began. It was a long service, the chapel damp and stuffy. When Heather thought her knees could stand no more, another bell rang out. Mass was over, but so was Heather's respite from the piercing green eyes. In a moment the woman was by her side again.

"My name is Lady Todd—Catherine to you," she said, as if their conversation had not been interrupted. "How are you called?"

So shocked was she at hearing the woman's name and remembering the queen's words that Heather could barely get out the words. "Heather. Heather Bowen."

The woman laughed. "Heather. Why, even your name is pristine. I wonder that Richard was ever attracted to you. He has always before been fond of more experienced women."

"Richard?" Heather stopped walking.

"Why, yes, Richard. Don't tell me he hasn't mentioned me to you." She reached up a slender hand, putting the fingers to her mouth. "Oh, I hope I haven't spoiled anything. I thought you knew. I'm afraid our Dickon is somewhat of a collector. You weren't the first woman, nor will you be the last. He moves from flower to flower like a honeybee. Is it any wonder he keeps his poor *wife* away from court?"

Heather fought against her fears, not wanting to

believe this woman. A spasm of pain moved through her—confusion, disbelief, and finally anger.

"Of course *I* understand. That is part of Dickon's charm, but an innocent young *child* like you . . . Well . . ."

"I am not a child!" Heather's voice, usually soft and pleasant, took on a shrill quality. It was as if this woman had slapped her.

Catherine Todd reached out her hand, placing it on Heather's arm as if in sympathy. "I'm sorry. I only meant to befriend you, not cause you any pain. By saying that you are a child I only mean that you are unschooled in the ways of the court." She smiled again, moving in quickly for the kill like a panther or a lion. "A man can love his *wife* very much and still seek the bed of a *mistress.* It is, I fear, the nature of the brutes."

Heather was helpless against the storm of pain which swept through her. There had been other women he had kissed; she had not been special to him after all. More than his wife stood between them. Her eyes asked the question that her lips could not form.

Catherine Todd smiled in answer. "Yes. Dickon and I are lovers. His wife means little to him."

So that was what the queen meant by cautioning her. In an effort to hide her pain, she whispered, "What is his wife like?"

Catherine Todd knew little of the matter, yet she expounded upon what she did know with the skillful mastery of the schemer. "From what I have been told, it was a match made in heaven, uniting two very powerful and rich families. John Renfred was one of King Henry's closest advisers, appointed by the king himself to be one of Edward's guardians. Our Dickon was wise to align himself with such a family."

Was that then what Richard had wanted to tell her? That he had married for political gain? Perhaps Edlyn did not love him. Heather's conscience was pricked to find that this thought was soothing to her.

Silently she scolded herself. Richard was married. It was something that could not be denied, and no matter what had joined him to Edlyn, the woman was his wife before God and the laws of the country.

"It was a marriage of convenience then," she murmured more to herself than to the other woman.

"Yes. But had it not been, Richard would still have strayed. One woman is not enough for him, I fear. But I am content to be his mistress and willing to share him with you."

Mistress! Share! The words rang in Heather's ears. Never! She was not like this woman who stood beside her. Heather would never be satisfied to be one of a collection, no matter how much she loved a man.

"I thank you for your concern, Lady Todd," she said, looking directly into the woman's eyes, holding her head up with a dignity that would have rivaled any queen's, "but I assure you that I am not nor will I ever be Richard Morgan's mistress." Heather walked down the corridor, fighting against the anger which threatened to spill over. Anger at Richard for playing her for a fool, anger at this woman for her smug attitude, but most of all anger at herself for being such a naive fool. She had loved him, had thought he felt the same, while all the time she had only been one more conquest, a diversion to keep him entertained while away from his wife and home.

Storming up the stairs, she ran headlong into Edward Courtenay, and it was only then that the tears which had been threatening became a flood of despair.

"Did I hurt you? Don't cry. I'm sorry," he fretted, running his hands lightly over her body as if to find the source of her pain. "I am a clumsy fool. I should have seen you coming." Usually so light of heart, he had no sign of a smile upon his face now, and his concern deeply touched Heather.

Through her haze of tears she looked up at him. "I'm all right, really. You did not cause me any injury."

He sighed in relief. "Thank goodness. I would

never have been able to forgive myself if I had harmed such a beautiful lady." Taking her arm, he escorted her up the stairs.

"I . . . I think I am just a bit homesick," Heather murmured, explaining away her tears. I will never shed tears over any man again, she vowed silently.

Courtenay laughed bitterly. "As am I. Homesick. How I miss London. It is so dreadfully dull here, though I know that I am fortunate to have escaped Northumberland's fate. He was beheaded yesterday."

Heather winced at the news, wondering what her father must be thinking right now. Was he still worried that a similar fate awaited him?

"I lived in fear that Henry would part my head from my shoulders, longed for the day when I might be free, and yet now . . . Strange, but after fifteen years in the Tower it seems home to me, prison or no."

"I'm sorry. I . . . I had forgotten about your confinement there." How she wished that she could take away those years. What kind of man had this King Henry been to lock away a young boy, to cheat him out of his life?

He laughed again. "Don't be sorry for me. I want another emotion. I want you to admire me, nay, to love me." They stopped before Heather's chamber door and he took her hands in his. "Could you?"

She shook her head. The pain of Richard's betrayal was all too recent. "I will never love again," she whispered.

Disappointment showed clearly on his face, but he was undaunted. "Never is much too long, Heather. I am not a man to give up when I want something, yet I will not pressure you. I offer you friendship with the hope that it may blossom into something more fruitful."

They stood there looking at each other, feeling serene in this new fellowship, just as Richard bounded up the stairs. At last finished with his paperwork, his matters of state and arrangements that dealt with the

Spanish ambassador, he sought out Heather to tell her once and for all the truth about Edlyn.

"Courtenay!" He swore aloud, filled again with jealousy. The man was harder to get rid of than a cold. "Has the queen given you no duties, man? Must you constantly moon about *this* door?"

"Richard!" Heather was infuriated. How dared he?

Courtenay pulled away from Heather to face Richard squarely. "I like *this* door, it has special appeal for me." His eyes were challenging. "I ask of you what you have asked of me. Have you a special claim to this territory? "

"Yes! Dammit, yes."

"I see. Interesting . . ." Edward Courtenay looked from Heather to Richard and then to Heather again as the truth dawned on him.

"You have no claim to me," Heather stormed, remembering all too clearly the words Catherine Todd had spoken. "Your duty is to your wife. Or had you forgotten?"

Her words were like the drops of a cold rain showering on him and washing away his anger. "It is about my wife that we must speak," he said, reaching for her hand. She pulled away from his grasp as if he had the dreaded pox.

"There is nothing that you can say—"

"But there is. You have to know. Things are not always as they seem."

"How well I know." Opening her chamber door, she was anxious to step inside before he created a scene. Already there were those who stood about looking over in their direction. Sensing her intent, he quickly stepped in front of her to block her way.

"You will hear me out!" As Edward Courtenay moved forward, Richard nodded his head in the Plantagenet's direction. "Tell him to leave. What needs to be said is between us and not for other ears."

Edward Courtenay casually toyed with the neck of his doublet, in no hurry to leave. "Shall I stay?" he asked Heather.

"No," she whispered, mortified at the gossip they were no doubt causing at the moment.

Courtenay bowed gallantly. "I will go, but if you have need of me, you need only call out my name." In five swift strides he had left them alone.

"What is it that you have to tell me?" Heather asked, retreating to her doorway, holding the door only halfway open.

"I was married by proxy to a woman I had never met. An arranged marriage—" he began.

"An arranged marriage. One of convenience, so to speak," Heather interrupted. "Yes, I know all about your marriage."

"You know about my marriage?" Her words confounded him. He had not been prepared for this, yet he continued on, forgetting all his flowery speeches that had been prepared for this moment.

"I have sought to have the union nullified—" he began, only to have his words drowned out in a ripple of feminine laughter. Sweeping forward, taking his arm, was Catherine Todd.

"Dickon. There you are, you naughty boy." She held on to him possessively.

"Catherine. Not now. Leave me," Richard ordered, a scowl masking his handsome features. Of all the times for this woman to make her entrance, just when he had begun to tell Heather his story. In annoyance he tried to shake off her clinging hands.

She pouted prettily, flashing her green eyes in Heather's direction. "Why, I only wanted to thank you for the flowers."

"Flowers? What flowers?"

"Why, the roses, of course."

"I didn't—"

"Red and pink. My favorite colors. You are so thoughtful. But then, you always were the perfect lover." She smiled at Heather. "I do hope I haven't interrupted anything, but I just had to see Dickon to offer him my gratitude."

"There was nothing to interrupt," Heather answered quickly. "We were quite through. Good day."

Closing the door, she locked it from the inside, ignoring his pleas for her to open it. At last he went away and she was reminded of those times when he had waited so patiently outside her house in London. To think that she had felt sorry for him, had nearly been ready to go to him. She had nearly been ready to offer him her heart again despite all he had done.

"Fool. That is what you are, Heather Bowen," she said aloud to herself. "Catherine Todd is right. You are a child. A stupid, optimistic dreamer." Her eyes swept to where the roses stood, red and pink petals opening to the light of the sun, just as she had opened to his love. How many other women at court had he given them to? A collector. That was what Catherine Todd had called him. Had he a blond amid his harem also? He was no better than some infidel sultan, and all the while he had a wife at home too.

I want no part of his gifts, she thought, reaching for the flowers in anger. They would be given to the chambermaid at the first opportunity.

29

In the next few days Heather skillfully avoided not only Richard but also Catherine Todd. She had no need of further heartache or any reminders of her naiveté. Yet even seeing Richard caused her pain—the pain of longing, of unfulfilled desire and the grief of her loss. She had never known that the sight of a man could cause such sorrow.

Of course, there was always a great deal to keep her occupied. The routine was always the same. Up early to help the queen dress and for morning Mass, breakfast, reading to Mary from among the stacks of letters which were always piled atop the large carved desk in the queen's solar, and then lunch.

In the early afternoons Heather was free to do as she pleased and often took advantage of the queen's generosity in allowing her ladies to ride horses from the royal stables. On the days when she did not ride, there was dancing or court games, which included a game called tennis, card games, and shuttlecock. Heather could sense Richard's piercing blue eyes upon her wherever she was and knew that he watched her. In these moments she felt her pain again, longing to be with him. What was the use of dancing? She only wished it were with him. How could she laugh when it was his smile she wanted to see? She fought hard against the love in her heart, but she was powerless, for when in his company for even the briefest of moments all was lost. Yet her pride would not let her reveal the sorrow in her heart. She laughed and flirted with Courtenay as if to show Richard that she would not be one of his collection. But how could she gain oblivion from this hopeless love she carried in her heart when she must be reminded of it daily? In a crowded room she was aware of his presence. Indeed, she did not have to look his way to know where he stood, what he wore, or what he was doing. Her senses told her and she was consumed with her love at every beat of her heart.

This evening she saw him gazing at her across the dinner table, and seeing that Catherine Todd was seated next to him, she looked hastily away. Dinner was always a lavish affair with a great many dishes to choose from, and Courtenay joked that they would both soon be "as round as the juggler's colored balls," and Heather tried to laugh.

Throughout dinner Catherine Todd was determined to remain the center of attention, and it did not escape Heather's notice how that green-eyed beauty constantly looked at Richard, smiling at him with her most scintillating smiles. She even went so far as to touch him every chance she got, with a familiarity that caused Heather to seek solace in Courtenay's attentions.

If Heather suffered, so then did Richard. Trying to remain the gentleman, aware of the queen's scrutinizing eyes, he loathed Catherine's touch. His eyes met Heather's and held for a moment as he tried to tell her that the woman meant nothing to him, that his love was for her, but she looked away, laughing at one of Courtenay's remarks.

Richard ate, but tasted nothing, drank glass after glass of wine and yet could not relax. He hardly heard the words even the queen uttered; he was aware only of Heather and the knowledge that she scorned him. Had he lost her?

After dinner there was merrymaking and more dancing and it was then that Richard could stand no more. Moving across the room with the intent of talking with Heather, he stood in the doorway, blocking her way, his face a mask of misery. Taking a step forward, he sought to talk with her and she found herself trapped, unable to get away.

"Heather," he said softly. Her body tensed in expectation, she deliberately looked away, but with every nerve of her body she knew he looked at her, a long look. Her pulse began to beat at neck and temple and she feared that he would sense how completely overcome she was at his nearness. She had not expected that being near him could cause her such pain, such longing.

When he captured her hand, his fingers gripping her slender wrist, she quivered at his touch, but too fresh in her mind was his betrayal of all she held dear, especially honesty. Instead of looking at him, she jerked her hand away and came quickly to Courtenay's side, and Richard could have sworn that he heard her say the word "collector" beneath her breath, and puzzled at her meaning.

Casting Richard a triumphant glance, Edward Courtenay followed close behind Heather, and Richard heard him say, "I have an excellent idea. Why don't we go riding early in the morning? There are many wonderful places we have both yet to see."

Heather started to refuse, but the memory of Richard's perfidy, her humiliation at Catherine Todd's words, quickly changed her mind. "I would like very much to go."

The sight of them together wounded Richard as no stab wound had been able to do. He cursed the blond-haired man beneath his breath, then walked to the door to be about his own duties. If she wanted Courtenay, let her have him! Yet as he watched them together his jealousy knew no bounds, and he resolved to himself that when they went out riding on the morrow he would be close behind.

30

THE SUN STREAMED in through the window as Richard opened his eyes, flexing his sore muscles as he tried to forget the sleepless night he had just spent. Fearful lest he somehow oversleep and leave Heather in the clutches of Courtenay, he had spent the night in a chair by the bed, from time to time, recalling the way she had moved, the tilt of her head, that glorious red hair billowing about her shoulders, and the sound of her laughter, the laughter she had shared with another.

"Courtenay!" he said in disgust. That silly, shallow, conceited rogue. He wondered that Heather should deem it pleasurable to spend so much time in the man's company, and again felt the sting of his jealousy. If only he were free he would marry her and take her far from here. He had been thrice a fool to suggest to the queen that Heather be called to court, but he could not undo the wrong now.

Quickly he got up. Having slept in his clothes, he had merely to wash himself and straighten his garments to be ready to go. Making his way to the stables, he saddled one of the horses, an ebony stallion, and readied the animal to ride. The horse flicked his long tail impatiently, eager to be off, and Richard gently patted the animal's black rump.

"Soon. Soon now." Hearing the sound of footsteps, he ducked into the shadows, thinking it to be Heather or Courtenay. He felt much like a thief, hiding in the stable, and cursed once more the circumstances which had driven him here. But he had to protect Heather. Only a fool would not guess Courtenay's intentions in getting her alone, and Richard was no fool.

"So there you are, Dickon," purred a voice he knew all too well. "I thought I saw you headed this way." Wrinkling her nose in disgust at the smell of the stable, picking up her skirts to avoid any contact with the dirt and offal on the ground, Catherine Todd swept toward him. She seemed to have a sixth sense where he was concerned, and sought him out at every turn, much to his annoyance.

"What do you want?" he barked, coming out of hiding.

"I wanted to talk with you." Bending over as if to pick up some object from the ground, she offered him a good view of her décolletage.

He threw his hands up in frustration as his anger boiled forth like a caldron. "How many times do I have to tell you that it is over between us? Your treachery killed whatever affection I might have felt for you. I am in love with someone else, as you well know."

Her answer was laughter. "That simpering flame-haired child? I find that unbelievable and laughable. You need a woman with blood in her veins, not ice water. Besides, I have seen the way she treats you, Dickon. Hardly the actions of a woman in love."

"Thanks to you. Your playacting about the roses was most skillful indeed. Too bad that you are a woman, for a stage is where you belong."

"Oh, Dickon, don't be angry," she said softly, coming up to him and boldly running her hand down the front of his doublet and fondling the thicket of hair there. "We could be happy together, you and I." Seeing Heather coming up behind them, she moved with the deftness of a striking cobra, throwing herself into Richard's arms. It was in this embrace that Heather found them, staring soundlessly as her eyes brimmed with tears. Did she need any further proof of the kind of man Richard Morgan was? No. Fleeing from the stables, she did not see Richard pull away from the arms entwined around his neck, did not hear his scathing words.

"Have you lost your mind?" he demanded, seeking to put as much distance between himself and the dark-haired woman as possible.

"Richard," she implored. "I dream about you . . ."

"Dream about someone else," he snapped. "Were you the last woman in England I would shun you!"

"So you refuse me again. Bastard!" Her honey-sweet tone melted as she vented her wrath. "Someday you will be sorry for what you have said today. I promise you that." As quickly as she had appeared, she now vanished, leaving Richard to face Courtenay, who had heard her parting words.

"Tsk, tsk. A lovers' quarrel. Hasn't anyone ever told you, Richard, that hell hath no fury like a lover scorned?" He stood with hands upon his hips enjoying Richard's discomfiture as with a triumphant smile he ordered two horses to be saddled. Leading the horses out of the stables, he tossed his mane of blond hair and tilted up his Plantagenet nose as if to issue Richard a challenge.

In impotent fury Richard watched from a distance as Courtenay helped Heather up onto her horse, knowing that there was nothing he could say or do to claim her for himself. He was married, and Courtenay, damn him, was free. He watched sadly as Heather rode off, her unbound red hair blowing in the wind. Following close behind her, Courtenay looked like a golden-haired satyr, that ancient deity of Greek myth.

Heather rode beside Edward Courtenay in silence, trying desperately to overcome her heartache, to wipe out the memory of seeing Richard in the dark-haired witch's arms. She would forget him, she had to.

"You ride quite well," Courtenay said to her, flashing her his boyish grin.

"I fear that it is not my skills," Heather tossed back at him, "but those of the horse." She felt the smooth rhythm of the horse's stride and fought to control her sadness. Courtenay was a handsome man. He had shown her kindness and attention these past few days, had made no secret of his desire for her. Perhaps in his arms she could forget Richard. So thinking, she gently nudged her horse closer to his.

They rode into the meadows and beyond, coming to the spreading trees of the forest. Riding side by side, they chatted comfortably about the latest court tattlings and mischief and Heather filled her eyes with the beauty of the forest, forgetting for a time all else as she gazed at the dazzling greenery. Side by side they rode, except where the path grew too narrow; then Courtenay followed her.

"Of course, were anyone to know that we were alone together without proper chaperon, we would be the talk of Greenwich," he said with a laugh.

"I don't care!" Heather called back, thinking of Richard's betrayal. Let the whole world chastise her, for all she cared. Riding amid the splendor of the forest was worth it. It was the first time in weeks that she had felt so free.

They headed far away from the palace, down a steep embankment, at last dismounting and leading the horses down the hill, careful to duck their heads to avoid being hit by the low-hanging branches. At last, coming to a small lake, Courtenay took her hand and led her to a large rock.

"Sit down, Heather," he said softly. "Do you like it here? I often came here when I was a boy. Before I was imprisoned in the Tower."

"It's beautiful."

"And you are beautiful." His eyes swept over her with a hunger which made her cheeks turn red. "Someday I will be king and all this will be mine, but I would trade it all for the words that you love me."

"Edward . . ."

He pushed her down upon the rock and knelt beside her, taking both her hands in his. "Let me love you, Heather. I can sweep away all thoughts of Richard Morgan from your mind." His mouth descended upon hers before she could protest, his kiss gentle. Heather opened her lips to his, reached up her arms, and sought to draw him closer, waiting for the sweet fire Richard's kisses always brought her. There was none, no matter how desperately she sought to lose herself in this man's caresses.

"Oh, God, Heather," Courtenay moaned, reaching up his hand to close over the curve of her breast. "I want you so." No longer the gentle lover, Courtenay was carried away by his desires, tugging at her dress in an effort to bare her breasts, and Heather stiffened in shock. She couldn't give herself to this man, no matter how wounded she was by Richard. She shoved at his hands; he was going too far, too fast. He had to stop.

"No!"

"Yes," he whispered, covering her mouth again with his own. Heather began to fight him in earnest, but the harder she fought, the tighter Courtenay held her. "I'll make you want me. I will. I will." Tearing at her bodice, he at last bared her breasts, and it was then that Richard Morgan bounded through the brush like some wild animal of prey.

"Leave her alone!" he growled, lifting Courtenay up by his doublet to meet him eye to eye. "You bastard. I ought to—"

"Richard. No." Heather sought to ward off the violence that threatened. "Please." Tugging at her dress, she cried out, "He didn't harm me. Please."

Faced with a man of great strength, Edward Courtenay cowered. "Don't hit me. Don't."

Richard thrust the man from him in disgust. "Get your royal ass out of here, Courtenay, before I change my mind. The queen has need of you, though I cannot say why."

Without a backward glance at Heather, Courtenay obeyed, mounting his horse and riding off.

"He would have made you his mistress but never his wife!" Richard chided. "He longs to wear the crown."

"And is it not your mistress you would make of me?"

Slowly he moved toward her, reaching out to capture her slender shoulders in his hands and pulling her toward him. "Such torture to see you in Courtenay's arms, but I will show you what a real kiss is." Ruthlessly his mouth came down on hers, engulfing Heather in the familiar sensations of ecstasy. To have him kiss her once again, to feel his heartbeat against hers, was intoxicating. Pressing her body closer to his, she sought the passion of his embrace. She craved his kisses as the flowers craved the sun. Warm, sweet desire fused their bodies together. Weakly she clung to him as his arms encircled her. Heather felt as though she were falling into a deep, dark vortex, felt possessed by their passion, and fought frantically to keep from being consumed by this power he held over her, this flame in the blood. If she let him touch her like this she would be lost. Lost.

"No!" Tearing herself away, she stumbled backward. "You will not force yourself on me again."

Her words stung him as bitter bile flooded his throat. "Force myself on you again?" he choked. "I have never . . ." He thought of the fever in the blood he had felt in the stables that magical night, but she had not fought him. "You were willing enough that night," he growled, lashing out at her because of his wounded pride. "Does it now make you feel better to think that I forced you?"

Putting her hands to her face, Heather burst into a storm of tears. "No. No. I don't know what I think."

Richard clenched his fists, not knowing what to say to her, what to do. A woman's tears could quickly unman one's anger. "Don't cry," he whispered helplessly. Damn, how he loved her. Even his anger could not do away with that feeling. Just the sight of her turned him into a quivering, witless fool, aching to possess her.

"Heather." He reached out to take her arm, and frowned as she shrugged off his hand.

"I don't ever want to speak to you again," she cried, seeking to still her longing with anger. How could she forget the sight of him in Catherine Todd's arms? "You are despicable. Married to one woman, lusting after others. I won't be one of your collection of women."

"My collection?" Remembering Catherine Todd, he knew instinctively that this was her doing, that she had prompted Heather's words. "I want only you. No other woman means anything to me."

"But Catherine—"

"Is a woman scorned. We were lovers, yes. But that was many long years ago. When I witnessed the woman's treachery firsthand, I no longer wanted her."

"I don't believe you. You have lied to me once, why not again?"

A muscle in Richard's jaw twitched in anger. "I have never lied to you! I tell you that she means nothing to me, and I tell you true."

She wanted to believe him. How she wanted to think that he told the truth, yet she knew what she saw. Besides, there was another who stood in the way. "Edlyn."

"Edlyn."

"Even if you did not love Catherine Todd, there is Edlyn to consider. One day you will go home to her arms."

"Not to her arms. Oh, Heather, I tried to tell you, but you would not listen to me. Instead you avoided me, never allowing yourself near me unless we were in a crowd. Do you have any idea how that tore me apart inside?" He reached up, combing his hand through the thick black of his hair. "I have no wife, no real wife. The woman who bears my name is insane."

She gasped. The thought was too horrible to imagine. All sorts of pictures danced through her head. "Oh no!" Her voice was hardly more than a whisper. "Why did you not get the marriage annulled?"

"I tried. A dozen times. I sought a divorce, but at every turn I have been thwarted. John Renfred is still a man of much influence, and now the queen herself, remembering her mother's woes, has denied me."

"Richard, I . . . I don't know what to say." Was this the truth? She knew that it must be. It would have been such a monstrous lie.

"Say that you love me, as I love you. Tell me that it doesn't matter. That we can be together. That my marriage is of no importance. That it will not stand between us."

She wanted to have him take her in his arms again, longed to tell him what he wanted to hear, but she could not. She needed time to think. Time to digest all that he had revealed to her. "I cannot."

"Then there is nothing more that I can say." It took every ounce of his strength to turn away, but it was a thing he knew he must do. "I love you. Remember that," he said softly. Then he was gone.

As he left her, Heather felt a cold wind sweep over her, like the wind that blew across the lake. She wanted to call him back, to tell him that she loved him too, but he was gone before she could say another word.

31

AFTER HER MEETING with Richard, Heather felt bereft. For so long she had avoided him, had dreaded what he might tell her, and now it was over and her world seemed suddenly empty.

"My wife is insane." She heard over and over again those words and her heart bled for him. Yet even so, could she come to his arms, be his mistress? The question was always in her brain. Even now as she came upon a small circle of ladies of the court.

"It is enough that we must attend Mass morning and night," Catherine Todd was grumbling, "but now she expects us to go to confessional as well. Must I spend all my hours in the chapel? What will we have to suffer next?"

Anne Fairfax, a plump distant cousin of Stephen Vickery's, laughed. "Poor dear," she said with mock sympathy. "You are so abused, but then a little beauty sleep *would* do you a world of good. I believe I can see bags under your eyes."

Heather tried to keep from smiling. Anne Fairfax was adept at putting the haughty green-eyed vixen in her place. Perhaps it was that which drew Heather to the brown-haired, brown-eyed woman. Anne was the oldest of the ladies-in-waiting and had the important position of sharing the queen's chambers. Sharp of wit, Anne was a match for anyone. She had befriended Heather and was one of the few ladies who did not remind Heather of her lack of "noble blood" or shun her because of Catherine Todd's words.

"I do not mind Mass," Heather confided to her new friend. "At home I was always up much earlier and went to bed at a much later time. Life at court is so frivolous that I sometimes feel guilty and lazy."

Catherine Todd looked daggers at both Anne and Heather before she walked away, taking her circle of friends with her, and Anne cocked her head. "Remember our dear friend Catherine is used to keeping late hours and sleeping late in the morning. Pretending to be a devout Catholic is most difficult work for her." They both laughed. "Ah, but one of these days she will forget herself and rattle her tongue too often."

Heather stopped laughing. "Anne, tell me true. What do you think will happen to us now with Mary as queen? It is confusing. I remember the king as head of the church. Will Mary take us back to Rome?"

"It is difficult to foresee. Papist. Heretic. Each side calls the other names. There are those who call the new faith Protestant, yet we in England consider the Protestants heretics and refer to ourselves as 'the reformed Catholics.' "

"Somehow I feel that God does not truly care in what manner we worship him as long as we love him in our hearts," Heather whispered.

"Well-spoken," Anne replied as they walked down the hall together to their rooms. "We sometimes forget the message to love one another that our Lord gave us. To love God and each other. Yet Catholics persecute Protestants and Protestants do the same to Catholics. Where will it all end?"

"At least Mary has shown tolerance," Heather answered.

"Yes, at least for the moment." There was a worried look in Anne's eyes, as if she sensed that the future might not be as calm as the present moment. "Mary is hopeful of converting those of the reformed faith back to the old ways. Let us hope that she will be as lenient when she learns that she may not be successful."

Heather was to remember this conversation in the months to come and wonder if at that moment Anne Fairfax had a premonition of her own tragic fate.

32

RICHARD MANAGED TO lose himself in his work, trying to forget his pain at losing Heather. He had done everything possible to see her alone, to press her for an answer, but she was always just out of his reach like an elusive butterfly. He had nearly given up hope that she would ever love him again. He had even begun to believe that perhaps she would be better off with Courtenay, yet one look at Heather swept such thoughts from his mind. He was selfish in his desire. The thirst for her love could not be denied.

"Richard, I like this not at all," he heard Stephen Vickery exclaim as he paced the floor of the library. Now that he was in residence at court, it was his friendship for this man that saved his sanity. "That man, that 'imperial ambassador,' oversteps his bounds."

"I don't like it either. We did not risk our lives to be ruled by such as he."

Stephen Vickery pulled at his red-gold beard in agitation. "Our hands are tied. You must understand Mary. All those years when her father had cast off her mother and declared Mary a bastard, she had only one sympathetic ear—her cousin Charles V. Spain, her mother's country, her kinsman, were her only friends. Is it any wonder that she still looks to Charles for guidance and advice and thus to this man Renard?"

Richard stopped his pacing. "I understand. But for the man to actually think to cut Elizabeth out of the succession to the throne. That is unthinkable."

He has not actually proposed such a thing to the council."

"No, but I have heard him talking with the queen. He will do so after the coronation. And as to this imprisonment of our archbishop, Cranmer. I know he instigated it."

Rising from his chair, Stephen Vickery sought to calm his friend. "Mary would have been tolerant, even with all that has been done to her, if not for Renard's constant suggestions. And of course Cranmer has preached against the Mass as an abominable blasphemy . . ."

"There have been aggressions on both sides. Bishop Bonner's chaplain had a dagger thrown at him in front of a crowd, a gathering that deeply resented his Catholic preaching. Damn! Many more instances such as this and Mary will cease to listen to us, to those who urge moderation, and turn instead to Seton's kind, who love to agitate." Clenching his jaw, he asked, "By the way, just where is Seton? Why has he not been to court?"

Vickery smiled. "I fear a touch of vanity has overcome him. While I was in London I noticed him spending an inordinate amount of time with a merchant. No doubt when he makes his entry here at Greenwich he will look like a peacock."

"With a merchant, you say? Which merchant?" A feeling a foreboding gripped Richard.

"Why, Thomas Bowen. Our lovely Heather's father." He laughed. "I have yet to forget the kiss that beauty gave to me in the Tower. It was nearly worth risking my life for. Of course my *wife* would have my head if she ever heard me say so."

Richard closed his eyes, remembering a time when he too had felt the softness of her lips, the glory of her body. How could she ever know how many times he dreamed of her, longed for her?

"At least we have not had to suffer Seton's foul temper, Richard. We should thank our good fortune. Let the merchant have him, I say. Seton can hardly do us much harm looking for cloth."

Richard was not as soothed. Seton hated him; this he knew all too well. The thought that the visit to Thomas Bowen was more than just a desire to purchase fine cloth was uppermost in his mind.

"I would not be too certain. Yet, like you, I much prefer Greenwich without him." It was enough to worry about Edward Courtenay without having to worry about Seton as well. Ah, Courtenay. If only he were safely married to the queen. He was English. There would be no threat of a foreign husband. England would be safe and Heather as well. But it was obvious that Courtenay was out of the question, definitely unsuited for any kind of responsibility. Mary treated him with the indulgence of an aunt toward a mischievous nephew. And much to Richard's relief, Heather was not in the scoundrel's company nearly so often now. Yet still he worried, knowing that she had not come to him either, though he had hoped. He had hoped beyond all else that she would.

"But as to this Simon Renard, we will have to watch him carefully. You are right in urging caution," Stephen continued, breaking into Richard's recollections. "We are wise to know that Protestantism and patriotism have become closely interwoven. I fear that the majority of people here in England think of Catholicism as foreign—Spanish, French. Why, there is hardly an influential family in England that does not hold property taken from the church during Henry's day. They will of course oppose any return to the old ways."

"Let us hope that Renard is as wise as you, Stephen," Richard said softly. As if speaking the name conjured up the man, Renard stood behind him, walking stealthily like a panther. Dressed all in black, he resembled that animal, his eyes dark and dangerous.

"Wise? In what way, Lord Morgan?"

Richard was caught, and thus told the truth. "In realizing that it will take time to change England back to the old ways, if it can be done at all."

The man smiled. "I have ever had the patience of

Job." He held a letter in his hand and this he crinkled slightly with his fingers, at last handing it to Richard. "This letter will cause you joy." His accent was so heavy that Richard could barely understand him.

The letter was from the city of Toledo, the imperial city and old Visigoth capital, the capital of Spain since the reconquest from the Moors. "It is from the archbishop," Richard said with surprise.

Renard smiled. "Yes. It concerns your brother, Roderick. Or rather Brother Stephen. Sent into exile, I believe, when your young King Edward was erroneously counseled to deport the priests. Brother Stephen is being sent here. To England. He is in fact already on a ship headed this way. He asked that you meet him at the London docks."

"Roderick? Here?" Richard was ecstatic, all thought of caution now gone from his mind.

"He is arriving tonight." So saying, Renard was gone quickly and as silently as he had come.

"Tonight?" Richard's happiness vanished at the thought of leaving Heather. Always he kept his eye upon her, watching out for her welfare. How could he leave her, even for a few days? Yet he must. Turning to Stephen Vickery he asked, "Will you watch over Heather for me and see that she is safe?"

The man nodded. "It will be a welcome task." He smiled knowingly. "I will see that she does not run off with Courtenay in your absence."

"Thank you. You have always been a friend to me. It means a lot to have someone whom I know I can trust." He smiled sheepishly. "I must leave you now. It would not be possible to leave without saying goodbye to her. I have to tell her something."

Intent upon finding her, he sought her right away in her chamber, only to feel the sting of disappointment when he saw that she was not there. Where was she?

Something, some inner sense, led him to the garden, fearing at first that he would find her again with Courtenay, but she was alone. He found her standing beside the pond, watching the reflection of the moon on the water, kneeling down, splashing her hands in the pond as if to catch a moonbeam. She was beautiful in the moonlight, her skin pale ivory, her hair hanging down her back like threads of dark red silk.

Heather seemed to sense his presence, turning around to meet his gaze. "What you are doing here?" she breathed, picking up her long skirts as if to go.

"Please, don't leave," he whispered. "I want to talk to you, tell you the whole story. Perhaps then you will understand. I was married by proxy while I was in Ireland. An only daughter of a rich and powerful man who was anxious to find a husband for his only child. He offered gold and land in exchange for his daughter's hand, and my mother saw it as the greatest of opportunities. Our own family, though wealthy and noble, had fallen from grace because of our religious views. The banns were posted, the betrothal confirmed, and the marriage ceremony itself conceived in silence with only a few in attendance. Even *I* was not there." He laughed bitterly. "When I arrived home I was given the news and met my blushing bride. A woman who is, as I told you, insane." He reached out and touched her hair with infinite gentleness and longing. "I couldn't go away without telling you the story and hoping that when I return you will give me an answer."

"Going away?" He could not go now, not now when she knew the truth. She wanted to be alone with him, to comfort him and atone for all her harsh words of the past weeks. Her body was on fire for his touch, she ached for his kisses.

"For only a few days. I am leaving on Renard's orders."

"Every day that you are away will be a day without the sun," she whispered. "Oh, Richard. What am I to do? I never wanted anyone but you. Never!"

"And I have never loved anyone but you. Remember that while I am gone." He pulled the whole soft, supple length of her against him, breathing in the fragrance of her hair and whispering her name as he kissed her, his mouth blistering her with its heat, with sweet wild desire. His hands caught in her hair, stroking it with a tenderness belying the passion which flared up between them; then he stepped away. "When I come back I want an answer, Heather. An answer."

33

WITHOUT RICHARD AT court it was a lonely place for Heather. Even their arguments had been more comforting than the knowledge that he was gone. At least she had seen him, been close to him. What worried her most of all was the total secrecy involving his absence. No one, not even Anne Fairfax, seemed to know why he had gone nor how long he would be away.

"How could I have believed Catherine Todd?" Heather asked herself more than once with self-reproach. "Loving is trusting, the two must go hand in hand." She remembered all the pain she had read in his eyes as she had snubbed him in favor of Courtenay's attentions. Knowing that she was causing him pain, thinking herself justified, she had flaunted Courtenay's obvious attraction to her. She had ended up hurting Richard, Courtenay, and herself. And now Richard was gone. It was a just punishment in itself.

Heather kept her inner turmoil to herself, spending long hours in her room trying to sort out her feelings. She loved Richard. How could she ever stop loving him? And he loved her. All her life she had been lonely, sensing that something was missing. Now that she had found love, could she turn her back on the man who made her feel so alive? Now that she knew what loving someone truly meant, could she be content as the merchant's dutiful daughter again? The answer was no, but therein was the problem which haunted her night and day. What was to be done about it?

At last she confided her secret to Anne, the one lady at court who Heather knew could be trusted. "And so there was no other place where I could take him to keep him safe, except my father's stable," she explained, concluding the story of their first and second meetings, encounters that would change her life.

Anne's eyes had widened to nearly the size of walnuts. "You kept him in a loft beneath your father's nose, knowing full well that they were enemies and you would be dealt with quite harshly were he discovered?"

"Yes. What else could I do?"

Anne smiled. "What else would *you* do? You are a brave person, Heather. Richard Morgan is a very lucky man to have your love."

"Perhaps not so lucky. These past weeks I have given him a great deal of pain." She did not spare any detail in telling Anne the whole of the story, her attraction to Richard, his words to her not to love him. They sat on a bench beneath an apple tree in the garden, hands folded on their laps.

"Don't you see, Heather, he told you not to love him because he didn't want to hurt you. How trapped he must have felt to be married to one woman, loving another. Loving you was like reaching for a star, knowing he could never have it. He didn't want to offer you a sordid relationship, though it meant his own pain."

"His . . . his wife is addled in her wits. What sort of marriage is it for him?"

Anne reached for Heather's hand. "I know about his wife. Perhaps I am one of the few who do. The others no doubt think her to be so beautiful that he fears to bring her with him."

"You know . . . ?" Heather felt somehow relieved.

"My cousin Stephen and I were at the proxy ceremony two years ago. To my shame we did nothing to stop it, though we both knew that it would bind him in a hopeless marriage. Had I known that telling you would have eased your mind, I would have done so. Now I know why you have been so sad."

"Catherine Todd told me . . ."

Anne's eyes blazed fire. "I have no doubt what *she* told you. She has always had her cap set for him, though I credit him with better sense. The woman is, pardon me for saying such, a bitch! Like a dog in heat she has panted after him all these years, giving the poor man no respite."

"I am no better, Anne." Heather cast her eyes downward, remembering the night out in the stables.

"Merry-come-up! To say such a thing," Anne admonished. "You and Catherine Todd are like comparing a demon and a saint."

"I am no saint. I . . . I have shared his bed." Blushing deeply, she whispered the story of that night in the stables, telling it as delicately as she could. "And now I am hopelessly in love with him. His very touch sets me afire."

Without saying a word, Anne put her arms around Heather, hugging her fiercely. "I am glad! So glad. You deserve happiness, both of you."

Heather pulled away slightly. "But what we did was a sin."

Anne shook her by the shoulders. "By what law? Man's law, not God's. God would not want a man so tied. I cannot believe him to be so cruel. You belong to Richard and he to you. It is as simple a thing as that."

"But what about the future? What kind of life can we have together?" Seeing a fly caught in a spider web in the branches of the tree, she flicked her finger to free it, watching as it flew away.

"A life filled with love. But you must be willing to sacrifice for that love. Can you? Will you? Can you suffer the scorn of others to be with him? Live day to day with the hope that he will be free?"

The tinkling sound of laughter wafted through the air and Heather saw the graceful figure of Catherine Todd floating by, walking with a group of her friends, ladies-in-waiting who shunned Heather because of her "common" blood. Leaving them, Catherine walked over to Heather and Anne. Dressed all in green, she blended with the leaves.

"Ah, the merchant's daughter. Tell me, is it your father who has supplied all the cloth for our gowns?"

Heather thrust back her head proudly. "Yes, it is. Nearly half of the cloth that will be used for the coronation has been purchased from him."

Catherine sniffed her disdain. "And his daughter will be riding in that same entourage. What has the world come to when nobility and common stock stand elbow to elbow? Why, the next thing you know, a stablehand will be made a duke." She laughed derisively. "Lady-in-waiting, indeed."

"I am proud of my father. He has the best cloth in all of London," Heather exclaimed. She would not let this woman humble her.

"Indeed? I have judged it to be of inferior quality myself. The wool makes me itch and the velvet is too thick, it makes me perspire." As if to emphasize her words, she reached for the fan which hung from the chain around her waist.

It was then that Anne Fairfax stepped forward with a wide and toothy smile. "Why, Catherine, I am so very sorry to hear of your discomfort. But I do think that I can be of some help if you will only come with me."

Heather looked at Anne, lifting one eyebrow to question her friend, but Anne only motioned for her to follow. Through the winding path in the garden they walked, coming at last to the pond.

Catherine looked about her in bewilderment. "How can a walk in the garden aid me?"

Anne came up behind her, her voice soothing. "It is all very simple really." Suddenly she reached out both her hands, giving Catherine a shove which sent her tumbling into the pond. The splash sent the ducks and swans scurrying. "You see. That should cool you off quickly so you will blame the merchant no longer."

Heather could not keep from laughing, for it was a comical sight to see such a proud woman up to her large breasts in water, her hair sticking out every which way.

"How dare you! How dare you!" she shrieked. "I shall tell the queen. You will be sent from court in disgrace."

Anne only laughed. "I think not. Not when I tell her all that you have been up to. Spying on her. Reading letters that are not for your eyes. I have seen you, and I promise you this. If you ever say another cruel word to Heather, if you ever do anything to cause her distress, you will reckon with me. Do you understand?" Anne stood with her hands upon her ample hips.

Standing up, wringing the water out of her dress as best she could, Catherine Todd nodded, but her eyes blazed hatred and Heather could not suppress the shiver which ran up her spine. Anne had made an enemy of a very dangerous woman. Heather heard her hiss, "If it takes me the rest of my life, I will see that you pay for this, Anne Fairfax."

"Come, let us go back to the palace," Heather whispered, taking Anne by the hand. It was not so comical to her anymore, for some instinct, some inner voice, whispered that there would be an act of reckoning for this one simple prank.

"I have wanted to do that for years." Anne laughed, tossing her head as they walked through the front door. "She has long had it coming, that none can deny."

"Perhaps, but I wish . . . I wish . . ." Heather shrugged her shoulders. "It does not matter." A page clothed in silver satin handed her a letter and she opened it hastily, hoping beyond hope that it was from Richard. It was not. She scanned it quickly, her face turning as white as the paper on which the missive was written.

"What is it, Heather?" Anne asked in alarm. "There is no illness in your family, I hope."

Heather turned to her in anguish, her hands trembling violently, her voice a croaked whisper. "It . . . it's from my father," she said. "I am to marry Hugh Seton before the month of September is out."

34

"YOUR MAJESTY. PLEASE. I cannot marry him! Is there nothing you can do?"

Heather knelt before her sovereign, heedless of the curious stares of Renard and the other councillors roaming about the chamber room. Seton was a monster. To plight her troth to a man who was capable of cruelty was frightening. Even without the love she felt for Richard she would have been loath to marry Seton. Her father had waited all these years, only to wed her to a churlish brute.

Mary's pinched features were unsmiling as she sat stiffly in her high-backed chair, her hands held rigidly in her lap. "I wash my hands of this matter. It is not for me to say whom you will or will not marry, child."

"But he is a cruel man. . . ."

The queen rose to her feet, denying Heather's words with a shake of her bejeweled head. "No, not cruel. Decisive perhaps. You could do far worse than to marry a man of his strength. Your father, your family, has prospered greatly by my favor. An advantageous marriage would bring them even more prosperity."

"But Seton . . ."

"In the first days of my victory I counted heavily upon his wisdom and loyalty. He is a good man. He will make you a good husband."

Heather could feel the blood drain from her face as a cold nausea gripped her. Was there naught that she could say to sway Mary? Could the queen truly be so blind to the man's character?

"Yes, your Majesty," she answered in a choked whisper.

The queen's cool hand touched her bare shoulder, bidding her to rise. "Is it that like all maidens you fear the marriage bed?" she asked softly. "I myself often tremble at the thought of my own wedding night. Now that I am queen there must be an heir to follow after me when I die." Her eyes took on a determined glow. "There must be!"

The *marriage bed*. The words reverberated in Heather's mind like a chiming bell. She would have to suffer Seton's loathsome touch. She would belong to him, would be his property. It seemed a sacrilege even to think of kissing him when her heart, her soul, her body belonged to Richard Morgan. How could she ever let another man, especially Hugh Seton, touch her? And yet she would be forced to bed him, were she to become his wife.

"No!" The word escaped her lips before she could stop it. She would not marry him. Never. Let her father do what he would.

The queen raised her eyebrows in dismay. "No! No what?" She regarded Heather critically. "Women must perform their duties. To marry well and bear children is what we were called to earth for. What more is there than this?"

"Love."

"Love? You are young and foolishly romantic. The troubadours' songs are just that. Songs. The perfect man does not exist except in our dreams. No, you will do what our women have done since the days of William the Conqueror, marry the man of your father's choosing."

Heather's eyes darted back and forth like a trapped animal's. "I will do what must be done. What must be done," she whispered, preparing herself to suffer all that her father might do in his anger.

Mary misunderstood her answer. "Good. Good. I will look forward to your wedding." She clapped her hands, signaling for her councillors to come to her. "I must get on with matters of great urgency now, Heather. A coronation awaits me and I want it to be a glorious one, heralding in our reign and God's glory."

The October festivities were fast approaching as September waned. The entire court would be moving back to the Tower to make final preparations, while Heather's life took a different direction. She would not rejoice. Heather's day of doom awaited. Her marriage. She remembered her father's letter. "Before September is out you will be wed to Hugh Seton."

Fleeing from the queen's chamber, she sought out Anne Fairfax in the garden. August had gone by so quickly and now the leaves displayed their bright hues of gold and flame, replacing the petals of the flowers which had bid their adieu until the next year.

"Oh, Anne, what am I going to do? The queen will not aid me."

"I feared that she would not." Anne kicked at a small pebble in her path. "It is the way of this *man's* world. They arrange our lives to suit themselves, with nary a thought to our happiness. I have been wed two times. Once to a man thrice my age and once to a drunken and cruel lout. In my stubbornness I vowed to outlive them both, and well I did. The next time I will marry for love or not at all."

"I will not marry Seton!" Heather's fists were clenched with determination.

"What about your mother? Is there any way in which she can sway your father?"

Hope gleamed in Heather's eyes, only to grow dim again. "My mother dances to my father's tune. All my life I have watched her bow and scrape to him. It's almost as if he held some power over her, some secret."

Anne shook her head, clucking her tongue in sympathy. "Alas, it is a pity. There are some women who have learned well how to dominate their husbands."

"Thomas Bowen is no henpecked spouse, though I wish to heaven that he were." But Heather would not bow to his wishes. Not this time. No, not this time.

They walked in and out among the yew trees in silence. It was so pleasant here. Heather dreaded the thought of returning, however briefly, to the hub of the city with its squalid poverty and noisy cobbled streets. Courtenay had been absent from the court quite frequently in the last days, and rumor had it that he was frequenting London's brothels.

"Fifteen years have been taken out of my life," he had told Heather. "I but seek to live the remaining years to the fullest." And from what Heather had heard from gossips in the palace, he was doing just that. She missed him, dear rogue that he was. Only Courtenay could take her mind off her troubles.

As if reading her thoughts, Anne Fairfax spoke his name. "Edward Courtenay. I think in his way he loves you. 'Tis a pity that his blood runs too royal. Better to wed him than this Hugh Seton."

"I can never marry anyone else. I love Richard Morgan with all my heart." Reaching out, she sought to catch a falling leaf and was successful, turning it over and over in her hands as if it were a valuable treasure.

"Richard Morgan. Ha. Just where is this man you love when you need him?" Anne snorted in disdain.

"I don't know. He left so quickly."

"If only I could get a message to him. His lady has need of her knight in shining armor."

"Yes, I need him," Heather echoed, knowing in her heart just how very true those words were. In just a few days her father would send Perri for her to take her back home. Home. The word had an ominous ring to it. For the first time she knew how Richard Morgan must have felt to find himself married to a woman he did not love. She was faced with a similar fate, and only her courage could save her.

35

THE CHILL AUTUMN wind blew fiercely, whipping Richard Morgan's cloak wildly about him as he stood at the dock. His eyes scanned the harbor for sight of the ship that would bring his brother home. Behind him the winding cobbled streets, gabled roofs, and church steeples of London offered a familiar sight to welcome Brother Stephen.

"Three years since I've laid eyes on him," Richard said to himself, squinting his eyes to the sun as sails of an incoming vessel came into view. The ship skimmed the waves like a dancer as screeching gulls circled overhead, swooping down toward the deck as the sails were furled.

The port was a seething beehive of noise as the sailors moved about, unloading the cargoes of riches arriving for London merchants from foreign ports. He couldn't help but wonder if any of these chests were for Heather's father.

Richard felt more at peace now than he had in a long while. Heather had now heard his story, knew the truth. She hated him no longer. It had been such torment to leave her after the kiss in the garden, but he had known that to stay for one moment longer would have meant that he would not have been content with just the taste of her lips.

"She loves me. I could see it in her eyes," he whispered to the wind. "Perhaps with my brother's help I can loosen these bonds of matrimony which tie me."

It was his only hope. All of the hours of pain

would be worth suffering if at the end he was united with the woman he loved.

Breathing in the salt air, he felt invigorated, hopeful. Stephen Vickery would watch over Heather until he returned to court, and then, when he returned, he would seek an answer from the woman he loved. Would she wait for him to gain his freedom?

The masts of the docked ships looked like tree trunks as he stood there, their brightly colored flags fluttering in the wind. He watched and waited as the Spanish ship glided into port to cast its anchor in English waters.

"The *Canción*," he exclaimed, remembering that the word meant "song" in Spanish. He watched as two figures came ashore first, a black-clothed priest and a man in fancy garments of bright vermilion. It was Roderick, that he could see in a glance, but wondered who the popinjay was. A Spaniard, but who?

Forgetting decorum, Richard broke into a run, excitement at seeing his brother getting the upper hand. Catching the priest up in a bear hug, he laughed and cried, "Roderick! Roderick!" Stepping back, his hands upon his brother's shoulders, he looked at him. He was thinner than he remembered, and a bit taller if possible. "How goes it with you, brother?"

Roderick laughed shyly, blushing a bit as he always had since early childhood and casting a glance in the Spaniard's direction. "It goes well. God has been good to me, to us all. It seems the sun shines in Toledo in more ways than one."

"So I've heard. Riches from the New World have no doubt been put to good use by the archbishop." He shook his head. "Seeing you is like looking into a mirror, except for your height and this." Richard pulled at his well-trimmed beard. One other difference marked the brothers; Richard did not have the small cleft in his chin that graced his brother's face.

Roderick laughed. "I remember how we always gave our father fits, changing places and pretending to be the other son. Even though I am a year younger, we gave him quite a time of it."

"Aye, I remember, Roderick." He caught himself. "Or rather I should say, Brother Stephen." As if suddenly remembering the other man standing beside them, he turned and raised his eyebrows in a quizzical gesture.

Brother Stephen stepped toward the man, putting a hand on his shoulder. "Forgive me, Rafael. The joy of seeing my brother again swept away my good manners. It is not every day that one returns home. *Sí?*"

"*Sí*, the man answered. Richard could see that the Spaniard was a handsome man with the dark brown hair of his countrymen. He had a sculptured nose and strong chin and carried himself with the air of one who recognizes his own importance. Dressed in the Spanish manner, in a jacket with a white ruff around the throat, hose and trunk hose, a tall pointed hat, and slashed leather shoes, this man was the height of fashion, even to the tips of his gloved fingers.

"Richard, this is Rafael Mendosa. Rafael, my brother." The two men acknowledged each other, quickly sizing up one another. At last they smiled at each other in the age-old expression of friendship. Richard suspected that there was more to this man than a handsome face.

"Don Rafael, let me extend my welcome to you on behalf of my countrymen." Richard nodded slightly.

"I am honored." Rafael Mendosa spoke with little trace of an accent, unlike Simon Renard, whose every word was difficult to understand. Richard reflected that perhaps the Spanish were not all alike after all.

They walked down the plankway, dodging in and out between the sailors and dockmen, who swore loudly until they saw a priest beside them. It seemed that even though the people of England had taken up the reformed faith, they still showed respect to those who wore the cloth.

"Rafael is here on a most pleasant task. A matter of the heart," Brother Stephen said at last as the three men walked down the cobbled stones toward an inn.

"Oh?" Richard stopped in his tracks.

"There are those of us in Spain who would deem it the highest honor to have Mary as consort for Philip, prince of Spain."

A warning shouted in Richard's brain. He had feared that something like this was afoot. So that was why his brother had been sent back to England. To soften the queen's heart. He had a premonition of misfortune, as if someone walked on his grave.

"I hate to disappoint you," he told Rafael sternly, "but I believe that Mary will take no man to husband. She has been without a man for all these years and is now in her late thirties."

The Spaniard laughed. "More reason to marry now, before she shrivels up like a Venetian grape, to blow away in the sun."

Richard eyed the man, appraising his attire. "Dressed as you are, my friend, you will be a tempting target for those who make their living at the point of a sword."

The Spaniard laughed heartily. "I may look like a peacock, but I assure you that I am a hawk. If we have any violence, let me put your mind at ease." He withdrew a knife from inside his boot, then replaced it in its hiding place. "My sword, my knife—I am well prepared."

"And I have my staff, Richard," Brother Stephen said with a wry smile. "I am quite skilled with it. Of course if all else fails I can pray for *their* souls as well as ours."

It was Richard's turn to laugh. "Having a priest for a brother does offer some benefits. I only hope that we will not be accosted." He thought of Heather as they walked along. Each moment away from her made him love her all the more. He was anxious to get back to Greenwich. There was so much to tell her.

Roderick was not blind to the change in his brother. It was not like Richard to be so quiet. "Has a cat taken hold of your tongue, brother?" he finally asked.

Thinking of Saffron, Richard winked at his brother. "No, though a cat very nearly was the cause of my death at the hands of an angry mother. Do not doubt that a broom can offer a man a threatening fate."

"A broom?"

Richard told his brother all, baring his soul to the man who had shared his joys and torments since they were both babes. Brother Stephen laughed with him and cried with him and offered a sympathetic heart.

"And so you love her?"

"Yes. I never thought it possible to love a woman so much. It's as if we lived in another time, only then we were blended into one person. I feel as if I have searched my whole life to find her, as if she is the other half of myself."

"Are you trying to tell me that you believe as those in the East do, Richard, that we have many lives? I must caution you on such a thought. You do not want to be called a 'heretic.' "

Richard shook his head. "No, I don't believe in past lives, but if I did I would want to have lived every one with her by my side." Richard's heart was already at Greenwich with the gray-eyed beauty.

For a moment there was mischief in Brother Stephen's eyes, as if he were suddenly transported back to those days when they had bedeviled the countryside with their pranks. "Perhaps we should change places, you and I, as we did when we were young. I would have a look at this Heather of yours. You can be ordained priest and I will console this woman you love."

There was no smile upon Richard's face. "I would not give Heather up, not even to you, brother."

"You make me believe that love really does exist," Rafael said, coming up behind the two brothers. Somehow Richard did not mind that the Spaniard had overheard his words. There was something about him he liked despite his manner of self-assurance.

"It does. Believe me."

"Ah, *amigo,* I have thought so myself, only to find disillusionment. I have made love with many beautiful *señoritas,* only to find that they are like gilt, golden on the outside only. Beneath the surface they are as nothing. *Nada.*"

Richard laughed. "Be patient. Love will find you."

They walked much faster now, anxious to reach the inn before the shroud of night descended. The only sounds were the clop-clop-clop of the horses passing by, the soft whir of the wind, and the soft clatter of pebbles striking the cobblestones.

Coming to a bridge that was missing several planks, Brother Stephen, stumbling over his long black robes, nearly missed a step and would have fallen into the water if not for the quick wits of Rafael Mendosa, who reached out his long arm to clutch at the priest in the nick of time.

"You saved me from a dunking," Brother Stephen said in gratitude. They reached the other side of the bridge, lulled into a false security by the sound of the water lapping against the rocks, the quiet of the night, and the fresh scent of the night air. Suddenly from behind the bushes came a giant of a man, his shiny bald head glistening in the moonlight.

"Your purses, gentlemen!" He brandished a sword, waving it about to signal for the others of his band to come from hiding.

Richard counted six men in all. Like their leader, they were huge men. "I hope that you have not boasted frivolously, Rafael," he shouted, reaching for his sword. "We have need of your skills tonight."

The Spaniard did not answer, but reached for his own weapon, swishing it through the air with an amazing agility.

"Ha. A priest. Papist dog," shouted a flame-haired bandit. He flicked the point of his sword to lift up the hem of Brother Stephen's habit. "He wears a skirt. Like a woman."

"A skirt!" laughed another. "Say your prayers, priest."

Still another circled around Richard's brother, seeing him as an easy target. Brother Stephen looked about for help, but Rafael and Richard were already occupied, Rafael with one robber and Richard with two, one at his front and one at his back.

Breathing in a deep sigh, the priest looked from one scraggly robber to the other. This was not the time for weakness. "I am your obedient servant, my sons. Let me pray for you."

Riotous laughter broke out. "Pray. The priest wants to pray for us. What think you, lads? I would say that we should pray for him," said one, coming closer.

Determined to do everything he could to avoid shedding blood, Brother Stephen stood calmly before them as the sound of blade upon blade sounded behind him. He watched as Richard wounded the man to his right and thrust against the bald man who came at him with a knife. The robber, incensed and kicking out frantically, seemed intent on drawing Richard's blood.

"Dear Lord, be with my brother," the priest whispered, clasping his hands together. "And with Rafael." Closing his eyes, he reached for his crucifix, only to feel it yanked from his hands and cast upon the ground.

"Here's what we think of you and all your kind, papist!" snorted one attacker.

Brother Stephen cried out, "How dare you so abuse God's badge!" Whirling and whirling, he struck out with his wooden staff, proving himself to be a fierce combatant until at last he had two men on the ground and one taking to his heels.

Finishing their own battles, Richard and Rafael looked upon their traveling companion with awe. "He had no need of us, *señor*," Rafael said with a laugh, watching as all the robbers made their hasty exit. "This priest fights with valor. It will be a long while before those *hombres* think to prey upon one guarded by Cristo." He nodded toward the fleeing forms.

Brother Stephen smiled sheepishly. "Shall we go into the inn? I think that we will be safe, at least for tonight."

Richard pulled open the heavy door of the tavern, the Cap and Crown, remembering that time when he had met pain outside its doors, the pain of an assassin's blade. He wanted peace for England now. Peace and freedom. Was it too much to ask? He tried to shake off the fear that Spain posed a danger to these ideals, but found it nearly impossible. The feelings against that country ran high. The fight tonight had proved as much. What would happen if Mary did indeed marry Prince Philip? Would the people of England then shout her name in praise?

The inside of the tavern was crammed with sailors quenching their thirst and loudly telling tall tales, making other conversation nearly impossible. Ordering three ales, Richard sat in silence, deeply troubled. Despite the fact that he liked him, this Rafael Mendosa could mean trouble.

"Tell me more about Heather," Brother Stephen said, tapping his brother on the shoulder in an effort to tear him from his musing.

"Roderick," Richard began, forgetting once again to use his brother's holy name, "you must help me. I cannot stay married to one woman when I love another. I want to marry Heather and have children to carry on our name. Surely God will be on my side in this."

Brother Stephen pondered for a time, then smiled. "Perhaps if I sought an audience with the pope. That is it! I believe there *is* hope. Give me time, Richard, to think on this matter. I desire with all my heart to see you married to this Heather of yours." He grinned, looking like Richard's younger brother and not like a priest. "I want nieces and nephews to bounce upon my knee."

"And I will give you many if you will but help me

undo these ties. My marriage is a mockery, as you well know."

"I will do what I can," his brother answered, his eyes showing the sympathy which he felt very deeply for the way their mother had so betrayed her own flesh and blood. "After I am made a priest at Canterbury, after I am truly Father Stephen, I will do all that is possible to free you. You will gain your freedom and take Heather Bowen to wive. Be patient."

36

A LIGHT DRIZZLE fell on the occupants of the old wagon as it lumbered along the muddy road, its wheels churning slowly through the mire.

"Fool nags!" Perriwincle shouted. "Move your arses." From time to time he would whistle loudly and jiggle the reins in an attempt to hurry the horses. "Sorry, Miss Heather."

Clutching her cloak tightly about her shoulders, Heather shivered. "I'm in no hurry to reach home."

The old man looked at her askance. "You'll catch your death, you will, if I don't get you back."

The sky was dark gray and a downpour seemed imminent. He watched as Heather sat staring at the road, her teeth chattering from the chill of the damp air.

"Home. Oh, Perri, that is the last place I want to go right now. If I had my way we would stay in this wagon and drive to the ends of the earth."

Slowing down the wagon, he looked over at her. Seated beside him, her hands folded demurely in her lap, she looked a pitiful sight, her red hair curling about her face from the damp mist, her face etched in misery.

"If I had me way I would take you there, but I don't think you would like it. You belong here with the people who love you." He flicked at the reins again, urging the horses on at a quick pace. "Your father's a bloody fool to give you to that Seton rogue."

"I didn't know that you knew!"

"Ha, that's all the old fool has talked about these

past few days. I had half a mind to beat some sense into his fool head, and will if you but tell me to."

Heather took hold of his arm. "No, Perri. It would only cause you trouble. I will handle this in my own way."

"You will not marry him?"

"No. I will never marry Hugh Seton. I love another." She lowered her eyes from his searching gaze.

"Richard Morgan?"

"Yes."

"I knew it!" In his excitement he let go of the reins for a brief moment, nearly sending the wagon into a ditch. At last, recovering his hold, he guided the wagon up the familiar path which led to the stables. He sat in silence as his conscience pricked him. There was something he had to tell her, but he didn't know how to begin.

"Father will most likely deal with me harshly when I tell him," Heather murmured, "but I cannot give myself to a man I don't love, especially after . . ." Blushing, she turned away from Perriwincle, having spoken too much.

"After lying in the arms of the man you do love," he finished for her.

Her eyes were wide as she gazed at him. "How did you know?"

Now it was his turn to blush. "Because I . . . I . . . I acted as cupid." His words came out in a frenzied rush. "I knew you loved him, and he you, and . . . and your father . . . He is such an old miser. I wanted your happiness. I . . . I thought that if only you two would make love to each other, he . . . he would take you with him. But bloody damn. It didn't work out that way, and . . . and I'm sorry!"

"Cupid?" Heather was confused, totally baffled by Perriwincle's babbling. "What on earth are you trying to tell me, Perri?"

"Red sage and summer savory," he blurted.

"Red sage and summer savory? Herbs, yes, but what have they to do with all this?" The wagon pulled up in front of the stables, but she held on to his arm to keep him from jumping down off the wagon. There were questions that needed answering. He must finish what he had started. "Go on, Perri, I must know."

"A love potion, it is. Potent, they told me. Red sage and summer savory. An aphrodisiac. I gave it to Morgan the night before he left."

A shocked gasp escaped from Heather's mouth. "An aphrodisiac?"

"Aye." He took her small hands between his large callused ones. "I'm sorry, Miss Heather. Forgive me. Forgive me. I meant you no harm. I only wanted the best for you. I thought he would take you with him, I did. I thought he would marry you. Forgive me."

Heather did not answer him; instead she started laughing. "Poor Richard. He never knew. And me, fool that I am, why did I never guess?"

Thinking her hysterical, Perriwincle sought to calm her. "It will be all right. It will be all right. Forgive me."

"Forgive you? No I shall not. I shall thank you, Perri. In my heart I will always thank you."

Now he was certain that she was daft. "Thank me?"

She was all smiles now. "Yes. He would have gone away without ever showing me what love is." And she had blamed him, said so many terrible things to him, when he was the most noble of men, her Richard. He loved her, but thinking of her, of her virtue, he would have left without ever showing her the sweet nectar of passion, if not for Perri.

Her smiles were contagious. Leaping from the wagon, Perriwincle felt light of heart. "Then he loves *you.* I knew it." Reaching for her hand, he helped her down from the wagon just as Thomas Bowen came out of the house.

"Ah, Heather. My darling daughter has arrived from court." Beaming from ear to ear, Thomas Bowen strode forward with a jaunty air. Seeing the smiles upon Heather's and Perriwincle's faces, he joined in their merriment, then barked, "Perriwincle, see to her trunks before her things are ruined. They cost me a fortune, after all." Taking her arm, he led Heather toward the house. "Rain. Abominable rain. How I hate the autumn."

Entering by way of the back door, they were met by Tabitha, who quickly took Heather's wet cloak and Thomas Bowen's hat. "It's so good to have you back," the blond-haired servant girl whispered.

Heather was silent, looking about her at the walls that had been so familiar while she was growing up. Now they looked foreign to her eyes.

"Well, tell me about your adventures at court, my dear," Thomas Bowen gushed. "I knew that sending you would be a wise investment. Just think, it will be my cloth upon the queen's back when she is crowned. My cloth. Mine. Why, I even bought a new carpet for the solar with the profits. Come and see."

So my mother finally has her new carpet, Heather thought. It made her happy to think that Blythe would now be content. Following her father up the stairs, she looked about her and could see the changes in the household. New furniture, a few paintings on the walls, wall hangings, all proved Thomas Bowen's prosperity.

"Look. See. It cost me nearly a fortune, but it was worth it. Nearly all the nobility have them now. This one comes from Persia." He gestured toward the floor, where a brilliantly patterned carpet adorned the wooden floor. "It makes the house warm as hot buns with the fire lit, even in the dampest weather." Kneeling down upon his hands and knees, he stroked it with affection. "Feel it. Bend down and feel it."

Heather gave in to his whim, feeling foolish on all fours. "Yes. Yes. It is soft." She pondered her fate as she looked at him, and was determined not to let him intimidate her as he usually did. After her experience at court she had matured and could not be so easily bullied. She stood up.

"Perhaps after you are married I will buy you a

carpet." There, he had said it. Said the word "married." It was time to tell him.

"Father . . ." Her mouth had suddenly gone dry and her heart was beating faster. She cleared her throat and began again. "I will not marry Hugh Seton, Father."

He looked at her as if she had spoken in French. "What?"

She bit her lip to keep from crying. She would be strong. "I said I will not marry Hugh Seton, Father. He is a cruel man and I bear him no love."

His fat face turned nearly purple with rage. "You will not! You will not? What have *you* to say about it? The marriage settlement is already drawn up."

"Then you will have to tear it up. I will not tie myself to a man like that. You cannot ask me to do such a thing." Without even knowing it, she clenched her fists so tightly that she had drawn blood. Now she looked at her wounds.

"I will cut you off without a farthing! I swear it will be so. I will cast you out on the streets, girl." He pulled at the collar of his long gown as if he were choking.

"Do what you must, Father." She was unable to hide the feelings of rebellion that she felt. Free. She felt free of all her childhood fears, of pleasing him, of causing his displeasure, of losing his affection for her, no matter how small it was. She didn't care what he thought, or said, or felt. This man had sold her. He deserved no loyalty.

He came to her then, walking around her in circles, surveying her as if she were one of his bolts of cloth. "After all I have done for you. You ungrateful chit."

"I am not ungrateful. You have fed me, clothed me, and taught me sums and reading, but I have repaid you time and again with my love and loyalty and by working hard in the house and with your ledgers. I will not give you myself to buy and sell. I am flesh and blood."

"Ha. What do you know of these matters? Marriage is the same as any other business. Profit is what matters. I will profit, as will you, from this match." He reached up to pull at the gray strands of his hair, what there was left of it. "I must admit that at first this Hugh Seton frightened me with his threats to tell Mary what I had done, but as we talked and it became apparent that it could be a profitable arrangement, I came to like the man. You will too when you get to know him better." He tapped his head. "A keen business sense, he has. The man will succeed. He is a crafty one."

"He is a brute and well should I know. He all but attacked me in the barber's courtyard." She shivered, remembering that day.

"It is just that he desires you so." Shrugging his shoulders, he grinned at her. "You will feel differently after he has bedded you."

"That he will never do. Hugh Seton will not touch me, nor will I be his wife. I am your daughter, not a bolt of cloth."

Again he pulled at the neck of his gown, his rage returning. "You are no daughter of mine! That Spaniard's brat, that's what you are. De Vega's spawn." As soon as the words were out, he regretted them, touching his mouth with his fingers.

"What? What are you saying?" Her gray eyes were enormous with her surprise, yet hadn't she always had the feeling that somehow she wasn't his child? Deep down inside, perhaps she had always sensed the truth. Now her mother's words made sense. That day she had found Heather with Richard in the stables, she had acted as if her outrage was for her own heartache.

"Foolish prattle, my dear. I did not mean a word of it. Of course you are my daughter." The anger had melted away, to be replaced by unease. He knew that this was the only hold he had on Blythe. She had done as he bid to keep Heather from knowing the truth. "Don't tell your mother. It is not true."

Heather shook her head slowly. "No, it is the truth. I can feel it. I am not your daughter. No wonder you have never loved me." She had a strange sense of calm. "But if I am not Heather Bowen, then who am I? Who is this de Vega?"

"I will not talk about it. I will not," Thomas Bowen shouted at her, striding for the door. Turning back to her, he announced, "As for this matter of the marriage, you will be locked in your room without food or water until you decide to comply with what I have asked of you."

Thomas Bowen took her to her room. Walking on legs that felt like wooden sticks beneath her, she reacted like a puppet, devoid of any feelings at all about her parentage. In many ways she was glad, for now she need not feel quite so guilty about not having her father's love, nor for her lack of feelings for him. Besides, this added a touch of mystery to her identity. She heard the door close behind her, and found Saffron in the room waiting for her. She would not be totally alone.

37

HEATHER AWOKE TO the sound of rain beating against the windowpane. The room was so muggy, so humid, that she felt damp. Damp and hungry. Her father had made good on his threat to keep her locked in her room without food, bringing her only water and some bread to keep her from starving. He jealously guarded the keys as if suspicious of everyone in the household. He knew, he said, how to deal with a daughter with "too much spirit."

Daughter! she thought. Ha: I am no daughter to him. His words echoed in her ears, that she was the Spaniard's brat, de Vega's spawn. Now she understood why her mother was so meek in his presence. She felt a loyalty to him for taking her in when she was with child. For marrying her. "De Vega," she whispered, remembering all that her mother had told her about the man she once had loved.

Rising from the bed, Heather paced back and forth, looking at the walls of this bedroom prison. Thomas Bowen had even been successful in keeping her mother away, at least for the moment, though Blythe Bowen had come once or twice to the door to talk with her daughter.

"Heather, dear, are you all right?" she now asked. Heather assured her that she was. "I have talked with Thomas on this matter, but he will not be swayed. He tells me that he is doing it for your own good, Heather. This Seton is a man of high social position, adviser to the queen—"

"I would not want to marry him if he were the King of England himself."

"Heather, I do not understand you. Marriages of convenience are the rule among the nobility and landed classes. You know that. Your father is not doing anything that any other father would not do."

"He is not my father!"

"What?" The word was barely a whisper.

"He told me so himself." Heather regretted her words as soon as they were out of her mouth. She had not intended to hurt her mother. Her anger was at her father. Now as the silence stretched out between them she longed to take the words back.

"How could he? How could he? He promised me." Heather could hear the tears in her mother's voice and for the moment understood the torment her mother had lived through all these years, the shame. Perhaps another reason she had danced to Thomas Bowen's tune was that she feared Heather would find out the truth.

"It doesn't matter, Mother. In fact I'm glad. Knowing the truth frees me. And it frees *you*."

"I had nowhere to turn, Heather. He took me in. We should be grateful to him for that. He gave us a home when we could very well have been homeless. In his way he loves me."

"He loves only himself *and* his money. The matter of my marriage is just the same as any other business proposal to him. He cares nothing for me."

"Heather, please . . ."

Heather swallowed her bitterness for her mother's sake. "I'm sorry, Mother." She leaned her forehead against the door, wishing that she were out of this stifling confinement. Four days. Four. She felt as if she would go mad at any moment.

"If it is any consolation, I know very well what you are going through." Her voice sounded husky, tormented.

"I know, Mother."

"Heather. Please think about this matter very carefully. Is it possible that you have not given this man a fair chance? Your Richard Morgan is married to another. Remember that. I did not love Thomas, and yet I have been content."

"Thomas Bowen is not like Hugh Seton. He may be selfish, but Seton is a cruel monster." Even her mother did not seem to understand.

"I must go now. Thomas is coming. My prayers are with you, child." Heather could hear the sound of her mother's footsteps.

"Oh, Mother. What would our life have been like if you had married your de Vega?" Heather sighed, returning to the bed to sit upon it in silence. She was hungry, so hungry. As if sensing her need for food, Saffron skillfully cornered a mouse, dropping it at his mistress's feet.

"Thank you, Saffron. You are quite the hunter." Reaching down, she fondled the cat, smiling at its offering. "But you take it." She nudged the rodent with the toe of her slipper." I hope that I never get *that* hungry."

Again, as she had before, Heather wondered about Richard. Where was he? Would he come for her? Did he know by now that she was gone from court, that she had been betrothed to Seton? No. If he knew, he would have come, of this she was certain.

"Oh, Richard," she sighed, closing her eyes. She had been such a fool. Why hadn't she talked with him that night she learned of his marriage instead of running away like a child to hide from her pain? He had stood outside her door and she had refused even to see him. And at court she had done the same, laughing all the while with Courtenay in an effort to flee her heartache. Richard had tried to tell her that his marriage had been forced upon him, just as her betrothal had been forced on her. Perhaps this thing with Seton was meant as a lesson. Henceforth she would not be so quick to judge another.

"My dear love, if only I knew where you were. There are so many things I want to say to you. Nothing matters to me anymore except you." What if she never saw him again? The thought was too painful, and she quickly put it out of her mind. Somehow, some way, somewhere, they would find their happiness together. Let Thomas Bowen do what he might.

Heather knew that so far Thomas had been lenient with her. Would he resort to beating her when she did not comply after a time? She had heard of such things happening, in fact it was commonplace. One young woman had been shut up in her room and beaten once or twice a week, suffering severe head injuries. At last the poor young woman had agreed to marry the man her father had picked for her, a man in his late fifties, only to die of her wounds shortly before the ceremony was to take place. Heather shuddered at the thought. Surely her mother would *never* let things go so far.

"Heather." The voice whispering to her through the crack in the door was familiar. Tabitha. Bounding from the bed, Heather stood at the door. "I have some bad news."

"Bad news?"

"Hugh Seton. Your father has asked him to come here this morning to talk with you. He should be here at any moment."

"Seton?" That meant that Thomas had become impatient, but feared to show her any violence himself. She could well imagine what the leering Seton would do to her.

"I must go now, though I wish that I could help you. May God be with you."

Heather was once more alone, remembering with abhorrence that time in the barber's courtyard when Seton instead of Richard had met her. He had shown a violence then that was frightening. The man seemed capable of anything.

"Well, he has met his match in me," she vowed, walking over to the mirror to peer within its depths. The face that met her glance was thin and pale, with dark circles under her eyes. Perhaps he would not want her now. That was her fondest hope, but just in case he sought to harm her in any way, she armed herself with the small china basin from the table. If she struck him with enough force, he would be rendered helpless, at least for a while. At that thought she smiled. A rose could well have thorns, or so Richard had once said.

Hiding the basin in the folds of her cotton gown, she sat down upon the bed to wait for Seton's arrival, only to hear the heavy tread of footsteps as soon as she relaxed. The time of reckoning was approaching. Gripping the basin so hard that her knuckles turned white, she waited.

The footsteps stopped in front of her door and for endless moments she stared apprehensively ahead, waiting for it to open. Without so much as a knock, Seton threw it open, nearly splintering the finely wrought wood.

"What is this horse manure about you saying you will not marry me?" he thundered, giving her a murderous glance. "I will brook no disobedience from my wife!"

"I am not your wife," she answered coldly. "Nor will I ever be."

Slamming the door behind him, he stood in front of that portal as if to block any chance of her escape, and for a moment Heather nearly forgot her resolve. This man was terrifying. Satan himself could not have been more threatening.

"I ought to break your neck, but if you were dead you would be of no use to me," he growled, taking a step forward.

Reaching behind her, Heather clutched the basin, but he did not come any closer. "You only want to marry me to hurt Richard. You have said as much. I loathe you. I would rather die than have you lay one hand on me. If you think that I will ever consent to be your wife, you are mad."

A dangerous expression, a narrowing of his eyes, contorted his face as he appraised her beauty and her shapely form. "It is you who are mad if you think you can deny me this satisfaction."

"Even you cannot force a woman to marry without saying the vows. A marriage under duress is not valid or binding."

"I will not use force." The evil grin that he gave her made her blood run cold. "You will give your consent."

"Never. Somehow Richard will find me and stop you."

"If he comes near you, I will kill him. What do you think of that?"

Heather gasped, horrified. She thought with fear that it was not an idle threat. Hugh Seton hated Richard Morgan. "You wouldn't!"

"Ah, but I would, and all would think me justified if I did. To trifle with another man's intended bride is a serious crime. Were I to strike the man down in a jealous rage, I would be forgiven, even by the queen."

Hatred choked her. Never had she truly detested another human being, but Seton was beneath contempt. "I will warn him."

"You will not leave this room until the day of the ceremony. If you speak one word, tell even your mother, I might decide to kill you as well." He lunged for her, his catlike movement so quick that he had her in his grasp before she could wield the basin. "I will stay here in the room next to yours and see to this matter of your marrying me." Tearing the basin from her hold, he shattered it on the floor.

"I hate you!" she hissed. She tried to shake him off, but he was strong. His beady brown eyes were angry and menacing as he forced her to look at him. "You're hurting me."

"That is nothing compared to what you will get from me, woman. I have long hated my brother and wished for his death, but I now see a better way to deal with him, by taking from him that which he values most dearly. However, if you give me cause, I will cut him down."

"Why?" she sobbed.

"Why? I will tell you why. He has robbed me of

my rightful inheritance by refusing to acknowledge me as his brother." His eyes took on a faraway look as he seemed to be transported to another time, years long past. "I lived in near-poverty with my mother. A gentle woman, she was raped by a noble and cast away by her family to fend for herself and her bastard child. Me. We lived on the charity of others, on scraps of food and kindness, while all the time your lover and his brother lived in splendor. How I hated them both, but especially Richard."

"Richard?"

"Our father's favorite. He took his own share of father's love and mine as well, leaving me nothing." In anger he pushed her down on the bed as if reliving his boyhood days. "I vowed someday I would live in that manor house. I did, but only after my mother died of the plague. I wanted her to live in luxury too, but they robbed her of any happiness."

She felt sorry for the boy he had once been, could imagine his pain, but that did not excuse him for the man he was now. Hatred and violence were ever-festering sores which would never heal.

"You did live at the manor. What more could you ask?"

Sparks nearly flew from his eyes as he answered her. "A name. The Morgan name. But that woman, Richard's and Roderick's mother, saw to it that I was denied. She had the old man wrapped around her finger, you see, and even on his deathbed he denied that I was his child. He tried to tell me that my mother, that sweet and gentle lady, had been a whore, sharing her favors with all the men in the countryside."

"Your hatred is misdirected. It is your father and his wife that you should hate, not Richard. No, not Richard. He is as innocent in this as you are."

He looked at her as if he would strike her down, but held his temper in check. "I will speak no more about it!" Opening the door, he turned back to her. "Remember what I have said, wife-to-be. Think on it when you rest your lovely head on your pillows. You will marry me or his death will be on your hands."

Even long after he left, Heather sat staring at the walls. She was doomed to marry a man she hated and feared because of her love for a man she must now protect. Such a travesty of fate. Such cruel mockery.

If only I could escape from here and warn Richard, she thought wildly. Was it possible that Tabitha could help her gain her freedom? Putting her face in her hands, she sought desperately for a way.

38

RICHARD LOOKED ABOUT him at the changing colors that September always brought, and smiled. His brother was on the road to Canterbury and Richard was on his way back to Greenwich and Heather.

He made his way on horseback down the rocky cobblestone road, feeling his heart quicken as he spied the familiar landscape which marked the grounds of Greenwich.

"I will tell her of Roderick's promise to take my case to the pope himself," he said aloud as the hooves of his horse clattered against the stones of the outer courtyard. Dismounting from his horse, he gave the animal up to the hands of a groom, then hastened up the walkway to the thick double door. Opening the door wide with his own hands, he strode toward the hall, his eyes scanning all those assembled for the familiar figure of his love. She was nowhere to be seen, and he supposed her to be upstairs in her bedchamber.

I will surprise her, he thought. I will take her into my arms and never let her go again. We belong together, she and I. I will make her see that.

He headed toward the stairs, but Stephen Vickery intercepted him. "Richard," he exclaimed. "Richard, I am sorry."

Richard looked at him with mild annoyance. "Stand aside, Stephen. Now is not the time to speak of court matters. I have been away longer than I intended, and I must see Heather."

"She is not up there."

"Not up there? Then she must be with the queen." Thrusting back his shoulders, he hastily brushed at his garments and pushed past his red-haired friend.

"She is not with the queen. Heather is gone, Richard. Gone. I told you I would watch over her, but I could not." The sound of his friend's voice filled Richard with foreboding.

"What do you mean, Stephen?" Thinking that perhaps Heather had suffered some accident, he reached out and grasped his friend's arm. "Tell me. Where is Heather? What has happened? What?" All sorts of thoughts ran through his head. "Is she hurt? Is that it? Where is she?"

Stephen's voice was soft, as if to spare his friend this necessary pain. "She is to be married, Richard."

"Married!" Richard's face turned deathly pale, as if all the blood had drained from him at the sound of the word. "No!"

"Yes."

"Damn Courtenay. I never thought he would actually convince her to marry him. Damn the man. Damn!" Richard fought against his sorrow, the unmanly tears which threatened to flood his eyes. How could he live without her? How? How could he come to terms with the fact that she was someone else's wife? In frustration and helpless defeat he strode up and down, wearing a path with his steps. He felt betrayed, angry, yet he knew that he was wrong in feeling this way. Courtenay had wooed her and won. Had he really expected her to tell him that she would wait for him to be free? That she would be his in spite of the scorn that their love would bring?

"Yes, dammit, yes. I wanted her to love me as much as I love her. Not give herself to Courtenay the moment I was gone." Anger replaced his sadness and he lashed out at the stairpost as if at Courtenay himself.

"It is not Courtenay," Stephen whispered.

Richard whirled about. "Not Courtenay." He knew of no other men who had courted Heather, though with her beauty it would not have been surprising if several of the men at court had longed for her. "Who?"

Stephen shook his head, not wanting to be the one to tell him, yet knowing that he must. "It is Seton. Hugh Seton has asked for her hand, and she is to wed him this very day."

"Seton!" The cry which tore from his throat was like that of a wounded animal. "Nooooooo!" Forgetting where he was, all the people staring his way, he sat down and grasped his knees, hugging them with his arms as he had when he was a small boy. Rocking back and forth, he sought to fight the demons which tore at his heart. "How could she marry? How? How?" At last his tortured eyes looked into Stephen's. "I can't let this happen."

"There is nothing you can do. The queen herself favors the match. She does not know him for the beast that he is."

"But he will destroy her." Slowly he rose to his feet, determined to do what he could.

"He will destroy you if you intervene. Marriages of convenience are commonplace. Your Heather will learn to be happy, much the same as other women have done. There is nothing you can do, Richard. Nothing."

Anger flared in Richard's heart. "Do not dare to say to me that I must stand idly by and watch the only woman I will ever love be sent like a lamb to the slaughter. I will think of a way to stop this mockery of a marriage. I might not have been able to save myself, but I *will* save Heather, though heaven and hell move to stop me." Flinging himself free of Stephen Vickery's restraining arms, Richard Morgan left the hall.

39

THE LAST DAY of September dawned bright and clear with hardly a trace of a cloud in the sky, but the beauty of the day went unnoticed by the young woman whose wedding day it was.

"I am lost. There is nothing I can do," she whispered upon hearing the cock crow. Long into the night she had been awake, tossing and turning upon her bed. She was trapped!

Heather began to weep, great sobs of anguish which poured forth warm and salty from her eyes until they were red and puffy from her weeping. Frustration and anger had brought forth this torrent.

"There is no escape. None. He has thought of everything." She had sought a way out of her predicament these last few days but had found none. Even the thought of jumping from the third-story bedroom window had come to mind. Ignoring the broken bones that might have been her reward, she had reasoned that she would at least have been able to attact attention and thus get a message to Richard. As if sensing her thoughts, her father had nailed the shutters closed.

Neither Tabitha nor her mother had come to talk with her since the day Seton arrived. Hugh Seton forbade it, as was his right as her intended bridegroom. She was trapped, caged as surely as the lions and bears inside the Tower that were kept for the amusement of the court. She was trapped and all alone.

Seton. The man was an animal. He seemed to

delight in being cruel to her, and her father, impressed at the thought of one of the queen's councillors as son-in-law, bowed to his every whim. With each passing day another luxury had been taken away from her. Light, the candles and oil lamps extinguished until it was almost dark; then even Saffron's company had been denied her. All the while Hugh Seton had growled his threats through the door.

"It will be your fault if I kill your lover. Your fault," he said over and over until it was an echo in her brain. She had neither consented to nor disavowed her betrothal, hoping that by stalling for time she could find some way to escape her sad fate.

"Oh, Mother, what am I to do?" she asked, talking to herself. Heather could not be angry with her mother. Not being a cruel person herself, Blythe was not fully aware of all that was being done to her daughter. No doubt she trusted her husband to do what was right.

Putting a hand to her face, Heather realized that she was thinner than ever, her cheekbones prominent, her face pale. It made her all the more beautiful in an ethereal way, but this she did not know. She knew only that she was desperately unhappy.

"What am I to do?" she whispered, her spirit nearly broken by the constant deprivation and fear she had suffered in the last few days. If need be she could wait until the actual words were to be spoken and then deny her consent before the priest. The priest would help her. Surely when she refused to say the words, told him what was happening to her, he would stop this mockery of a marriage. This thought was all that sustained her. That somehow all would be well. Seton could not marry her in front of wedding guests who witnessed her refusal.

The sound of her chamber door opening signaled her doom, as the light from the hallway nearly blinded her. She was like a mole who had been too long away from the light.

"For the love of God, don't frown so, girl," came her father's voice. She felt his hand on her arm and winced. "Do you want all the guests to think that I have beaten you?"

She turned slowly. "That torment at least you have spared me," she said sarcastically. "You no doubt leave that for my husband to do."

Her father eyed her with worry. "I do what is best for you, girl. Someday you will thank me. As Seton's wife you will receive one-third of all his estates. You will be a wealthy woman and someday when he regains his rightful lands and title you will be a woman of great renown."

"Do you think I care about that?" Her voice was hardly more than a whisper. She was weak and had not the strength to argue with him. "I feel sorry for you. You do not know what is truly important in life. All you care about is money."

He did not answer her, but held his tongue, and for a moment Heather had the hope that perhaps his conscience might lead him to stop this thing he had brought about. Her hopes were dashed by the entry of her mother and Tabitha bringing her wedding dress. Thomas Bowen had sold his so-called daughter and would not renege on the bargain.

"Heather! Heather, are you all right?" The anguish in her mother's voice was heartrending. "Here, drink this. It will calm you and make what you must do easier to bear."

Trusting her mother, Heather reached for the cup of herbs in wine and drank it. It went to her head quickly because of the lack of nourishment in her stomach and she felt strangely as if she were floating.

"Your eyes," Tabitha whispered. "I shall fetch cucumber slices to take down the swelling. If you will but lie back for a few moments they will soothe you."

Tabitha's words, her pitying glances, only served to start Heather weeping anew, and her mother came to her instantly to offer her loving arms to soothe her.

"Please, don't let him make me marry that man. I can't. I can't. He told me that if I do not, he will murder him. I have to warn Richard. Send someone to find him. That is all I want now. Please," Heather babbled between sobs. Her tongue was thick and she could hardly get the words out, but somehow she managed, yet by the look in her mother's eyes she could tell that Blythe Bowen didn't want to believe Hugh Seton capable of murder and thought her daughter merely distraught about the pending marriage.

Leading her daughter toward the bed, Blythe sought to calm her. "Lie down for a few moments. Rest before we dress you."

Heather did as she was bid, exhaustion and the power of the drugged wine taking effect. Closing her eyes, she felt the cool chill of the cucumbers which Tabitha had brought.

"She is overwrought," Blythe whispered. "She is not making sense. Trying to say that he threatened to murder someone. Thomas is not a violent man. He would not kill anyone." Her eyes looked toward her husband. "Thomas, what have you done to her?"

"I have but kept her locked in her room as is my right. Do not blame me for the girl's stubbornness."

"I did not think that you would starve her! Oh, why did I not take a hand in this?" Reaching for her daughter's hand, she held it in her own, chafing the wrist as if hoping to bring back at least a little color into her daughter's face. "Tabitha, bring up a bowl of hot oats, honey, milk, and barley. I would not have my daughter go to her wedding pale and hungry. Men. Such fools at times."

When Tabitha returned, Heather ate the cereal with the frenzied urgency of those who have been deprived, washing the bites down with gulps of warm milk. "I never realized just how good food could be," she said between mouthfuls. "I will never be finicky again."

Blythe watched with a sad smile, which turned to glowering rage when she turned toward her husband. She was no longer the mouse. Her daughter's welfare was her prime concern now, but though Heather pleaded with her mother to stop the marriage, this Blythe would not do. Perhaps she thought that in the long run it was in Heather's best interest.

When at last Thomas Bowen's sister came sweeping into the room, Heather was dressed in her finest linen chemise. There would be no special bridal costume, merely the finest dress in Heather's wardrobe, which ironically was the white velvet with red brocade underskirt. The same dress she had worn when first meeting Catherine Todd.

Pushed and pulled, scolded and coaxed, Heather was soon fully dressed, even to the fine leather shoes upon her feet. These were new, a gift from Anne Paston, her father's sister, and while they were beautiful, they pinched her toes.

"Why, she is a little pale, Blythe," the woman remarked, eyeing Heather up and down. "You had best pinch her cheeks a mite."

A bridal garland woven of wheat, rosemary, myrtle, and late-blooming flowers were thrust into Heather's hands. Magenta corn roses, white shepherd's purse, and violet and blue delphiniums made a colorful bouquet.

"The wheat is a symbol of fertility," Blythe explained, blushing a little. "Let us hope that this marriage will bring forth many children, for I would so love having grandchildren."

Casting the garland from her, Heather looked at it as if it were poison. "No!"

"Perhaps she fears they will make her sneeze," Anne Paston said with a questioning stare. "Many women keep them all their lives as a treasured reminder of this moment."

"To me it will be a reminder of the unfortunate plight of women in this world," Heather replied bitterly. Nothing she could say could convince these two women of her abhorrence of marrying Hugh Seton. Only Tabitha with her kind blue eyes knew what Heather was suffering. Somehow Heather had to get the girl alone so that she could seek her aid.

Tying the bridal knots, Blythe whispered, "You are the most beautiful bride London has ever seen."

"Would that I were as ugly as an old crone," Heather hissed in reply. "Rather than marry that one, I would as soon remain a spinster for all eternity."

Hugh Seton heard her words as he met the bridal party at the door. His piggish eyes warned her to hold her tongue. "Such sweet words of modesty from my future bride," he mocked with a low bow. "I find you, however, lovely."

Like Heather, he was also dressed in his best, a chocolate-colored doublet, tan hose, white shirt with lace at the throat, brown trunk hose, and leather shoes.

"The queen has sent her regrets, my love," he said. "Because of the coronation tomorrow, she is too busy to attend our nupitals. However, she has asked that after the wedding we come to visit with her at the palace."

"I'm certain that she would like to hear everything about the wedding." Heather said by way of veiled threat, though she well knew that no one, particularly the queen, would believe her. Mary had already told Heather of the high esteem in which she held Hugh Seton.

Walking down the stairs, Heather found a large throng of guests awaiting. They would accompany the bridal party to the church.

"The bridal cup," Thomas Bowen exclaimed, handing it to Heather. With its sprig of rosemary and trailing colored ribbons, it looked like some pagan offering and Heather could not help but wonder if some ancient Celtic bride had held such an object in her hand.

As they rode to the church, a small troupe of minstrels preceded them, playing on flute, viol, harp, and bagpipe. Behind rode Blythe and Thomas Bowen and Anne Paston and her husband, with the wedding guests riding in the rear. All along the road the Londoners gathered to watch, loving pomp and ceremony.

When they arrived at the square in front of the church, all dismounted from their horses to walk up the stone steps of the chapel. Heather watched as the priest stepped out from under the portico, the open book in his hand, the wedding ring resting on a satin pillow. At last Heather's chance had come. This priest would ask her the standard questions: if she was of age, if she swore that she and her betrothed were not within the forbidden degree of consanguinity, if her parents consented to the marriage, if the banns had been published, and finally if she herself and her groom both gave free consent to the match. She would tell him no to the last and put an end once and for all to this farce.

"I have chosen a Catholic ceremony to please the queen," Hugh Seton breathed in her ear. He was no fool. A ceremony spoken by a priest would be that much harder to break. There would be no divorce.

Pushing past him, Heather flashed Hugh Seton a triumphant look. "I am here against my will," she said to the priest. "I do not want to marry this man and would have spoken sooner if not for his threats to the man I love. He has vowed to kill him if I do not comply with his demand to enter into marriage. Please, you must help me. You must get a message of warning to Richard Morgan and keep this would-be murderer confined."

Hugh Seton's evil laughter drowned out her words. "He does not speak English or Spanish. Did you think me to be a fool? He does not know what you are saying, my dear wife. Your words are just so much gibberish. He needs only to say the Latin Mass to make our marriage valid. That he can do, though he is a Frenchman."

Heather couldn't think clearly. She had not foreseen this. To ensure his safety, Seton had made certain that Heather could whisper no words of her plight into the priest's ear. Pushed and shoved into the candlelit chapel, she fought the urge to swoon. She would not give in to that womanly weakness.

Speaking in his churchly Latin, the priest babbled words Heather could not understand while all the while Hugh Seton looked upon her with eyes that seemed to devour her. Was he imagining what it would be like to ravish her when this was all over?

I will never forgive Thomas Bowen. Never, Heather thought bitterly as the priest held forth the ring for her hand. She was whiter than the gown she wore as she pulled her fingers away from the priest's outstretched fingers.

Suddenly, before the final vows could be spoken, the chapel doors were thrown open as the assembled guests gasped in shock.

"In God's name, stop!" came a voice from the back of the church. Standing there like an avenging angel was none other than Richard Morgan.

40

"RICHARD!" HEATHER SOUGHT to run to his side, but Hugh Seton's strong arms detained her. Still she knew that a glorious miracle had occurred. Richard was here. He had saved her from a disastrous marriage.

"What is the meaning of this?" Hugh Seton thundered, making all assembled tremble. "This woman is to be my wife. You have no rights here."

"Your wife! I think not. I would see you in hell first, Seton." Reaching for his sword, Richard brought forth the weapon and strode forward to take Heather's hand. Weaponless, Seton could only glare in murderous rage. He was not one who was used to being thwarted, and Heather wondered if he would seek revenge.

"Now, see here, whoever you are," Thomas Bowen spluttered, stepping forward to reach out for his daughter. "What right have you to—"

"Every right. I love this woman. She is mine. By all that is holy she belongs to me." As he drew Heather into the shelter of his arms, his eyes were filled with love and longing.

"And I love him," Heather said softly, looking into those love-brimmed eyes.

From the back of the chapel the assembled throng craned their necks to see what was happening. Soon the story of what had happened here would be whispered on the corner of every street in London, but Heather didn't care. She only knew that the man she loved was here, shielding her from all that might harm her.

Hugh Seton's face turned several shades of red as his eyes swept over the two lovers. He could nearly imagine them locked in the throes of love. Once again Richard Morgan was taking that which Seton thought to be rightfully his, and as before, he was powerless to stop him.

"Damn you to hell!" he shouted. "I will see you pay for this if it takes me a hundred years. You are a dead man. This I swear before all assembled!"

At his words Heather shivered. "He told me that if I would not marry him he would kill you."

Richard brandished the sword threateningly at the man who claimed to be his half-brother. "You told me once that I should kill you. Now I wish I had. If I had known what pain you would cause this woman, I would have done so." Circling the blade in front of Seton's eyes, Richard barked, "Now get out of here before I *do* kill you."

Without a word Hugh Seton stormed from the chapel, pausing only long enough to look back once and raise his fist in anger.

"Let us leave too, Richard," Heather pleaded, clinging to him. "Before he gathers armed men to harm you." Hand in hand they fled, without looking back, leaving the room buzzing with whispers. As they made their way past Tabitha, Heather heard her cry out for their happiness and caught a glimpse of the servant girl's smile.

"I drove the horses off. It will be a long while before Seton can follow us. We will ride north," Richard said at last, helping her onto a horse tethered in front of the church, then mountng his own beside it.

"I would ride anywhere with you," she answered. "To hell and back if you asked me. I have learned the meaning of love and happiness, though it was a hard lesson."

They rode through London in great haste, leaving the crowded streets far behind them. Heather was laughing and crying at the same time as they traveled, her tears drying quickly in the warm sunlight. Richard, glancing over at her, was startled by the sight of her crying.

"Heather, what's wrong?" he asked, urging his horse to a halt beside her. "Do you want to go back?"

"Go back? No. I weep for joy, Richard. I am happier than I have ever been in my life. How many times have I dreamed of going away with you. Now my dream is a reality."

He leaned over and gently touched the silken strands of her fiery hair. "I cannot ask you to be my wife until I am free. That freedom may never come. What can I offer you except my heart?"

She smiled at him, her lips quivering as she spoke the words: "That is all I want. Your heart. Your love will be my sun and moon."

His face grew grim. "I can give you nothing but love. For your own sake I should turn you free, but how can I when I am only half-alive without you? I am a selfish man, Heather. I took your virtue—"

"I would rather be your mistress than any man's wife," she exclaimed with a toss of her red hair. "And as to my virtue, it was red sage and summer savory that was to blame."

"What?" he asked. His eyes probed her face, and seeing the mischievous smile, he cocked his head in bewilderment.

Gales of laughter escaped from her mouth. "It was Perriwincle. He came upon us with Cupid's bow and wounded both our hearts. Thinking to bring us together, he gave you a love potion."

"A potion?" Remembering now the taste of the brew, Richard looked at her as the truth dawned on him. "Why, that scoundrel. And here I have been torturing myself for weeks with bitter recriminations . . ."

"And I blaming you for all sorts of ill-doings." She nudged her horse forward so that she could reach out and touch his hand. "I have learned much this past month. I never should have doubted you. I will never do so again. When I thought that I was to be married to Seton, I suddenly realized what you have been going through all these years. Now the vows of marriage are not important to me. It is what is in our hearts that truly matters. I love you and you love me."

"Oh, Heather," he groaned. "If only you could be my wife."

"But perhaps it cannot be, will never be possible. I will try to live with that. With you beside me, loving me, it will be an easy matter."

"Always." Words could not whisper what the look on their faces said. Looking over the city of London, holding hands, love flowed between them as swiftly as the Thames. At last he said softly, "We must go. Seton will be after us. There are many miles to travel before night." His smile was seductive. "And when we reach a proper inn, wench, there is much that we must make up for."

Past the fertile fields of newly sown wheat and rye they rode. Michaelmas had just passed, signaling the winter season. Soon the rains and frost of winter would be upon the land. But that was the furthest thing from Heather's mind as she looked over her shoulder. Seton. She must not forget his fury or his hatred. He had threatened to kill Richard and her if she escaped him. Shuddering in fear, she touched her heels to her horse's flanks. Masking her fear from Richard, she managed a smile.

"Come, love. I am in a hurry to reach this inn that you speak of."

41

THEY REACHED THE inn by nightfall as they had intended, the Rose and Thorn. Completely surrounded by rosebushes, it was easy to see where it came by its name. It was a charming half-timbered, whitewashed building with a thatched roof and boxed windows that looked out on the rolling hillside.

Helping her down from her horse, Richard's hands lingered on the soft curves of her body and she tingled at his touch. They had waited so long for this moment, it seemed. Too long.

"I feel like a young boy again," he whispered in her ear, gently taking her hand. The horses were safely stabled and then they entered the inn.

An old man and his wife greeted them, the woman nudging her husband as if to say, "Newlyweds." At Richard's request for a room, she smiled and led them up the stairs to where a large, low-ceilinged room awaited them, as if it had been built for their comfort. It had a fireplace, a carved oak bed and matching table and chairs, wall hangings, and a window with a wide expanse of glass.

"Perfect!" Richard exclaimed, thrusting several gold coins into the woman's hands. Thinking that Hugh Seton might seek to find them here, he said, "We do not wish anyone to know that we are here. I will pay you well for holding your tongue."

"Yes, sir." She grinned. "I know how to hold me tongue."

"We would like a bath first and then to be left alone."

"Yes, sir."

Slamming the door, Richard bolted it securely as a warm smile played about his features. "I love you. I want to say it again and again."

"And I love you!"

"We have dared much for our love. Even the queen will be against us now. She will be loath to have such a scandal touch her court."

"I don't care. All I want is you. Kiss me, Richard." He complied gladly, his lips soft and gentle, his hands caressing over her with infinite skill. A knock at the door interrupted them.

"I intend to bathe with you. What think you of that?" He raised an eyebrow at her.

Flashing him a seductive smile, she answered, "I would like nothing better, my Lord." Reluctantly he unbolted the door.

A tall strapping youth lugged in a large round wooden tub and behind him came four other boys carrying water buckets. Making several trips, they soon had the tub filled to the brim.

Looking down at her once-white gown, now splattered with mud and dirt from the road, Heather could almost hear her father saying, "Look at you, girl. Have you no idea of the cost of that gown?" In spite of herself she smiled.

Richard, seeing that smile, smiled himself, thinking how angry Seton would be to think that Richard was enjoying his supposed wedding night. What might have been a tragedy had turned to victory.

At last, with a wave of Richard's hand, the young boys were gone and he and Heather faced each other across the room. "Let me start a fire," he said.

Watching as he threw wood onto the grating, then lit the firestick, she looked at him. He was so handsome. As the fire blazed in the hearth, its flickering flames dancing against the blackened stone, she thought to herself that as he had sparked the fire, so had he inflamed her very soul.

"There. That will keep us warm," he whispered, standing up to strip off his garments. He let them fall where they might, then looked at her with a smoldering gaze. "Now you."

Heather stood up and unfastened her gown. "I need help, my love," she breathed. He stepped forward, standing before her, so close that there was barely an inch between them, just enough space for the gown to slip from her body and fall to the floor at her feet. Standing in her chemise, she tried to banish her fears of Seton. What if he were to find them? Would the woman keep their secret? She shuddered to think what would happen if she did not. "I won't think of that now."

Tugging at the chemise, Richard watched as it too slid to the floor. The sight of her sweet high breasts, narrow waist, and slender hips was well worth waiting for.

"I'm sorry that I am so thin," she whispered with a slight blush, covering her breasts with her hands. She told him of how her father had tried to force her to marry Seton by locking her up without food.

"My God, Heather." He was infuriated at what had been done to her, but fought his anger, seeking now to comfort her. "You are beautiful," he whispered, bending down to kiss each soft peak as if this way he could take away her suffering. Caressing one breast, he whispered, "A perfect fit. You are just the right size."

Heather moved her body against him, feeling the burning flesh touching hers. "There is always magic between us," she said in wonder. "Such wonderful magic."

"You were created to be loved," he answered. Picking her up in his arms, he deposited her in the warm water. She leaned back in the soothing scented depths and closed her eyes.

Watching her in her bath aroused Richard and he joined her quickly, the water nearly overflowing as he settled into the already brimming tub. "Scrub my back, woman," he said with a teasing smile.

Hesitating for only a moment, Heather set about lathering him, noting with pleasure the broad chest, the muscles of his abdomen, and the throbbing manhood which proved his desire for her.

"You may touch me there if you like," he said with a laugh, noticing the direction of her glance. "It will not bite you, in fact you will remember that it gave you the greatest pleasure." Heather did touch him with the gentle probing hands of the curious, marveling at the strength his manhood portrayed.

"It likes my touch."

"Yes," he answered. "There are many things that I must teach you. Let us begin now." His hands closed around her shoulders, pulling her to him. In the small confines of the tub it was difficult maneuvering their bodies, and in exasperation he stood up in the tub, taking her with him.

"Enough of this torture," he breathed. Reaching for a large linen towel near the tub with which to dry her, he acted as lady's maid, drying her soft curved body and then his own. "We must get you to bed before you catch a chill."

Burying her face against his chest as he swept her up in his arms and carried her to the bed, Heather thought again how much she loved him. He was always the gentle lover, never cruel or forceful.

With a sweeping movement he tugged at the covers and laid her down upon the linen. He kissed her then, molding his lips to hers, his tongue exploring the recesses of her mouth with great tenderness. Heather's lips parted to his mouth, enjoying the taste of him, the feel of him, and yes, the very smell of him. It was as if they had been fashioned, molded each for the other. Could any wine taste as sweet as his kisses? She knew it could not.

Caressing her, kissing her, he left no part of her free from his touch, and she responded with a natural passion. It was as if they were all alone in the world. Adam and his Eve.

Smoothing back a strand of her hair, he pressed a kiss against her warm skin. Lying there, her red hair billowing out around her, she looked so fragile, but he knew what strength she possessed.

"I love you, Heather."

Staring up into the mesmerizing depths of his eyes, Heather felt an aching tenderness for him. This was love, not lust, that they shared. Something that transcended the body and joined the souls. Reaching up her arms, she clung to him, drawing in his strength and giving hers to him in return. She could feel his heart pounding and knew that hers beat in matching rhythm.

"Richard," she whispered, touching his face with her fingertips. "Never in my wildest dreams did I imagine that I would feel like this."

"Nor I," he answered.

Reaching out her own hands, she explored his body as he had done hers. His flesh was warm to her touch, pulsating with the strength of his maleness.

"Love me. Love me now," she whispered. The frantic desire for him was nearly unbearable. She writhed in pleasure and pain as he covered her body with his own. His manhood entered gently, teasing the petals of her womanhood.

"You are warm and damp and inviting," he said, covering her mouth in a searing kiss as he thrust into her softness.

Heather locked her pale, slender thighs about him. There was nothing in the world but this man filling her, loving her. She wanted time to stand still, the earth to stop its spinning so that they could be entwined like this forever.

Welcoming his thrusts, she moved with him until they were engulfed by wave after blessed wave of ecstasy. For a moment they both hung suspended in time as blue eyes met gray ones.

"Heather!" Richard's cry was like a benediction. With a shudder he was still, yet buried deep within her. "You will always be mine."

Sighing with happiness, she snuggled within the cradle of his arms, happy and content at last.

42

HEATHER AWOKE AS the first rays of the sun warmed the room through the large glass window. Lying with Richard's strong body entwined with hers, she felt a fierce surge of desire to again feel his hands caressing her, his mouth upon her own. Last night had been an ecstasy beyond belief, even more beautiful than the first night they had joined their bodies in love. They had made love yet again, had fallen asleep cradled in each other's arms, and then had made love once more.

Richard looked so young in the depths of his slumber as she studied his face in the bright light of the sun. Like a boy, handsome and vulnerable. His eyelashes were so thick and black. Perhaps someday she would have a daughter with the beauty and strength this man possessed, or a son. Someday.

Reaching out, she gently touched his beard, the soft bristles tickling her hand as she stroked his face. How could she ever forget the first time she had seen him, standing so tall and strong before her? Even then she had begun to love him and had felt the urge to protect him, despite the risk of Northumberland's ire.

Heather lay back down upon the bed and snuggled once again into the warmth of his arms, her head against his chest. She found herself wishing that life could always be as peaceful as it was this morning. If only she could remain in his arms forever, safe from the cruelty and ignorance of the world.

"What are you thinking?" His voice was barely more than a whisper.

"How happy I am here with you, that I wish it could always be this way."

He didn't even need to touch her to be overcome to bursting with his desire. Just the thought of her inflamed him. Reaching out, he caressed her. Her body was perfection. How he loved the smooth soft skin of her body, the peaks of her breasts, the taste of her skin, the fragrance of her hair.

"Are you hungry?" she asked innocently.

"Aye. For you," he answered, opening his eyes to look at her smiling face. "I long to find myself nestled in your velvety softness." Feverishly he kissed her, his lips teasing hers until the assault left her breathless.

Reaching up to fasten her arms around his back, she clung to him, pulling him closer as she returned his kisses with wild abandon. His hands and mouth moved over her body, bringing forth a rippling fire of pleasure, and she in turn stroked his back, her soft hands at last sliding down to touch, to explore his male hardness.

Wrapping his fingers in her hair, he buried his face in the long silky strands, inhaling deeply of the sweet rose fragrance. "Heather," he mumbled hoarsely.

Gently he pressed her down among the pillows, his mouth tracing a path of flame across the flat plain of her stomach. There was not an inch of her he did not know already, but he wanted to rediscover the glory of her, arouse her to the highest heights, bring her the greatest of pleasure.

Heather felt the ripples of desire course through her blood like the sparks of a radiating fire consuming her as he probed gently between her legs. His manhood was sheathed within the moist softness of her body like a sword in a scabbard. This time their joining was filled with a frenzy as they surged together. Heather held on to him tightly as the world seemed to quake beneath them, arching to him, moving with him as powerful shudders swept through them both. Clinging to each other, they glided slowly back to earth to drift off into a contented slumber once again.

When Heather awoke it was to find Richard sitting on the edge of the bed looking down at her. "Breakfast awaits you, my lady," he said with a grin, gesturing toward the oak table. Spread out on a white linen cloth was a veritable feast.

Achingly aware of her disarray, she sat up in bed. Her hair was a mass of tangles, her face needed washing. Instantly Richard was aware of her needs, bringing forth a small mirror mounted in a wooden frame and a brush.

"I knew that you would have need of these when you awoke, so I asked the innkeeper's wife if she could procure them for me." He nodded toward a small basin and pitcher. "And there is warm water with which you can wash."

Clutching the linen bedcover to her bosom, she was suddenly shy. How foolish to feel that way after what had already passed between them, she thought, and yet there was something so personal about grooming oneself and going about the morning necessities. It had been different when he was with her in the stables. Then she had always left him when the need arose.

Richard sensed her feelings and said quickly, "I see that they forgot the wine. Let me leave you just a moment, my love. Would you prefer the white or the red?"

"The red," she answered, watching him walk toward the door. As soon as the door closed behind him she was up and about, washing her face, brushing her hair and teeth, and going about her morning toilette. Donning her chemise, she looked at the white gown, soiled beyond repair and totally inappropriate for her present needs. She would be better off dressed only in her undergarments than to have to bother with the gown and farthingale. For once she longed for the simple dresses she had worn at home, comfortable and easy to keep clean.

Entering the room, Richard saw her standing by the window deep in thought, her hair billowing around her shoulders, her head thrown back to reveal the slim column of her neck. He had a longing to make love to her right then, but just cleared his throat to make her aware of his presence.

"Red wine and red roses," he said as she turned around. "I had the devil's own time finding them at this time of year. All the other bushes were bare, and yet, there these were on a bush behind the inn, as if waiting for me to pluck them for you."

She was deeply touched by his gift, remembering the other time he had made her such an offering. Somehow that time seemed long ago, ages ago, when in fact it had been only a few weeks. Roses would, from this day forth, always be a reminder to her of trust. She would always trust him and love him.

Sitting down to eat, Heather eyed the dishes before her: beaten eggs with herbs—tansy, mint, sage, parsley, and ginger; a roast gull basted in honey; spiced milk; bread; fig pudding; and an assortment of fruits—apples, plums, and pears.

"Heavens," she exclaimed with a laugh. "If I eat all of this, I will grow fat as a toad."

"Fat or thin, I would love you," he answered, taking a seat opposite her. The food was delicious and as they ate, they talked. There was much that each needed to hear and to say.

"How did you know where to find me?" was Heather's first question. "I thought I would faint when you broke into the church that way. My hero. Always you will be my hero."

He shrugged his shoulders. "When I came back to London, I went right away to court with the intention of telling you how much I love you. Finding you gone, I nearly went wild with worry. Then Stephen told me that you were gone and that you were to be married to Seton. My worry turned to rage. If Seton had been before me at that moment, I would have killed him with my bare hands."

"And I would have cheered you on."

"I went to your house but found it empty. All the time a voice was shouting in my ear that I was too late, that you were married to that bastard. I didn't know where to go, where to turn, and then, as if fate was on my side, a little old woman started jabbering to me about the wedding procession that had just passed by a few moments before. 'Such a lovely red-haired bride,' she said. She pointed in the direction of the chapel and I rode as fast as I could to try to stop the ceremony. It makes me tremble to think that I might have been too late."

"But you weren't, and now we are together." Reaching out, she clasped his hand with hers. "We have our whole lives before us."

He told her then about his mission to Canterbury and about his brother Roderick. "He is to be ordained a priest there, although there are those who have called him by that name already. Brother Stephen is the name he has chosen, after that Stephen who was stoned to death because of his faith. After he is ordained I will have to get used to calling him Father."

Heather realized how little she knew about this man she loved, and with an eager frenzy to know everything about him, she questioned him as they ate. There had been three children, two sons and a daughter. Richard's sister Elizabeth had died of a fever.

"Seton has always claimed to be my father's son, but I don't know. I just don't know. There is nothing of my father that I can see in his face, and yet it is not an uncommon thing for a man to seek love outside of marriage."

At his words, Heather turned white. "No, I don't suppose it is," she murmured. Quickly he was at her side to gather her into his arms.

"It was not the same thing, my love. I love you. I would marry you in an instant if only I were free.

My father only lusted after other women, although after tasting my mother's treachery perhaps I cannot blame him."

"Your mother, is she . . . ?"

"She is dead. She died early this summer. Her gluttony was the cause of her demise. A chicken bone caught in her throat and she choked to death. How outraged she would have been at such a death. But let us speak no more of her, let us talk of much pleasanter subjects." He told her the tale of his brother's valor at the inn, and she giggled to think of the priest swinging his staff with such force that he could overcome three men.

"How surprised they must have been."

"Aye. He took them completely unawares. Roderick has always been one slow to anger, but when aroused, he is a tiger." He laughed, remembering all the antics of the young brother he had grown up with.

"What does he look like?" This priest had piqued her interest. As Richard's only living relative she was eager to meet him.

"He looks a great deal like me, without the beard of course. Same blue eyes and dark hair, but he has a small indentation in his chin that I do not have." Pulling at his beard, he winked at her. "I will see that you soon meet him, but what of your life?"

Heather told him about her childhood, and about her constant intuition that the man she knew as her father might not truly be her sire. "And he is not, Richard. In a fit of anger he told me that I am not his daughter."

"Not his daughter?"

"No. He said my father is a man named de Vega. To think that all this time I have been half Spanish and didn't even know it. My father was an explorer. Someday I will look for him and find him. He has much to answer for." Reaching for her wine, she tasted of its warmth, though it was not any more intoxicating than were his kisses.

"Perhaps I can help you find him." Holding up his

glass, he said, "To the future, to our happiness, and to our love." They drained the goblets dry and Richard set about clearing the table, calling one of the young men who had brought water for the bath to take the things. "And ask the innkeeper if perchance he has a harp."

"A harp?" Heather asked with a whimsical smile.

He gathered her into his arms, stroking the soft skin of her back. "I intend to sing to you. You bring out the romantic side of me." His mouth traveled to where the pulse beat rapidly in the hollow of her throat, and his hands cupped the full swell of her breasts, fondling them until Heather felt once again the ache of desire.

"You have turned me into a wanton, I fear, my lord," she whispered.

He answered by kissing her, moving his hand along the indentation of her waist, holding her closer as the hard evidence of his own desire pressed against her. At last, leading her to the bed, he drew her down upon its softness with him, and whispering words of endearment, made gentle love to her once more. He watched her eyes as he brought himself within her, saw the wonder written upon her face that anything could be this sweet, and he knew within his heart that he would love her forever.

43

THE NEXT FIVE days were spent in loving, drinking, eating, talking, and loving again. The world had ceased to exist for them, so caught up were they in their love. There was so much they wanted to know about each other, opening up their hearts, their minds, and their souls.

With each day their fears of Seton diminished and their lovemaking grew sweeter as Richard taught Heather all the ways to please him as well as how to enjoy and respond to his touch. Always there was an exploding sensation, a wild passion between them. He aroused feelings in her that no other man could ever possibly awaken, and she knew instinctively that it was the same for him.

They hardly left their room except when it was absolutely necessary. There was always the chance that Seton could be lurking about, and besides, they relished this world of their own. Once when Heather had been listening to the sounds of the courtyard below, standing at the open window she had heard words which made her blush.

"How long have they been upstairs now?" asked a male voice.

"Five days. Nearly a week," came a woman's answer, no doubt the inkeeper's wife.

"Has anyone seen them?"

"Hardly anyone. They are in a world of their own."

"Do you suppose they are all right?"

Deep giggles of feminine laughter. "They are all

right, James. Don't you remember how it was with us once?"

Silence, and then, "Yes, I remember."

"The boys have seen them when they bring food, drink, and water to bathe. Kit even brought up a harp."

"A harp?"

"He sings to her. Love songs. Ah, to be young again."

Heather smiled now as she remembered the words. They had been at the Rose and Thorn almost a week, and in all that time, Richard Morgan had proven to be the perfect lover. With him the sun was suddenly brighter, the grass was greener, the air more fragrant, the rain and mist a cloak of enchantment. She had never been happier, yet once in a while a thought pricked her. Could it always be this way, or would what they had done soon catch up with them?

"What are you thinking, Heather? I watched your smile turn to a frown just now." Coming up behind her, Richard wrapped his arms around her.

"That we are just too happy. I'm afraid that somehow something will happen to end this joy. We have been able to shut out the world, but for how long?"

"Forever." He drew her closer, as if to assure her, his hands seeking the warmth of her slim body. He thrilled to the magic, the flame that always consumed them both just at the touch of one another. How he had once laughed at the minstrels and troubadours who had sung the praises of love, and now he was throwing roses at her feet and warbling those same love sonnets.

"Where will we go, Richard? We cannot run away forever. Someday we will have to stop and turn around."

He kissed the silken softness of her hair. "Hush, let us not think about that now. We have today. We will have to be content with that for the time being."

He started to kiss her, but a loud knock on the door cooled their passion and sparked their fears.

"Who in blazes can that be? I paid a good price to ensure that we would not be found. I have not asked for food or drink. Then who?"

Heather's hands trembled. What if it were Hugh Seton? What if he had found out their whereabouts?

"Richard. Richard, are you in there?" came a voice. Heather's heart stopped beating for a moment, until she recognized that voice. Drawing Richard's cloak about her shoulders, she raised an eyebrow at her lover.

"Stephen Vickery. What is he doing here?" It seemed that the world had found them sooner than they had foreseen. Walking to the door, Richard cast her a glance over his shoulder as if to reassure her, then opened the portal wide.

"Thank God I've found you," the man exclaimed upon seeing Richard's face. "I have been searching everywhere for you these last two days. Then I remembered you telling me of this inn."

Richard looked at him in annoyance. "Obviously I did not want to be found!" He sought to block the entrance, but Stephen Vickery merely pushed him aside and smiled at Heather. "Oh, don't be embarrassed. The story of your escapade is all over London. The queen is livid. Nothing I could say would sway her. As for myself, I am delighted, though I daresay you have incurred Seton's wrath."

Heather blushed as red as the doublet Vickery was wearing. "I would have rather died than marry Seton. Richard—"

"Saved you from your fate. I always knew that beneath his cool exterior was a spark of passion." He made himself comfortable, sitting down on one of the oak chairs. "I applaud what you have both done. Too long has marriage been relegated to a matter of finance." His eyes took on a sudden sadness. "But that reminds me why I am here. It's Edlyn. She is ill."

"Ill?"

"Yes, a message came for you at court. You must go home right away. If you do not, I am afraid it will compound your already compromising situation. I know you were trapped into that marriage, Richard, but she is your wife."

"I know that. I would not want anything to happen to Edlyn. She is a harmless enough creature and I pity her. What has happened to me is no fault of hers." He gave Heather a searching look, then asked, "Will you come with me?"

She nodded. "From now on, wherever you go, I will go." Motioning for Stephen Vickery to turn his back, she gathered up the white velvet dress, and slipping off Richard's cloak, dressed quickly.

"The coronation was lavish and splendid," Stephen Vickery was rattling on. "Though most eyes were turned upon Elizabeth. I'm afraid that whenever she is around poor Mary looks dowdy. I wonder just how long it will be before Renard convinces her to put her poor sister in the Tower."

"She would never do that."

"Perhaps not, particularly when things seem to be going her way. Secluded up here, you have most likely not heard. The council has passed two statutes. It seems that they have informed her majesty that she is no longer 'illegitimate.' The divorce of Henry and Catherine of Aragon is hereby invalid."

"That must please the queen, to no longer be considered a bastard!" Richard said sarcastically. "Though now Elizabeth will be considered one again."

"Elizabeth is wise. She will look after herself. Don't forget the time she begged Mary to allow her to be instructed in the Catholic faith, only to pretend to have a stomachache so that she could sit through Mass with a frown upon her face, thereby assuring those of the reformed faith that she had not truly espoused Catholicism. No, she will flow with the tide."

As Richard and Heather prepared for their journey to the North, Stephen Vickery told them all the latest rattlings of the court. "Courtenay has taken up his debauched ways again. Without you there to guide him, Heather, I fear that young man will come to ruin."

"He must not," she exclaimed, receiving a scathing look from Richard, still overly jealous when it came to the memory of seeing her constantly with that man.

"There are some who say that now that he has been rejected as a suitor for Mary's hand, he schemes to marry Elizabeth." He reached for an empty glass, pouring himself some wine and drinking it quickly. "Ha. He has little knowledge of how difficult it would be to dominate that strong-minded miss."

Heather offered her back to Richard so that he could help her with the lacings on her petticoat and gown. The thought of seeing Edlyn, Richard's wife, was unnerving. Still, she must go with him and do what she could to help. With the skills she had learned from her mother, perhaps she could do something to heal the woman. The proper herbs could often accomplish what doctors could not.

Stephen Vickery stood up, still thinking about court doings. "But I have not told you the half. The council has restored the Mass throughout England, while *The Book of Common Prayer* has been suppressed and Protestant rites are severely frowned upon."

Richard clenched his teeth. "It is as I feared. Mary will go too far. She does not realize that there are those who do not wish to return to the old ways."

Heather thought about her father. So proud of his *Book of Common Prayer* with its letters of gold. He would never give it up. It was one of his treasures.

"Except in London and a few large towns, the popular feeling seems to be with the queen. The country in general seems to favor a return, though I might add that no one seems prepared to return their lands to the church. Their loyalty does not extend that far." Stephen Vickery chuckled. "The purse, the purse, always it is the purse that truly does the talking."

He accompanied Richard and Heather to the door, noting the sadness which came to their eyes when they took one last look around them. Impulsively he reached for Richard's hand.

"God speed you, man. If ever you have need of me, call me."

"I will. You have proven to be a true friend, Stephen."

The older man smiled sheepishly. "May I kiss your lady good-bye? For luck?" At a nod from Richard, he gave her a peck on the cheek. "Take care of him, Heather. See that he does not get in too much trouble."

Leaving Stephen Vickery behind them, Heather and Richard went to the stables, mounted their horses, and rode off once again across the meadows and down the roads to Norfolk. Ahead lay the dotted fields and winding roads of the future, behind them the memory of stolen hours of bliss.

II

The Pain and the Passion

Norfolk, London, and a Ship Bound for Spain

On life's vast ocean diversely we sail,
Reason the card, but Passion is the gale.
—Alexander Pope, *Moral Essays*, I

44

It was a long and tiring journey to Richard's estates in Norfolk. Anxious to arrive as quickly as possible, they rode much of the day, stopping only at night. Often they made love, but more often than not, they would fall exhausted into each other's arms to sleep cradled together during the night. As they rode, Heather was haunted by the thought that they would not arrive in time. If anything happened to Edlyn, the guilt would tear their love asunder.

From Chelmsford to Colchester to Norwich they rode, staying at so many different inns that Heather felt quite like a Gypsy. Always there was the ever-present danger that Hugh Seton would pursue them and claim his vengeance. Still, being beside Richard was her heart's desire. She was with the man she loved, and the countryside with its fields, moorlands, and sweet inland waters was a wonder of beauty.

When at last they arrived at the manor house, Heather was suddenly beset with nervousness. What would Richard's household staff think of her? She was now his mistress. The word had a lurid ring to it, but the love they felt for each other was real. She would fight to see that it remained untarnished.

Richard sensed her inhibition immediately, though he did not know its cause. "What is the matter, my love?" he asked gently, helping her from her horse.

She smiled at him, trying desperately to hide the foreboding feeling that had swept over her. Was it the fear of seeing Edlyn? Yes, it was. "It's just that it is such an imposing structure," she answered. And indeed it was, though nowhere nearly as grand as Greenwich had been. Still, there was a rustic beauty about the manor that tugged at her heart. Richard told her that it had been built by his grandfather during the reign of Henry. Of red stone, it was three stories high with tall, rising gables and chimneys. Innumerable windows from story to story seemed to promise that the inside would be well-lighted. And of course being up north where rain was plentiful, the grounds were magnificent with greenery everywhere.

Putting his arms about her waist as if fearful lest she flee, Richard maneuvered her to the double oaken doors and pounded upon them with such force that those inside would have been deaf not to hear. Even so, it was several moments before the door was answered by a grossly overweight gray-haired woman in a black dress and white apron.

"Yes?" she said stiffly, looking them up and down. The dust of the road, the snags and tears in their garments, must have made them look like paupers, for it was a while before she recognized the lord of the manor. "Richard?"

"It is I, I am surprised that you should wonder. I received a message about Edlyn, that she is ill? It has been a long, hard journey, Agnes." Taking hold of Heather's hand, he led her into the room.

"Message? I sent no message," the woman named Agnes stated, her eyes narrowing. Looking at Heather, thinking her to be some tavern wench, she asked, "Who, pray tell, is this?"

"This is Heather."

"Heather?" Her manner was insulting as she blatantly looked Heather up and down and snorted in disapproval at what her eyes could see.

"I fully expect you to show her the same courtesy and respect that you show to me. Is that understood?" Richard commanded, his eyes unwavering as they looked at the woman.

"Yes, sir!" she snapped, turning her back quickly to hide her disdain. It was obvious to Heather that she had already formed her opinion of Richard's red-haired guest.

Ignoring the woman's reaction, Richard led Heather up the semicircular marble stairs. She marveled at the statues of two griffins on either side. They looked so real that she fully expected them to leap upon her.

"Edlyn's room is on this floor," he said, leading her down a narrow hallway when they reached the top floor. His face was etched with worry and perhaps remorse. "They are not always kind to her, though I have ordered Agnes and Charles to do their best. Edlyn, I fear, can be quite a handful."

"Could it be because they abuse her in any way?" Heather asked.

He shrugged his shoulders. "I cannot say. I try to protect her when I am here, but I cannot always be by her side. I have duties in London, as you well know." He paused for a moment to look at her, and she could read sadness on his face. "Duties which the queen will relieve me of ere long."

"Richard . . ." She wondered if there would ever come a day when he would regret his decision to flaunt their love and run away together. For so many years he had been loyal to Mary and her brother, Edward. How would he feel if his queen now openly displayed her anger?

"Come." Opening the locked room, Richard stepped inside, Heather following close behind. "I have always had bitter memories of this manor, no matter how beautiful it is, and have sought to absent myself as often as possible, but with you here that will change. This I know."

It was dark inside and Heather strained her eyes against the gloom. The room had a foul odor of unwashed human flesh, and stronger smells of body wastes.

"What on earth!" she exclaimed, immediately outraged by what she suspected. She looked at Richard but the look on his face told her that he had not expected to find the room in such a state.

"Usually I let them know when I am coming. This time I took Agnes by surprise it seems." He ran down the hallway and shouted to Agnes. Hurriedly entering the room, the fat woman tried desperately to explain the situation.

Meanwhile Heather searched for a firestick and lit the wall sconces. The figure lying on the bed shrank back from the light, looking up at them with fever-glazed eyes. Putting her hand upon Edlyn's forehead, Heather glared at the woman called Agnes. Gone now was any shyness.

"She is burning up with fever! Why has something not been done for her?" Heather snapped.

Agnes looked down at her feet, unable to meet Heather's eyes. Still her manner was hostile. "We tried everything. We called in the doctor to put leeches to her, and bled her once or twice."

"Put a kettle on at once and gather some camomile and thyme from the herb garden. And while you are at it, have some hot water and a basin sent up here." The woman hesitated, standing in one spot, opening her mouth as if to explain again the situation, fearful of what Richard would think. Heather had lost all patience. "Go! I hope that God can forgive you for your lack of human charity, for I fear that I cannot."

Her eyes filled with tears as she looked down at the dirt-streaked face of the woman on the bed. It was difficult to judge her age, for her face was filthy, her dark hair matted and unkempt, but Heather supposed her to be about twenty.

"How could anyone do such a thing? How?" she whispered.

"Heather, I didn't know. I swear I didn't," Richard said hoarsely. "When I have come before, Edlyn has appeared to be well taken care of, clean, and well dressed. She has never been like this. I do not love my wife, but neither do I hate her. I would never, never have allowed such treatment."

Reaching out to take hold of his hand she whispered, "I know. I know. You would never be so cruel as this. But whoever sent the message obviously wanted you to know of Edlyn's harsh treatment. I want that woman, Agnes, to answer for this when all is said and done."

"She will. I promise."

A shudder swept over her as she looked down at the bed. "This poor woman is being kept a virtual prisoner. I would even venture a guess that she is ill-fed as well." Her eyes blazed anger as Agnes returned to the room, bringing a cup, a kettle, and the herbs that Heather had requested. Putting the herbs in the hot water to steep, Heather prepared a warm drink and coaxed Edlyn to drink it. "Where is the tub? I want to wash her. No one should be allowed to wallow in her own filth."

Agnes answered Heather's look of dislike with one of her own, resenting this interloper who was telling her what to do. "We have a hard time keeping her clean. She has no interest in washing, nor is she interested in proper clothing. It is all the same to her."

"She is a human being and must be treated as such. I would not treat my cat in this fashion."

"Begging your pardon, *miss*," Agnes said with a slight bow. "I will see to the tub and the water."

At last the tub was brought in and Heather gently washed the young woman. "How old is she?"

"Twenty-five. It was a high fever that nearly killed her when she was a child," Richard explained. "Instead it took its toll on her mind. Let us pray that this fever does not kill her. I want her to live, Heather."

"So do I," she whispered. "So do I."

Heather stayed with Edlyn all night, forcing her to drink more of the hot herbal tea and applying cool cloths to her head. By midnight the woman's condition had worsened. She twisted and turned on her bed, lost in her own frantic dreams. It was a torture for Heather to watch her, feeling helpless to chase away the demons that seemed to pursue the young woman. Her body was like a raging fire.

"She is going to die," Richard groaned. "Will I

ever be able to forgive myself for neglecting her as I have done?"

"She will not die!" Heather cried. "Not while I have breath left in my body. I will not give up." If Edlyn died now, her death would be a constant reminder, a wall between her and Richard. She would not let that happen. Frantically she tried to think of anything that might be of help. The physician was too far away and would never arrive in time. It was left to her.

Suddenly it came to her. Snatching off the heavy linen coverlet, she undressed the woman on the bed as Richard stared at her in disbelief. "Heather, have you lost your mind? She will catch pneumonia as well."

"Trust me in this, Richard." Sponging Edlyn with cool water, letting the water evaporate, she also forced cold water down the woman's throat. All through the night until daybreak she kept up the treatment, sponging Edlyn as soon as she felt warm to her touch again.

At last Edlyn's forehead grew cooler and her eyes fluttered open as she looked around her in confusion. Seeing Heather, she tried to speak, but the sound was more of a groan.

The vigil was over. Edlyn's fever had broken. "Thank God," Heather whispered, touching the woman's face. "Thank God." The fever was gone but not the storm which raged in Heather's heart. Always before Edlyn had been just a name, a being whose existence had been the obstacle to Heather's happiness with Richard. She had somehow not seemed real during those passionate nights in the inn. Heather had been able to hide away from the truth, to push the thought of Edlyn away. But now, after having seen the woman, after having saved her from the fever, it was impossible to act as if she did not exist. Edlyn was real, and instead of being a woman to resent, she was a creature to be pitied. She could not be blamed for what had happened. She was as much a victim as Richard, a poor tragic prisoner of her mind.

"You saved her life," Richard said softly, looking at Heather with admiration. He tried to gather her into his arms, seeking more to comfort her than to love her, but for the first time since he had told her the truth about Edlyn, Heather drew away from his arms.

"I'm tired, Richard," she said weakly, leaving the room, wandering around until she found an empty chamber. There in the solitude and darkness she fought desperately with her emotions. Their love had been a blending of their bodies and the forging of their hearts.

"I love him," she murmured, "but how can I stay with him in *this* house?" She knew that she could not. Somehow their love seemed sordid here with Edlyn beneath the same roof. She remembered Agnes and the other servants eyeing her up and down, judging her, and knew that she longed to be away from here, to seek the sweet comfort of Richard's arms away from these walls. Away from the wagging tongues of those who would condemn them.

She slowly became aware of the murmurings of the servants in the hall and strained her ears to hear their words.

"Bring her here! Men are such insensitive brutes."

"She is a beauty."

"Fah. She is most likely some wench with the morals of a stray cat."

"Such lovely hair. I liked her. She must be a fine woman to stay by that poor thing's side and nurse her so gently."

"Oh, Matty, you would see goodness in the devil himself! I say she has her eyes on snaring our dear Richard. Like a vulture, I imagine that one will wait as long as it takes until he is free, though only by another's *death* will she become mistress of this home."

Heather could not bear to hear any more. Covering her ears, she sought out the bed and her slumber. Could she blame them for their resentment?

No. "Vulture." The word pounded in her brain. "Only by another's *death* will she become mistress of this home."

"No," she moaned. "I would not want her to die." Burying her face in the pillow, she wept. How could love so perfect, so sweet, be wrong? "We must get away from here," she resolved, fearful of what others' chattering tongues could do to her love.

At last exhaustion overcame her and she fell into a deep sleep. Not an untroubled sleep, but a restless slumber, one disturbed by dreams. She ran alone, terrified, through a misty fog while a voice shouted to her that Richard was dead. Seton. His evil face leered at her, his hands reached for her as he threatened again to kill the man she loved. He was coming closer and closer, and she screamed, reaching out imploring hands to those who stood and watched. But they would not help her, instead called her "whore."

"No!" She awoke with a start, trembling as if from a chill, plagued by the fear that somehow Hugh Seton's evil hand would reach across the miles to tear their happiness asunder.

"But where can we go?" she whispered in the darkness. "We cannot go back, yet neither can we stay here. Where? Where?"

45

IT WAS LATE. The candles in Richard's chamber were burning low as he paced the floor. "Why did she pull away from me? Why?" he asked himself. He had expected her to be loving as before, and yet she had pulled away from his touch as if it were poison. "I never meant for Edlyn to be so abused," he swore. "I would not want my happiness to come because of her death. I was relieved when the fever broke. Relieved." Did Heather understand all the emotions which were now tearing him apart? No. Her actions tonight showed that she did not.

He was exhausted. His bones ached after being on horseback for so many days, yet when he lay down he could not sleep. He kept remembering the way Heather had looked at him, the reproach in her eyes. Her face swam before his eyes until he could stand it no more. Rising from his bed in the early-morning hours, he stormed through the house searching for her. Her place was by his side.

At last he found her, sleeping soundly in the room which had been his mother's chamber, curled up like a kitten amid the blankets. She looked so lovely in her sleep, her breasts rising and falling with each breath she took. He remembered how silky soft they were to his touch and ached to caress them.

"Heather . . ." He knew that he ought to let her sleep, yet he wanted to settle quickly this sudden unease between them. "Heather."

She opened her eyes slowly, scanning the room

with wide-eyed confusion until she remembered where they were.

"My estates, my love. Remember?" Richard whispered, giving in at last to his urge to touch her. With slow exploration he slid his hands over the soft contours of her body. "I missed you last night. It is not right that we sleep apart." He noticed that during the night she had removed her gown and had slept only in her chemise, and he smiled to think how easily that garment could be removed. He was well-practiced in undressing her from their stay in the inn. Slipping it from her shoulders, he gently cupped one breast as his lips sought hers.

Weakly Heather clung to him as he gathered her into his arms, forgetting all her resolve of the night before in his embrace. His lips trailed kisses down her throat to the throbbing hollow of her neck, sending delicious ripples of heat through her blood.

A clatter in the hallway, the chatter of voices brought her to her senses, and she fought to escape from his spell. What power he held over her. He had only to touch her for her to become lost in the wild vortex of her passion for him. One kiss and she was lost.

"No!" She tore herself away, pushing at him so hard that he nearly toppled from the bed.

"No? Heather, what in God's name is wrong with you? First last night, and now this morning . . ."

"I can't! Not here. Edlyn and . . . and the servants. It isn't right." She hoped that he would understand what was in her heart. "Richard, I want to go away from here."

"Away? We just got here. I can't leave so soon. I have responsibilities. Winter is coming. I've spent too much time away already." He sought to take her in his arms again. "We can't go back. Seton will be waiting for us."

She shrugged from his embrace. "Then we will go back to the inn. Anywhere but here. I thought that being your mistress would not bother me, but I was wrong. Here in this house I . . . I just can't let you touch me."

He swallowed hard against his anger, saying only, "And so you will refuse me?"

"Yes." She wanted to reach out to him, to tell him that she loved him, but instead she turned her back to him.

"Women!" he growled, remembering suddenly his mother's refusal to share his father's bed. He remembered the way his father had begged, but he would not do likewise. Already he had done enough groveling for her love. "So be it, then." He walked to the door, then turned back. "Sleep alone in your bed, Heather."

She reached out to him, knowing full well that were he to come to her again, take her in his arms once more, she would not resist him a second time. "Richard. Please. Understand how I feel. Take me away from here."

He wanted to tell her that he would, that he had been wrong to bring her here, but stubbornness made him hold his tongue. She was only giving in to foolish feminine emotions. After they had been at the manor awhile she would change her mind and let him love her again. Had he not been so confident of that, he never would have said the words "We stay." Slamming the door behind him, he left Heather once again, alone.

As he took the steps two at a time, his emotions raged in turmoil. "What more must I do to prove to her how much I love her?" he stormed, remembering all the times he had waited outside her father's house in London and then again outside her chamber door at court. He had even suffered Courtenay's scorn and laughter. Yet as he walked about the main hall his anger cooled. How would she feel to be beneath this roof? Even though Edlyn was insane, she still was legally his wife. "Time. It will just take time," he murmured. Heather was the woman he loved. It was only right for her to be mistress of his house. In his heart *she* was his wife, didn't she understand that? "She will in time," he answered.

"Richard, who you be talking to?" It was Agnes who came up behind him, touching his arm with the familiarity that she had shown during his boyhood.

He whirled around. "Myself, I fear." A frown marred his handsome face as he remembered the abuse Edlyn had received at this woman's hands. Agnes had been his nurse. He had trusted her and she had betrayed that trust.

Before he could reprimand her, Agnes clucked her tongue. "I know what you must be thinking. But you are wrong, Richard. It was not my doing that caused the fever. I give you my word on that." She sighed. "She must be watched constantly or she gets into mischief."

"Is that why you locked her in that foul room?"

"Your *wife* has a violent temper, I fear. Like a raging child, she has fits of tantrums, swearing and throwing things. It was my way of subduing her. If I was wrong, then I beg your forgiveness." She looked up at him and he remembered all the kindness she had given him in his youth. All the love his own mother had kept from him, Agnes had bestowed freely. "Her two boys," she had called Roderick and him. How could he believe that she would willfully show cruelty to anyone?

"Just don't let it *ever* happen again!"

"I promise you that it will not. I will see to that." She grinned at him, a gap-toothed smile which he remembered well. "Now, come. I have prepared your breakfast. All your favorites. Even Yorkshire pudding."

He couldn't hide his smile. "Ah, Agnes, you do spoil me."

"That I do, Richard. That I do. It's good to have you back home again." She took his arm to lead him to the kitchen. He belonged to her again, just as he had as a child, and neither his gibbering wife nor that whey-faced redhead would take him away from her.

She, Agnes, was mistress of this household and would always be. How she loved to be the queen bee, issuing her orders. No London whore would sweep into this manor and tell her what to do. She would soon have that one on her way. So thinking, she smiled again.

46

TIME DID NOT change Heather's mind, nor wear away Richard's resolve. October blended into November and Heather feared that with each day they were drifting farther and farther apart. Richard was busy from dawn to dusk during the ensuing weeks, meeting with his stewards and manorial officers who totaled up their accounts, giving him his share, and Heather felt totally ignored, little realizing the agony Richard himself was going through. A thousand times he cursed himself for a fool and longed to do as Heather bid him and take her away, but just when he had decided to leave, he would find one more thing that needed to be done.

Feed was too scarce to keep most animals through winter, and so many of them were killed, their meat smoked and salted. In the north country it was not possible to obtain foodstuffs from foreign ports easily, and so many people's lives depended upon Richard now. Without a proper store of food his tenants and servants would die, and this he could not have on his conscience, no matter how he loved Heather Bowen. Londoners were spoiled, their comforts and hungers easily satisfied, but in the North it was a far different matter. Thus he kept himself from his heart's desire, paying for his noble decision with the pain which stabbed through him every time he saw the sadness in Heather's face.

Over and over again Heather wondered what would have happened if Richard had not been called back to his estates. The new surroundings had caused a conflict in her emotions. She loved Richard, that she could not deny, and yet here in Norfolk she felt estranged from him. Guilty. Unwelcome. The woman named Agnes did nothing at all to make her feel at home, but instead, seemed to take every opportunity to taunt her, at least when Richard was absent.

When Richard was in the manor, the woman smiled and fawned over him until Heather clearly understood that for some reason he was in the woman's power. Clearly Agnes considered herself mistress of the manor and Heather the interloper. She repeated over and over that Heather was not Richard's wife.

Nor am I his mistress now, Heather thought sadly, closing her eyes against the ache in her heart and the longing to have Richard love her once again. This time she would not push him away. No, not this time.

But Richard did not come to her; instead she found herself clashing over and over again with Agnes over one matter or another. It became obvious to Heather that as mistress of the household Agnes had been lax in her duties. There were cobwebs on the lofty ceilings, dirt on the windowsills, dust on the floors, and the buttery and pantry were ill-stocked. Rats in the cellars had eaten up the winter's store of grain and Heather wished that Saffron were with her to chase away the bold rodents as he had at her father's house in London. But there were no cats, for Agnes hated the animals.

When Heather approached Richard with the truth of Agnes' slovenliness, begging him to dismiss the woman, it merely seemed to widen the differences between them.

"Agnes has been in this household since before I was born. She knows what must be done," he snapped, tired from his long days of working out in the cold. "If there are things that have not been accomplished, then I am certain that it is because of her constant attention to Edlyn."

"How can you be so blind!" Heather had gasped, turning her back on him in outraged anger.

"If you would take your rightful place as mistress here, perhaps all could be set to rights," he snapped at her then, issuing her a challenge.

Before the day was out she had tackled the responsibilities with a vengeance, examining every room for any sign of disrepair. She would prove to him what could be done. In rooms without carpets, the rushes were freshly strewn, mixed with herbs, the old rushes thrown out and burned. New sacks of grain were bought from local farmers to replace the grain the rats had eaten, and several cats were given a permanent home to guard them, despite Agnes' protestations. A large garden for vegetables and herbs was outside the kitchen door and Heather made certain that it was kept thriving until winter snow would bring an end to anything green or fresh. With each day she came to feel affection for this household. Gone now was her feeling of not belonging as her efforts worked magic. She was strong and would put up a fight. Even Agnes' hatred did not stop her.

As All Saints' Day arrived in November, Heather found out that she had indeed made an enemy of Agnes, yet she was unprepared for the venom of her anger. The woman even blamed Heather for a raging thunderstorm, saying that she was a witch. Having at first envisioned Heather as weak, Agnes now came to realize the full depth of Heather's strength and fought hard to force her to leave.

Her stories turned Richard's tenants against Heather, for they were susceptible to such tales. The household servants, having always been ruled by Agnes, were also hostile to Heather, and more than once she thought she heard the word "mistress" being bandied about, yet Heather managed to hold her head up. Somehow the word did not sound as sordid now. She at least could count two of the servants as her friends: Cook, a middle-aged woman whose cap was always askew, her hair straggling down around her ears, first in command of the kitchen, and Matty, a plump round-faced woman with kind brown eyes and a turned-up nose. Right from the first Matty had been the only one to show kindness to Heather. It was Matty's duty to keep the scullery maids in line. Heather gave her authority over the other servants as well, two house maids, two grooms, a stablehand, and the gatekeeper. All the servants had their separate rooms at the long end of the servants' hall, except Matty, who lived with her gardener husband in a separate cottage across the courtyard. It was here that Heather often fled when the atmosphere of the manor was more than she could bear.

It was not difficult to confide in this woman, particularly when Matty vowed that if it was the last thing she ever did she would soon have the other servants flock to Heather's side. Matty had gone against Agnes once before. it was she who had sent the message to Richard when Edlyn was ill, hoping thereby to have him discover the evil woman's perfidy.

"I love him, Matty. But I think I may have lost him. He has been so busy of late that I hardly ever see him."

Matty wiped her hands on her apron. "You have not lost him. He loves you, lass. Of that have no doubt. He is just a man, and as such has a stubborn streak of pride in him. I would wager that he is waiting for you to come to him. Men don't like being rebuffed, you know."

"What can I do?"

Matty giggled. "Ah, lass, if you do not know, then I cannot tell you. I will let intuition be your guide." She smiled mischievously, looking like a little girl despite her years. "But I will lend a hand. They say the way to a man's heart is through his stomach. . . ."

Matty showed her how to make frumenty, a pudding made of wheat boiled with milk, currants, raisins, and spices. It was, Matty promised, a dish that Richard was inordinately fond of. Heather made the dish for the feast of the plowman, Martinmas, and watched anxiously as Richard tasted of her efforts.

"Tell Cook that this is excellent. The best that she has made," he said as they sat at dinner. As always, he did his best not to look at Heather as he spoke.

"Cook didn't make it, I did," she said shyly.

"You?"

"Matty told me that it was your favorite. I . . . I . . ." She started to look away from him but the magnetism between them was too overpowering. In the silence they sat staring at each other as tides of longing washed over them both. Heather wanted to cry out, to tell him how much she missed his arms about her as she slept. How lonely she was in the large bed without him. The weeks had seemed like years without his love.

Richard wanted to say so many things, but as he opened his mouth he found that he was tongue-tied, like a small boy again. He loved her more than anything in the world and yet when she had asked him to take her away he had stubbornly refused. He was a fool and now wanted with all his heart to have things the way they were before.

"Heather . . ." he breathed, but the sadness in those large gray eyes of hers made all his words tumble about hopelessly in his brain and so he said only, "If I had known that first day I met you in your father's storeroom that you could make frumenty, I would have forgotten all about my duty to Mary and abducted you right then and there."

It was all Heather could do to maintain her composure. She wondered what the servants would do if she now sauntered across the room and threw herself into his arms, begging him to love her, but said only, "Ah, you would have, my fine rebel? And what of poor Mary then?"

"Mary? I know of no Mary," he answered with a half-smile. Her hair, he thought, glows like fire in the candlelight. How I want to reach out and entangle my fingers in its silken glory. "Heather . . ." Leaving his half-eaten portion of the pudding, he came to her then. Her nearness was his undoing. Ignoring the shocked look of Cook, he gathered her into his arms, claiming the softness of Heather's lips.

"Richard, your pudding."

"The pudding can wait," he breathed. "I want only

to taste of you. Lord, how I have missed you!" Before she could protest he picked her up in his arms to carry her up to his chamber. "This is where you belong. Here! Please don't deny me again. I love you." He unfastened her gown, one of many he had had sent from London, letting it slip to the floor to expose the chemise and petticoats beneath. With slow exploration he slid his hands over the soft contours of her body until Heather tingled with desire. The chemise and petticoats soon followed the gown to lie in a heap at her feet.

How could she deny him when she loved him so? Did she really want to? No. She had been wrong and now she admitted it to herself. This manor *was* Richard. It had not been fair to make him choose between them. Let the servants cluck their tongues, let Agnes look down her nose. This was where Heather belonged. Here in Richard's arms. How could she have lived without his love for so many weeks? Edlyn was not his wife, she was.

Boldly she stepped forward to face him, pulling off his doublet and shirt with the ease of one who has had much practice, yanking at the rest of his clothing, anxious for him to join her in his proud naked glory. Tugging at his hand, she led him over to lie with her before the fire on a soft sheepskin rug, where they clung together, their bodies embracing, caressing as they kissed, his lips lightly tracing the outline of her mouth with his tongue, then claiming the whole softness of her lips.

Pulling away slightly, Richard let his eyes linger on her body. It was a familiar sight, and yet she never failed to stir him. How could he have waited so long before claiming her again?

"You are so lovely." Her breasts were perfect, her legs long and shapely, her hips just wide enough. He stroked her silken flesh, feeling desire arise in him as it had the very first time he had made love to her. He needed no love potion now to set his pulse to pounding. Her breasts brushed his chest as she reached her fingers up to twine them in the dark curls of his hair, pulling his face down to hers. Their lips moved softly against each other's at first, only to grow fevered as their very flesh seemed to meld together.

"I love you so, Heather," he whispered against the fragrant skin of her throat.

"And I, you," she answered, reaching down to feel the strength of him, the power of him. He was everything she had ever wanted. "I was wrong . . ." she breathed.

"No. It was I. I should have understood how you would feel and not been so stubborn."

"I should have realized how you loved this manor. I should never have asked you to take me away. I have learned to love it here too, these past days. From now on I will heed Ruth's words. Whither thou goest, I will go." His lips silenced any further words between them as they ignited a flame in each other.

As he slowly filled her with the sweet length of his manhood, she wrapped her arms and legs tightly about him as if to hold him to her forever.

There was no sound, no words between them, for the rhythm of their passion, the meeting of their gaze as they looked at each other, said all that needed to be said. Heather felt the emptiness that had been with her since they had arrived here burst nearly to overflowing with the love she bore this man. She would never be lonely again. Shaking her head in mute joy, the wonder of it all glowing in her eyes, she captured his hand and drew it to her lips.

At last Richard spoke, his arms tightening about her, his fingers tracing the strong jawline of her face. "I will never let you go."

She smiled at him. "Perhaps we can stay just as we are all winter."

"Mmmmm, it would be nice, though I fear that we would not get much done. You are all too tempting, my love."

For just a fleeting moment a shadow passed in front of Heather's eyes, the reminder that to others, theirs was a forbidden love, and she clung to Richard as she sought to chase away her fears. In the aftermath of love, she thought about the coming winter, wondering what it would bring. Seton had not followed them. Had his threats been only idle boasts? It appeared so. The memory of him dimmed as the days marched on.

47

DECEMBER WAS RELATIVELY mild in Norfolk, with rain and sleet but very little snow, but if the fury of a storm had avoided the countryside, the same could not be said for London, where winds of turmoil seemed destined to sweep forth. At last Heather and Richard could close their eyes no longer to what was happening at court. Stephen Vickery spelled it out for them in a letter sent posthaste by messenger.

As they sat before the fire, Richard read parts of the letter to Heather. "He begs me to return. He tells me I am needed. Needed. As if I didn't know."

"And the queen, is she still angry with you?"

Richard shook his head. "Aye. But Stephen thinks that she still trusts my advice and will forgive me in due time." He read on, "Please do not leave her in the hands of such as Renard and Seton, who flatter her constantly and play on her basic trusting nature. It bodes ill for us all if they are to gain absolute power. Did we fight so long and hard only to find ourselves victims of other Northumberlands?"

"Seton in power?" The thought was too horrible to imagine. What would happen to Richard and her then?

Not wanting to alarm Heather further, Richard read to himself. Early in December a dead dog with its ears cropped and the head shaved like a priest's was thrown into the queen's presence chamber at Whitehall. There were those angered at Mary's decision to replace bishops of the reformed faith with

Catholic prelates recalled from exile: Bonner, who had been made Bishop of London, and Gardiner, who was now Bishop of Winchester and a close adviser to the crown.

Heather was piqued as he read silently, wanting to share in what was happening at court. "Richard, please, read the letter aloud. I must know what is going on."

Richard complied, allowing her to read over his shoulder. "Further rumblings have been caused by the rumor that a man named Rafael Mendosa is near to convincing Mary to accept the emperor's son and heir, Philip of Spain, as her husband. Is this your Mendosa? Let us hope that he does not succeed. We need no Spanish kings! Again, I beg you to consider all that I have told you. Stephen Vickery."

Richard tore up the letter angrily. It was just as he had feared. The many would suffer because of a few impetuous men.

"Stupid fools. Can they not see that such acts will only harden Mary's feelings toward those of the reformed church? They play into Seton's hands." He told her quickly about the incident with the dog.

"Perhaps you *should* go to London. If Mary seeks to punish anyone for what is between us, it will be me. I was the one who ran away—you did not have to kidnap me, I came freely." The thought of his ill-favor was like a crushing blow, though not a surprise. Would Mary ever forgive him? Would she welcome him back to court?

As if reading her thoughts, he swept her into his arms. "I will not leave you! You are more important to me than the world. Mary will do very well without me by her side."

She pushed him gently away. "No. You must go. Could you ever live with yourself if you turned your back upon her when she so greatly needs you? You love me but you love your queen and country as well. I am willing to share you with these two rivals, but no others." She kissed the tip of his nose. Strange how she had been the one to want to leave not long ago. Now the thought of leaving Norfolk pained her, but she must think of what was best for Richard. He had given up much for love of her. Would he ever regret it? No. He loved her. She was secure in that love.

Richard thought for a long while. "Christmas is coming. I cannot leave you at such a time, nor my tenants. When the new year has come we will speak of this again. What difference can one month bring?" Without realizing it, this question would come back to haunt him in the months to come.

48

THE FLICKERING FLAMES from the Yule log seemed to pulsate with the rhythm of the music, mirth, and merriment which echoed throughout the manor. It was Christmas Eve, a time of celebration. Heather had taken a hand in decorating the manor for the holidays. Holly and mistletoe hung from every bower to bring good luck throughout the following year, and the fires and candles twinkled along the tables, illuminating the veritable feast laid upon them.

Dressed in her emerald-green velvet gown with gold brocade underskirt and white-fur-trimmed sleeves, Heather was lovely and looked every inch the lady of the manor.

"You have outdone yourself, my lady," whispered a short, tiny young scullery maid. " 'Tis happy I am that you have come to us." Her words touched Heather's heart, for it had taken much patience to win the trust of the girl. One by one the servants' hostilities were melting away.

Viewing the heavily laden trestle tables with a critical eye, Heather decided that there was certainly enough to feed all that were present. Richard was giving a Christmas dinner for all his tenants, making use of the special rents that he had been given of bread, hens, ale, and the like. It would be a splendid feast, for the villeins had been overly generous this year.

There would be merriment until Epiphany, or the Twelfth Day, the sixth of January, and the services required of the tenants would be suspended. It was whispered that Richard had been most generous this year. All manorial servants were to receive extra bonuses of the food, clothing, drink, and firewood which comprised their traditional Christmas due. All eyes turned upon Heather, as if everyone knew that she was the reason why the perquisites had been most bountiful.

"Ah, such a feast we will have," Matty said with a chuckle, rubbing her ample waist.

Only to Matty would Heather have confided her fears. "I'm so nervous, Matty. For so many weeks Richard's tenants have shunned me, calling me Richard's whore, and now I must face them as hostess of the house."

"Fah. Don't worry your pretty head. The servants all love you, you have won them over one by one. You will do likewise with the tenants. You have not only been good to us but to poor Edlyn as well. No one has such patience with her tantrums. You seem to have the skill to soothe her."

"I only undo what Agnes has done. Edlyn has been treated like an animal, and so at times she reacts like one. But all will be ended."

"Ha, I would be so bold as to say that it is time Agnes got her due. For too many years has she reigned as 'queen' in this house, fooling poor Richard with her endearing ways. Like all men, he fails to see her true nature. She is spiteful, lazy, and the Lord knows what else."

Heather sighed. "Richard and I have argued time and time again over Agnes. I have pleaded with him to send her away, but he won't do as I ask. Why?"

Matty put her hands on her hips, meeting Heather's eyes. "Richard remembers the old Agnes. The one who sat him on her lap and told him and his brother stories. Starved for love, those two were, and she had plenty to offer them, being childless herself. I wonder if there wasn't a reason for her being so kind to the boys. Perhaps in truth she is no better than their mother was."

"What was Richard's mother like, Matty?"

"Beautiful, with hair like ebony and eyes like the sky, but her beauty did not go beyond her face. She was selfish and thought only of herself. Why else would a mother bind her own son in marriage to a woman who would never be a wife to him?" Tears shone in Matty's eyes as she reached out to touch Heather's hand. "I'm so glad you came, God bless you. I knew the moment I saw you that you were the one who could make Richard happy. He's had so little happiness in his life. Someday you two will be man and wife, as it was surely meant to be."

"Perhaps someday, Matty. I can only hope that Mary will listen to Richard's brother and grant him his divorce. Richard plans to take his case all the way to the pope."

Matty's eyes grew as large as saucers. "The pope! Imagine that. Merry-come-up." She giggled. "Oh, how I would like to see Agnes' face when you marry your Richard." Her eyes searched about the room. "Where is Agnes?"

"Richard instructed her to watch over Edlyn tonight. Whenever there are people about, she is edgy and at times can even be dangerous."

Again Matty chuckled. "She will be livid. This will be the first time since the death of Richard's mother that she has not been the hostess for the Christmas festivities. Serves her right, I say."

Heather left Matty without offering a reply. Walking toward the hallway, she sought out the hiding place she had chosen for the presents. There were presents for Matty, Edlyn, and of course Richard, hidden behind a large indentation in the wall, which was covered by a wall hanging. It was there that Richard found her.

"Merry Christmas, my love," he whispered, kissing her lightly on the cheek. He eyed her suspiciously. "And just what are you about?"

She kissed him back. "Wouldn't you like to know?"

Pushing her gently aside, he found her hiding place and brought forth the packages. "I used to hide presents in that very same place," he said with a smile. "Which one is mine?"

Heather started to answer him, when suddenly her eyes grew large in fright as she saw Edlyn perched high above the solar on the balcony of the stairs.

"Edlyn!" she gasped. Leaning against the stair rail, the woman was reaching out her hand to try to touch a sprig of holly fastened there. "Dear God, she will fall!"

Picking up her skirts, Heather ran with Richard up the two flights of stairs, they reached out just in time to catch Edlyn before she fell crashing to the wooden floor below. Shaking herself, Heather nevertheless managed to calm the young woman.

"What in God's name is she doing out? I told Agnes to watch her." The sound of his voice startled Edlyn, who now thrashed about, holding her arms up as if he would strike her. His voice softened. "I won't harm you, Edlyn. For God's sake, there is no one who will harm you here." He reached out a hand, turning her face to look into her fear-glazed eyes, and it was then that he saw the bruises.

"There you are, you fool idiot!" Agnes shrieked, running from one of the upstairs chambers. Seeing Agnes coming toward her, Edlyn cringed in stark terror, leaving no doubt as to the source of the bruises.

"Oh, Richard, can't you see?" Heather cried. "It was Agnes who harmed her. Open your eyes to the truth of what the woman is. You are not a child now, Richard."

Agnes narrowed her eyes, hissing, "What do you know, you whore? How can you seek to judge me? You! You, of all people. How I hate you. Why don't you go back to London where you belong? I got along very well without your interference." She raised a hand as if to strike Heather, but Richard's grip stayed her.

"That's quite enough, Agnes," he shouted, his eyes pools of sorrow. "I want you out of here by tomorrow."

"Out of here? No. You can't mean—"

"I should have listened to you, Heather. I was blind. So blind!" Although Agnes tried every way to change his mind, this time Richard was firm in his resolve.

"It is your fault!" she shrieked at Heather. "You have not heard the end of this. I will see that you pay for what you have done." Heather was stung by her words of hatred and had the sudden fear that Agnes would make good her threat.

"Come, my love. Our tenants await us," Richard said, seeking to ease Heather's troubled mind. He led her back to the tables, where the air was rich with the aroma of the sauces made from herbs and wine and spices from the East.

Heather went about her duties as hostess, watching as the tenants quaffed their ale and ate heartily of the roast beef and plum pudding, the goose and bread stuffing. After the main courses had been eaten, Richard passed around loaves of bread cut in three parts for the ancient Christmas game in which a bean was hidden in one of the loaves. The person who found it became king or queen of the feast. Much to everyone's delight, it was Matty who found the surprise and got to wear the paper crown upon her head. Bedecked in red wool, she looked like the spirit of Yuletide.

A gesture from Richard sent the minstrels forward to play their instruments and lead the assembled tenants in singing carols, and while the others were occupied, Richard gave Heather a gift.

"I have one for each of the twelve days of Christmas," he said, watching as she unwrapped the present, "but this one is special."

It was a ring, a gold ring inscribed in tiny letters that said "I love you" on the inside. "Richard!"

"Until that day when my brother convinces them to free me of my matrimonial bonds and I can give you a wedding ring," he whispered, slipping it upon her finger.

Deeply touched by his gift, she knew of no words

that could express her love for him at that moment. Not even the arrival of a group of mummers, that band of masked pantomimists who paraded through the countryside and visited dwellings to play at dice and dance, could break the spell. As the others sat in rapt attention to watch the sword dance, Heather and Richard stood hand in hand, content just to be together.

"Christmas, such a blessed time," Heather whispered.

Richard's expression was loving and tender, but as he looked at the pantomimists his expression changed. "Bigod, what is this?"

Instead of the famlliar St. George and the Dragon play, which symbolized the death and coming to life of all growing things, it was a more sinister theme. Richard recognized at once that one of the mummers was depicting the queen kneeling in prayer and giving fond looks to another of the characters. It was obvious to Richard that this person, wearing a tall hat, was supposed to be a Spaniard. The female character stood beside this Spaniard moaning and weeping as a black-robed mummer pretended to strike him with a sword. Clearly the moaning figure was Mary; the Spaniard, Philip of Spain.

"What is the meaning of this?" Richard asked in anger, pushing forward through the crowd. "I will not have you make fun of my queen."

The mummers all turned to him in surprise. " 'Tis all in fun. Only our way of saying that we will have no Spanish king," said the black-garbed mime.

"King?"

"Aye. Where have you been, sir? It seems that Prince Philip will give his consent to marry our queen. The news from London is that a Spanish emissary has just brought confirmation of acceptance of the marriage contracts," answered the man dressed in queen's attire.

Richard was dumbfounded. "Acceptance of the marriage contracts?" He did not know that things had gone so far. Surely the council would never approve the match. Under the terms of Henry's will, Mary was obliged to obtain the council's consent before she could marry.

Sweeping off his tall hat, the pantomimist who was dressed as Philip bowed low to Richard as if to soothe his anger. "I, sir, like you, am a loyal Catholic and long with all my heart to see this land once again brought under the blessed rule of the pope, but as long as I draw the breath of life, I will not see England bow her head to a Spanish yoke." Throughout the hall Catholic and Reformer alike hurrahed the man's statement.

"No Spanish king!" came the chant, echoing over and over again, drowning out the din of the minstrels. Only after the mummers had been long gone did the hall calm down.

Heather knew exactly what must be done. Richard could no longer hide himself in the country. They must return to London before open rebellion threatened the security and peace of the kingdom.

"Poor Mary. To wait so long for a husband, only to cause such discontent with her people over her choice," she whispered to Richard. "Can they not see that though she is a queen she is also a woman? She has feelings, a need for love, for arms holding her tight, just like any woman of common blood. I could sense that she was lonely, so lonely." The memory of what the queen had said to her that day about marriage came to her mind.

"They do not see that, they only fear that by this marriage England will become involved in Spain's hostilities against France. There has been enough bloodshed."

Heather took hold of Richard's hand, placing the palm against her cheek. "On the morrow you will leave me. My heart tells me that it is so."

"If I cannot persuade her to say no to this alliance, at least perhaps I can make her see that she and she alone must have sole royal authority over English affairs." He looked at her wistfully. "You did not ask to go."

"I know that in this you must go alone."

"If only I could take you with me, but I cannot. I will return as soon as I can. I make you my promise on that." It was a promise that he would be forced to break.

49

FROST COVERED THE ground like a blanket of white as Richard guided his horse along the slippery road to London. He peered up at the dark clouds overhead with a feeling of frustration. What else could go wrong to hinder his journey? He had sent an urgent letter to Stephen Vickery informing him of a meeting place where they could sup and discuss this matter of the marriage. The Cap and Crown was the appointed place, but if the weather continued at this gale, Richard would be late in arriving.

"Damn!" he swore beneath his breath.

He was cold and tired and hungry. Pulling his cloak tightly about him, he resigned himself to push on.

"I have grown soft," he scolded himself beneath his breath. "Good food, leisure, and the arms of the beautiful woman I love have spoiled me." And indeed it did seem as if he had left the gates of heaven to tread the pathway of a cold and frozen hell.

How long or far he rode, he did not know; he knew only the feeling that the wind was at his back driving him forward as if to hurry him along. But if the wind was his friend, the sleet and snow were his enemy, nearly blinding him as they fell to the earth in a blur of white. At last he could go no farther, and coming to the shelter of a ruined building, an old abandoned abbey, he guided the horse inside. The roof was in serious disrepair but at least it would shelter him until the storm quieted. The storms of December had blown into January full force. It looked to be a long time before the skies would clear. A long while.

"I will have to content myself to wait," he mused, seeking out the driest spot in the abbey. It was strange to think what a grand structure it had been. Now it was little more than a pile of gray stones, many of which had been pilfered to build some noble's estate. The threat of a Spanish king was doubly threatening to these lords, for surely Philip would seek to force these nobles to give up their ill-gotten gains from the church.

Closing his eyes, he thought of Heather, as he whispered her name reverently. It was much pleasanter to think of her than of what awaited him. Mary would not be easy to persuade, and her anger at him would complicate matters.

"Heather," he whispered again. Many times he had dreamed of her these last four nights, aching to hold her in his arms. If only he could have taken her with him, but during the winter months that was impossible. Instead he would hope that he could return to her before the month was through. Drifting off into a deep slumber, he saw the face of his gray-eyed lover and smiled.

The pressure of hands grasping his shoulders awakened Richard from his sleep. A rude awakening. Through the haze of his awareness he watched as a grinning youth reached to take away his sword, plucking it from his belt as easily as Richard had picked the summer roses. In anger Richard struggled with his captor, only to be set upon by two others, brawny men who pushed him back down upon the ground.

"My, my, our traitorous friend certainly longs for a fight, eh, Julian? Methinks he has no liking to see his bloody head rolling upon the straw."

"He should have thought of that before he sought to stir up his followers in revolt. It is a good thing that we were warned of his intent. 'Tis bad enough that Thomas Wyatt has escaped us. At least we come away with one prize." This man was older than the others, with the appearance of an old weathered soldier, and Richard scanned his face for any sign of recognition. There was none. This man had never seen him before.

"I do not know who you *think* I am," Richard said indignantly, trying to pull free of his captors, "but I am in fact a loyal follower of the queen. One of her advisers."

The young man laughed. "You expect us to believe that? The next thing you will be telling us is that you are the bloody King of England."

"I tell you the truth! I am on the way to London to talk with the queen. There—" a kick in the ribs was his answer.

"Think you that we would let you get within three miles of her royal person? Ha! We have been told to watch for you. Courtenay spilled his guts to us about what is planned, fool that he is."

"Courtenay? What has he to do with this?" Richard forgot his pain as he heard this bit of information.

The soldier grabbed him by his doublet, pulling him up to a face-to-face position. "As if you didn't know." Letting his hold loosen, he thrust Richard to the ground again, sprawling in a heap.

"He thought to marry the Lady Elizabeth, since Mary had spurned him, and set himself up beside her as king and queen. Lucky for Mary it was that Bishop Gardiner wormed the details of the plot from him. They were prisoners in the Tower together, the bishop and Courtenay, but it appears that this time that foppish lord will reside there by himself," said the young soldier.

"Cease your jabbering. He doesn't need to be told about the plot."

"Plot? What plot? I must know." Somehow Richard had to convince this tattered group of soldiers of his innocence and get posthaste to London. The queen had need of his loyalty once again.

"What plot?" mimicked the older soldier, scowling down at Richard. "As if you weren't in on it." He walked up and down, his eyes raking over his prisoner. "Where were you headed before we caught you unawares? Not to Kent. 'Tis said that Thomas Wyatt is to lead the revolt there. Not to Warwickshire. No, that is the territory laid out for the Duke of Suffolk. Is it that you intended to rouse the Londoners?"

"No! I seek audience with no one except my queen." Richard sought to rise, but the booted foot of the brawny ruffian stopped him.

"Bloody heretic! May you all rot in hell. London is a good place for you. Damned reformers all." The brawny soldier motioned to the older one. "Take him to my Lord Seton. He will know what to do with him. This looks to be the one he told us to watch for."

"Seton? Seton has his hand in this?" Disgust mixed with anger ached in Richard's belly. Why must he be met with the man's treacherous interference constantly? His eyes darted back and forth for any sign of escape, but he was only one unarmed man against three soldiers.

"Don't get any ideas, you bloody fool. We will cut you down if you but blink an eye," said the brawny soldier as all three pointed their swords at him. "Get his horse."

Richard's hands were tied behind his back and he was pushed and shoved to where his horse awaited. It was a difficult task to mount the animal, and seeing his predicament, his captors at last flung him upon the horse's back like a sack of wheat.

"Seton is my enemy," Richard croaked. "He will not tell you the truth about me. Take me instead to the queen. Please. I beg you."

Laughter met his words. "Seton is the enemy of all who would seek to harm our queen," said the young soldier.

"Buffoons!" Richard cursed beneath his breath. "At least they take me in the right direction." With the wind once again at his back, he set off along the London road.

In a few hours' time the small band arrived at their destination and Richard was thrown into a small windowless cell-like room. Trussed up like a Christmas goose, helpless to fight, he had been delivered into the hands of the man he detested above all others.

"Forgive me for being so inhospitable," came a mocking voice. "Perhaps a cup of wine . . ." Seton stood in the doorway, grinning.

"Go to hell, Seton."

Seton waved his hands about, motioning for the youngest man to light a candle in one of the wall sconces, then motioned the soldiers to leave. Slamming the door shut, he turned the key in the lock. "I want to keep you safe until I see what is going to happen. I may have need of a scapegoat, and you will do nicely."

"Scapegoat?"

Again a grin. "I am walking a tightrope for the time being. There are those who say that Mary's days are numbered. Fool that she is, she insists upon her Spanish prince." He laughed mirthlessly. "Why, you should see her. She kisses that painting of him that they sent her as if it were the prince himself. Think you then that *you* can sway her? For I know that is your mission, is it not?"

"Yes. She is a wise woman. She will listen to reason when she learns of the consequences of this union." Richard tugged at his bonds, wishing that he could get loose and wipe that smile off Seton's face.

"She is a shriveled-up virgin who sees the answers to her maidenly prayers. For all her acting the nun, I have no doubt that she is a woman who lusts for a man in her bed the same as any other female. Time is running out on the queen. Already her looks, what little she might have had, are fading. So I have no desire to align myself with Mary, but neither do I want to find myself on Tower Green with my head bowed to the axman were she to be victorious. Clever, no?"

"Does that mean that you are to remain neutral in this matter?" Richard eyed the man before him warily, wondering just what was in his mind.

"It means that I have men fighting on both sides.

If the tide shifts to Wyatt's supporters, I will be prepared. No matter which side wins, I will be with the victors."

"You vile traitor! Bastard!"

Hugh Seton turned red with anger, his small beady eyes filled with hate. "Do not call me traitor, nor bastard. I will have none of your insults."

"You cannot silence the truth."

"Brave words for a prisoner. Beware lest I change my mind and kill you after all. You are not in a church this time, Morgan. I am not unarmed as I was when you stole my bride." His hand brushed his sword.

"She was never yours to steal. You merely wanted to use her to hurt me." He kept his eyes riveted on Seton, watching as the man paced back and forth, his hands folded across his chest.

Seton stopped his walking to stare again at Richard. "Make no mistake, she will be mine one day, or if she refuses me, then she will die." He laughed, an evil sound, as if entertaining some private joke.

"What do you mean?" The fear that Seton had another sinister plan up his sleeve coiled in Richard's stomach.

"You will see. You will see. I have a surprise planned for her which will most likely be arriving at your door in Norfolk. Let us hope that your *lover* will be amused."

Richard fought uselessly against his captivity. "If you harm one hair on her head, so help me God I will see you in hell, Seton." How in God's name had he fallen so easily into this man's trap? Now it seemed that Heather too was destined for some kind of villainy.

"You can struggle all you like. You will never be free. You are at my mercy." Seton walked toward the door.

"Wait." Seton turned around at the sound of Richard's voice. "How did you know that I would be on that particular road at that time? Was I betrayed?"

Seton laughed. "You told me."

"I told you? Absurd."

Seton opened the door and stepped through, but said over his shoulder, "It was your letter to that imbecile Vickery. It was intercepted by one of my retainers. I thought it would not be long before you would seek to meddle again in court affairs. My patience was rewarded." The door closed with a resounding bang.

Alone in the dimly lit room, Richard closed his eyes. He dared not think what the consequences would be if he stayed in Seton's grasp much longer.

"Heather." What was the surprise Seton said awaited her?

50

HEATHER SHIVERED AT the cold in the room. Winter was full upon them, with freezing, long nights and dark, clouded days. Pulling her chair closer to the fire, she looked down at the tapestry held in her hands and tried her best to concentrate once again upon her stitches. Richard had been gone over a week now and she had yet to receive any word from him. Why? He had promised that he would send her word as soon as he reached London.

"He is safe," she whispered aloud. "I am merely being foolish and impatient. Of course the weather will slow him in his journey. He will send me word when he can." She rose from her seat to throw another log on the fire, basking in the warmth and glow it gave as the fires consumed it.

"Shall I prepare us all a hot herbal drink?" a voice asked behind her, startling her. It was Undine. She was always coming up behind Heather as if she were one of the fairy people, quick to appear and disappear. The old white-haired woman was in charge of taking care of Edlyn now, and her soothing herbs and gentle gnarled hands were of great help. Only she and Heather could control the raging tantrums that so unnerved the household.

"Please do, Undine. The chill in the air seems much worse today. Perhaps because of the dampness." Heather smiled at Undine, wondering what she would have done without her these past few days. The woman had come to the manor begging for shelter from a storm and Heather had not the heart to turn her away.

The old woman toddled away on her short legs, to return in an instant holding forth mugs of steaming, aromatic liquid and Heather reached for the one farthest away.

"No. That one is for Edlyn," the old woman said sharply, pulling it from Heather's grasp. Her wrinkled face quickly recovered from its angry expression to turn again to a smile. "I put a sleeping potion in hers so that she will get her rest this midday."

"A sleeping potion? Again? I do not think it wise to give her such a thing so frequently, lest she become dependent upon it to sleep." For just a moment Heather had a twinge of misgiving about this woman, but it melted away quickly as Undine looked at her and smiled.

"It will do her no harm. Believe me. I had twelve children and gave the potion to all of them with nary a sign of harm. I have seen others with that poor woman's condition. Sleep is what heals them. Deep sleep. Trust me in this."

"I will trust you, Undine." Taking sips of her own drink, Heather felt the hot liquid seem to radiate heat throughout her entire body, until she noticed the chill of the room no longer. Again she thought of that day when she had first seen Undine in her tattered rags, her hand reaching out to implore shelter. It was not right that anyone should be so wanting while others enjoyed such comforts. Was it any wonder that Heather had offered the woman a permanent home at the manor? She remembered Undine's words to her: "I believe you will find me to be a *surprise*, my fair lady. I am useful for more things than you will ever imagine. You will see. You will see." And indeed Undine had proved to be most useful. She had nursed many of the servants when they had taken ill, her cooking was perfection, and she was a skillful storyteller. Heather wondered what Richard would think of the old woman.

Richard. Had she given him enough provisions?

What if he found himself snowed in somewhere without much to eat? The clip-clop of a horse's hooves against the stones in the courtyard and the nickering of that same horse caused her elation.

"Richard! It is Richard!" she exclaimed, running to the door and throwing it open, expecting to find him waiting for her. Instead it was Stephen Vickery who dismounted from his horse and came to greet her.

"Damnable cold! It is days like this that make me wish I had been born in Venice. How I long for the warmth of the sun." He looked about him. "Is Richard inside? I would think on a day like this he would be sitting before the fire with a mug of hot spiced cider."

Heather looked at him in confusion. "Richard is not with you?" Her eyes looked down the road as if expecting any moment to see him riding over the crest of the hill. A joke, that was what they were playing on her, and it was not in the least amusing.

Stephen Vickery strode forward to place his hands on her shoulders. "It is freezing out here. Come, let us go in." A feeling of foreboding crept along his spine as he sought to calm not only Heather but also himself.

"No! We must wait for Richard. Where is he?" Despite her protests, he led her inside the door and closed it behind him. The warmth of the room enfolded them like a cloak and he savored its comfort for just a brief moment. What a fool he had been to venture north at this time of year, but then, he had hoped to convince Richard to return with him. Perhaps both of them together could convince the queen to adhere to a few sensible measures in this question of the marriage. He had a few suggestions. Philip should be named after Mary on all official documents so that it would be Queen and King of England; no foreigners, no Spaniards should act as advisers on English affairs; and the military alliance between the two countries should be defensive only, so that England should not become involved in any Spanish hostilities against France. He was certain that Richard would agree with him. But where was Richard? He put this question in words, only to be met with Heather's horrified stare.

"He was to meet you at the Cap and Crown. He sent you a message over a week ago. He himself has been gone a week and two days."

"Gone? Message? I received no message, nor did I meet anyone on the road. It is most strange."

Heather put her hand on her head to keep from fainting. She had been right to worry. Some inner sense must have told her that Richard was in danger, but she had refused to listen. She had not been foolish and impatient to feel apprehensive about not hearing from the man she loved.

"Something has happened!" The blood pounded in her brain, her arms and legs felt like sticks of wood, yet somehow she managed to think clearly and calmly. "We must leave at once. Together we will retrace the path Richard rode. I will bring several of the tenants with us to comb the area."

"Leave? I just got here. Have mercy, woman, I am frozen stiff." He sought to calm her. There had to be an explanation. They had merely missed each other along the way, that was all. The messenger was most likely still waiting at Stephen's door, obstinate as they always were and eager to collect his gold coin.

"If you will not go with me, I will go alone." Heather fled up the stairs to dress in her warmest clothing. She could not stay in this house another moment when there was a possibility that Richard's life might be in danger.

Stephen Vickery followed after her, trying to change her mind. It was something he could not do. "You cannot travel about the countryside in the dead of winter. You will come to harm and Richard will have my neck."

"I can and I will go. Do you think that I care for my own safety when Richard's is in peril? Come with me, or stay. The decision is yours." Frantically she dug through her clothes chests until she found the necessary woolen garments. "Well?"

Vickery shrugged his shoulders. What was to be done with a stubborn woman? The possibility that she might very well be right tugged at his consciousness. Women always seemed to have second sight in these things. "We will go together, though I want you to be witness that this was your idea and not mine. I do not want to bear the brunt of Richard's anger when we find him!"

"*If* we find him!" Heather breathed. The thought that they might not was a torture to her very soul.

51

SEVEN MOUNTED FIGURES bent over their horses, nearly swooning with fatigue as they neared the gates of London. The rhythmic pounding of the horses' hooves met with the pulsing of their heartbeats. Both horses and humans alike had been driven hard by the urge to reach the city as soon as possible.

"Heather, are you all right?" Stephen Vickery asked, casting her a worried glance. It was a difficult enough journey for the men. How could a woman have fared well? She looked cold, hungry, her face was drawn and pale, though she was still beautiful.

"I am fine, but will be far better when we find Richard," she said, reining in her mount. They had searched along the road for any sign of him, only to be disappointed at every turn. It did not aid their cause that the freshly fallen snow had wiped away any possible sign of tracks, human or animal. Two of their party had stayed behind to scour the countryside further, but it was at best a meager hope they held of finding him. Their only hope lay in arriving to see him already within the city's walls.

"I pray God that he greets me with a smile, asking what took me so long," Stephen Vickery croaked. He was soon to be disappointed. It was as if Richard Morgan had vanished into the mists of the London fog. There was an added problem as well. Heather and Stephen Vickery found themselves in the middle of panic.

Rebellion blew in the very winds about London, for although Courtenay's words to Bishop Gardiner were said to have forewarned of a conspiracy, though Courtenay himself had been arrested, the revolt had flared up in four counties at once.

"It is what Richard feared, I think," Heather whispered, her voice nearly lost in the din of the London streets.

"Aye. It is my fear as well. It seems that these leaders of rebellion prefer to die in battle rather than on the block."

Riding through the London streets, they heard the latest tattlings. Even now, it was said, Sir Thomas Wyatt, son of one of Henry VIII's most talented advisers, had gathered together some five thousand or more men and was marching from Kent to London. His stirring cry "We are all Englishmen" seemed to echo all the way to London.

Fearing for her family, Heather threw away her pride and went straightforth to her father's home. If all else failed, she knew that she could count on Perriwincle and Tabitha to aid in her search for Richard. It was Thomas Bowen himself who opened the door for her, standing with his eyes and mouth wide open as if he saw a ghost before him and not a woman of flesh and blood. At last he spoke.

"God's blood! It is you. Why are you here?"

"Hello, Thomas," Heather answered without a trace of a smile.

Thomas Bowen recovered his composure. "Go away! You are not welcome here! Haven't you caused me enough trouble? I am nearly ruined. No more am I the queen's merchant, thanks to you."

"Please, let me in!" In answer, he started to close the door in her face, but a voice behind him stayed his hand.

"Thomas, I thought I heard Heather's voice just now." Blythe pushed him aside and looked at Heather with her gentle blue eyes. "It is Heather. My Heather! Oh, thank the Lord!" Gathering Heather into an embrace, she wept and laughed at the same time, as their tears of happiness mingled. "Are you well?

Blythe asked at last, pushing Heather an arm's length away.

"I am well, Mother, though I beg you, if you have seen Richard, please tell me."

Thomas Bowen snorted his disdain. "So he has left you already, trollop that you are. You foolish harlot!"

Blythe turned on her husband with a fury that Heather had never seen before. "Hold your tongue, Thomas! Say no more hurtful words or I swear I will leave you."

"Leave me?"

"Yes, by God's gentleness, I will. I suffered many long nights knowing that it was partly my fault Heather ran away. I should never have let you have your way, and will not again give you free rein over *my* daughter's destiny." Taking Heather's hand, she brought her inside. "Now, tell me all that has happened."

The story poured forth in a torrent of words and emotions that left both women engulfed in its tide. "And so you have been happy."

"Yes, until now. I fear for Richard's safety."

Blythe shook her head sadly. "Let us hope and pray that he has not been a victim of the storm brewing in the countryside. It seems that fear of Spanish rule has many of our London citizens sympathetic to these rebels." Her voice lowered. "Even your father has expressed his intent to open the gates to this Wyatt if need be. It seems that all those of the reformed faith are tempted to do so, should the need arise. A pox on them for their treachery."

"But they welcomed her accession but five months ago."

"I cannot speak for the others, but I do know that your father was incensed by Mary's export levy on cloth and import levy on French wine. She meant well, thinking to help the poor by her measures. She denounced 'rich clothiers' for their low wages and seems to have tried to stop the corruption in the administration. And now this matter of a Spanish king."

Heather smiled grimly. The Spanish could not be too bad after all. She herself was half Spanish, if what Thomas Bowen had told her months ago in his anger was true. "Has Mary no friends in London?"

"I fear not. Even the lord mayor and his aldermen seem to be loath to side with their queen. This Wyatt is appealing to all citizens to join with him to prevent England from becoming an appendage to Spain."

"Who is this Waytt? What is known of him?" Heather asked in anger. If he was the cause of any harm to Richard, he would regret that he had ever been born.

"Perriwincle knows of him. You had best ask him to answer you."

Heather fled to the stables, to find the old man at work repairing an old weather-beaten door. His face lit up with a smile as he hugged her to him.

"It's bloody glad I am to see you, Mistress Heather. Bloody glad." His eyes swept over her. "Are you happy with your lad?"

"Yes, oh yes . . . but, Perri, you must help me. Richard rode to London to see the queen and meet with Stephen Vickery. He has not arrived yet. I fear foul play. If you can find out anything at all, I would be most grateful!" She looked him straight in the eye. "Could this Wyatt be in any way responsible? Tell me what you know of him."

"Wyatt? I knew him in his youth. A hot-tempered one he was. We fought abroad together. He was a good soldier, but his stay in Spain and near-torture by the Inquisition as a heretic turned his heart to hatred for anything Spanish. Why, he even disliked poor Queen Catherine, dear Mary's mother. Just because of her Spanish blood, he did."

"Will he succeed, do you suppose?"

He shrugged his shoulders. "It is hard to say, it is, most hard to say." He wrung his hands and shook his head sadly. "I have heard it said that the old Duke of Norfolk—in his eighties, mind you, but still one of the best military men in this kingdom—has been sent to Rochester. He will show these young upstarts a thing or two. You wait and see."

They did wait, two days in fact, but Perri had been wrong. Many of the queen's men deserted to the opposition, and Wyatt and his soldiers marched even farther, to Southwark. They would soon be outside London itself. Perriwincle, ever on the alert for news, now told all he had learned. There were constant rumors.

"The western rising has collapsed. At least we have one victory for our one defeat. A lord named Sir Peter Carewe has fled to France, where it is said he will command an invading army of French soldiers. The Duke of Suffolk, Lady Jane's father, has disappeared into the Midlands. Sir James Croft has gathered forces in Wales. It seems that our Thomas Wyatt has threatened to imprison the queen when he comes through the gates. Let him try, the braggart. I for one will stand beside her, God bless her!"

"But there is no word of Richard? Has no one seen him?" At his denial, Heather's heart sank. She could no longer put from her mind the terrifying thought that Richard might very well be dead. Not content just to sit idle, she ran to the Guildhall in the city, hoping to gather some information. Standing in the back, she was surprised to see the queen herself in front of the lord mayor and assembled company. It grew so hushed as the queen began her speech that one could have heard a needle drop.

She told the gathered assembly that she was ready to abandon the Spanish marriage if the Commons so wished, and would indeed abstain from marriage while she lived, but that meanwhile she would not allow them to let the issue be a "Spanish cloak" for political revolution.

"I cannot tell how naturally the mother loveth her child, for I have never been the mother of any; but certainly if a queen may as naturally and earnestly love her subjects as the mother doth her child, then assure yourselves that I, being your lady and mistress, do as earnestly and tenderly love and favor you. And I, thus loving you, cannot but think that you as heartily and faithfully love me; then I doubt not but we shall give these rebels a short and speedy overthrow."

Heather felt pride for her queen swell her heart. Surely neither Henry VIII nor Edward VI had spoken more eloquently. How could the people not be on Mary's side now? The thunderous applause confirmed her thoughts. It was promised that London would arm itself, and Heather knew that this time the battle would be right within the walls of London.

"God save our queen," she whispered, "and Richard as well."

52

RICHARD SEEMED TO lose track of time as he languished in the cell-like room that he had been thrust into. Four times a day Seton came to see him, to toy with him as a cat does a mouse and to taunt him all the while with his victory. He made no secret of his hatred nor of his wish to see Richard pay for the many slights and imagined hurts he had suffered as a boy, and most of all for sweeping Heather out from under his very nose the day of their wedding. At least Richard knew that Seton would not kill him; he was having a better time of it by keeping him alive.

Tedium and boredom were perhaps the worst thing about it all, and the dampness, the lack of good food, and his longing for Heather. But at least he had the satisfaction of knowing that she was safe in Norfolk. Seton would never be so bold as to march to the manor and come up against the people of the village. The northerners were a hardy lot. Armed with swords, hand guns, and pitchforks, they were a formidable host.

He was not kept tied up now, at least not at night, and this helped him to sleep, at least when that sweet slumber came to him, which was seldom. Always he was awakened by the anxiety and the all-consuming passion to be free.

"Freedom," he whispered. "Such a beautiful word." He had tried every way to escape this cell. Trickery, force, violence, and even by taking a metal spoon and chipping away at the stones. It was useless. Until that time when Seton saw fit to release him, he was his "guest." Yet the hope always seemed to remain in his heart that somehow, some way, he would gain his escape. He had promised Heather that he would return to her soon. Lord, how he wanted to keep that promise.

As always when his eyes closed, it was of her that he dreamed. There was not another woman like her, nor would there ever be again. She protected all of those she loved, even Edlyn, whose very presence stood in the way of her happiness and heart's desire. But to harm that child-woman would never even enter Heather's thoughts.

"Lovely, lovely Heather," he murmured, at last trailing off to sleep.

The pressure of hands on his shoulders awakened him, and for a moment he thought himself to be back in the abandoned abbey. He struck out with his hands. They would not take him this time. They would not!

"Leave me be. I am on my way to see the queen. I must see her, I must," he mumbled, struggling against the hands that fought him.

"Shhhhhh. You will be both of our undoings," came a young man's voice. "I am here to help you. Be quiet or you will bring Seton down on our heads."

"Who are you?" It was pitch black in the room, yet he seemed to recognize that voice.

"It was I who set upon you with the others. They think you guilty, but I do not. My conscience has bothered me these many nights. There is something about Seton that I do not like. The man has shifty eyes and a false smile. I will give you your chance to see the queen and hope to God that you will not prove me foolish."

"God bless you, my lad. God bless you," Richard whispered, feeling the young man's hands push him along. Blinding light met their eyes as they opened the door, and for a moment Richard feared that they would both be found out as the tread of footsteps sounded in the hall. Quickly they ducked back inside.

"The guard is sound asleep. Lie back down on the cot. I will keep myself out of view by leaning against the door when it is opened." Richard made a dive for the bed, snoring loudly as if in the depths of his dreams.

"That one is sound asleep," came a low voice, chuckling as he passed by. Richard hardly dared to breathe as his heart thundered in his chest, but the foosteps passed on and at last the time seemed right to make his escape.

"There is a horse, your horse, hidden in the hedges at the back of the castle walls," the young man whispered. "We are at Saint Albans. You need to ride straight south and should be near London before tomorrow at this time. God speed you, my friend."

"And God bless you. You will not regret this act of kindness, that I promise. I am ever loyal to the queen. I would lay down my life for her." Opening the door, he fled up the stairs with the young man close behind him. The building that had housed him was a drafty old castle, no doubt belonging to Hugh Seton. Hadn't he always thought the bastard to be ambitious? Mary had rewarded him well, and all the while he sought to betray her if the need arose.

"Damn you to hell, Seton. This act will be your undoing. You will be unmasked for the traitor you are, to join those other traitors whose heads will be lost on Tower Green." Running up the long, winding stairs, he at last reached the main door and slipped into the shadows until he could make certain that the coast was clear. It was, and the door was unlocked as well. Slipping through the portal, he turned to wave once again to the young man who had proved to be his friend.

Freedom. After weeks in prison it was a heady draft. Tethering his horse, tossing his head back with a feeling of triumph, he headed in the direction of London.

53

RICHARD SPURRED HIS horse along the London road, not even deigning to look behind him as he rode. If he was being followed, well, so be it. It would be no easy task to take him captive again. At last he reached the city, seeing the stones of the old Roman wall before him. He was not prepared for what he found beyond. Total chaos.

More than a hundred people crowded the streets while others peeked from shuttered windows, all crying out questions. "Is it true that Wyatt's troops have marched into Southwark? How many men does he have with him? Will we be safe?"

Children clung to their mothers' skirts, wives held to their husbands' hands, seeking to keep them from joining battle, and voices of young as well as old blended in a tumult of chatter.

"Who would have ever thought that I would live to see such a thing as this?" Richard said aloud, his voice blending with the noise of the crowd. "Be damned to Wyatt and his rabble!" He rode up and down the street, gathering information. The old Duke of Norfolk had been relieved of his command for having been beaten at Rochester, and Bishop Gardiner had convinced Mary to appoint the Earl of Pembroke and Lord Clinton in his stead. Their orders were to blow up the bridges if it became necessary.

"We'll blow up the bridge. Blow up the bridge . . . hold back the rebels!" came the shout of the throng. It was as if there was magic in the air, a feeling of unity that made the barriers of social position, religious or political views, vanish for the moment. Even those who had been known to view the Spanish marriage with alarm, who had condemned Mary, now shouted out her praise and the view that they would fight any invasion.

"Thank God Heather is safe in Norfolk," Richard murmured beneath his breath, looking about the crowd. What would she think of all this? He tried to second-guess this Thomas Wyatt. What would be his plan of attack? Would he row boats across the Thames? Would he try to take the Tower? Or was it his intent to march his men across one of the many bridges? If so, which bridge?

"London Bridge," Richard swore. He could hear a sound like thunder and knew instinctively that it was the noise of guns and cannon. Despite his chattering teeth, his fatigue, and the frost upon his eyebrows and eyelashes, he rode in the direction of the sound, intent upon doing all he could to offer protection from the invaders. Not since the Wars of the Roses had London been so endangered.

Reaching the bridge, Richard saw that Wyatt had indeed reached London Bridge. Joining the throng of hundreds of men who stood upon the northern bank, daring the rebels to cross, he looked sadly at the floating pieces of the center drawbridge. So that had been the cause of the explosion he had heard. He watched and waited to see just what would happen now. As cold as it was, he could be certain of one thing: they would not want to try to swim the river.

"Why, they seem to be diggin'," shouted one old man, shading his eyes with his hand. "Do they hope to reach Cathay? Ha! 'Twill be a good place for 'em after we are through with 'em."

Richard strained his eyes to see what was happening. They were indeed digging. He was amazed to see that there were even some of the enemy who were attempting to repair the bridge, ignoring the blast of the cannon. Digging, pick-and-shoveling at the frozen earth, they looked like worker ants, their numbers growing all the time.

From somewhere came the shout: "Rise, you Londoners! To the aid of the queen! Rise!" Looking behind him, Richard could see that the words were having their effect. The number of men who offered their response to the cry was staggering. Wyatt would find that London Bridge would be stoutly held against his attack.

As if sensing that he was defeated in this phase of his attack, Thomas Wyatt gave the signal to his men to turn back.

"They're leaving. We showed them what stout-hearted Englishmen can do when provoked!" shouted a youth in triumph.

Richard was not so fooled. Being older and wiser than the young man behind him, he knew that they had not seen the last of Wyatt and his band. Where were they marching? Surely they must realize that each of the bridges crossing to the city would be just as difficult to cross and just as rigidly guarded. His question was answered in just a few moments. Thomas Wyatt was headed toward Kingston, to make his way from there into the city.

"To Kingston!" Richard shouted, leading a band of men that way. When they arrived they could see that Wyatt and his men had marched upriver, crossed the Thames at Kingston, and were now marching down the north bank through Westminster. They were armed with gun carriages and a few handguns, and Richard damned the advantage gunpowder would give them. He and the men riding behind him had only swords, clubs, and stones.

The black of the storm clouds rolling over London set a mood of gloom as the men of the city gathered along the banks of the Thames. A few of the defenders were shot, and some of the invaders were wounded by those most brave souls who ventured forth with fearless frenzy.

"The French are coming to our aid!" shouted Wyatt, as if to bolster his men's courage. They had no doubt heard the news that the Duke of Suffolk had turned tail and hidden in the forest of Warwickshire. Richard could not help but admire the man's courage and the way he sat his horse, like a prince. How sad that it had come to this. Men like Wyatt should have been fighting for the queen, not against her.

"Englishman fighting against Englishman. Aye, 'tis a sorry sight for these old eyes," shouted a man near Richard.

The fighting was raging through the streets of London. Striking out with his sword and felling an opponent, Richard was surprised to see the old man Perriwincle up ahead, riding in his wagon.

"Perriwincle!" he shouted, feeling an instant fondness for the old man. "Over here. Perriwincle!"

The old man took off his hat, waving it frantically in the air. The sound that he emitted from his throat was a poor attempt at a war cry, a whoop more comical than threatening. It was as if he sought to frighten these men with his hollering.

"Perriwincle!" Richard shouted again, riding in the man's direction. This time the old man heard him. Leaping from his wagon, he ran to Richard, pushing and shoving his way through the crowd, grinning from ear to ear. It was as if the years had been suddenly washed away and the old man was a young and spry soldier again.

"We'll hold 'em, we'll hold 'em," he shouted, striking out at a man twice his size who tried to block his way. He looked in Richard's direction, judging him friend or foe, and only then did he recognize the man astride the horse. He stopped yelling and fighting and stood with his mouth wide open in shock. "Richard?"

"It's me, though I doubt that you can recognize me with all this mud splattered about my head and shoulders. Are you ready for this fight?"

"Aye, I'm ready. But you? Mistress Heather has been worried nigh out of her head over your whereabouts."

"Heather? She has written to you?"

"Written? No! She is here. In London. Searching all over for you, she be."

"In London?" He reached down to grab hold of the old man's leather doublet. "Are you certain? Have you seen her?"

"Aye. She's staying at her father's house, if you will. Though I doubt it not that she is running about the town asking everyone if they have seen you." Perriwincle clucked his tongue. "A woman in love is hard to manage. She is nigh frantic, she is."

"Running about London? She'll be caught up in this and injured." Richard's face turned pale. He could think of nothing else but that Heather might be in danger. "I must find her. I must." She would not know of the danger which swarmed in the city streets.

Leaving Perriwincle, he rode in the direction of Ludgate Hill with the rebels at his heels.

"There's one of them now!" came a shout. Blocking the way were several robust Londoners armed with stones and clubs. "Leadin' his traitorous bastards."

Richard was not prepared to be met by resistance from the front. His fear for Heather's well-being had made him careless. He twisted away just as a wooden club struck forward, knocking him from his horse.

"Get him. Get the traitor. He will not get the best of us." Voices. Noise and tumult and pain. Two hulking giants jerked his arms up high behind his back, forcing him to his knees. He bucked and struggled like a wild stallion, only to feel a searing pain, agony, as he was struck full force upon the head. His body convulsed and grew limp as blackness closed over him. Down, down into a darkened pit he seemed to fall, plummeting into the depths of oblivion.

54

HEATHER PUSHED IMPATIENTLY at the corpulent form of the richly clothed banker who blocked her way. She had to reach Whitehall before Wyatt and his followers did. If Richard was anywhere in the city he would be near the queen.

"If." The word tasted bitter on her tongue. Where else could he be? The possibility that some ill had befallen him made her shiver, and she reached down to pull her cloak tightly about her. "He has to be all right. He has to be." The all-consuming urge to find him pushed her on.

She found Mary where she had expected her to be, in the chapel, down on her knees in prayer. Mary's guards were even now begging her to flee, imploring her silently from beyond the door. Mary would not do so. Rising from the ground, she looked them squarely in the eye.

"I will not turn cowardly now," she said with furious zeal. "God will not turn his back on me. I promised him that if he but gives me the strength I will bring England back to him. It is my fault that this tragedy stalks us. I have been too weak, too soft on heretics. No more the gentle queen. No more." Her eyes were gleaming as she jerked at the crucifix. "Kneel! We will ask again for his protection and divine help."

Without thought to propriety, Heather rushed forward. "Your Majesty. Richard. Is he with you? Where . . . ?"

Mary's eyes narrowed as she looked upon the intruder, and her face turned pale as she crossed herself. "You! How dare you enter thus?" There was no trace of kindness, only pain. "I thought you a sweet and virtuous child, but you are as evil as Salome, that evil temptress."

Heather bowed so low that her forehead nearly touched the floor. "Think what you will of me. I care only that Richard is safe. If you know his whereabouts, please tell me. This I beg of you."

Mary's voice was low and hoarse. "I have not seen him for months. Not since he fled with you to the northlands. If you seek him, it must be elsewhere." She flung her hands about in frustration. "Go!"

She had not seen him. It had been Heather's last hope. Putting her hand to her mouth, Heather stifled a cry of desperation. Why had she ever let him leave Norfolk alone? "My fault," she whispered. "My fault." The sound of the queen's voice saying her Paters and Aves drowned out the words.

Heather walked to the doorway. The gust of winter wind nearly took her breath away as she left the palace, but she hardly noticed. It was as if she walked in a trance, as if the sights and sounds around her were not real, only a cruel pantomime. Only the sound of Perriwincle's voice could cut through her silence.

"I found him. He's here. I found him, or rather he found me, he did." Over the rocky cobblestones he ran until he was by her side. "Richard. He's here. I should have bloody well known he would not let her queenship down."

"Richard?" It was as if some fairy godmother had waved a magic wand. Laughter bubbled forth from Heather's lips. "Richard? He's all right? He's safe?" She hugged Perriwincle with such a ferocity that he nearly lost his breath.

"He's looking for you, he is. I thought for certain he would find you before I did."

"I was inside with the queen." Heather gestured toward the palace. "She has not quite forgiven me yet, but then, I am not surprised. Perhaps someday she will know what it is like to love beyond all reason."

Perriwincle led her to the wagon, helping her up on the high wooden seat beside him. "We had best go home. Things are getting a bit rough, they are. Besides, that is the best place for Richard to find you."

His reasoning was sound. There was scuffling and fighting everywhere. The streets had become a battleground. "Perhaps when we get home he will be there to meet us." She smiled, wondering how her father would react to Richard. He had been as a lamb lately, after his wife's threats to leave him if he uttered one unkind word. It had been pleasant around the house for once, without his moods and tantrums.

Tabitha met them at the door, her blue eyes wide with fright. "I thought you might have been injured, Mistress Heather. I was worried nigh unto death."

"Where is Mother?" Heather asked, looking about her.

"Up in her bedchamber, looking at the carnage from her window. She sent me to find you, but I was afraid to go too far down the street. The rebels are everywhere!"

"Ha. They are outnumbered," Perriwincle growled. "They will soon be put in their proper place. Why, there must be at least twenty-five thousand men who have come to Mary's aid. That brave lady's words have mustered a veritable army. We'll bloody well show these rebels, we will." He fled out the door again, anxious to be back in the midst of the fighting.

"Richard's here," Heather exclaimed to Tabitha. "Perri saw him. He's safe."

"God be praised!" Tabitha squeezed Heather's hand with a familiarity she seldom expressed, then quickly let go, as if suddenly rememering her station. "I'm sorry, Mistress Heather."

"Don't call me Mistress Heather, Tabitha. We are friends, you and I. Let there be no barriers between us. When I go back to Norfolk I would like you to go with me. It is not right that you must stay here and work your life away. You are young and pretty and deserve much more. You deserve happiness and a man to love you."

Tabitha shook her head. "I am not pretty, I am plain. No man will ever want me. I am content here, really I am."

"You are pretty! Your hair shines golden in the sun, your eyes are wide and the most beautiful shade of blue I have ever seen—"

"I am too tall and gangly. I tower over all the stablehands, the butcher's son, and the baker's brother. Who would ask for me?" They walked up the stairs to the solar and stood before the warmth of the blazing fire. "But I would like to go with you. I have missed you, Miss . . . Heather."

They sat before the fire with hot mugs of cider, and Heather told Tabitha all about Richard's homeland, about the broads—those open expanses of water which dotted the mainland.

"And there are the dearest cottages with thatched roofs made of reeds. Oh, Tabitha, you would fall in love with the countryside and the people as I have. I am no more the city girl. London can be cruel at times. Come with me."

Tabitha leaned back in her chair and closed her eyes as if imagining herself there. "My very own cottage." Only the sound of banging on the door disturbed her reverie. With a start of fright she bolted up from her chair. "Oh, dear, dear me. What if that is one of those rebels? What if they march in here and kill us all?" A log snapped in the fire and she cried out, thinking it to be gunfire. How she hated the sound of it. It was a rarity. Few men had guns. Most were content with their swords, but this night . . .

"It's Perri, Tabitha. I can tell by the rhythm of the knocking." Heather fled down the stairs to open the door for the old man. "What is it, Perri . . . ?" she began. The look on his face alerted her to the fact that something was very, very wrong. Tears trickled down the old man's face. "What is it?"

"How could they? Fools. Bumbling fools." He struck

out at the doorframe with his fists. "Bloody idiots. How could they think such a thing? A terrible, terrible mistake it is."

Taking him by the shoulders, Heather led him inside. "Who are fools? Who are idiots? What has happened?" she asked gently.

"We have to tell the queen. She has to set him free." He shook his head in disbelief. "How could it have happened?"

"What, Perri?" Heather was unnerved by the way he was acting. Were the rebels winning then after all? "Whom does Mary have to free? Don't tell me that you are suddenly growing soft for these followers of Thomas Wyatt's." She tried to maneuver him up to the solar, but he shook free of her. Never had she seen him in such a state. "They must pay for what they have done, Perri. I know that Thomas Wyatt thought to save England from Spanish influence by what he tried to do, but he was misguided. Mary is the rightful queen, not Elizabeth, not Lady Jane Grey." She shook him by the shoulders. "What is wrong, Perri? Are the rebels winning?"

"He's in the Tower. He's in the bloody Tower like some criminal, like some traitor. Richard."

Heather felt the floor seem to sway beneath her. Reaching out to grab for the doorframe, she clung to it for support. "Richard? What are you saying, Perri? What are you saying?"

His eyes were glazed in shock. "It can't be true. It isn't true. I saw with my own eyes the way he fought for Mary. Bloody, bloody fools."

She nearly screamed at him. "Perri! What are you saying?"

"It's Richard," he answered. "He's been taken to the Tower with those of Wyatt's ilk. They are calling him a traitor."

55

IT WAS COLD. Cold and damp. Richard reached up to pull imaginary covers over himself, only to be confused when his fingers came back empty. He tossed and turned upon the rock-hard straw mattress, trying to clear the mists from before his eyes.

"Where am I?" he mumbled. He tried to move, but it only intensified the pain in his head. His nostrils inhaled the room's stale odor and he tried with difficulty to focus his eyes. "Gray stone walls. What the devil?" He was confused, thinking himself again Seton's prisoner. But no. He had been freed, freed by that young lad.

Slowly he looked about him, the throbbing in his head growing worse as he tried to sit up. "Bars on the windows. I am in prison." Had he merely exchanged one cell for another? Moaning, he struggled from the bed, making his way slowly to look at the world through the small opening in the wall. "The Tower! What the . . . ?"

Slowly the events of the previous night danced before his eyes and he remembered. "No!" He was not alone in this his prison. Two other men sat in their respective corners looking at him with wary eyes. Their expressions seemed to tell him that they thought him "touched."

"We've lost," said one of the men.

"Aye. It will be our heads or worse."

Richard paced about, trying desperately to ignore his headache. He had to get out of here, and quickly, before the world tumbled about his shoulders. Clinging to the door, he rattled it back and forth with a clamor that sounded through the stillness of the early morning.

"Pipe down, you blighters!" A guard appeared at the door of the cell to scowl and grumble.

"Let me out of here. This is a mistake!" Richard demanded.

"Yes, your mistake," came the answer as the guard started to walk away.

"Come back! Please. I should not be here."

"That's what they all say."

Richard clenched his jaw in impotent anger. "I am ever the queen's man, loyal to her majesty. I fought for her, not against her. This is a mistake. Open this door at once."

The guard chuckled. "My, my, my, if we ain't hoity-toity. It is no mistake, my fine lord. We have been told about you." With that said he disappeared, leaving Richard more confused than before.

Sitting back down on his straw bed, he heard one of his fellow cellmates say, "Did you hear what he said? Do you believe his story?"

"Of course not. What would you have him say? He's just trying to save his own neck." The dark-eyed man frowned at Richard and began mumbling to himself.

The words of the guard echoed in Richard's ears: "We have been told about you." What did he mean by such a statement? Was it possible that Seton was involved in this? No. It was only ill fate that had put Richard in this position. Somehow he would get a message to the queen and all would be well. Mary would never believe him to be a traitor. He thought of Heather, praying fervently that she had not been harmed in all of this. Somehow he must get word to her.

"You there." It was the voice of the man who had frowned at him, a wizened old man who reminded him strangely of Perriwincle. "Just who are you?"

"My name is Richard Morgan. I am, or was, one of

the queen's advisers. I was swept along with the tide of rebellion while searching for someone. Attacked from behind by men like myself who were fighting for the queen." He laughed sarcastically, bitterly. "Tell me, what was the outcome?"

"Wyatt was overcome near Temple Bar. Like you, like us, he is in the Tower."

"And the queen?"

"She is safe. She will marry her Spanish prince and bring us all under Spain's thumb." He cast Richard a glance which told him he did not want to talk more about it. Neither did Richard. It was like some monstrous cruel joke. That he who had constantly been loyal to Mary should be thought a traitor was beyond belief.

Not content just to sit and wait, he again banged and rattled the door to his cell. This time his commotion was answered quickly, the guard accompanying another man.

"Calm down. Calm down. I got a man here to see you," growled the guard.

Richard looked at the face of his visitor. "Stephen!" Never had he been so glad to see another man in all his life. Stepping out of the way of the door, he stood silently by as the guard issued his friend through the door.

"You can have until I'm finished with my rounds to talk." The guard stalked off.

Stephen Vickery's voice was no more than a whisper. "What in the name of heaven is happening? The word at court is that you are one of Wyatt's rebels."

"You know me better than that, Stephen."

"Aye, I know you would never turn against Mary. But there are others, Seton among them, who are crying for your head."

"Seton? I should have known he was behind this. He abducted me on my way to meet with you in London. I sent you a message and he intercepted it. I spent more than a week in his castle dungeon before I managed to escape." He kicked angrily at the straw on the floor.

"So that's where you were." Stephen Vickery pulled at his beard as he always did when pondering a matter. "But how could he have been behind your being captured? I tell you that he could not."

"Fate. Fate and ill fortune, my friend. I had just learned from Perriwincle that Heather was in the city and I was trying to find her when I got lost in the scuffle and brought down by one of my own. Seton could not have planned it better." Realizing that the two other prisoners were staring at him, Richard lowered his voice and drew Stephen with him to the far side of the small room. "He is the traitor. Seton. Sitting on both sides of the fence just in case Mary was the winner."

"Seton is calling for your death. He claims that you are a traitor, and he has brought forth several witnesses to so testify. Even, I regret to say, your old love Catherine Todd."

"But Mary would never believe—"

"Mary is angered still by the fact that you ran away with one of her ladies-in-waiting. To her mind Heather is no better than Anne Boleyn, and you no more her trusted adviser. Had that not happened, I have no doubt that she would still believe in your loyalty." He shook his head sadly. "You will, I fear, pay dearly for your love of Heather."

"And so the joke is on me." Richard's laugh was mocking, more of a sob than sound of mirth. His bitterness showed plainly upon his face. To have put his thoughts, his loyalty, his very life into the cause of Mary's safety and well-being, he felt betrayed that she could now turn her back on him just because he had run off with the woman he loved. She turned her back upon him who was ever her loyal servant and turned instead to the man who at every turn had sought to bring her down. "Seton is the winner. He has had his revenge upon me."

"It is not just you, Richard. Nor is Seton the only one crying for blood. Renard is crying out for the

Princess Elizabeth's arrest and Courtenay is languishing in his cell. Lady Jane Grey and her husband are to be executed tomorrow, though the poor child had naught to do with this uprising." Stephen Vickery toyed nervously with the sleeve of his doublet.

"So it seems that the innocent as well as the guilty will suffer from this Wyatt's rebellion. What of Heather? Is she safe?"

"I have not heard from her or seen her since we arrived in London, but I believe that she is well. It is you I am worried about now. Many of Mary's advisers have censured her for being too merciful."

" 'Merciful Mary,' some have called her."

"I fear that she will be called that no longer. Not if Renard and Seton and the others have their way. Renard is telling her that as long as there are any enemies in this land Philip will be in danger. Bishop Gardiner has argued that mercy to the nation requires that traitors should be put to death." The footsteps of the guard sounded down the hall and Stephen Vickery stiffened in anticipation of being ordered out of the cell, but the footsteps passed on by.

"And you fear that I will be a casualty?"

"Yes, Richard. Yes. Mary is as besotted by her love for this Spaniard as you are by the love you bear Heather. As you would seek to protect the woman you love from all harm, so would Mary seek to protect Philip from any who might think to cause him harm."

"I am no traitor!" In anger and frustration Richard pounded his fists into the hard stone of the wall.

"But if you are perceived as such, if your enemies triumph, you will suffer for it. I have tried to talk with Mary, but she will not listen. She is in a frenzy of religious zeal. She had a Te Deum sung in St. Paul's and in Westminster Abbey, both to calm the people and to give thanks to God for her victory."

Again the footsteps sounded but this time they did not walk down the hall. "You. Your time is up."

"No. Wait. Stephen, I have an idea. My brother.

He is a priest now. Perhaps she will listen to him. We must try. I beseech you to bring my brother to London." It was his only hope, his only prayer. "And Rafael Mendosa as well. If Seton can bring forth his witnesses, false though they be, then so can I."

Vickery nodded his head as he walked through the doorway, and Richard knew what he was thinking. It would be Richard's only hope, his only salvation. "God willing, they will arrive in time," he whispered before the door was shut once again to silence.

56

"A TRAITOR. A traitor. You align yourself with a traitor." Thomas Bowen clucked his tongue and rubbed his nose in agitation. "What were you thinking of, girl? To go off with such as him when you could have been married to a fine, upstanding citizen like Hugh Seton."

"Don't call him traitor. Don't you ever call him traitor!" Heather shouted. The weeks of Richard's confinement, not knowing his fate and being denied access to him, had taken a toll on both her health and spirit.

"He is a traitor. The queen calls him so. Seton calls him so. I call him so."

Heather looked him straight in the eye. "And yet as I recall, it was you who were of a mind to open the gates of the city to Wyatt and his men, just because you do not favor the queen's economic policies. Richard is no insurgent, no betrayer. I will go to my death saying that he is as free from guilt as a newborn babe!"

Thomas Bowen looked at Heather with apprehension, fearful of causing her further anger. If it were known outside these walls that he had thought, even for a moment, of taking Wyatt's side, it would bode him ill.

"Hush, hush, daughter. Do not carry on so. Do you want half of London to hear you? I have my business to think of. If you want to pine away for some man who is as good as dead, then do so." Turning his back upon her, he walked away.

There had been no further mention of what he had told her so many months ago of not being her father, but Heather remembered it well and felt as if the tie which had bound her to him for so many years, the years of longing for him to love her, was finally broken. If she had made excuses for his heartlessness and selfishness before, she did not do so now. There was no love between them, only perhaps a truce, an unspoken bargain that neither would push the other too far. Blythe Bowen deserved at least a little peace in her own house. But upon the matter of Richard's guilt or innocence Heather would not keep silent.

"He is wrong. I know that he is. Richard Morgan is no traitor," Tabitha whispered, stepping out of the shadows. Wiping her hands upon her apron, she sought to calm Heather's frazzled nerves. "Perriwincle saw what happened. Why won't someone believe him?"

Heather picked up a long spoon to stir the soup, swishing it about with such strong strokes that it splashed onto the kitchen floor. "Because he is a stable-keeper. His word is as nothing against such testimony as Hugh Seton's or Catherine Todd's. There was such confusion that day that there is no one who can come forth and say for certain that Richard was not fighting on the side of the rebels. Richard's trial is coming up soon and I can do nothing but stand by and wait."

"They will not let you see him?" Tabitha's voice held a great pity.

"No. The queen has forbidden it, though I do not think she realizes how cruel she is being in denying me."

Tabitha looked shyly at the floor, not wanting to seem overbold. "If it is the queen who stands in your way, why not go to her and make her see that Richard could not be guilty in this matter?"

"The queen hates me now. It would do no good." Heather stopped stirring for a moment, remembering how angry the queen had been in just the short span of time she had talked with her in Whitehall. Of course there had been danger then.

"You must try," Tabitha mumbled.

Heather pondered the matter. "If I were to throw myself on her mercy, beg her to at least listen to reason, what harm could it do? Stephen has talked with her, Anne Fairfax has reasoned with her, and now I will go to see her." Stephen had sent for Richard's brother and the Spanish emissary, Mendosa, but with winter engulfing the land just now, it could take weeks for them to arrive. Tossing the spoon aside, Heather clenched her fists in determination. "I will do it! Let her frown and snarl at me, I do not care. She will listen to what I have to say. She must." Looking over at Tabitha, she could see that the servant girl was smiling, and it struck her that despite her shyness, Tabitha seemed to have an inner strength, the ability to gently prod one into doing what was necessary.

Taking off her apron, straightening her hair, Heather readied herself to go before Mary. It was now or never, for time was of the essence; every moment that Richard spent in the Tower meant more danger for him, more confirmation of his supposed guilt.

Dressed in a plain dark blue woolen gown, her hair drawn back in a bun, a thick cloak thrown over her shoulders, Heather walked through the mud and snow to Whitehall. She had not bothered to change her clothes, reasoning that to appear plain and dowdy just might wipe away her "harlot" image in the queen's eyes. She would plead for Richard as friend, not lover.

Walking up the steep steps of the palace, she whispered over and over the words she would use to soften Mary's heart. Pushing past the guards, several of whom recognized her from her Greenwich stay, she entered the hall.

"Why, if it isn't the merchant's daughter," a familiar voice purred. Catherine Todd, hovering as always before a mirror. "Have you come to sell us more of your father's cloth?" The hall twittered with laughter.

"I have come to see the queen," Heather answered, holding her head high and ignoring the malice in the green-eyed beauty's voice.

"The queen?" Catherine Todd walked around Heather, eyeing her up and down with a mocking smile. Her eyes did not miss Heather's plain garments. "You wish to see the queen? Have you an appointment, merchant's daughter?" She turned to her companions. "It appears to me that *she* has need of a merchant. Dressed as she is, she would do better to come before a baker than a queen. Of course, keeping the company she has of late, perhaps she has fallen onto hard times." She lowered her voice and hissed, "Traitor's whore!"

It took every fiber of Heather's being to maintain calm, to keep from striking out at the woman with the vicious tongue. It could only harm Richard to create a scene. "It is not for you to judge me, Catherine Todd. God alone decides what evil we have done. As for me, I would rather stand in my shoes on judgment day than in yours. And as to traitors, I know of none. I only remember a man who risked his life for his queen and his country. Can you say as much for what you have done?"

"I have done nothing," Catherine Todd retorted.

"That is exactly the point," Heather answered, stepping past the brightly clad woman. Announcing herself to Mary's guards, she waited until they beckoned to her, and then entered the presence of the queen.

Mary seemed to have aged overnight. Her face, always pale and drawn, now seemed nearly white and much thinner. Sitting in a chair at the farthest corner of the large room, she eyed Heather without even a hint of a welcome. "Well?" was all she said.

Heather fell to her knees before the queen, bowing her head in a gracious gesture of humility. "I come to beg mercy and justice from a wise and worthy ruler," Heather began.

"I know what you would have of me, that I release

your lover." The queen's voice was harsh, and Heather had no doubt that the expression matched the tone.

"My friend and your loyal servant," Heather said adamantly. "Your Majesty."

"What games are you playing with me?" The words were shrill. "Oh, do get up. How I hate to talk to someone groveling before me."

Heather rose to her feet, looking the queen square in the face. "I play no games, my queen. I merely come to seek justice for one who has always been loyal to you. Richard Morgan."

The queen's eyes blazed with fury. "Richard Morgan, Richard Morgan, Richard Morgan. He was once my friend and my most trusted adviser, but like all the others in my life that I have cherished, he too has betrayed me. It was Thomas Wyatt's side that he was on when delivered into the hands of this justice you talk about."

"No. He would never seek to betray England, nor you. My servant tells me that he was worried after my safety and riding back to London to see to my well-being. Can a man be called a traitor to show concern for another?"

"I have heard testimony of those who would call him traitor and deny your words, child." It had been so long since Mary had called her "child." For just a moment Heather had hopes that perhaps Mary had given her forgiveness.

"They are mistaken. False words do not make facts. Remember, your Majesty, how valiantly Richard, your servant, fought for you, even suffering a near-mortal wound to bring your letter to those who would fight your enemies and declare you rightful queen?" Heather's eyes did not flicker. "As you needed him then, he needs you now, to fight against his enemies, those who would seek to bring him harm."

Mary Tudor reached for her cross, fingering it as if it would help her know the truth. For just a moment her expression softened and she looked like the gentle queen again, but just as quickly her expression turned grim.

"They have all betrayed me. Courtenay, Richard, Wyatt, and even my own sister, Elizabeth. I do not know whom to trust. I only know that I cannot risk harm coming to this land again. There must be no more strife, no more battles. I must make England safe for Philip, so that we can rule together in peace. I must wipe away all who defy God's will in bringing us back to Rome." A flush spread over her face. "He desires me and loves me, this Philip, though I am over eleven years his senior. Together we will bring forth an heir to unite England's future."

"And Richard will help you make this a peaceful land. He has always counseled you wisely, has he not?" Heather took a step forward, her arms outstretched, imploring.

"Yes, he has always been most wise." The tone of her voice was gentle, as if she remembered all the times when he had been at her side. "Perhaps I should at least hear him out in this matter. I am ever a just queen."

"As well as a wise queen." Heather scarcely dared to breathe. Was it possible that Mary would change her mind concerning Richard's guilt? Surely if she at least heard Richard's story, all would be well.

"Ah, if it is not my dear betrothed. Do you seek mercy for your lover's treachery? If so, you are well wasting your time." It was Hugh Seton's voice and Heather shivered at the thought of his presence. He swept into the room with the air of one very sure of himself.

Heather stood up, facing him. "I am here to speak with the queen and not with you."

His smile was a snarl. "The queen listens to me in all matters; therefore you *will* need talk with me."

Heather turned toward the queen. "Richard will never get a fair hearing from this man. His hatred runs too deep. Please, your Majesty, let us speak of this matter alone."

The anger had now returned to Mary's face, no doubt at the reminder of what Richard and Heather had done. Hugh Seton now appeared to be the wronged party, a man wounded deeply by the heartlessness of the woman he was to have married. "Hugh Seton will stay. He *does* have a say in this matter. And as to his hatred, I would say that it is warranted." Her eyes flashed at Heather in warning to keep silent. Turning to Hugh Seton, she asked, "You will give him a fair hearing, will you not?"

He bowed gallantly. "Despite my wounded heart, I have pondered this matter of Morgan most deeply. I have prayed for guidance fervently, and God has spoken to me. I will admit that Morgan has in the past been a steadfast pillar of strength, but Satan is ever the evil tempter leading men into sin and betrayal." He cast his eyes toward Heather as if saying that she was the instrument by which the devil had worked. "Thomas Wyatt also has been up to this time a loyal subject, but he too must be punished for his treachery. They are of like kind, my dearest queen. Let them live, and like the serpents of hell, they will tear the realm apart with their poisonous fangs."

The queen gasped and cradled her hands at her breasts. Seton's speech had clearly undone all that Heather had tried to do. Beneath her breath Heather cursed the man, knowing the fiery sting of hatred.

Seton continued, coming in for the kill. "I ask that in your wisdom you see fit to execute those who seek England's downfall. Make them an example before all who would seek to harm thy royal personage. Only then can we have a strong and peaceful future."

"No!" Heather cried out, her knees trembling, her pulse pounding. "Richard is innocent. He is not a traitor. He is not. He is not. He has never sought England's downfall, only her glory." She touched the hem of the queen's gown in supplication. "Please, your Majesty. Please."

But Mary was not of a mind to offer mercy. Her temper broke as she remembered how close she had come to losing her crown and her life. Years of misery and mistreatment now boiled over like a caldron. All of her gentleness now turned to fury, her affection for Richard Morgan to rage at his supposed betrayal. "He will stand trial at this same time on the morrow. Richard Morgan will be judged by men for his earthly misdeeds, and may God forgive him for his sins."

57

HEATHER CLOSED THE door to her bedroom behind her, reaching up to draw the folds of her cloak securely around her.

"Where are you going?" The sound of the voice startled her.

"Tabitha!" she said, whirling around. It was a relief to see that it was the tall blond servant girl, for had it been her mother, there might have been a scene. "I'm going to the Tower to see Richard. Even the queen herself cannot keep me from him now."

"The Tower? You must be insane to attempt such a thing!" Tabitha blushed at the boldness of her words.

"Perhaps there are those who would call me so. Others would call me a woman in love," Heather answered with a smile.

"You may well sacrifice your own freedom just for a moment with him."

"I would sacrifice my very life! I love him." Heather walked toward the stairs with Tabitha following behind. At the top of the stairs Heather paused to look into Tabitha's wide blue eyes. "It is a thing which I must do."

Tabitha looked at her in awe. "I have always thought you the most beautiful of women, but never have I admired you as much as I do now. I can only hope that someday I will feel such a love as this."

"I hope that you will. It makes life worth the living." She thought a moment, then said, "Come with me, Tabitha. At least as far as the Tower entrance. Please."

"I would be proud to come with you, Heather. Besides, they will be on the lookout for one woman, not two. Two servants should be able to sneak past the guards." She hurried up the stairs to her own quarters, and when she came back she too was wearing a hooded cloak.

The dark gray shadows of the clouds clung to the moon as if to the arms of a lover as Heather and Tabitha walked along. Dressed in dark brown and black, their hoods hiding their faces, they seemed to blend with the night.

I know that even if this meeting with Richard is but brief, it is well worth the risk, Heather thought. To see Richard before the ordeal of his trial was an all-consuming desire. One sweet moment of ecstasy that might well have to last forever. But she would not think of that now.

The sight of the grim gray fortress rose before them and Heather remembered another time when she had trod this same path. Another time long ago. A lifetime ago.

"The Tower," she whispered, wondering how many other women had loved ones imprisoned there. It was said that no one ever escaped from its dungeons. Only death or a pardon would bring a man beyond its walls. But if she could help Richard escape, she would, she vowed. "Though my very own life be forfeit."

There were many other towers besides the White Tower—the Bloody Tower, Constable Tower, Bowyer Tower, the Salt Tower. In which one was Richard imprisoned? she wondered.

As they approached the river, Heather could smell its dankness. Her heart leapt with the thought of laying eyes once again upon the man she loved. So long since she had seen him, so very long. Nearly eternity, it seemed.

They neared the doors to the fortress and banged

upon the door, to be met by a guard who gruffly asked their business.

"We are faithful servants of the prisoner Richard Morgan," Tabitha stated, holding forth a basket of food in front of her, that which Heather had prepared. "His trial is tomorrow and we have brought food for him."

"Food? I can take it to him!" The guard licked his lips and it was obvious that the basket would not get much farther than beyond the door.

"No. Please. We want to see him and give it to him personally. As his servants he will need to tell us things that must be done to look after his estates," Heather quickly interjected.

"He has been ever a kind lord and we would be with him on this night," Tabitha whispered.

The guard started to protest, but seeing that it would be easier to comply than to argue, he mumbled, "All right. All right." No doubt he had been disturbed from his dice game or other such entertainment and thought the two women a bother. Nonetheless, he led them up the spiral stone stairs. Surely no harm could come from one visit, he undoubtedly thought. "Watch your step," he barked, but Heather could think of only one thing: she was going to see her lover. Tripping, she nearly fell, but Tabitha quickly helped her regain her balance. "I told you to watch your step!" he growled.

The guard presented the two women to a surly-looking prison guard who led them through winding passages until they came to a thick iron-studded wooden door. Jiggling his many keys, this guard at last found the right one and opened the door.

"Only one of you can see him. Which one be it?"

Heather quickly stepped forward.

"I will wait for you downstairs," Tabitha announced, fleeing down the stone-floored corridor before the guard could change his mind. In her hurry she nearly collided with a tall handsome man with hair the color of dark wood. He touched her gently on the shoulder with hands that made Tabitha quiver. Looking up, she met his sparkling brown eyes and felt a tidal wave of emotion sweep over her.

"You are in a great hurry, *Señorita,*" the man said in a voice lightly touched with an accent. "Do you flee to or from a lover?"

Tabitha blushed hotly. "Neither. I accompanied my friend to see the man she loves on the day before his trial. He is innocent, yet we fear he will be condemned."

He looked at her with interest. "I too have a friend imprisoned within these walls. We have much in common, you and I."

"A friend? Who? Perhaps I have heard of him."

"Richard Morgan is his name. Rafael Mendosa is mine."

Tabitha stared at him. "Richard Morgan? That is the man Heather has gone to see."

He shook his head. "Ah, I see. Then perhaps it would be better if I spoke with him later. Three would be a crowd, no?"

"Yes," she answered, feeling an instant liking for this man with the face of an angel and the body of a Greek god. Now more than ever she wished that she were beautiful. What would it be like to love a man like this?

"Then let me escort you home," the man said.

"No. I promised I would wait. I would not want Heather to be alone. The night offers many dangers." Tabitha started to leave him, but he quickly caught up with her.

"Then we will wait together, you and I."

Tabitha cast her eyes in the direction that Heather had walked, wondering what was happening. "We will wait together."

Heather heard the heavy door close behind her and tried desperately to grow accustomed to the dim light of the cell. "Richard," she called out softly. There was no answer, and for a moment she feared that he was not within the room, but the familiar warmth of his arms encircled her waist, drawing her near.

"Heather! Heather! My God, I must be dreaming. If so, I hope I never wake up."

Heather put her arms around his neck, clinging to him, burying her face in the strength of his chest. "Did you think I could stay away?"

He kissed her then, a kiss which spoke of his love. Her mouth searched blindly for his and found it, her lips parting beneath the caress of his mouth, arousing them both to hunger.

"You taste of honey. So sweet, my love." He touched her face with gentle, probing fingers, as if to memorize her features. "I hunger for you every day, every night. You fill my thoughts and my dreams. My need for you is like a fire in the blood."

He kissed her savagely then, with all the flame of his longing. At last he said, "If I must die, at least I will die happily, having loved you and been loved by you."

Heather felt the warmth of his mouth, the hardness of his body, the rapture of his roaming hands caressing her. The hunger of her own desires overwhelmed her. It was as if the world fell away beneath them in a shower of sparks flaming into fire.

"Make love to me, Richard," she breathed, bringing him down with her to the hard stone floor. "Take me . . . only so can we live."

He groaned, his mouth moving to the softness of her throat, his hands cupping her breasts. "Yes. Yes." Suddenly he moved away. "No, I cannot take you here. Not here. I do not want to put you in any danger. It is not good to be within the arms of a traitor."

"You are no traitor. I know that as surely as I know that I breathe. But I would have come to you even if you were." She felt for his hand and laid it against her cheek. "My dearest love, I want you so."

"You must forget me," he whispered.

"No. Never," she denied his words fiercely. "I will remember you until the day I die."

His hands stroked her hair. "You have your entire life before you. You must marry and raise the children we were denied, with a man who is free to give you his name." The very thought tore at his soul, but he must think of her happiness.

She sobbed softly. "I want no other man, no one else's children." She reached out to touch him. "Oh, Richard, what is to become of us? I cannot live without you. Not for one hour, not for one more day!"

"If I am judged a traitor and beheaded, it will be necessary for you to do so," he murmured in her hair, fighting back his own tears.

"If only we were back at the manor in Norfolk. We were happy there," she cried. "We will find some way. You have done nothing wrong. God cannot turn his back on you. No. You will not be judged guilty."

"But if it happens, if it is God's will—"

"Hush! I won't hear of it."

"You must. If something happens, I want you to seek aid from my brother Roderick, from Father Stephen. Do you promise?"

Her voice was choked with misery. "Yes, yes, I promise. Though I will not live without your love." She thought of the man who had brought them to this. Seton. She hated him with a fury that was overpowering. "Seton! How can a man like him triumph? It is a travesty of all that is holy. He speaks of God, though he himself is godless!"

"He has had his revenge upon me in the cruelest of ways, for he takes me from the world I love, now that I have found you." He held her tightly, murmuring words of love.

The footsteps of the guard sounded like the thundering of a cannon. "You will have to leave now, miss. You can stay no longer."

"No." Heather clung to Richard. "I will stay with him. Imprison me too."

Richard put her from him roughly. "No. Go, Heather. Take my love with you. If God wills, I will see you on the morrow. If not, pray for me and remember how deeply I have loved you."

One last embrace was granted to them before the guard stepped forward to stop them. "You must leave!" The words echoed in Heather's ears like the drumbeat of the executioner's song. Tears stung her eyes, blinding her as she walked away.

58

THE LARGE ROOM was a veritable sea of faces: the curious, those who were to be tried, witnesses, and those who would offer up life or death with but the nod of a head.

Heather sat between Tabitha and her mother, with Perriwincle sitting far behind in the back of the chamber. As Richard entered by a side door, Heather reached out and squeezed her mother's hand as hard as she could to keep from crying out. She wanted to run to him, to beg the court's mercy, but she knew that this was a thing that she must not do. Instead she must sit and watch this ghastly mummery and pray that God in his wisdom and mercy would reach out and touch the hearts of those who sat in judgment.

The queen entered through the large double doors at the far end of the room, and all heads turned to look upon her. Dressed all in black and gold, she looked awesome and unforgiving. Her eyes swept the crowd before she sat down, and Heather felt a thrill of fear.

"You may begin," Mary said in her mannish voice, nodding toward the black-robed judge sitting at the front of the room on a high dais. Along one side sat the nobles. Richard would be judged by his peers.

It ws a living nightmare, a mockery from start to finish. Richard would have no justice; Hugh Seton had seen to that. Up and down, the evil man walked, smiling at the nobles who would have the power of life or death.

"Is it possible that he can convince this entire council of Richard's guilt?" Heather asked herself. He seemed so sure of himself, so jovial and at ease. It was as if he were at a cockfight or other social gathering, not at a trial.

Hugh Seton offered up his own evidence against Richard, stating that he had jailed him earlier for his suspected part in the upcoming rebellion. "I was having him carefully watched," he said, offering up Richard's message to Stephen Vickery as support to his claims. The letter had been torn in half, only the words which were damaging to Richard remaining. It put Stephen Vickery in danger as well, though since he had never received the message, his life and liberty were not at stake.

"My dear Stephen," the letter read. "I must meet with you to discuss this most unfortunate matter of the queen's marriage. Something must be done to stop Mary in this unwise and most foolhardy venture. I have been so blinded by my own happiness that I have failed to do my duty to God and to my country, but now it is evident that action must be taken. Meet me at the Cap and Crown on Wednesday next so that we may decide what steps to take." It was here that part of the message was missing, torn away. Heather knew that it was here that Richard had told Stephen about the pantomime that the mummers had given, but to the court it would seem most damaging because the words read, ". . . to kill Philip by striking him with a sword." Again parts of the writing were missing, ending with only Richard's name. Hugh Seton insisted that in the struggle to obtain the message, it had been torn asunder, but Heather knew the truth. Hugh Seton had doctored the missive to suit his own ends.

A young soldier was questioned next, admitting that he had set Richard free. "I believed him when he said he was innocent of plotting against the queen, but I was wrong. May God forgive me for what I did. I showed mercy where none was due." Looking in Richard's direction, he spat, "Traitor."

Two other men in Seton's employ, would-be soldiers, were called forward to testify that they had indeed taken the man named Richard Morgan prisoner. "He is as guilty as Wyatt himself," the brawny one swore, pounding the arm of the chair with his fists. Heather watched the attacks as if in a trance. Only when Catherine Todd came forward did her anger bubble to the surface.

"Richard pretended to be a good Catholic in front of Mary," the dark-haired bitch said loudly enough for all to hear, "but he was instead bitter toward the church for tying him to a woman he did not want. He often talked of how it was Mary's fault. He thought her a fanatic and—forgive me, your Majesty—a simpleton. 'I can wind her around my finger as easily as a weaver winds thread around a spool,' he said to me many times. But I had no idea to what lengths his bitterness would lead him. Still, his talk completely turned me against him. I swore I would have nothing more to do with him, and thus he turned his attentions in other directions." Her eyes settled upon that spot where Heather sat. "A merchant's daughter, of all people. A known Reformer. I have little doubt that *she* has a part in this."

Heather wanted to pounce upon the viper-tongued woman and tear out every hair on her head. "The witch. The foul, lying witch," she said beneath her breath. Only her mother's firm hand upon her shoulder kept her from rising from her seat. "How could her jealousy be so potent as to take a man's freedom from him, his very life?" It was obvious to see that the woman's testimony had had an effect; the rumbling in the room attested to that. "And all because he spurned her, because he loved me and not her."

Anne Fairfax was next to speak, rising eloquently to her feet in defense of Richard's character. She spoke of him as a most loyal subject, a devout Catholic. "Only the strength of his country, the well-being of his queen, concerned him. He was never an ambitious man, though some"—her eyes focused upon Hugh Seton—"might have flattered the queen to gain their power. Never Richard. He loved Mary.

Deeply. Mary and England." She said again and again that he was innocent, but Catherine Todd's testimony just moments before had spread its venom. It was impossible to turn back a tide once it had begun to flow in.

Stephen Vickery also spoke in glowing terms of Richard's character, praising him for his valor in the struggle against Northumberland, risking his own life to warn the queen of the duke's intentions the night Edward VI died. He denied that the message sent to him was in any way meant to incite rebellion. "As I was worried about what a Spanish king might mean, as many of us were, he too was concerned, out of love and affection for Mary and loyalty to our country. If there are any of you sitting out there who have not had like worry, rise to your feet now and speak out." He gestured to the room, but none rose to their feet. "If Richard Morgan is guilty, then we are all guilty." He swore again and again that Richard had been riding in defense of his country, not against it that fateful day. "His love for the woman sitting in this room bade him seek her out. Is it a matter of treachery to love? Are there any of you who might not have done the same? It was cold and dark and a mass of confusion that night. Is it not possible that these men who say that he was riding with Wyatt were mistaken? Think on this, gentlemen, before you condemn this Richard Morgan. If you have any doubts, then I beg you to offer your voice up to free him."

"Bless you, Stephen," Heather whispered under her breath. His statements had seemed to turn the tide. The chamber room was silent now, as if each man was in deep and contemplative thought.

Hugh Seton rose to his feet again, anxious to remove the red-haired, bearded Vickery from the room and the mind of those in judgment. Seton motioned to one of the guards, the doors were again opened, and all eyes turned in that direction.

"Courtenay," Heather breathed. "Edward Courtenay." She remembered well this man who had been her friend at court. Surely he would not say anything to harm Richard, even though he himself was deeply implicated in this plot of usurpation.

Playing on the drama of the moment, Hugh Seton asked, "What is your name?"

"Edward Courtenay," came the obvious answer.

"And you are the same Edward Courtenay who is of the blood royal?" Courtenay nodded. "That same Courtenay who has been judged to be guilty of plotting to seat himself upon the throne of England beside the Princess Elizabeth."

"I wanted to marry Mary!" Courtenay objected, not one to condemn himself before so large a crowd.

"But when Mary spurned you, your thoughts were to be king without her." Courtenay started to protest, but Hugh Seton put up his hand. "Enough. You are not being judged this day. I only want you to tell me whether or not the man sitting there"—he pointed directly at Richard—"is a fellow conspirator, and if so, what part he was to play."

Courtenay was silent a long while, and Heather thought that perhaps he was wrestling with his conscience. It would be difficult to send a man to his death by telling a lie. She prayed that he would look at her, and at last he did, his eyes strangely sad, as if he really had no stomach for what he was about to do. Still, that did not excuse him when he said, "He was."

Richard Morgan had been silent through all the testimony, but now he rose to his feet in rage. "Liar!" he spat. "You are a treacherous liar." He was quickly subdued.

"What was his duty to be in all this?" Seton continued, relishing his victory like one in his cups relishes his drink.

Courtenay looked down at the ground. "He was to rouse London against the queen. London and Norfolk."

Heather listened to the rest of the testimony in a daze. How could he have lied as he did? What kind of a man would do such a thing? As he walked to the back of the room, he passed by her and she could not hold her tongue.

"How could I have ever liked you? You are selfish and spoiled and think nothing of ruining a man's life!"

He looked at her with all the sadness of a wounded puppy. "Do not judge me too harshly, Heather. A man does what he must to survive." With that he walked away, and Heather wondered if he had been promised that he would keep his head if he would cause Richard to lose his. Surely there had been no love lost between the two men, all because of her.

Richard could say little in his own defense. It was written upon his face that he realized that his doom was sealed. His eyes sought out Heather with a gentleness which touched her soul. Even with his world tumbling about him he was concerned for her welfare.

"I can only say that as God is my witness, I never plotted against my queen. I was, I am, and I will always be your most humble and loyal subject. May God forgive those who have perjured themselves this day."

The judge declared Richard guilty. It had not taken long for them to come to such an agreement. Turning toward Mary, they saw her nod her head, saying that she too thought Richard guilty. There was nothing more to be done. "You will be taken to Tower Green and there you will be beheaded in two days' time."

"No!" Heather rose to her feet, not being able to keep her silence any longer. "You are sending to his death an innocent man."

The judge thundered in anger, "God has given his judgment."

"God? What has God to do with this mockery? It is the devil who rules here. How he must be laughing now." Her eyes turned toward Seton, to find that he was indeed smiling in his triumph.

"Take the prisoner away," he shouted.

Richard stared at the crowd. He was glimpsing his last moment of freedom. Now he would be taken back to a dark, cold cell and then to the scaffold on Tower Hill. "Heather," he whispered. "Heather."

She heard him call her name but was silent as the grief of the moment shattered her. All she could do was look at him, watching as he was taken from the room and out of her life. People spoke to her, but she did not hear them. Her mother and Tabitha pushed her toward the door, but she did not feel their hands. She only knew that her life was ending, that her heart would be severed from her body with the strike of the headsman's ax.

59

HEATHER STARED AT the letter the messenger had brought to her, remembering Richard's words in the courtroom. Truly the devil was in command, his laughter rumbling forth with the thunder and lightning which raged forth in a furious storm. He was mocking them even now.

"Edlyn is dead," she whispered, reading the words again. She could hardly believe it. Sadness tore at her heart. The poor, poor woman, never to have tasted truly of happiness, and now she was dead. "How did she die? What killed her?" she asked the messenger, a tall skinny lad she remembered well from her days at Norfolk. She could not help but feel a twinge of guilt at having left Edlyn behind, but there was naught that she could do. Everything had happened so fast, and she had thought that Undine would take care of the young woman. Again she asked, "How did she die?"

He looked at her without expression in his eyes. "Just wasted away, seems loike. Cain't roightly saiy."

"Wasted away?" Heather's gray eyes widened in horror. "Did Undine not tend her?" The remembrance of the indignities that Agnes had made the poor childish woman suffer flashed before her eyes. Had she replaced one woman's cruelty with that of another? Undine had seemed so kind, so solicitous of Heather's approval, and truly fond of Edlyn.

"Old Undine tended her, all roight," he said, averting his eyes. "Was by her bedside day and noight. It was the Lord's will, it was."

Heather shook her head, tears stinging her eyes. "The Lord would not take from this earth a being so completely innocent of any wrongdoing." She brushed the tears away with the palm of her hand. "Edlyn was as guileless as a child." Closing her eyes, she crumpled the note. First Richard and now Edlyn.

"Now you be free to marry wi' the lord," the young man said, barely realizing just how cruel and heartless the words sounded.

"Don't say such a thing!" Heather exclaimed, drawing back from him. That others would echo his words tore at her soul. "I mourn for Edlyn, truly I do."

He studied her face before he spoke, and seeing that she meant the words she spoke, the young man held back the torrent he had nearly uttered, the congratulations that Undine had bidden him to say. This woman before him did not gloat at her good fortune as Undine had said she would; instead, she seemed on the verge of despair.

" 'Twas the 'king's disease,' old Undine told me," he said instead. "Edward."

"The 'king's disease'?" Heather thought back to remember that ailment which had taken the king's life. There had been those, Richard included, who had whispered that the boy-king had been poisoned.

"Aye. Her hair fell out of her head, it did, and her body shriveled up to near nothing. Took a long time to die, but she breathed her last and gave up the ghost on Wednesday last."

So while Richard had lain in his prison cell awaiting his fate, Edlyn had been dying, wasting away in a torturous, agonizing manner. And now Edlyn was gone and Richard doomed to the headsman's ax. Surely none of God's doing, but the devil's instead.

"I be going now, mum. Be you all roight?"

"Yes," she murmured, reaching in her pocket to pull forth a gold coin. Handing it to the lad, she looked into his face once more, and he was taken aback at the misery written upon her face.

"Shall I tell them that the lord will be comin' for

the funeral?" he asked, feeling the hurry to put this unpleasant errand behind him.

"No. Richard will not be coming home." She knew that since Richard had been declared traitor his lands would be forfeit. Would Seton get his hands upon that which he had so long looked upon with evil jealousy? Yes. The land would soon be his. The people might just as well be prepared for what was about to happen. "Tell them that the lord of the manor has been housed in the Tower, that they will soon have a new lord."

He stepped back as if she had struck him. "New lord? What of our Lord Morgan?"

"He has been wrongly accused of treason and unjustly sentenced." She could say no more, too fresh in her mind was all that had been spoken in court against him.

He stepped forward as if to comfort her. "What can we do to save him? It will be the ax. I will raise the countryside and we will swarm like bees to save our roightful lord. You have but to saiy the word."

She was tempted to do just that. So very tempted. Damn Mary Tudor to hell and back, damn Seton and all the others who had betrayed Richard, and a pox upon Courtenay for turning his back upon their friendship, thus taking from her the man she loved above all others. Let the bastards feel the sting of the sword, let them quiver in fear of their lives as she had trembled in fear of the death sentence for Richard. " 'Vengeance is mine,' saith the Lord," she thought, and yet reality grasped her. To do such a thing would mean more killing, more bloodshed, and most likely the heads of all Richard's followers. Not even for Richard could she so doom them. There was no hope.

"Go home, boy," she cried. "Go home and pray for him, tell them all to pray for him." She watched him leave through the fog of her tears.

The ax, she thought, managing only barely to control the hysteria which threatened to consume her. My Richard's noble and handsome head to be severed by the executioner's ax. She had to do something. She would not stand by and allow them to so mutilate him.

Visions of his rescue darted through her mind. Perriwincle could aid her. They could steal into the prison and free him and hide him in the wagon as they had that night when he had been wounded. She would risk anything, do anything to save the man she loved. And yet even as she thought of these things, her heart knew the truth. There was nothing that she could do to save him. Nothing. She could only be there by his side and tell him that she loved him ere he died. And yet . . .

Falling to her knees, Heather closed her eyes and prayed.

60

It was dark in the prison cell. Dark and silent. Richard looked out the tiny window knowing that when the sun loomed again in the sky he would meet his death.

"At least the headsman's ax is quick and painless," he murmured, remembering his uncle's execution. The only thought that really pained him was how Heather would react to his death. She was a young and beautiful woman with her entire life before her; she must not let his death blacken her heart. He cringed at the thought of her seeing his head perched atop a pole on traitor's gate. "I who was the queen's most loyal subject."

Walking back to his cot, stumbling in the dark, he felt numb, as if his head had already been severed from his shoulders. The anger was gone and in its place was a lethargy, a deep sadness for the follies of mankind. On a small table by his bed was a plate of food, but he had no appetite. What use was it to eat? Instead he lay down and tried to envision all the pleasant memories and moments of his life. Closing his eyes, he fought against sleep, longing only to think and to dream. So lost to his own private visions was he that he did not hear the scuffle outside his door, nor the voices until the door opened. Standing before him, robed in black, was his brother.

"Roderick!"

"Father Stephen," the priest corrected him with a sad smile. He cast his eyes in the direction of the guard. "It is his right to be forgiven for his sins. Leave us alone."

The guard shook his head. "I can't. I've been given my orders. You shouldn't be here at all. There is time enough tomorrow to give this one his last rites. If you hadn't put up such a fuss, I would have forced you to leave."

"I am this man's brother as well as his priest. Can you not show common decency and let him confess his sins in private?"

"But you might do something to help him escape, and it would mean my head." The guard nervously toyed with the keys.

"I am a priest. A man of God. I give you my word that I will not use force to free this man, nor will *I* take him beyond these walls." He touched his cross as if to seal the vow.

"Well . . . You being a priest and all . . ." The man crossed himself as if to ward off any guilt for what he was about to do. Being himself a loyal Catholic, always most respectful of monks and priests, he decided that there could be no harm in allowing the man to soothe his conscience. "You may stay a few moments." The door shut with a resounding bang.

Father Stephen waited a long while before he spoke, just long enough to make certain that the guard was not listening at the door; then he whispered, "Listen to me and listen well. There is only one way that you will leave this Tower, and that is to die."

Richard's eyes widened in surprise. He had thought his brother was here to offer comfort or to listen to his sins. He was not prepared for this. "To die? What in God's name do you mean?" It was against the laws of the church to take one's own life, and surely Roderick would not want to endanger his own soul by taking the life of his brother. Murder was a most grievous sin.

Blue eyes met blue eyes and Richard could swear that he saw a gleam of mischief in his brother's eyes. "I have a certain root with me, a potent herb which when chewed and swallowed gives the appearance of death to him who has partaken of it." He reached into his pocket and withdrew it, holding it forth for Richard to take. "You must use it. Only thus will you have any hope of cheating the headsman."

Richard twirled it over and over in his hands, fascinated by it, mesmerized by the thought of its power. It could give him life by bringing him the appearance of death. Life from death.

"This will still your breathing. There will be no sign of a pulse. You will to all men appear to be dead. I will come quickly to claim the body and insist upon taking it back to the family estates in Norfolk."

Richard grimaced, the thought not a pleasant one. "But what if they should decide to take my head anyway? Seton would no doubt love to see me grinning at him from atop a pole on traitor's gate. If I am in this trance you speak of, what is to keep me from losing my head anyway and not having the strength to defend myself?"

"That, dear brother, is up to me." Father Stephen ran quickly to the door to peer out. There was no one outside; the occupants who had shared the cell with Richard had already met the hangman, so there was no one to tell the tale. He walked back and sat upon the edge of the cot, whispering in Richard's ear, "There will be no time for them to do so once you are beyond these walls. I will insist on being left alone with the body, and while we are thus isolated, you will quickly shave off that beard of yours and don my priestly attire. As Father Stephen you will have no trouble in escaping. Rafael Mendosa has a ship waiting at the London docks which will take you to Spain."

Richard bolted up from the bed. "That is the most ridiculous plot I have ever heard of. It will never work. You will get yourself as well as me killed!"

"Shhhhh. Richard, keep your voice down." Father Stephen's voice was stern and full of authority.

Richard's voice quieted. "We will be found out."

"Not if there is a commotion to draw the attention of those who might offer us resistance. When they come back in the room, they will find the coffin weighted with sandbags. Before it is discovered, I will hope to make good my own exit. If I am imprisoned, well, that will just have to be. Mary would never execute a priest, particularly one who is on the verge of being named bishop."

"Bishop!"

"Yes. But come, we have no time for chatter. The guard is coming back. All I can ask of you is that you trust me. God will find a way to save us both, Richard. This I know in my heart." Bowing his head, he took his leave, whispering, "Take the root tonight when the moon is high in the sky." Then he was gone.

Richard tightly clutched the rough object in his hand. "The root. The root." It seemed to echo in his mind, taunting him with death, promising him life. The thought of chewing it was unpleasant, frightening. It was difficult to understand the ways of nature, yet he knew the magic of many herbal remedies.

"What else is left to me?" he whispered to the darkness. There was no chance of Mary changing her mind. At sunrise tomorrow he would face the headsman unless . . . unless. . . .

As the moon rose overhead to shine brightly down upon the earth, Richard raised the bitter herb to his lips. His last thoughts were of the woman he loved, with the prayer that they would meet again.

61

AT THE FIRST rays of day's dawning two guards walked down the stone-floored corridor toward the door of the condemned prisoner. They were jovial. There was always a sense of excitement on the day of a beheading. Crowds of people, anxious to view the spectacle, would mill about, there would be drinking, in secret of course, and both guards hoped that when the wine flowed they would have their share. There would be bribes from those anxious to get a closer view, as well as from those members of the victim's family whose only desire was to make the death as painless as possible.

"I got me a bit of that nightshade just in case the bloke's loved ones think to spare him some pain," said one, reaching in his doublet to make certain it was safe. "Lady Jane Grey refused even a touch of it, brave one she was, but her husband paid me a small fortune so that he could have his share. It's glad I am that he was not our king."

The other man grinned. "That rebellion seems certain to fill me pockets. Fifteen hangings in only three days, and seven beheadings. All in all, it has been very rewarding, yes indeed. I only hope that I can profit from this one as well."

They came to the iron-studded door and brought forth the key. "I'll lay you odds that this one don't cry out. He looks to be the sort who will keep silent. A real man, this one is. Too bad. Too bad."

"Ah, we all got to go sometime. At least it's the ax

and not the hangman's rope." He turned the key in the lock, opened the door, and stepped inside.

"Hey, you. Get up. It's time to meet your maker," yelled the first guard. He wondered if there were any possessions that this one would leave behind that he could get his hands on quickly. Eyeing the other guard warily, he supposed that the same thing had touched his companion's mind.

"Oddsbody, I never seen a man sleep so peaceful-like on the day they was to die. Gives me the willies, it does. Usually they are pacing about." The older guard nudged the shoulder of the sleeping prisoner but he did not move. "Now, you take Anne Boleyn. She must have worn a path from one wall to the next. Hoping against hope that old King Harry would give her a last-minute reprieve. I saw her lose her head, I did. Thought at the time that it was a great waste of beauty." Again he jostled the prisoner, but again there was no response.

"He ain't movin'." Leaning down to put his ear to the man's heart, he looked at his fellow guard with surprise. "He's dead."

"Let me see." Bending down, the man took Richard's wrist in his great big hands. "No heartbeat." Taking a knife out of his belt, he put the blade before Richard's lips. There was no moisture on it when he drew it away, no sign of breath upon the metal. "I don't think he's breathin'."

"Of course not. I told you he's dead. This one has cheated the executioner. I would like to see the look on that man Seton's face when he learns of it. Seems to me he was relishing the sight of seeing this one lose his head. I'll lay you two to one that he'll throw a fine fit, that one."

The older guard looked frightened. "Hope they don't lay this one on us. Them nobles are a strange lot." As if making absolutely certain that the prisoner was dead, he kicked his leg with the toe of his boot. There was no response.

"What are we going to do?" His question was answered by another's lips. Standing in the doorway to the open cell was a dark-robed priest.

"If he is dead, then I will handle this, my son," he said.

The older guard shook his head. "This ain't none of your concern."

The priest walked into the room. "Ah, but it is. He belongs to God now and not to any earthly master." He bent over the prisoner. "He is indeed dead." Bowing his head, he spoke in long flowing Latin verses and intonations, ending with, "*Requiem aeternum dona eis Domine. Et Luceat eum requiescat in pace.*"

The old guard stepped forward. "I've got to send for this man Seton right away. He told me to watch over this one and make certain he didn't get away." Looking down at the man on the cot, he laughed. "Don't suppose that be our worry now." He quickly sobered. "Now we got to think of what's to be done. It ain't no fun to kill a dead man. All thems what's expectin' to watch the gory sight will be angry."

The younger guard wrung his hands, obviously agitated and frightened. "They'll be havin' our heads, they will."

The priest, Father Stephen by name, stepped forward quickly. It appeared that this was going to be much easier than he had ever imagined. Like taking honeyed milk from a babe. "My sons, do not worry. I will aid you in this matter. This Seton that you fear will hear from my lips of your innocence. The man died of natural causes and not from foul play. If you will but help me move the body to the chapel . . ."

"No. It stays here. We are in enough trouble already." The older guard was steadfast in his duty.

Father Stephen smiled. "My son, let me have the say on what is to be done with this poor soul. Do you deny his soul peace?"

"No. I only seek to assure my own. Never in all my years has a thing like this happened, 'cept once when a bloke was poisoned." Sudden fear crept over his face. "Could it be? Who would . . . ?"

The priest shook his head. "We may never know,

my son. Unless of course there is a full investigation." He raised an eyebrow at the older guard.

"Ah, Jack, let the father take the bloke. If you ask me, the sooner he's outta here the better," exclaimed the younger of the two watchmen, his eyes darting back and forth with anxiety. As if to hurry the process along, he picked up the man on the cot by his feet. "Help me."

The one named Jack hesitated for a moment, then with a shrug of his shoulders complied. Carrying the man down the winding stairs with the priest close behind them, they came at last to a small, darkly lit chapel. "Do what needs to be done, Father. I wash my hands of this." Tossing the body none too gently on the floor of the chapel like a sack of wheat, they left the priest alone with his charge.

As soon as the door was shut behind him, Father Stephen acted with the speed of lightning. There was the chance that these two might come back, might change their minds, or that Seton would make an appearance. It had all gone a bit too smoothly. He must not be puffed up with false confidence; his brother's life hung in the balance and depended upon the decisions he made now.

He tried to rouse Richard but it was no use, it was too soon for him to come out of the drugged state he was in. Father Stephen had thought it would be a much longer time before he could get Richard alone and thus had timed erroneously that moment when the root's effects would wear off.

"And so I must do all this without your help, dear brother," he whispered, taking from beneath his own robes some of similar appearance. Stripping off his brother's doublet, hose, shirt, and boots, he found a hiding place beneath the small altar for the garments, then dressed Richard in the black robes of a priest, tying a hempen girdle about his slim waist.

"If we are caught now it will be both our heads, Richard," he murmured, glancing uneasily at the door. There was no one beyond it and he prayed that God would be with them now in their hour of need.

There was one other matter that needed to be taken care of, Richard's beard. It clearly marked him as no priest. "I am no barber, brother, but I will do my best," Father Stephen mumbled, drawing forth a razor from a purse that hung beneath his habit. Hacking away at the thick coarse hair, he was soon glad that Richard was still in his peaceful trancelike slumber and not subject to the pain his small nicks would surely bring.

At last he stood back to view his handiwork. There would be few who would not swear that lying here was the same priest who had entered only a short while before. But he had to get Richard to awaken. They must get safely out of here before they were caught. Again he tried to rouse his brother, but it was no use. The thought came to him then that he must at least drag Richard to another chamber to hide until they could leave the Tower. So thinking, he cautiously opened the door, but it was too late. Coming down the hallway was the younger of the two guards.

Father Stephen stifled a curse, raising his eyes to the heavens for God's forgiveness for the oath that nearly passed from his lips. He was trapped. There was nothing that could be done. Unless he thought quickly.

Dragging Richard's sleeping form behind the altar, he picked up a candlestick and held it behind him just as the door opened.

"Hey, you. Priest," came the voice. Father Stephen stepped forward to greet him, thankful that the man had come alone.

"What is it, my son?"

"Lord Seton is on his way here at this very moment. Me and my companion, we think perhaps it best if we put that bloke back in the cell where he belongs. He wanted me to tell you to hurry and say your prayers for the man. When he comes back down here, we'll carry the body back up the stairs."

He looked around him anxiously. "Say, where is he?" He had no chance to ask more questions. With all the strength he could muster, Father Stephen rapped him on the head, rendering him unconscious.

"Forgime me, my son," he whispered, dropping the candlestick and hurrying back to where he had left Richard. Dragging him down the hallway into the safety of another darkened room, he returned for the guard, putting him in yet another room.

"God help us," the priest prayed, staring down at his brother's inert form. Their time had nearly run out.

62

RICHARD WAS COLD, so cold. He shivered and wondered at the feel of the warm hands that touched him. "Heather?" he croaked, fighting to open his eyes. "Make me warm, Heather." Twisting his head in a restless struggle, he reached out to the hazy shape beside him. His mouth felt as dry as sand, his head throbbed with pain, every muscle in his body felt stiff and sore. He seemed to hear a voice talking to him, pleading with him, but he could not understand the words, so foggy was his brain.

With terrible slowness he opened his eyes, puzzled by his surroundings. His eyes tried to focus, sweeping painfully about the room, taking in the gloom and darkness. Where was he?

Again the voice, a man's voice. His eyes turned to the dark shape looming beside him, a black-robed specter, and he shuddered, thinking it Death himself come to claim him. "No," he mumbled. "I'm not ready. Not yet." He struggled with new energy as that form reached out to touch him. His teeth chattered, and he began to shake violently as if stricken with Saint Vitus' dance. At last he quieted, reaching up to take hold of his aching head. Had he partaken of too much wine the night before? Was that his trouble? If so, he would never drink of the grape again, this he vowed.

Weakly he tried to rise, feeling that there was somewhere he had to go, something he had to do, but his legs would not support him and he felt the room spin as strong arms steadied him.

"I know that you are weak, Richard," that same voice was saying. "But you must call upon every reserve of strength that you have to leave this place. Even now Seton is at the gate. Please. We are so close to freedom."

Richard recognized that voice now. "Roderick?" he asked, licking his lips in an effort to quench their parched dryness. He was confused. Why were they here? Were they playing hide-and-seek? Yes, that was it.

Again the voice repeated, "Seton. He is nearly here. Listen to me. You are Father Stephen. Father Stephen. Do you understand?"

"Father. Father will find us." He felt his legs give way beneath him and fell to the hard floor. When he looked up, the face before him seemed blurred. Strong arms picked him up, shaking him roughly.

"You are Father Stephen. Listen to me and listen to me well, Richard, if you do not want to part with your head. Seton had you condemned as a traitor and imprisoned. Remember? I gave you a root to chew so that they would think you dead."

Through the mists of his brain the truth slowly dawned on Richard. "Seton."

"And he is coming for you now. We will both be punished if you do not do as I tell you. You are me. Remember how we would play that game when we were little? Only we are grown now, Richard. You are me, Father Stephen. You came to see the prisoner, to offer up the last rites. Now you are leaving to return to the queen. The queen has called for you. Remember?"

"Father Stephen. Yes, I am Father Stephen," Richard repeated. Slowly reality was returning to him and he had a brief flicker of knowledge of the danger they were both in.

His brother raised his eyes to heaven, thanking God for returning his brother to his senses. He wondered if that guard had awakened yet. Well, it made no matter. The priest had returned to the man to tie him up with the ties of his own girdle and to stuff a cloth in his mouth to keep him from crying out. It was the other guard who posed a danger. He led his brother out the door and pushed him into the corridor. "The London docks. Go. Hurry."

Richard started to leave but turned back. "Heather. You must get a message to Heather. I will not leave without her." His brother nodded, giving him his silent promise.

Richard did not know how he walked down the stairs, but somehow he managed to do so despite the weakness of his limbs and the haze before his eyes. It was all coming back to him and perhaps then it was his anger which drove him on. He would cheat Seton of his victory. He would thwart that bastard!

"You, there. Halt." It was a voice he seemed to recognize which called to him. The guard. Now he remembered. Slowly he turned around to face the man, expecting full well to be recognized and dragged back into his cell.

No. I will fight if need be, he thought grimly. Let them kill me now. But the guard merely looked at him.

"Where in blazes is Simon? I've looked everywhere."

Richard shrugged his shoulders, remaining silent.

"I sent him to see you. I want that body back where it belongs. I looked in the chapel and there is no one there. Where is he, where is Simon?"

This time Richard pointed toward the stairs. "Back where he belongs, my son," he murmured, trying to imitate his brother's manner of speech. "I helped him carry the poor soul."

"You helped him? Well, why not? You have the look of strength about you." He started for the stairs, but turned back. "You will tell Seton, as you promised, that we are not to blame?"

"Yes, my son," Richard intoned, making the sign of the cross before him. "I will tell him." He hurried down the hallway, his heart pounding like the hooves of his stallion. At last, after passing several guards who did nothing at all to detain him, he came to the front portal. The taste of freedom was like that of fine wine. He was so close to being safe, so close. He smiled, that expression changing to one of suppressed anger as the door was opened and he found himself face to face with his enemy. Seton, he thought with alarm. If there was anyone who would see through his disguise, it was this man. Seton knew both Roderick and Richard, had seen the two as boys together, knew of their fondness for trickery, for changing places. Seton alone would know well that he was not his brother. He would look at his chin and see clearly written that which marked him as Richard. There was no cleft to his chin. No cleft. Desperately he sought to turn away his face, burying his chin in the folds of the cowl of his habit, bowing with humble servitude before this ambitious bastard.

But Seton seemed not to notice that it was not the priest his eyes beheld. Too puffed up with his own importance, he grinned at Richard. "I told you that one day all would be mine, you sniveling eunuch. I only wish that our father was alive to see which of his sons now wields the power." He pushed past him. "I am not surprised that you have no stomach to watch what I have wrought. Flee, then, and go back to your prayers, you foolish priest. I have won. I have won it all!" He hurried up the stairs, laughing victoriously.

Richard cast one glance behind him, anxious for his brother's safety, then hurried out the door. "The London docks," he whispered, and was gone, fleeing in that direction, looking much like the ravens that nestled in the rafters of the Tower.

63

HEATHER SAT UP in bed with a start. What time is it? What time? As if to answer her question, twelve tolls of the bells sounded in the distance.

"No!" Like the cry of a wounded animal the sound escaped her lips. They would have already taken him to Tower Green, to the hill, to Tower Hill. The thought was too hideous to imagine, yet she knew that it must be true. They would have murdered him by now, severed his handsome head.

Hugging her slender arms about her body, she rocked back and forth, moaning over and over in her own kind of mourning for the man she had so deeply loved.

"I'm too late," she sobbed. "Too late." She had wanted to be beside him, to see him one last time, to let him see the look of love on her face before he met his end, but she had been denied this. Why? "I wanted to be with him."

Rising from the bed, she walked about in a daze, seeing his face before her eyes, feeling the touch of his hands, hearing the sound of his voice. Tears streamed in rivulets down her cheeks; she could think of nothing but her loss. Such a brief time of happiness they had shared. Such a short time of ecstasy. Now he was gone. How could she live without him?

Closing her eyes, she seemed to envision the grisly scene before her eyes and began to scream uncontrollably. Richard was dead. Richard was dead. Was there nothing she could do to dispel her living nightmare?

She did not even hear her mother come in. Only the sharp slap to her face by her mother's hand stopped the tortured cries.

"Stop it! Stop it this instant!" Blythe called out loudly, fearing for her daughter's sanity.

Heather was mute in her grief, curling away as if to escape into her own private world, a world where such pain did not exist. With her hands hanging down at her sides, she stared blankly before her.

"Get some more of the poppy juice, Tabitha. Quickly," Blythe ordered. Heather looked up at her, suddenly knowing why she had slept so deeply this morning, why she had missed the execution.

"You gave me something in my milk."

"There was no reason for you to suffer any more agony. I knew that if I did not give you the juice you would have moved heaven and hell to be with him this morning. I thought to spare you that pain."

"I should have been with him! She pushed her mother angrily away. "Where is he? What have they done with his body? I want to go to him. I must." Struggling with the arms which grasped her, she was like one touched in the head. Again her mother struck her, a gesture which caused Blythe as much pain as it did Heather as she took upon her own heart her daughter's grief.

"Stop struggling with me and listen! He wouldn't have wanted you to suffer this kind of grief. He would have wanted to spare you the sorrow of watching him die. I know. I know. He loved you as I do and I would have wanted to shield you."

"I wanted to tell him how much I loved him. One more time. One more time." Heather collapsed in tears against the warmth of her mother's enfolding arms, hugging her tightly as if afraid that she too might be taken from her.

"He knew how much you loved him. He knew." Blythe felt tears sting her own eyes. "And he loved you too, so much." Rocking her daughter back and forth like a child, she keened softly in their mutual sorrow. It broke her heart to see her child suffer so. Why was the world such a cruel place? Why couldn't one just go about life, and love and be loved? Why wasn't she able to protect her daughter from the evil in the world? She had wanted to do so, so much, to keep Heather from all hurt, all harm. Only sunshine should have touched this beautiful red-haired girl, not such black clouds of despair.

For a long moment the two women stood in their embrace; then Heather stepped away. Remembering the heads so often displayed upon London Bridge, she shuddered. "I must see him. I must. I won't let them put his head on traitor's gate for all London to see. He was no traitor. If I could not save his life, at least I will see that in death he is not so abused. Even if it means my own life, I will have my way in this."

"No. Heather, think. He would not want you to so endanger yourself."

"I must." Pulling away from her mother, she sought to find her plain linen gown and a cloak. "I should have been there," she murmured, yet she knew that he would not have wanted her to suffer such pain. He would have approved of what her mother had done. Richard would have applauded Blythe Bowen's actions, but that did not make her heart ache any the less.

Stepping out the door, she was surprised to see that the city was engulfed by a fog. How appropriate, she thought, that the sun should be blocked out on the day that he died. Richard Morgan had taken the sun with him as surely as he had taken her heart.

Heather walked down the cobblestones to the Tower, groping her way through the fog and through the mists of her own tears. She was assailed by memories of him with every step: their first meeting, when he had hidden from Northumberland's men in her father's storeroom; that time she had witnessed his near-death at the hands of an assassin; her fight to save his life. Could she ever forget how he had looked lying on the cot in the stables, so young and defenseless in his deep sleep, so handsome? Even then she had loved him. Even then.

Turning off the main road, she trudged along the path to the river, remembering that time when she had taken the letter to the council. She had wanted him to think her brave, as brave as Mary. He had been her hope, her dream come true, her future, her love. "And always will be. I will never forget him. Never. He will live in my heart until the day that I die."

When at last she stood at Tower Hill, she looked about her, wondering if even now Richard Morgan's blood stained the snow. "He gave his blood to England, and this is how he was repaid," she breathed, trying desperately to keep her anger and resentment in control. "Seton. If it takes me forever, he will pay for what he has done." How she hated the man. It was like a canker sore on her heart.

Seeing two bedraggled men walking about, clutching their cloaks about them for some measure of warmth, Heather approached them. She had to find out if they knew anything about what had happened to Richard. If they were workmen, perhaps they could tell her where his body was.

"Excuse me, kind gentlemen," she said, touching one upon the shoulder. "Can you tell me what has been done with the body of the condemned man?"

The man chuckled. "Which one? There have been many whose lives have been lost on this hill."

Heather swallowed her tears. "The man named Richard Morgan. He was to be executed this morning. A dark-haired man over six feet in height. Handsome and proud. A nobleman. Wrongly accused of treason against the queen."

The white-haired workman scratched his head. "Don't remember such a man being beheaded today. There was old Thomas Wyatt, a blond-haired bloke, an old man, and some crazy woman who insisted she had visions, but no tall dark-haired man."

Heather thought she had surely stopped breathing; her hands shook as she reached out again to the man. Was it possible? Had Richard been given a reprieve? "Are you certain?" she asked in a trembling voice.

"Yes. But if you don't believe me, ask one of the guards," the white-haired man answered peevishly.

Heather ran over the slippery ground, stumbling and falling more than once in her haste. The old man's words were ringing in her ears. By the time she reached the guards she was hysterical in her joy. If they had not taken his life, perhaps that meant that he would be free. Dared she to hope?

"The prisoner Richard Morgan. Where is he?" she asked, recognizing one of the guards as the one who had let Tabitha and herself in the door several nights before.

The guard winced when she said the name, and drew back from her as if he had not heard her talk to him. She repeated her question, and this time he answered gruffly, "Dead."

"Dead?" All her hopes were shattered in the most brutal of ways. "But I talked with a man and he said that the man I seek was not killed today."

"He wasn't. Blimey if he didn't just up and croak last night. Mysterious death, it was. Scary, if you ask me. A man doesn't just up and die. Something evil about it all. Something frightening. Unless of course he was poisoned."

"Poisoned?"

"There are those who say it was that. Or perhaps the devil himself took a hand in the matter. That would explain it all." He wondered what she would say if he told her that the body had disappeared, vanished into thin air. Already it had been said that the man's ghost was haunting the Tower, along with the ghosts of the past. He had been told not to mention what had happened, and it took all his self-control not to say something. It bothered him. A man didn't just up and vanish. But he bit his tongue.

"Where is he?" Heather whispered.

Again he was tempted to tell her the story, but

merely said, "Out back, in potter's field. That's how it is with traitors."

"He was not a traitor!" Heather snapped.

He ignored her outburst, turning his back upon her. "I've told you all I know," he said.

"Is his grave marked in any way? I would like to see him buried upon church grounds. He was a most loyal Catholic. It would be important to him."

He flushed. "Unmarked. The grave is unmarked. All the prisoners were buried at one time. Now, away with you. There is nothing that you can do for him now." He strode away, looking back at her once or twice to make certain that she would cause no more trouble.

It was as if the pain of his death now struck her anew. She grieved for him a second time. Dead. He was dead. Where was he buried? Where?

Turning her steps homeward, she wandered aimlessly along the streets of London, feeling lifeless, not caring what happened to her, wishing in fact that she too would die and be relieved of this overwhelming pain and sadness.

64

TABITHA STARED WITH fascination into the flickering flames of the fire, waiting anxiously for Heather to return. As usual, she was daydreaming about the handsome Spaniard she had met at the Tower, imagining him smiling at her again as he did then. She had been so tongue-tied that she hardly said a word to him, only looked at him with her adoring eyes. She thought of Heather, feeling her pain. How sad to love someone as much as Heather loved this Richard Morgan, only to lose him in such a way. How would she feel if she and the man named Rafael Mendosa were lovers, only to be so parted?

"Oh, Heather," she sobbed, feeling the full force of the pain the other woman must be feeling. "To have found love, only to have lost it." And what of this Mendosa? "I will never see him again," she sighed. The man had been polite to her, perhaps even friendly, and of course concerned for her well-being, but a man as handsome as he would never give a second look to a tall, gangly, awkward servant girl. It would be just as well if she put from her mind any foolish dreams. And yet . . .

"Dreaming again by the fire instead of going about your chores. Get to your work, girl." The obese figure of Thomas Bowen stood in the shadow of the door, his hands folded in front of him in a surly manner.

"I'm sorry. Forgive me, sir. I . . . I . . . was only . . ."

"I know well what you were doing, you lazy chit."

He cocked his head toward the doorway. "There is someone downstairs at the door. I presume that you have the good sense to answer it?"

Like a frightened mouse, Tabitha hastened away, taking the stairs two at a time and nearly tripping in her haste. Reaching for the latch, she pulled the door open, gasping in surprise at the sight of the tall imposing figure of the man whose face had haunted her dreams these past nights.

"You!"

He bowed gallantly, his eyes raking over her tall, slim form. He seemed just as surprised to see her as she was to see him.

"Señorita Tabitha. How pleased I am to see you again. It is like beholding a blossoming flower in the early-morning dawn."

Wiping her hands on the folds of her apron, she stepped back from him. Embarrassment flamed in her cheeks as she raised a trembling hand to brush back the stray curls which framed her face. The night they had met, she had not told him that she was the Bowens' serving girl. Luckily she had on a fresh gown and apron that were not too tattered or torn. Thomas was not overly generous, and only Heather's charity to the girl in giving her some of her own dresses to wear saved her from being ragged, but the dresses were too short for her, hitting her well above the ankle. Now she could see that the Spaniard's eyes were focused on just that area.

Tabitha winced in her humiliation, fully expecting to see scorn upon his face, but his warm, gentle smile stirred her heart.

"Is your friend Heather Bowen in?" he asked, looking anxiously about him. It was obvious that he was worried about something.

Tabitha shook her head no, looking down at her feet in an attempt to avoid his searching brown eyes. "She . . . she has gone to the Tower to . . . to try to find out what happened to Richard Morgan."

"*Caramba!*" He threw his hands up in frustration. "I was afraid such might happen."

"What is it? What has happened?" Forgetting her usual shyness, she touched his arm, then drew her hand back as if regretting her familiarity.

Rafael Mendosa's voice hushed to no more than a whisper. "It is about Richard that I am here. He has escaped and is even now waiting for her aboard my ship. Though his own life is in danger, he will not leave without her."

"Escaped!" Tabitha covered her mouth with her hands as the word bubbled forth. In joyous mirth, she seemed to dance on air as she twirled around in a circle.

"Please, you must find her! We cannot wait much longer. All of London will be searching for him." The somber tone of his voice sobered Tabitha's levity.

Looking at him with wide blue eyes, she promised, "I will look for her and send her to you. On this you have my word." Their eyes met and held for only a moment, but in that moment she was totally lost and knew that she was hopelessly in love with him. He was so tall, so strong, so handsome, and his smile seemed to turn her very bones to pudding.

"I will trust you in this, Señorita Tabitha," he answered, reaching for her hand and drawing it to his lips. As he kissed her hand, the touch of his mouth sent shivers up her arm. She wanted to reach out and touch the dark brown hair of his beard, bring his face close to hers and feel his lips brush her mouth. What would it feel like to be kissed by those soft lips? She could only wonder, speechless, unable to answer him as he turned away from her to walk through the doorway. She wanted to call him back, to cling to him, but merely watched as he walked away. A ship. He would be leaving England and she would never see him again. The thought brought a sob to her lips, and he turned to look at her, saying, "It will be all right. Richard will be safe. But hurry." Then he was gone.

"Tabitha! Tabitha! Who was at the door, girl?" The booming sound of Thomas Bowen's voice thundered down the stairs, shaking her out of her lethargy. Years of faithful service seemed to mesmerize her, and she drifted toward the stairs, eager to be at the man's beck and call, but as her foot touched the step, she shook herself free of his spell. She couldn't take the time to answer him now. She had promised Rafael that she would find Heather and send her to the ship.

"Tabitha! Get up here quickly, girl!" he called again. At the sound of his angry voice she winced, remembering the sting of his wrath. Pausing for only a moment, she remembered that the Spaniard had said he would trust her; she thought also of Heather's kindness over the years. Heather's happiness depended on her now. Without a backward glance, she flew from the house and down the cobbled streets of the city.

65

DRESSED IN PLAIN leather jerkin, coarse sailcloth trousers, and shaggy fur hat, the sleeves of his shirt rolled high above his elbows, Richard Morgan resembled neither the noble lord who had fought for his queen nor the saintly priest who had so recently left the Tower of London behind him. Indeed, he blended well with the other seafarers who swarmed across the deck, climbed the rigging, and made ready to sail upon the *Canción.*

Balancing himself against the rocking and swaying of the deck beneath his feet, he scanned the shore, watching for any sign of a red-haired young woman. The docks were bustling with early-morning activity: suntanned and red-faced sailors loading their ships with cargo destined for Spain, young women saying good-bye to the men they might not see again, and the more imposing and threatening queen's red-clothed guards searching the docks for a bearded noble who had escaped from the Tower of London on the very day he was to have been executed.

One such guard had questioned Richard, but by fate or God's will the man had believed Richard when he said that he had not laid eyes on the escaped man. The guard had been totally unaware that his quarry had been right beneath his nose. For the time being Richard was safe.

Weaving in and out among the Spanish sailors, Richard moved to the back of the ship to stand upon the poop deck and look again toward the shore. "Heather, where are you? Where are you, my love?"

The thought tormented him that she might not want to leave her country. He was asking a great deal of her. The queen had been incensed with her for leaving her bridegroom at the altar and running off with Richard to the north country. How much more outraged would Mary be when the tale was told of the merchant's daughter sailing off to Spain with a man judged to be a traitor? Heather might never be able to come back to the land of her birth. Richard was now a fugitive. A man with no country. What could he offer her now? Would their love survive?

And what of Mendosa? What would Philip of Spain think to know that a man who was judged the enemy of his intended bride, the Queen of England, was at this very moment standing on the deck of a Spanish ship ready to set sail for Spain? Mendosa put himself in the clutches of danger in the name of friendship.

"And I, who sought to keep England from Spain's clutches, am now forced to seek safety in that very land I would have defied," he murmured to himself. He should have been angry, filled with outrage at what Mary had nearly done, but he felt only sorrow that she had been so blind. His heart would always be in England, no matter where he went, no matter how long he was gone from her shores. He was and always would be an Englishman.

As an English ship left port, its sails billowing in the breeze, he was conscious of yet another worry. Privateers. In the last year they were becoming bold and were ever a source of dread to every sailor. There was the risk of danger upon the sea, and if he brought Heather along with him, he might put her life in jeopardy as well. Spanish gold was a tempting prize, but so was a beautiful woman. Heather's beauty might well mark her for danger.

"If I were any kind of man at all I would leave her behind, but I am selfish. The thought of living without her is not to be borne," he said to himself. His emotions were at war with each other as he paced the deck of the ship.

Mendosa had still not returned. What if he could

not find Heather? What if something had happened? Was Seton even now holding *her* prisoner in exchange for the one he had lost? Knowing the man as he did, he knew there was nothing the bastard would not do.

"I should have gone to her myself, despite the danger," he swore so loudly that a wizened old sailor turned to look at him, mumbling words in Spanish which Richard could not understand. The ship was ready to set sail, and neither Heather nor Mendosa was on board.

When at last Richard was about to lose all patience, when the temptation to go in search of them himself was at its strongest, he saw the familiar figure of the brightly clad Rafael striding toward the ship with his jaunty air, pausing to talk with another velvet-bedecked figure, one that Richard recognized as one of Seton's men. Ducking behind the mizzenmast, he shrank from sight lest somehow the man recognize him despite his sailor's attire. Looking out to the waters, he resolved himself to let the crystal blue channel take him before submitting again to the confines of the Tower or the threat of the headsman's ax.

He was still in hiding when he felt a hand on his shoulder. Flinching, he half-expected to find himself prisoner again, but it was Rafael's face that greeted him.

"Heather was not at home."

"Not there? Where . . . ?"

"Looking for you, *señor.* A brave one she is, or so it seems. She has gone to the Tower."

Fear was clearly written upon Richard's face. "The Tower!"

"And that is why I must leave you again. I have told the captain that we cannot sail yet. I must find her. Her life is now in danger."

"What do you mean?"

"That man Godfrey that I was just talking to, Señor Seton's man, told me what Seton is about. It seems that your wife has died and some have claimed that it was poison that killed her."

"Edlyn? Dead?" He shook his head sadly. He was free now. Free. No more bound to Edlyn, to his childish, insane wife. If only he had been freed in another manner and not by her death. "Poor Edlyn."

Rafael gripped him by the shoulders. "You do not understand, *amigo,* just what I am trying to tell you. Mourn your wife as you must, but listen well. Seton is even now sending out guards to go to your Heather's house to arrest her."

"Arrest her?"

"For the murder of Edlyn Morgan, the murder of your wife."

"What! That is absurd." In his anger he forgot all the danger, and as he looked over his shoulder, he could see that his outburst had stirred the interest of Godfrey, the man Rafael had been talking with.

"Calm yourself, *amigo,* or we are all in danger," Rafael hissed, reaching out to slap the Englishman on the face, acting out a drama for the eyes of the man named Godfrey. "You will do as you are told or find yourself upon another ship."

Bowing his head in a gesture of meekness, Richard shook his head. "*Sí. Sí.*" Looking out of the corner of his eye at their enemy, he saw that now the man had lost interest in their conversation, thinking it only a dispute between sailor and Spanish nobleman and of no consequence. "Mendosa," he whispered, "what are you telling me? How could anyone believe Heather guilty? She has been in London these past weeks." Seeing Godfrey turn around again to look, Richard busied himself by pulling the ropes of a hemp loading net, easing a cargo of gold down into the opening of the treasure hold.

Mendosa pretended to be directing him, jabbing his finger in the direction of the deck as if to tell the sailor to hurry. "That does not matter, *amigo.* In a matter of witchcraft there is no logic. This Seton is drawing the trap tightly about your *señorita,* thinking it a way to cause you to play foolishly into his hands. That you must not do. You must wait here! Let me try to find her and bring her here to safety."

"I will go to find her. Do you think me a coward?"

"No, *señor,* no coward, but a fool if you do other than wait here where you are safe. I do not want to have to rescue two." Richard started to argue, but Mendosa shushed him. "I will be back within the hour with your Heather. Meanwhile I would advise you to look busy." Without a backward glance he stalked off, leaving Richard in a haze of bitter anger.

"Damn you, Seton. Damn you to hell," he swore beneath his breath, pulling with all his strength upon the ropes. The chest of gold rose out of the hold to swing like a body on a gibbet.

"No, no, *señor.* The net is to go in the hold, not out of it," chided a nearby Spanish sailor, smiling as if to say "This landlubber is loco." Richard carefully eased the netted chest back to its resting place.

Now Heather *must* come with me. Our fate has been cast to the winds, he thought to himself. They would be two wanderers, two fugitives, but at least they would be together.

66

HEATHER WANDERED AROUND the streets of London like a lost soul, torturing herself with the memories of Richard. Nausea churned in the pit of her stomach at the thought of his death. She was silent, her grief welling up inside her like a dam, ready to burst at any moment. She resolved to be brave, but it was a difficult task.

"How will I go on living without him?"

Passing by a gibbet from which hung a grotesque body of one of the rebels, she stared in horror.

"Serves him right," said a passerby. "If you ask me, all traitors should be hung, beheading's too easy. Hang them all, I say, and as to heretics, burn them."

A wave of sickness washed over Heather at the words, and now the tears which she had been holding back rolled down her cheeks. Fiercely she dashed them away, sobbing as she sank down in a heap upon the wet grass. Huddled in a ball of misery, she gave vent to her grief until her tears were spent. Anger overcame her sorrow, anger at the injustice of the world.

A town crier walked by warbling the news that Mary would be married by proxy to her Spanish prince ere two weeks had passed, and Heather couldn't help but feel bitter. The queen had robbed her of the man she loved.

"And now she is to be a bride."

Looking about her, she tried to judge the time of day. How long had she wandered about? The fog was continuing to roll into London, enveloping her like her grief. Rising to her feet, she collided with a rotund woman as she walked along. She could hear the crying of the street vendors as she entered the marketplace.

"Any old iron take money for," chanted the rag-and-bone man, his bag slung over his shoulder. He tipped his hat to Heather and moved along his way.

Traveling musicians strolled along with their lutes, fiddles, and drums, but the songs could not cheer Heather. They only made her more melancholy. How could the world be happy when Richard was dead? How?

The pudding-and-pie man pushed his one-wheeled cart up to her, his eyes kind, his voice gentle. "A hot puddin', baked as I go. You be wantin' one, miss?"

Heather's stomach rumbled in answer but the thought of eating disgusted her, even though she had not eaten a bite all day.

"Pies, puddin's, and tarts, warm from me oven." He held one forth as if to tempt her. The aroma was tantalizing, yet Heather shook her head no and the man moved on.

Passing a clump of rosebushes, Heather paused, reaching out to the budless stalks as if they were filled with flowers, remembering when Richard had brought her roses. She had been angry with him then, thinking him a scoundrel, married to one woman and seeking the favors of another, and all the while he had loved her. How could she have wasted so much precious time? They could have been together then. . . .

"Fool. I was a fool," she whispered.

She wandered aimlessly for a long while, lost in her broken dreams and memories. How dashing he had looked upon his horse, riding at the queen's side when she came victoriously into London. And at the church that day of her wedding, she had thought herself lost to Seton's trickery, but Richard had been there. Always he had thought of her well-being above his own, and in the end his love had been his undoing. If only he had not ridden in search of her that day. . . .

A tolling bell struck twelve times. The noon hour. She knew that she should go home; she could not walk the streets of the city indefinitely. Walking through the fog, she started in that direction, only to hear the sound of a frantic voice calling out behind her.

"Heather! Heather! Heather!"

Turning, she saw that it was Tabitha. Sweet, loyal Tabitha, who always tried to share her grief. This was one time when her words could do nothing to soothe her, yet out of common courtesy she paused and let the young woman catch up with her.

"Tabitha, I . . . I don't mean to sound unkind, but I want to be alone."

Tabitha didn't answer at first, merely threw her arms around Heather's neck. Heather stepped back, her face etched in anger. "How can you be joyful?"

"He's not dead. Richard Morgan is not dead."

"What mockery is this? He is dead. I just left Tower Hill and they told me—"

"He escaped. Rafael Mendosa came to the house to tell you." Her voice lowered to a whisper. "He is on a ship, waiting for you to come to him. A ship bound for Spain!"

Heather was afraid to believe. She had thought this morning for only a brief time that he had been spared, only to be cruelly disillusioned.

"Tabitha, please. I know that you are trying to be helpful, to give me hope, but there is none. There is none!" Shrugging off the other's woman's hands, Heather walked along by herself.

"No. No. I am telling you the truth. Richard Morgan is alive. We have no time to talk about it. Come with me. The docks. You are to meet him at the docks." Tabitha tugged at Heather's arm, pulling her in the opposite direction from which she walked.

"Alive? Alive?" Like a sleepwalker she followed after the servant girl.

"You cannot take the time to go back to the house

for your things. I will tell your mother what has happened. She will understand. And if she does not, well, it is what you must do anyway."

The fog was much thicker now, like wisps of smoke, curling around them as they walked. It was nearly impossible to see one's hand before one's face, and had Heather not known the city streets so well, they might well have been lost. It was a long walk to the docks, with nary a light to guide them; still, the smell of the water beckoned them on.

"I can't believe it," Heather said aloud, looking toward the heavens to offer up her thanks. "Richard alive." Even a figure stepping out of the fog to block their way did not take away her smile.

"Who goes there?" asked the voice.

Heather answered without a second thought, "Heather Bowen." At her words the man reached out to grab her. She shook free of his arms.

"It's her," he yelled to another. "The one we're after. Catch her." As Heather fled down the cobblestones, the two men gave chase, Tabitha following in Heather's tracks. They didn't stop to question why they were being pursued; for the moment, that did not matter.

The fog proved to be Heather's friend as she ran across the street to crouch behind a large hawthorn hedge. The sound of running feet passed by her and she peered through the foliage to watch as the darkened figures sped by.

Who are they? she thought in panic. Why are they after *me*? Had they mistaken her for someone else? No, she had spoken her name quite plainly. Had it something to do with Richard? Yes, that was it. They thought she would lead them to Richard. Never!

Filled with the need to protect Richard, to see him again, she slipped from her hiding place as soon as it seemed to be safe. Running down the roadway, darting in and out among the bushes, she felt like a mouse trying to escape from a cat. Brambles clutched at her skirts, roots and branches seemed to reach out and trip her. Once or twice she turned her ankle on the rough and stony ground, only to get up again to renew her flight.

She was afraid to call out to Tabitha, fearful that her voice would fall upon the wrong ears and she would be caught, thus she sped down the cobblestones in silence. Here and there a flickering light led her way, but for the most part the fog seemed like an immense gray cocoon.

"I have to reach the docks!" she whispered as she ran. It was the thought that kept her going, even when she tripped over one of the cobblestones and hurtled to the ground with a shriek. The fall knocked the breath from her body, and she lay upon the damp ground, pain streaking through her, fighting with every ounce of strength and courage she had to get back up again.

"Heather?" The voice was faint, barely more than a whisper. From where she lay, Heather could see the shadowy figure of Tabitha hovering above her. "I heard you cry out. Are you all right?" Reaching out her hand, she helped Heather stand up.

"My ankle. I can't walk on it. I must have sprained it." She tried to walk but could manage only a limp. "We must hurry. If you heard my cry, then whoever is trying to subdue me must have heard it too." She hobbled a short distance, only to wince in pain. "Ohhhhhh." What a time to be injured.

"Lean on me. Together we can make it to the docks." Much like revelers at the fair indulging in the three-legged race, Heather and Tabitha made their way down the roadway, ducking into doorways from time to time or dodging behind trees and hedges. Heather breathed in the scent of triumph in the smell of the waters.

Turning to Tabitha, she laughed with the pure tinkling sound of happiness, only to collide full force with a man blocking her way. "Who are you?" he asked, clutching her arm. This time Heather was not so foolish as to answer. "I said, who are you?" Struggling against the arms that held her, Heather found that this man was well-muscled and strong. She was no match for him. She was trapped.

"Please . . ." she whispered, all her hopes tumbling about her.

Again he asked, "Who are you? I am looking for a young woman. I must find her."

"I am not the one you are seeking. Let me go." He would find that she was indeed the woman he searched for in a moment. Her heart pounded in her breast as she tried to pull free of his hands. Where was Tabitha? As if answering her question, the tall girl pushed between Heather and her captor.

"Leave her alone. Let her go!"

"Tabitha!" the man exclaimed in relief. He looked down at Heather, turning her loose. "And you must be Heather. Come, we have no time."

"Rafael!" Tabitha's voice was tinged with worship and happiness. "Heather has twisted her ankle."

"Ah, poor *señorita,*" he said, picking Heather up in his arms. "Follow me, Señorita Tabitha." With his help they made it to the docks, only to hear the man with them curse loudly in anger. "I told them to wait. I told them not to sail without us."

Heather tried in vain to see the reason for his ill temper. All she could see was a ship slowly pulling away from the docks; then she realized. "Richard's ship!" It was leaving without her.

"Keep your arms around me, Señorita Heather, tightly." He took a leap forward, grabbing hold of the ship's tiller as if by superhuman effort. Hanging there, pulling himself up on the thick pole of the bonaventure mast, he watched as the sailors pulled Heather aboard the ship, then reached down his hand to clutch Tabitha's hand, drawing her upward. Her last thoughts were that it was crazy, what she was doing. She had no business being aboard this ship. What madness possessed her? Thomas Bowen would give her a sound beating for this foolishness, and yet at this moment all else was unimportant except that she was going with Rafael Mendosa.

Heather too felt the exhilaration of the chase, giving herself up now to the host of strong arms which reached to help her onto the deck of the ship. So close, she had been so close to disaster.

"Heather!" She recognized the voice of the man she loved, and succumbed to the overpowering emotions she felt at that moment. As she was swept into his strong arms, her mouth ached to feel his lips, her body burned to have him hold her again. A wave of happiness washed over her as she fell into Richard's arms.

67

BLUE SHIMMERING WATER, as far as the eye could see, the changing colors of the vast ocean—turquoise, pale blue and the deepest blue of the same hue as the summer sky. Heather sighed with happiness as she stood beside Richard at the rail of the *Canción*. They were headed south with the wind at their backs. South to Spain and a new life.

The breeze tore at her hair, and the salt spray splashed her face as she gazed out at the ocean. She felt the strength of Richard's arms draw her closer. It was as if it were the most natural thing in the world to stand at the railing and kiss each other. The sailors rushing about them only turned to each other and winked as if to say: Ah, to be so in love.

"Will you be glad to have your feet again upon land?" Richard asked, nuzzling her neck as he whispered the words.

"On land or on the sea, I am happy as long as we are together," she answered, admiring this handsome man of hers. She looked upon him with admiration. His face was sun-bronzed from the days at sea, making a startling contrast together with his blue eyes and black hair. She liked him minus his beard; his jaw was firm and strong. If his face was thinner from his weeks in prison, well, it only seemed to make him all the more attractive.

Heather admired his narrow hips and well-muscled chest, his strong legs which now stood slightly apart as he kept his balance on the rolling deck. The fabric of his shirt molded to his muscular chest, and she remembered the feel of those arms as he held her. Even though he was dressed as the others, in the same sailor's garb, she could always tell his tall figure as he walked about the deck or climbed the rigging. She loved him so. Each day of pain, each moment of sadness and disappointment had been worth enduring, for now they were together. There was only this time, this place, and the arms of the man she loved. Looking up at him, she met his eyes boldly and smiled.

"Ah, when you smile at me that way, I forget everything, Heather. I love you. And yet the fact remains that we are homeless, you and I. I have naught to offer you but myself."

"That is all I want, all I ever wanted," she whispered, reaching up to entwine her arms around his neck. "Perhaps all is not lost for us. We have Mendosa's friendship, and if my father is still alive, I will seek him out and see if he can be of any help to us in our new life."

"Yes, your father. I had forgotten that you are of Spanish blood, my love."

"Mother told me all about him while you were locked in the Tower. We shared our heartache, she and I. Rodrigo de Vega, that is his name. He sailed with Francisco Pizarro and Hernando de Soto in search of new lands, leaving my mother with the promise to return. He never came back, leaving her with empty promises and a child in her belly. Me." Her voice was tinged with bitterness. "All these years I wondered why she was so meek and mild with Thomas Bowen, and now I know the reason. It was because she was so grateful to him. He married her and gave her child a name."

"A beautiful child," he whispered, stroking her hair. "I feel sorry for this de Vega not to have watched you grow into a beautiful woman."

Her eyes were as stormy as the sea. "I feel no sorrow for him. I will never forgive him. Never. If it were not that we are fugitives, I would not want to see him, but circumstances often melt away one's pride." She shook her head sadly. "No doubt he will not be too anxious to see the proof of his perfidy, but he cannot deny I am his child. My mother has told me that it is from this Rodrigo de Vega that I come by my red hair and gray eyes."

He touched her face gently. "Then I thank him with all my heart." There was silence between them for a long moment as he gazed at her, at the slight widow's peak he loved so well, her upturned nose, the flawless skin of her complexion. He remembered that first night he had seen her. Had he loved her even then? Yes.

"Ah, the lovebirds," Rafael Mendosa said with a smile, coming up behind them. "What think you of the sea, Señorita Heather?"

"It is beautiful, Rafael, so peaceful and serene."

He laughed. "For the moment, *señorita.* Like a beautiful woman, it is unpredictable and full of spirit at times. Let us hope that you do not witness first-hand its temper." He looked about the deck, his eyes searching for someone. "Señorita Tabitha. Where is she?"

"In one of the smaller cabins below. I fear that she is not as fortunate as I. The sickness of the sea ails her." Actually Heather suspected that part of the blond woman's problem was nerves. Nerves and shyness. The way she blushed and trembled whenever Rafael Mendosa was near had not gone unnoticed by Heather. She has fallen under his spell, Heather thought. How I hope that he will not break her heart.

"She is ill?" His voice was filled with concern and tenderness, easing Heather's fears. "Is there anything that I can do for her?"

"Tabitha is resting now, but there is something you can do for me."

"Anything, Señorita Heather."

"Have you heard of Rodrigo de Vega? He sailed with Hernando de Soto to the New World."

"De Vega?"

"Yes. Rodrigo de Vega. He is my . . . my father."

If he was shocked by her revelation, he did not

show it, maintaining as always his undeniable charm. "Rodrigo de Vega. Yes, I have heard of him. He is one of Philip's most trusted nobles. A man of great renown. I have met him once or twice while in Castile."

"Philip's noble? I'll be damned," Richard swore. "It seems that all is not as bleak as we thought, if he will help us."

Heather brushed at her skirt with agitation, asking the question that had to be asked. "Is he married now?"

Rafael shook his head no. "But I believe that he was several years ago. He has always been a man of subtle mystery, this explorer noble, as if he bears a great sadness in his heart.

"Or guilt," Heather said, ignoring Rafael's quizzical look.

"Will you help us find him, Rafael?" Richard asked, trying to soothe the tension which had suddenly sprung up between his friend and the woman he loved.

"*Sí, amigo,* I will help you." He swept Heather a most gracious bow. "And now I must go below to look upon another fair face, the Señorita Tabitha. I have just the thing to soothe her." Smiling at the two lovers, he took his leave of them, walking upon the swaying deck as if upon solid earth.

"An interesting man, our Mendosa," Richard exclaimed.

"I like him. I hope with all my heart that he proves to be the man Tabitha has longed for all her life. A woman needs a man to love, as I love you." In answer he reached out to cup her face in his hand, bringing his lips down to hers for a kiss that mingled gentleness with desire.

"I love you. The thought of never seeing you again wounded me more deeply than the wrongful cry of traitor." The stark emotion in his voice touched Heather's heart. "When we get to Spain, I want you to marry me, before a priest and before God."

"Marry you." The words sounded so precious to

her. How long had she waited to hear him say them? "I will marry you."

Pulling her into his arms, he crushed her against the warmth of his chest. "Only death will part us now."

The creak and sway of the ship kept Tabitha awake. She opened her eyes as the cabin door swung open. "Heather?" she asked softly, stifling a groan. Never in all her life had she felt so miserable. This horrible seasickness robbed her of any poise and dignity.

"No, *señorita,* not Heather. Rafael."

She buried her face in the pillow, refusing to look at him. What must he think of her? He would surely think her weak and sickly as well as plain of face. Fighting the urge to cry, she remained silent and unmoving until she felt a hand on her hair, stroking the soft curly strands with a gentleness that was surprising for someone so large and so strong.

"I am so sorry that you are not well," she heard him say.

The motion of the ship seemed to tie her stomach in knots, yet she managed somehow to turn over on her back and gaze up at him. "I'm all right. Really I am," she lied, only to clasp her hand over her mouth at the sudden motion of the ship. Running from the bed, she was just barely in time to reach the chamber pot before her stomach emptied its contents. In humiliation she was sick in front of the very man whose admiration she so longed to obtain.

"Poor *señorita,*" she heard him say as he moved about the room. The next thing she knew, he had dampened a cloth with water from a pitcher near the bedside and was wiping her face and forehead. Bright splotches of red blazed high on her cheeks to have him see her like this. "Lie down, *señorita.* I have something which will help you in this first time at sea." He handed her what appeared to be a handful of weeds. "Chew these. I promise you that they will make you feel much better."

She would have taken them if he had given her wooden pegs to eat. "Thank you. You are very kind."

At her quizzical look he answered, "A rare blend of strawberry leaves, spearmint, and just a bit of sage. My mother's concoction. She often gave it to me when I was a small boy and we sailed upon my father's ship."

Tabitha looked at him shyly, wondering what he must have been like as a child. Handsome even then, she thought. "They taste good together," she stated in surprise.

When at last she had chewed them a long while, he put forth a small linen handkerchief. "Spit them into this. Don't swallow them."

Again she was embarrassed, but did as he said. He left the bed for a moment and came back with a cup of water in his hand and bade her drink it. She sipped it slowly, her eyes riveted upon his face all the while. When she was finished he pushed her gently down upon the bed and pulled a woolen blanket up over her.

"Sleep," he said to her. "If you need anything, anything at all, call me."

"Thank you, Rafael," she whispered. He closed the door, leaving Tabitha to her dreams.

68

FROM THE DECK of the *Canción* Heather watched the ocean, so peaceful now. But as Rafael had said, it could be violent. Last night there had been such a storm that she had feared lest the ship topple over and throw them all into its mighty depths. Richard and Rafael had not shown panic, but she and Tabitha had huddled together in Tabitha's tiny cabin, clutching to the very beams for support in a world gone topsy-turvy. Now all was calm again.

Heather's eyes sought out Richard. She never tired of looking at him. As he worked, he removed his shirt. The wide expanse of his bare chest always stirred her emotions as the sinewy strength of his muscles rippled with his every movement. Was there a more handsome man anywhere?

Sensing her eyes upon him, he turned to look at her, his eyes smoldering, flashing her a devilish grin, his teeth as white as the pearls the Spanish galleon carried on board.

"Heather."

Heather was surprised to find Tabitha standing behind her. So Rafael's gentle ministrations to the girl *had* healed her. Heather smiled at the way Tabitha looked at Rafael and at the fond look he returned. There was a flash of attraction that sparked between the handsome Spaniard and the blond-haired young woman. Gone was the meek servant, and in her place was a woman of poise and natural charm.

Why, she is almost beautiful, Heather thought, looking at Tabitha standing by the railing with her long hair blowing in the wind. It was like the change of a caterpillar into a butterfly.

Sensing Heather's eyes upon her, Tabitha turned and smiled. "I feel as if I was only half-alive before now. I've never felt this overpowering love before. Even thinking about him makes my heart flutter. I will never forget how kind and gentle he was to me. Now I fully understand your feelings for your Richard."

"Rafael is a fine man. I'm happy for you, Tabitha."

"I know that he is as high above me as the stars above the earth, and yet somehow I sometimes think he feels the same about me. Yet perhaps it is only a dream. Sometimes if you want something so very much you imagine that your dream has come true."

"I think he cares for you, Tabitha. Why wouldn't he? You are a very pretty young woman."

Tabitha clasped her hands to her breast and her blue eyes widened. "No. No, I am not. I am plain and tall, yet when he looks at me I feel beautiful."

Heather shook her head sadly. Thomas Bowen had chided this sweet girl so often that he had convinced her of her unworthiness. "You are beautiful." Beauty was deeper than just the surface, an inner glow from the soul, a gift that Tabitha had been given by Rafael's love.

From behind them the women heard the sounds of the Spanish sailors talking, their voices raised in agitation.

"Por allí, por allá. Un barco . . . otro barco. Siguiente detrás."

The words stirred fear in Heather's soul. "Ships! Following us." Searching for Richard, she saw him striding toward her.

"You and Tabitha go below at once!" he thundered. "There are two ships headed toward us and we know not yet whether they be friend or foe." He didn't say the words, yet Heather knew that he feared that Seton followed them.

"I will not leave," she answered stubbornly.

"I said go below. Now!" Tabitha scurried off, used

to doing as she was told, but Heather stood her ground, sensing the danger they were in.

"If I am to die, it will be by your side."

He looked at her in anger, but his emotion melted away at the look of love in her eyes. "If it is an English ship, I will carry you down below myself if need be. Stay until we see what ship seeks us."

Looking out toward the ships, she sought to judge for herself. The *Canción* was said to be faster and more maneuverable than most ships. Although she was built for trading and carrying gold from other lands to Spain, still the *Canción* was equipped with small cannon.

"Surely we need not worry. The cannon . . ." she thought aloud.

"Are not good at a distance. We can only hope to keep them from boarding us if they are enemy." As the captain issued his orders, Richard left her. The sound of tramping feet sounded as the sailors too hurried to obey.

They were English ships. Heather knew full well what that meant. "Seton!" It couldn't be true. Not when everything was going so well. Not when they had at last found peace and contentment. "No!"

But it was true. Men swarmed the deck brandishing their weapons. It seemed as if all hell had broken loose. She watched three men scramble into the rigging, trying their best to fully unfurl the sails. The wind was blowing against them, holding the ship still. There was no way that the *Canción* could outrun the pursuing ships. Puffs of smoke billowed from one English ship as it fired upon them. The deck shuddered as wood splintered from the railing.

"Damn bastards. Damn bloody bastards!" Richard shouted in frustration. "We have been hit."

The *Canción* struck her colors and topsails to show nonaggression to the other ship, yet the English ships moved steadily onward. Another shot brought damage to the rigging, and still another sent wounded sailors sprawling to the deck, smeared with their own blood.

"We must surrender. I want no trouble with these English," shouted the captain. "Philip wants peace between our countries, not war. Even now he is King of England by proxy marriage."

"No. No surrender!" Richard yelled, overcome by his desperation, his will to survive. The other sailors glared at him, knowing full well the reason for this confrontation. They were not willing to die for an Englishman. Muttering among themselves, scowling in his direction, they made it clear what the outcome of this battle would be.

"Surrender!" came the shout.

Rafael rushed forward. Unlike the others, he would not admit defeat. "No. No, we must fight!" The roar of a cannon sounded just as he stepped to the beakhead, the force of the explosion hurling him to the deck of the ship.

"Rafael. No," Heather shrieked, seeing him fall. Ignoring the danger, she ran to him. He was holding his side in pain.

"I am hit!" he breathed, seeking to stanch the flow of blood with his hands.

Tabitha ran to his side, having heard Heather's cry. "Rafael. Rafael," she sobbed, gathering him into her arms. "No. Please no." Gently she tended his wound as Heather rushed to Richard's side. The Spanish were now flying the flag of surrender, allowing the Englishmen to board.

"We can hide, Richard," she whispered, reaching ou to him.

"Hide? Where? No. No more running. It is time we faced Seton. Surely God cannot let a man like him be the victor. It is against all that is holy."

"He will kill us both!" She fought against her all-consuming fear. "But we will die together. I will never again be parted from you, Richard. Not again. Never again."

They stood together on the deck like two carved figureheads, fearless in their love. It was thus that Hugh Seton found them, the sound of his laughter floating in the wind like the cry of the devil himself.

"I have you. I have you. I knew that you would take to the sea." His eyes blazed with hatred as he stood before them. "This time it will not be the painless executioner's ax for you, Richard Morgan," he hissed. "I will see to it that you face the fiery flames of the stake!" He gestured to one of his men, who took hold of Heather, pushing her roughly along before him. Only then did Richard fight like one possessed.

"Do what you will to me, Seton, but leave her alone! She has naught to do with this hatred between us. Set her free." Lashing out with flaying fists, he struck Seton once before he was subdued.

"Free? I think not. I will not rest until I see you both aflame at the stake." Gesturing again, he watched with glittering eyes as two well-muscled men inflicted punishment upon Richard for striking him. Standing with feet apart, Hugh Seton appraised his alleged half-brother. "Take him away."

"May you rot in hell, Seton!" Richard spat, struggling with his captors. "Some way I will be free of you."

"There will be no priest to save you this time," Seton shot back. "I would have had Roderick's head if not for the queen and her fondness for priests." He would take them back to England, this traitor and his heretic, witchly lover. The taste of revenge was like the sweetest of wines. "For dressing as a priest you will burn, Morgan. You and your lover will burn!"

III

The Law of Love

London

Who can give law to lovers? Love is a greater law to itself.

—Boethius

69

THE STALE ODOR of rotting straw assailed Heather's nostrils as she looked about her at the cold stone walls of her prison cell. Clasping her hands together tightly, determined to be brave, she discovered that it was easier said than done, for the thought of the fires was terrifying. That she would be found guilty, she had no doubt, for after having witnessed Richard's trial, she had no faith in the justice of trial by one's peers. Perjury and bribery were all too common. Seton would win his guilty verdict by such measures.

And what of the queen? Heather knew that there would be no mercy for either Richard or herself in that quarter. Mary Tudor had changed from a gentle queen into a fanatic whose only thought seemed to be the punishment of those she considered heretics. There were those who were calling her "Bloody Mary" behind her back. No doubt Seton had taken a hand in her zeal to burn all those who might make England unsafe for Philip. Hadn't he said as much when Heather had gone to the queen to plead for Richard? All might have been different now if he had not interfered. Mary had begun to soften toward Richard until he had spoken out. On the ship he had said that Richard would burn as a heretic because he had disguised himself as a priest. His eyes had blazed with hatred as he had said, "This time it will not be the painless executioner's ax for you, Morgan!" The echo of his words still sounded in her ears.

"Oh, Richard, where are you? In which cell are you entombed?" Closing her eyes, she recalled the ordeal of their arrest. Arriving back at the London docks, she and Richard had been jeered by the crowds which had flocked to see the traitor and his "witch" lover. No doubt Seton had spread the word of their arrival. In the dark of night they had been rowed up the Thames to traitor's gate, and Heather could not help but remember that other time she had entered by way of this entrance. If only she had known then what awaited her now, she would never have risked her life to carry forth that letter.

"A pox on Mary," she whispered in anger. How could Northumberland have been any worse a ruler? Or Lady Jane Grey? At least that personage had shown her mercy. Mary seemed not to know the meaning of the word, at least in these days. Even Perriwincle had turned against her in a fit of righteous anger when he had visited Heather only a few days before. He had told her then that it was rumored that the council was debating a bill at the very moment which would reenact the Heresy Act of 1401, whereby heretics could be burned alive unless they recanted. So how could Heather think that she or Richard would be spared?

The walls were cold and damp and she clutched her woolen cloak tightly to her body. It was the only possession she had been allowed to keep with her. Even her jewelry had been taken from her.

Sitting down upon a small wooden stool, she fantasized ways to escape from her cell. Remembering all that Richard had told her of his own escape, she had to smile at the thought of the daring of his brother. But he would not be able to help Richard now.

Cold, hungry, and miserable, she fought against her tears. Richard. Was he all right? Was he suffering similar pangs of hunger and thirst? What she would have given to have his strong arms enfolding her, keeping her warm with his body, but of course Seton had insisted that they be parted. How she loathed that man!

Rising from the stool, she sought the hard contours of her cot. Closing her eyes, she gave herself up to dreams and memories.

A rattle of keys jarred her from her reverie. Looking up, she saw the face of the guard peering at her through the grille of the wooden door. "I have a visitor for you."

"A visitor?" If it was Seton, she would soon tell him what she thought of him.

But it was not Seton. Blythe Bowen's face appeared at the opening of the door. "Heather, oh Heather, are you well?"

"Mother!"

The guard opened the door with a grunt, pushing the merchant's wife within. "Only a few minutes now, mind you."

Heather ignored the guard's gruff voice and ran to her mother's arms, clinging tightly to Blythe. Always as a child she had felt so safe in her mother's arms, and now was no different. Her mother would protect her. She would see that no harm touched her.

"I want to get you out of this place," Blythe whispered, crying softly, the tears mingling with Heather's own. "A witch. What utter nonsense. We are no longer in the Dark Ages."

"It is Hugh Seton, Mother. He is responsible." She looked into Blythe's eyes. "I would never have harmed Edlyn, though I *would* have profited by her death. I pitied her and sought to bring her what kindness I could."

"I know. I know, my poor darling. You would not even seek to harm a mouse, and yet they are saying that you poisoned her. How can people be so stupid, so cruel?" She broke away from their embrace and held her daughter away from her, looking deep into her eyes. "You must tell me everything. Surely there is something that can shed some truth on this evil lie. Who would profit from that poor woman's death?"

"Hugh Seton. She died long before Richard was judged a traitor. I think that he wanted to make certain that the manor would be his, one way or another. It would not be a difficult thing to bribe someone to do his bidding." She bit her lip, trying hard to think of who might have done the deed. Agnes was gone, Matty would never have done such a thing, but what of Undine? The old woman had come from out of nowhere, throwing herself on Heather's pity. No, Undine had treated Edlyn with tender care. Hadn't she even thought to give her a potion to help her sleep? "A potion," she breathed. Now she remembered the way the old crone had pulled the cup away from her hand that one day when she had reached for the brew meant for Edlyn. Could it have contained poison? Had the woman been poisoning poor Edlyn under Heather's very nose?

"Yes." The answer had to be yes. It was the only answer. How could Heather have been so blind, not to see the woman's intent, despite her flowery words and smiling glances?

"Heather, what is it?" Blythe asked, sensing her daughter's stiffening movement.

"I think I know who poisoned her. Undine. *Undine.*" The messenger who had brought the news of Edlyn's death had remarked that the old woman had stayed by Edlyn's bedside, but that had not been out of affection, it had been to be certain the poor childish woman was dead.

"Undine? Tell me who she is and I will have Perriwincle seek her out at once," Blythe said angrily. "Let us hope that somehow he can find her."

"She is an old woman with the face of a shriveled-up apple and a head of white hair," Heather said softly, seeing the woman before her eyes as if she stood in front of her. "Small, like a dwarf, short legs. She has a nervous tic to her left eye and a nose which slopes down like the awning of the baker's windows."

"If anyone can find her, Perriwincle can," Blythe whispered. "But tell me, are they feeding you enough?"

"One guard has been kind to me, but the other has given me only moldy bread and water."

Blythe clenched her teeth in anger. "Well, I daresay that shall soon be stopped. Money seems to speak very loudly here. These guards are as money-hungry as your father. I'm certain that with enough gold exchanged you will soon find the food fit for the queen herself. I will see to it."

"Mother . . ."

"Yes?"

"Please make certain that the same is done for Richard."

"It shall be done," Blythe said with a wink. Hearing the footsteps of the guard, she looked sadly at her daughter. "Have you heard about your friend Anne Fairfax?" she asked.

"Anne? No." Heather thought her to be at Whitehall with the queen.

"She has been found guilty of heresy. It seems that her views on God do not hold with Mary's. Tomorrow at dawn she is to burn at the stake."

"Anne? No. No. Never was there a woman who was closer to God. How can they call her a heretic?" Heather shook her head in shock. Anne Fairfax, the queen's own lady-in-waiting, keeper of the bedchamber? "Has the entire realm gone mad? What is to become of us all?" The news shook her perhaps more than her own danger, for Anne had always been so wise, a woman far beyond her time. Now she would be burned, and for what reason? What had she done?

"She was found with a copy of Cranmer's *Book of Common Prayer,*" Blythe whispered, looking around her, lest someone overhear.

"The Book of Common Prayer . . ." Heather thought of her father. He too owned the prayer book. It was his treasure, with its letters of gold and fine leather cover. There must be, in fact, many people who had one in their possession, despite the foolish law that had been passed a few months ago. For years Londoners had read from its pages. Now Anne Fairfax was to die for doing that which half of London was guilty of doing. It was absurd.

"Nor would she denounce Bishop Latimer. She has spoken out against the queen's intent to burn heretics. Now she will burn."

"And I suppose Catherine Todd has again worked her evil."

"Yes. Her testimony was very damaging. She spoke of how Anne talked against the queen."

"There was never a more loyal servant of Mary. Anne but spoke the truth, but it seems that to do so now brings one death," Heather answered bitterly. She shuddered at the thought of what awaited her friend. It was too horrible to imagine, and yet she and Richard faced the same fate.

The guard came to take Heather's mother away, but Heather seemed not to notice. Her eyes were vacant in her shock. Anne Fairfax. Laughing Anne, who had pushed Catherine Todd into the pond, who had been the only one besides Stephen Vickery to speak out for Richard at his trial. Anne Fairfax, her friend. With a dismal cry of outrage Heather beat her fist against the prison door.

70

THE SMALL BEDCHAMBER was swathed in light from the many oil lamps hung about as Tabitha tended the wounded man on the bed. She had cared for him with infinite tenderness these past days, her soft voice and gentle hands the only blessed thing he was aware of.

Surprisingly, Thomas Bowen had been overjoyed to let Tabitha bring him to the Bowen home to recuperate from his wounds, and had even shown Tabitha great kindness these last days. He constantly fawned over their guest, and though she had the suspicion that it was more than human kindness which caused this shift in Thomas Bowen's mood, she hastily pushed such thoughts aside. The only thing that mattered was that the Spaniard regain his health.

"Rafael? Are you awake?" Tabitha asked now, leaning over the bed.

"*Sí.* I am awake," he answered hoarsely. Swathed in bandages, he looked somehow ghostly, but underneath the linen was the man she loved. She could still envision that moment at sea when she had seen him lying on the deck of the ship covered in blood. At that moment she had thought him dead.

Rafael struggled to sit up. "Richard Morgan . . ." His voice trailed off as he asked the unspoken question.

"He and Heather have been taken to the Tower. Heather's trial is to be in but two days." She sighed. "Richard has been charged with heresy. By this time the entire city knows that he masqueraded as a priest to escape his death. Seton has seen to that. As a heretic he will burn."

"Can he be blamed for such an act? He is no heretic, only one who loves his life." Rafael remembered well what Richard had done. He and Father Stephen had both formulated the plan.

"We do not blame him, but there are those who call it heresy in these troubled times." As she put a glass of cool water to his lips, his fingers tightened upon hers in a gesture of thankfulness and caring.

All his life Rafael had searched for a woman who was truly beautiful within her heart, one who was not gilt but gold, and now he had found her. "How can I ever thank you?"

"Just get well," she whispered, averting her eyes. Reaching down, she sought to pull a blanket up over him lest he catch a chill from the open window, her eyes lingering like a caress upon the strong planes of his body. He was all strength and beauty. "Let me close the window."

The fragrance of her skin, like fresh morning flowers, assailed him, but it was her voice, that low, melodious lilt, that drew his heart. He could listen to her for eternity and never tire of hearing her. And her eyes. If the eyes were indeed the mirror of the soul, then she was truly beautiful.

"No. Don't move. Stay by my side." He reached out and took her hand, longing to gather her into his arms. He wondered if her lips would really be as soft as he imagined, as sweet. It was thus that Blythe Bowen found them, looking deeply into each other's eyes, but Tabitha quickly moved away as her mistress entered the room.

"You have seen Heather?" Tabitha asked.

"Yes. She is pale and thin and I worry . . ." Blythe Bowen broke down in an uncharacteristic flood of tears. For so many years she had been the strong one, a strength underneath her gentle disguise. Now her strength was crumbling as she thought of the fate which awaited her daughter.

Tabitha tried to soothe her. "All will be well. They cannot prove her guilty. They cannot."

Blythe shook her head. "They can and they will, just as they did with Richard Morgan. I brought her into this world only to witness her suffering. God give me the strength." Burying her face in her hands, she gave vent to her anguish. "Oh, that I had not met Rodrigo de Vega, never borne Heather to suffer this pain."

"Rodrigo de Vega," Rafael repeated, remembering his conversation with Heather that day on the ship. "Of course, I should have remembered."

Blythe looked toward the bed with confusion. "You know him?" she asked.

"Yes. Heather and I talked about him. She had thought to find him so that he could help Richard and help her as well, in their new life in Spain, but fate was not kind to them."

"Rodrigo de Vega!" Blythe spat in anger. "Is he still sailing around the world in search of his fortune?"

"No, he is now living in Spain. He is Philip's closest adviser. I heard it rumored that he would be accompanying Philip to England."

"To England after all these years," Blythe breathed, trying without success to push away the bitterness the years had brought. "I shall tell him that he is too late to see his daughter. I will watch his face when I tell him of her fate."

Forgetting his pain, Rafael sat up in bed. "Of course, I should have thought of this before, *señora.* It is said that your queen is insanely fond of her new consort, that she dotes on his every word. Would she then put to the torch the daughter of one of her husband's advisers? And what of Philip? Surely he would show leniency to this half-Spanish daughter of yours?"

"We have no time. The trial is in a few days," Blythe answered. And yet, if it was possible . . . She would throw away her pride if it would save Heather's life. Surely no father would stand by and watch his own daughter burn at the stake. But could she get a message to him in time? Could she stay Mary's hand for just a short time? She had to try.

Tabitha, silent until now, remembered a bit of gossip she had heard on the street. "I heard it said that a Spanish envoy is to arrive in four days' time. Dare we to hope? There was talk that it is for the purpose of arranging the wedding ceremony that this envoy is to arrive in London. I heard it said that Mary fears that they will be pelted with stones as the other envoy was in January when they arrived."

"A Spanish envoy," Blythe Bowen repeated. "It is perhaps our only hope." She who had been meek for so many years was now to take a hand in saving her daughter's life.

71

THE TRIAL HAD gone much as Heather had supposed it would. The verdict was guilty before the jurors sat upon their benches along the far wall, before the judge took his place at the front of the large room. Now Heather had been returned to the Tower to await her doom.

"Please, let me stay with her. For just a few moments. Please. I am her mother," Blythe pleaded, wiping away her tears. The guard grunted in answer, opening the door, and Heather felt the warm comfort of her mother's arms wrap around her.

"Guilty. I am judged guilty," Heather whispered tonelessly, wondering what dreadful evil could have brought about such a travesty of justice.

"I had prayed for a miracle. Oh, if only Perriwincle could have found Undine, but perhaps she has vanished into the fog."

"Perriwincle will find her. He has to. He must. It is our only hope!" Time was running out for Heather and for Richard. Only Hugh Seton's desire to make them suffer a long while had kept them alive this long; otherwise they would have been burned days ago.

Blythe looked at her daughter, hiding her own fear. After talking with Rafael Mendosa she had begun to have hope, had tried in vain to find Rodrigo de Vega, to plead with him if necessary, but just like Undine, he was nowhere to be found. If Perriwincle could not find that old woman, if Blythe could not locate Rodrigo in time, what hope was there for her daughter's life? It was a thought which sent chills of fear up her spine. Heather was her life, her baby. How could she bear to see her suffer such a torturous agony as death by fire?

"How could they have lied? How could they have whispered such evil things about me?" Heather sobbed as the proceedings floated before her eyes. It was a mockery. She could still see the woman called Agnes leering and pointing her finger as she told of how Heather had boasted openly that she would soon rid them all of Edlyn.

"Right from the first she made it clear that she was to be mistress of the manor," Agnes had said. "Why, she even had me fired. *Me*, who was ever loyal to his lordship. It was plain to see that she had bewitched him. She is a witch!"

Heather had risen to her feet in indignation. "I am no more a witch than you are!" she had cried out. "I wanted you to leave the manor because of your ill treatment of Edlyn. She was ill and you—"

Agnes had stood up, her eyes pools of malice. "She poisoned that poor dear child with her evil concoctions. I say burn her for her sinful transgressions, let her suffer the pangs of hell!" Agnes had told of seeing Heather fly, her shadow blocking the moon. She had blamed her for causing stomach cramps and for the death of her stillborn grandson. At the conclusion of her testimony there was a clacking of tongues and a shaking of heads as the assembly bent their heads to look upon Heather. Testifying in her own defense, Heather was constantly interrupted with reminders of how she had run away with the man, the traitor and heretic named Richard Morgan.

Hugh Seton insisted that it was by magic that Heather had called forth Richard Morgan that day of his wedding. "She enchanted him as she did me," he exclaimed, waving his fists above the air. "Death to the witch!"

Silence had pervaded the courtroom, an eerie silence. When at last the sentence was passed, Heather was not surprised by the outcome. She had little doubt that the jurors had been bribed by Seton. The way they averted their eyes attested to that fact.

"I was not tried for murder, nor for witchcraft," Heather whispered, clinging to her mother, "but for going away with the man I love. What is the crime in that? Is it evil to love?"

"No," Blythe answered sadly. "Only to be beautiful." She squeezed her daughter tightly, then pushed away from her, looking deep into her eyes. "Now, listen to me, and listen well. Plead your belly. Tell them that you are with child, whether it be true or not . . ."

"I have just had my monthly time."

"It does not matter. Tell them. It will save your life for at least six months' time. Meanwhile I will see that we find this Undine and your father as well. Rodrigo de Vega. Perhaps he can save you. Please, Heather."

Heather was adamant. "No. Not and let Richard die alone. Without him I have no life."

"Heather, you must! You must!"

"No." The look in her eyes told her mother that there was no use in arguing further.

A rattle of keys and the harsh voice of the guard tore Blythe from her daughter's arms. She wanted to scream at the injustice of it all, but that would only have caused her daughter pain, and so instead she maintained her self-control.

"Good-bye, Mother." Heather's voice was a choked sob.

"Good-bye . . ." The harsh reality struck Blythe in the chest. "No. Not good-bye. Somehow—"

"Come along with me!" With hands that were far from gentle, the guard pushed the merchant's wife from the cell.

Blythe lashed out at the guard with flinging hands, helpless in her misery. "They sold their souls by this act. She is innocent. Innocent." Her eyes met those of the guard. "And well you know it, too. I only pray that God will forgive them, for I know well that I cannot."

As Blythe was pushed down the flight of stairs the word "guilty" rang in her ears. Guilty of witchcraft and heresy and sentenced to die in flames at the stake. As she was pushed out the door she fell in a heap to the ground.

"Tomorrow. They will kill my child with the dawn." She could not let this happen. She must save her lovely daughter. Somehow. Tears welled up in her eyes as she buried her head in her hands and sobbed.

72

ALONE IN HER tiny cell, Heather thought of Richard. If only she knew which cell he was in. "What hour is it?" she murmured. Time moved so slowly in the darkened cell that she could not be certain.

"If only I could see him. If only I could be nestled in his arms one more time, I could die bravely," she breathed. Her love for him was the only reality in this tiny room.

Looking through the grille of the wooden door, she could see the shadow of her jailer coming toward her. He was an older man of about her father's age, and unlike the others, he had been kind to her.

Is he bringing me my dinner? she thought bitterly. How could she eat when with the first light of the morrow's dawn she would be burned into cinders? At the thought she wept softly, not even turning around as she heard the creak of her door.

"Come with me," said a gruff voice. "Quickly now." She turned around with a start. Was it already morning? Had he come to take her to her doom? She had thought she would be brave, but now all her resolve crumbled and she fought to still the trembling of her hands.

"So soon I am to die," she whispered. "I had not thought it morning yet."

"It is not morning," came the answer. "I do not come to take you to your death, but to your lover."

"To Richard? Why? How?" She searched his face for the answer and found only sorrow there.

"I have a daughter about your age," he replied to her questioning gaze. "I am of the reformed faith. I have no stomach for this burning. I . . . I heard what you said to your mother, about not pleading your belly, about wanting to die with the man you love, and I . . . somehow I . . . well . . . I can't save your life, nor that of this man you love, but I can at least bring you the comfort of being with him during this last night. I can give you that."

Heather touched his arm. "You have given me the greatest gift of all. You have shown me kindness and given me hope for this world."

He looked quickly away. "Come. We must hurry. If I am found out, it will be my head. If anyone asks you, please do not tell them how you came to be with your lover." He hurried her along the dark corridor, glancing over his shoulder from time to time. When at last he pushed her into another cell and shut the door behind her, Heather found herself standing before the tall, erect figure that she recognized so well.

"Heather?" He looked at her, hardly believing his eyes. "How?"

"It is said that love can move mountains and calm oceans. Just see what magic our love can bring," she said softly. She had hope now. Love *could* bring forth miracles.

"The guard?"

"The guard. He overheard me telling my mother how much I love you and has sought to bring me comfort in these last hours."

"Comfort. Oh, if only he would free you. I could die knowing that you were spared. But how can I bear to see you suffer?"

"Hush!" She ran to his arms and buried her face in the warmth of his chest. "I love you. Always remember that. Our love will free us."

He kissed her savagely then, with all the hunger of his soul. "We have only tonight, my love. Tomorrow they will take our lives, but we will love, you and I, with a flame brighter than those that will claim us."

Heather's heart hammered so loudly that she feared the guards outside would hear it and come to take her away. Her eyes were huge as she looked at this man she loved. After all that they had been through, she wanted only to feel his hard warmth against her, reassuring and strong.

She moved against him in a manner that wrenched a groan from his throat. They couldn't waste any of the precious time they had together. Reaching down, without any trace of modesty she pushed the bodice of her dress from her shoulders, baring her breasts to his gaze and to his touch.

"Beautiful. So beautiful," he breathed, cupping her full breast in his hand. With hands and mouth he explored her soft body, searching out her most sensitive places as she writhed under his touch. Like a flame his lips burned over the soft peaks of her breasts. He stepped away only long enough to strip off his garments, and when he came to her again he was all naked power and throbbing strength.

She had been accused of being a witch, and yet it was he who worked a powerful magic, he who was the weaver of spells. She felt as if she were floating. Let the sunrise come, she thought with a smile. They had the nighttime, and for now that was enough. Pulling the remnants of her gown from her slim body, spreading it upon the straw for their bed, she reached up to bring him down to her.

"Your beard is growing back," she whispered, wondering why of all things she had noticed that.

He grinned at her. "Makes me look more the rebel, don't you think?" His voice sounded toneless, belying his smile. He kissed her again, slowly with a fierce yet tender power. Her insides turned to molten fire at his kiss and her desire raged like an inferno. Naked and burning with passion, she flung her arms around him, holding him close as her mouth returned his kisses with a frantic urgency. All the days of anguish, of searching, of wanting, all the questions in her mind drifted into oblivion as he stroked her. He was maddeningly gentle, bringing her to a fever pitch before he covered her body with his own. So entwined, she slid her fingers across the broad hard-muscled shoulders, thrilling at the ripples of strength that emanated from him. She never got tired of touching him. Her hand explored, stroked, and enclosed the shaft of his manhood, arching to him, wanting him. She was like a blossoming flower, opening to him.

He took her with a powerful surge as she drew him to her, needing him as she had never needed anyone, anything before. He sheathed himself in her searing satiny flesh. They were man and woman coming together, driven by their passion as man and woman had been since the first moment in time.

Heather cried at the wonder and beauty of their love as together they plunged over the chasm and into the flames of ecstasy. Over and over she called out his name as he took her with a tender fury. Clinging to him, her arms about his neck, she answered his movements with her own. She was like a wild thing, like the witch she had been accused of being. In the beauty of their joining, the darkness of the outside world was forgotten, and only the magic of the moment was real. Lying naked, their limbs entwined, they sealed their vows of love and knew at that moment that though they might die, the love they felt at this moment could never be destroyed.

73

BLYTHE BOWEN FLED down the streets of London with the wind at her back, heedless of the dangers. She had only one thought—Heather. She had to find Rodrigo. She had to. It was the only chance that Heather had for life, for happiness. So far it had been like a wild-goose chase. She seemed to be just one step behind this Spanish envoy as they swept through London. Even now she could see the first rays of dawn lighting the sky. How much time did she have? How much time to save her daughter?

"Whitehall," she cried aloud, remembering what the queen's guard had told her. Philip was to arrive during the second week of July, and his Spanish advisers had much to do to get ready for his arrival. It was to be his wedding day. "His wedding. Bah. My daughter's funeral it will be if I do not reach Rodrigo in time."

Would he help her? He must. Surely no man would turn his back on his own daughter. She would plead with him by the love he once bore her.

Running up the steps, pausing only long enough to catch her breath, Blythe ignored the shouts of the guards as she swept into the hall. Aglow with lights which had not yet been extinguished, it was a breathtaking sight. A fire flamed in the fireplace, and wall sconces flared with light.

"Rodrigo de Vega. Where is he?" she demanded of an elaborately dressed young woman. At the woman's stupefied glance, Blythe grabbed her shoulders. "I must see him."

Wordlessly the woman pointed to the stairway, and before she could blink an eye, Blythe had already reached the steps. Taking them two at a time, she sought the right chamber. Two of the doors were locked and she prayed fervently that they were not the ones which housed the man she had once loved. She ran on a little farther, wondering what her punishment would be for so bold an act as entering the queen's palace without invitation. It did not matter, if she could save Heather's life.

She thought she heard voices down the hall. "Please God, let it be him." Her lungs were nearly bursting, her heart thundered in her breast so hard that she feared she would die, still she continued until she was standing before the thick wooden portal. Taking a deep breath, she pushed it open with all her might.

The queen herself stared at the merchant's wife, mouth open, eyes agog. "Who dares to enter unbidden?" she asked in full anger.

"Rodrigo de Vega. I must speak with him," Blythe gasped. From the corner of the room a man stepped forward.

"I am Rodrigo de Vega," he exclaimed.

"Rodrigo. Rodrigo." She could not quite find the words as she looked once again at the face of the man she had so loved. He had changed very little. Wasn't that the way of men? She had grown heavy and gray and yet he looked as if the years had scarcely touched him.

"Who are you?" he asked, searching out her face in the dim light. He reached for a candle and held it in front of her face. *"Cristo Glorioso!"*

"Hello, Rodrigo. We meet again," she managed to choke.

He looked at her as if he had seen a ghost, his face paling beneath his tan. "It is not possible. It is not possible. You are dead," he cried.

"Not dead, very much alive," she answered, wondering at his look of agony.

"But he told me you were dead. Señor Bowen. He said that you and the child were dead."

Blythe's heart lurched in her breast. What vile lie was this? Was this Spaniard trying to save his own conscience? "Perhaps you wish I were dead. Only then would you be free of your guilt. You left me with a child and a broken heart. Did you find your golden land? Was it worth it to leave the woman who loved you more than life itself? Tell me, was it?" Tears were running down her cheeks and she hurriedly wiped them away.

"I didn't know. I didn't know. He told me you were dead. By the blessed Christ, I swear this to be true!" They were oblivious of the staring eyes of the others in the room: there were only Rodrigo de Vega and Blythe Bowen upon the earth at this moment.

Blythe felt as if she could not breathe. She could not think, only feel. She had been betrayed, but not by Rodrigo de Vega. Thomas Bowen had told a most vicious lie to her and to this man she had once loved. Rodrigo had thought her dead all these years. He did not desert her after all. She wanted to laugh, to cry, but there was no time. She would take Thomas Bowen to toll after Heather was safe.

"Our daughter," she murmured. "She is in danger. Even now she faces death. Please, I beg you to save her. She is not a witch, she is not. Heather is innocent."

Before the queen and all assembled, Blythe went down on her knees. She asked for an extension of time for the man named Richard Morgan and for her daughter. Rodrigo de Vega voiced his own plea. "At least let me gaze upon the face of my child once. How can you deny me this?" he asked of Mary.

"This Heather, she is your child?" the queen asked, touched by the scene before her. It reminded her strangely of her own mother to see this woman down on her knees. She would grant this request for this woman, for this man.

"Yes. A better daughter has never been granted to woman, except of course for your Majesty. I beg of you to hear her out. And Richard Morgan. I know well that he fought for you, my queen. You are known for your wisdom and your mercy . . ."

"One week. I will give them one week. If at the end of that time they cannot prove to me that they are not guilty, I will see that their punishment is carried out." Turning her back, Mary swept out of the room.

The rays of the sun shone through the window of the hallway and Blythe looked with horror upon its beams. Morning. Heather would even now be facing her terror alone. Taking Rodrigo's hand, she said only one word. "Come."

74

HEATHER NESTLED IN Richard's arms, dozing peacefully on the straw in the aftermath of their love. She looked as if she had not a worry in the world as she lay beside him, and he too had the look about him of a happy man. It was thus that the guards found them.

"God's blood! What is this? How?" sputtered one guard, the one who had taunted Heather for so long.

"Oddsbody. Surely she *is* a witch to so come to her lover through stone walls." He stepped away as if fearful that just looking at her would bring him misfortune.

The sound of their voices woke the lovers, and instinctively Heather sought the warmth and security of Richard's arms, clinging to him as if their love would keep her from harm.

Recovering his nerve, one guard stepped forward to pull her away from the man beside her, while the other bound Richard's arms behind him. There was no need to struggle; they would die peacefully and bravely side by side.

"Heather, I love you," he whispered, longing to hold her at least one more time. She looked so vulnerable standing between the two guards as they bound her wrists too. If only he had the power to protect her. Her cloud of red hair hung about her shoulders like a halo, making her look more angel than witch, and yet these men did not seem to see her innocence.

"She even has the hair of a witch!" said the largest

of the guards, pulling at the fiery strands until Heather winced. As she turned to scowl at him, he stepped hastily away as if fearful of her ire.

A dark-robed priest came forth, his eyes staring into Heather's own as if to see into her very soul. She met his gaze unflinchingly, determined to be as brave as Anne Fairfax had been. He rambled on and on, much of the time in Latin, but she heard him say, "Repent of your evil!" Crossing himself, he too seemed afraid that she might cast a spell on him.

"I have done no evil. I have loved and been loved. There is only beauty in love, only beauty and peace." Her eyes met Richard's and she smiled.

Pushed and shoved along, Richard and Heather were led down the steeply winding stairs of the Tower to the gate below. Unlike Richard's sentence when he was to have been beheaded, the burnings would not take place on the Tower Green but in one of the Squares of the city instead. With this in mind, the guards had arranged to have two barges waiting which would take the procession downriver to the carts which were waiting beyond London Bridge.

Heather felt Richard's eyes on her and turned to meet his piercing gaze. His expression told her more than words could have ever done. He loved her beyond life itself, just as she loved him. If God were merciful they would be together in the next life.

Shoved onto a waiting cart, driven through the marketplace, Heather tried to keep from looking at the goggling crowd, but it was difficult. Their hissing and booing was louder than the sound of the drums. Elbowing each other, pushing and shoving in their attempt to look at a red-haired witch, they seemed more demon than human. Some threw stones, others sticks, and all jeered as they looked upon the two beings in the cart. The burning of a witch was quite a spectacle.

The procession weaved through the throng of onlookers with a priest at the head, holding aloft his cross. His chanting was nearly driving Heather wild, but each time she seemed close to hysteria, she had only to look at Richard for her calm and love to be renewed. Nothing could harm them if they but believed deeply enough in their love and in God's mercy.

Following behind the priest were two acolytes, the priest's assistants, and behind them the mayor of London himself, strutting proudly as a rooster. The guards, all four, followed the wagon, looking from time to time at Richard and Heather as if fearing they would vanish at any moment.

The raised platform was clearly visible as they rode along. It was raised high enough so that the crowd could view the proceedings. Two stakes were already set up as if to welcome the victims, and the platform was piled high with faggots.

Heather walked with deadly calm to that place, her eyes meeting Richard's with dignity and peace as she stepped upward to the platform.

"I love you," she whispered as they tied her to the stake.

"And I you," she heard him reply.

Heather could see the barber looking at her from the crowd. There was great sympathy written in his eyes, as if he understood how deeply she loved the man beside her. Was he remembering that time when she had brought Richard to him to save his life? No doubt he was.

The faggots were piled around her, waist-high. Looking in Richard's direction, she could see that he too was being surrounded by the large piles of firewood. A black-robed man stood ready to set them alight. Although her knees felt as if they would give way, Heather managed a brave front for Richard's sake. If he sensed her fears, it would only make the ordeal that much harder for him to bear. Brave, she must be brave.

From out of the crowd Hugh Seton stepped forward, a scroll in his hand. He eyed both Richard and the woman at his side with equal malice. His voice was little more than a mumble to Heather's ears.

Over the din of the crowd she heard only ". . . witch . . . God . . . good of the realm . . . Mary's decree."

Richard looked at the man who had so often taunted him. Strangely enough, he felt no hatred. He was too filled with love and concern for the woman bound beside him. She was amazing, this woman of his. Brave even unto death. If only they had had more time together. If only. . . .

Usually bags of gunpowder were placed between the legs of the condemned prisoners so that the flames would cause a speedy death, but Hugh Seton would allow no such reprieve this day. He wanted to watch them suffer the agonies of the fire. "Light the fire," he commanded.

The priest in the crowd chanted words to ward off evil, holding forth his golden cross like a charm. "The soul of a witch may well escape into the rising smoke," he whispered to the crowd. "See that you do not stand too close." Like ants on a disturbed anthill, the throng scurried back.

The dark-robed executioner stepped forward to light the fire, and the crowd began to cheer. What kind of devils were they to so enjoy another's misery? Heather wondered. She felt the heat of the quick-scorching flame and whispered a prayer. It was as if her life flashed before her eyes, all her days of loving the man beside her. He was her life and now she would join him in death.

The smell of burning wood came to Richard, the pungent aroma of the smoke as the fire crackled and sparked and choked Heather. It was as if the flames licked up to caress her. The smoke stung her eyes, leaving them burning and watery.

"I will never see the summer again, never share the smell of the flowers with Richard. We will never see the light of another dawn. Never more will I feel Richard's arms around me, hear his words of love. And yet, I have loved and been loved," she whispered.

Closing her eyes, she imagined that she heard voices. Am I already dead? she wondered. It seemed that she felt someone cutting her bonds. Looking up, she saw a face which was familiar to her and yet unknown, a man she had never seen before. His red hair and gray eyes mocked her.

"Release this woman and this man at once by order of her Majesty, Mary, Queen of England, and of Philip, her consort," she thought she heard him say. What mockery was this? Fighting the dark clouds which hovered before her eyes, Heather at last succumbed, fainting as the arms of the red-haired man reached down to pick her up.

75

HEATHER OPENED HER eyes as gray mists swirled before her. Where was she? Was she in heaven? She could smell the odor of smoke and realized that it was coming from her hair, her clothing. It was then that she remembered. That man. Who . . . ? Was she home?

"You are awake, my love," came a voice.

"Richard?"

"It is I." He grasped her hand and held it to his breast. "We are saved, at least for the time being. Your father—"

"Thomas?" The fog in her brain had not quite cleared yet. Somehow she could not seem to understand. The man. He had looked like her somehow.

"I am your father," came a deep masculine voice. Hovering over her, he looked awesome. Tall and regal, he looked to be some foreign prince. "Rodrigo de Vega is my name." He looked at her with such sadness that she felt pity for him. "Your mother told me of your plight. I had no idea that I had a daughter. A beautiful daughter. I was told that both you and your mother had died."

She wanted to believe him. Somehow she did. He had not the face of a liar, yet she asked, "Who would tell such a lie?"

"The man your mother married. It seems he loved her so much that he broke both her heart and mine to possess her. He took all that was precious from me and left me only half a man. How can I ever forget or forgive his great wrong?" He brushed the hair from her forehead in a fatherly gesture.

Anger swelled within Heather's breast. Anger for the misery her mother had suffered, for the lonely years she had spent, and for the pain this man standing beside her had endured. Thomas Bowen was a miserable, miserly wretch. "I will never forgive him!" She could not help but wonder what her mother would do now, being reunited with the man she loved once. Would she leave Thomas Bowen as she should? Was it possible to recapture the years spent away from a man? Did he still love her mother, this red-haired giant?

"Now at least I know the truth. I have found you, sweet Heather. We must atone for so many years."

Heather could not help the words which spouted from her lips. "Are you married? Will you and mother perhaps . . . ?"

"That is for Blythe to answer," he whispered, looking in the direction of the door. "I still love her and would marry her if she would have me." His eyes grew tender as she walked into the room.

"I am flattered, Rodrigo. You always were a handsome man and you still are. What woman would not want you?"

He took a step forward, gathering her into his arms. "We will go to Spain. I have a grand hacienda there with trees and a fountain. . . .

She shook her head. "No. My place is here."

"Then we will stay here," he said, his brows drawing together in a frown.

"I am a married woman, Rodrigo. Thomas Bowen, right or wrong, liar or saint, is my husband. I spoke vows before God, and I would seek to honor them. If I cannot fully understand what he did so many years ago, if I cannot forgive, I must at least try to forget."

"Forget? How can you forget the love we shared?" He seemed shattered by her words, and Heather's heart went out to him.

"Mother . . . !"

"Hush, Heather." She turned to Rodrigo. "We loved with a passion that outshone the stars, you and I, but that was many years ago. I have made a life and so have you. Let us remember our precious memories and treasure them always. I hope that we can always be friends, if not lovers."

Heather could not believe her ears. Her mother was throwing away her happiness, resigning herself to stay with an ugly, miserly man who had ruined her life by his treacherous lies. She could have had love, passion, and she was turning her back upon it for honor. How could she do such a thing? How? Her mother's words answered her question.

"You see, Rodrigo, you never really needed me. You had your ships and your gold, and though you loved me, I never truly came first with you."

"Blythe. . . ."

"Thomas needs me. He does not know that he does, Heather does not realize that he does, but it is true nonetheless. He needs me and in his own way he loves me. I cannot throw away the years I spent with him because of a dream. You are Heather's father and I hope you will show her the love that you once felt for me." Tears brimmed Blythe's eyes as she stood looking at him. It was as if the years were stripped away and Heather could see the woman her mother used to be. If everyone had choices in life, Blythe had just made hers.

"You are saying that we cannot bring back those years we shared." Rodrigo de Vega sighed. "Perhaps it is true. Yet oh, how I wish that for just one moment we could be young again." He reached out to touch Blythe's cheek, wiping away her tears. "This Thomas Bowen is a very lucky man. What he has is more precious than gold." They stood gazing into each other's eyes as if for a moment the years were stripped away, but a clamoring noise out in the courtyard shattered the spell.

Richard looked out Heather's bedchamber window. "It's Perriwincle. What in the name of all that is holy . . . ? He has a woman with him. Matty!"

Heather remembered Matty. She was the woman who had befriended her and spoken such kind words to her at the Christmas festivities. Surely if anyone would attest to her kind treatment of Edlyn, it was Matty. Standing up and walking to the window on her wobbly legs, Heather looked below. The old man had a bundle of some kind in the back of the wagon. It looked like a bag of shorn wool bobbing up and down. No. It was a person.

"Undine!" she gasped. Cursing at the top of her lungs was the old woman. Perriwincle had arrived a bit late but nonetheless a hero.

"That woman. She is the same one who tended Edward when he was ill. There are some who whispered that she poisoned the young king. How do you know her?" Richard questioned, remembering well the visage of that evil hag.

"She came to the manor begging for shelter. I took her in. I thought she would be good to Edlyn. Instead, she murdered her. I have no doubt that somehow Hugh Seton is involved in the matter."

"Seton? Yes. He told me that he was sending a surprise for you. Now I know what he meant. An evil surprise, one which nearly cost you your life." Putting an arm about her waist, he helped her back to the bed. Grinning mischievously, he bowed low before Rodrigo de Vega. "I would ask you for your daughter's hand in marriage. I love her very much and swear to bring her happiness evermore."

Rodrigo looked from Heather to Richard and then back again. "Daughter, what say you of this?"

"I say that I love him with all my heart and that I will die if you do not say yes." She threw her arms around Richard's neck, holding him close. Now that Undine had been found, she had a feeling that all would be well.

"Then I say yes," Rodrigo de Vega answered, looking at Blythe to see if she also gave her blessing. She nodded. It was then that Thomas Bowen entered, his hat in his hands, the light from the sun casting a glow on the top of his shiny head. All eyes turned toward him and the room was suddenly hushed to a silence.

"I'm glad that you are feeling better, Heather," he said softly, looking from Rodrigo de Vega to Blythe and back again. It was clear by the sorrowful look in his eyes that he thought he had lost the woman whom he had taken to wive. "Hello, Rodrigo."

"You little weasel!" Rodrigo hissed. "I ought to—"

Blythe held up her hand. "Let me deal with this, Rodrigo. "Thomas has much to answer for, as well he knows."

Tears filled the merchant's eyes as he fell to his knees before Blythe. "Forgive me, wife. I did wrong, I know that now, but you were so lovely and I so besotted by you that I told but one small lie—"

"One small lie! You ruined three lives. Blythe's, Heather's, and my own," Rodrigo thundered, looking as if he would seek to skin Thomas Bowen and hang his carcass from the ceiling. "You told me that they were dead. Dead!"

Thomas bent his head in shame until his nose was nearly touching the rush-covered floor. "I know. I know. Think you that I do not know that I have lost everything now? Everything. It is punishment enough that I suffer at this moment." His eyes raised to Blythe's and Heather was stunned by the love which shone there. "You will leave me?"

Blythe was silent, letting Thomas feel the full force of his well-deserved retribution. He answered for her. "You will. I do not blame you. I have shown you little love these past years, though it *was* in my heart. How tragic that until this moment I did not realize that you are so very dear to me. I need you, Blythe. Please do not leave me. I would give up all my earthly possessions, my gold, my house, my cloth, if you would but stay and learn to forgive me. Forgive me. Please. I beg of you." Tears ran in rivulets down his fat cheeks.

"Oh, stop blubbering, Thomas," Blythe scolded, bending over him and wiping the tears away. "If it is forgiveness you want, you have it, though I cannot speak for Rodrigo or for Heather."

"I will never forgive you," Rodrigo answered. "You have taken all from me. What I cannot understand is how she can choose to stay with *you.*"

"Stay with me?" The merchant was upon his feet in an instant, hugging his wife to his massive chest. "Oh, you will not regret it. I love you so much."

Blythe pulled away. "But there will be some *changes* around here, dear husband." She cocked her head and winked in Heather's direction, only to see that Heather was oblivious of all that was taking place around her, kissing Richard with all the tenderness of her heart.

"I believe we should leave the young ones alone, no?" Rodrigo said. Without a backward glance, they all did just that, leaving the two lovers locked in each other's arms.

76

TABITHA HEARD THE tumult in the courtyard, heard Heather's voice welcoming old Perriwincle back, but she resisted the temptation to join in the merry-making. Rafael needed her by his side.

"What is going on, *señorita?*" he asked, straining his ears to the voices below.

"Perriwincle has returned, bringing the old witch woman with him. I heard him say that she can attest before Mary what a monster Hugh Seton really is."

"So our lovebirds will be free to fly away. I am happy for them." He leaned his head against the back of the chair, basking in the warmth of the sun. Soon he would be healed and then he would go away.

"Love is a very beautiful thing," she murmured, glancing at him and aching to have him hold her in his arms. She wanted to tell him that she loved him as Heather did Richard, but fearful that he might shun her, she did not say the words. But Rafael spoke, and what he said shattered all her dreams.

"You should find someone to love you, Señorita Tabitha. A lovely young woman should not spend her days alone."

"I am not alone," she said softly. "I have you to care for . . ." All her life Tabitha had considered herself plain and awkward until Rafael Mendosa had looked upon her with a smile; now his words brought a feeling of rejection. Little did she know of the love raging in his heart. He had grown to love this woman with the soft hands and the gentle voice. She was the woman he had always dreamed of finding, a woman to share his life with, a woman totally devoid of selfish vanity, who thought of others before herself. But he could not tell her. What if his love was not returned?

"Soon I will be gone."

"Gone." He had spoken the words that broke her heart. "Gone. Then truly I will be alone." She turned to him, meeting his eyes with a boldness that was rare for her. "And you think that I should find a man who befits my social station, is that it, Rafael? A baker or cobbler or tinker will do for the servant who is plain of face. But I tell you that they will not do. I may be humble of birth, I may not be pretty, but no one could love you more."

"You love me?" His voice was soft, belying the tumult in his breast.

"Yes." She turned away, fearing what he would say now. She had made a total fool of herself by telling him what was in her heart.

Rafael turned her around to face him, searching out the softness of her mouth. He could not deny the spark which flashed between them. He felt her love and reached out to it as a low moan came from his throat.

"I love you too, Tabitha," he said at last. "It was meant to be. We were meant to be. I have waited all my life for you. *Querida.*" His mouth swept across her cheek to the silky strands of her hair, and he buried his face in that soft treasure. It was in this embrace that Richard and Heather found them.

"Sorry, my friend," Richard said as he looked at the two lovers. "I meant not to intrude, only to tell you of our news. We are soon to be wed, Heather and I. Perhaps our marriage will not be the only one of this household." He flashed Rafael an approving grin. "Undine has confessed all, though I wish not to know the reason. It seems that the man who claimed to be my half-brother is not any kin of mine at all, but the illegitimate son of a gardener."

"Your gardener?" Rafael asked. "But why did he say . . . ?"

"Seton's mother had dreams of rising above her station and so she concocted a fantasy about a man who had shown her kindness, and thus told her son that he was the child of the lord of the manor. Undine was the midwife who delivered Seton and she knew the truth, yet she kept the secret well."

"But why?"

Richard shrugged his shoulders. "She lied to Seton all of these years to fan the flames of his hatred and make him a useful tool in her hands. It was an evil deed, but it worked well. And later when she came under the employ of Northumberland, they both could see how Seton's hatred of my father, of my family, could be used well. All this time Seton's hatred has been misdirected. It was not my father who shunned him, but the man whose foul deeds he acted upon who was his true enemy."

"And what of this charge that you are a traitor?" Rafael asked, holding Tabitha close.

"Perriwincle found two of Seton's men, the very ones who held me prisoner. They were comrades in the wars and Perriwincle has persuaded them to tell the truth of the matter. It was Seton who was traitor and not I."

Richard enfolded Heather into his arms. They had their entire lifetime to be together, many sunsets, many dawns, rain and sunshine. Love truly had conquered all.

Epilogue

November 1558

THE BELLS OF the nearby church pealed. The queen was dead, long live the new queen. Heather stood at the window of the manor in Norfolk, looking at the snow. It promised to be a hard winter this year; already it was unseasonably cold, with the frost in the early morn and the shivering, dazzling powder of white now touching the earth.

Had it really been four years since she had thought her life ended? It hardly seemed possible and yet it was. Four years. Four.

But I am happy, she thought. I can withstand any storm now that Richard and I are together. They were married now, with two little ones in the cradle. First had come little Anne, named after Heather's friend who had suffered martyrdom, and next had come the son Richard had so wanted—Edward, named for his uncle, who had also been a victim of others' treachery. Walking from the window, Heather peered down at their sleeping faces. Anne had a head of black hair and blue eyes like her father, while Edward seemed to be the image of Rodrigo, with Heather's gray eyes and red hair.

"My family," she heard Richard say, and turning around, welcomed him into her arms. Reaching down to touch the soft hair of their elder child, they said a prayer of thankfulness, remembering the events of the last years.

Undine had confessed that under Hugh Seton's orders she had poisoned not only Edlyn but also Edward VI. There were others who had testified to

Seton's treachery and villainy, and at last Mary Tudor had seen the truth, turning *from* the man as surely as she had turned *to* him. Richard had been given back his lands and Hugh Seton condemned for all his misdeeds. It was he who lost his life by hanging, and though Heather hated to see anyone suffer, when she remembered all that Seton had done because of his hatred, she had conceded that justice had been done after all. Matty had stepped forward to tell how kind Heather had always been to Edlyn, and Mary, who had once scorned Heather, had taken her once again to her bosom.

Again Heather heard the bells and felt a great sadness for the woman who had been queen. In many ways Mary had been a good queen. Her reign had begun with such hope but it had ended in disillusionment. Now she was gone. What would Elizabeth bring to England? Only time would tell. Heather wondered what would be written of Mary's reign. Would only the evil be recorded for posterity? Would none remember Mary's gentleness, her forgiveness in those early months? She had been by nature merciful until the rebellion which nearly took her life and caused so much heartache for everyone.

Heather felt Richard tighten his arms about her and looked into his eyes. "I was thinking about how happy Mary was to welcome Philip in that summer when we were pardoned and taken again to court. Remember?"

"How could I forget? The weather in England was dreadful, and when Philip landed I remember thinking that the pouring rain might be a bad omen somehow. Our new king was drenched to the bone as he reached Winchester. A tragic beginning to a sad marriage."

"Poor Mary. She was not to be as lucky as I. There was none of the love in Philip's eyes that you show to me. Queen or not, I pitied her." If it was a marriage of convenience as far as the new king was concerned, one look at Mary's face had proved that it was a matter of adoration for her. She had finally met her husband, a man from her mother's beloved country and therefore so much more precious to her, a dream come true. Married at last after a lonely life of suffering.

"Pity her? I suppose. And yet it is difficult for me to forget what she did. The burnings." Heather felt Richard's muscles tighten and remembered how tortured he had been. Two hundred and eighty-three had been burned in less than four years, and while he had been able to save many lives he still felt that on this matter he had been a failure. Some of the reformed faith had fled into exile, but many had stayed and died, those of humble origins as well as scholars and people of renown. What had prompted the renewed vigor of the burning of heretics? Was it because the queen thought herself with child and wanted the dynasty well secured? Or was it her zeal after restoring the pope once again as head of the English church? Would they ever really know for certain? And now Elizabeth was queen.

Heather picked up her son in her arms. Poor Mary, to have been denied this blessing, the wonder of motherhood. She had died childless, leaving England in the hands of the sister she had resented.

"Heather, let me hold my grandson," Blythe said softly, coming up behind them and taking the baby. The change in her mother was staggering. No longer meek and mild, she spoke her mind freely and was even known to disagree openly with Thomas upon occasion. As for Thomas, he was no more the overbearing and miserly man. Fearful lest he lose Blythe's love, he now treated her like the Queen of England herself. Nothing was too good for her. Where there had been only two servants, now there was a household staff of ten, as befitted their prosperity, he had said.

"He is going to be another Rodrigo," Blythe murmured, looking at the baby. "A charming man who will steal many hearts, eh, Richard?" She cradled the baby close to her breast as if remembering another baby, a time long ago.

Heather wondered if her mother ever regretted her decision to stay with Thomas and decided she had not. She was happy now and told Heather often that she would never have been happy in Spain even with Rodrigo. Perhaps she might have been happy in her youth, but she had made her home in England and was no longer an adventurer, but a settled matron. Rodrigo had returned to Spain, saddened by the fate which had torn him from the arms of the woman he loved, but happy to have found his daughter at last.

As if reading her daughter's mind, Blythe whispered, "I still love Rodrigo. He is your father and will always be the love of my youth, but I made the right choice. I am content."

"As am I," Heather said softly, looking into the eyes of her husband. She felt an overwhelming sense of peace and happiness. She had everything she had ever hoped and dreamed of. If only the new queen would not tear her husband from her arms and bring him far away to the court. "Richard . . ." He silenced her words with a kiss. Even after four years of marriage his very touch caused her heart to stir.

At last he pulled away and she was shaken by the passion she read in his eyes. "I know what you are thinking, my love. That Elizabeth will bid me to come to court. But have no fear on that score. I have served one queen faithfully and now it is my time to live my life in peace. No longer will I be the queen's rebel. My heart is here and will always be." The bells rang again and she knew in her heart that all would be well.

About the Author

Katherine Vickery lives in Boulder, Colorado, where she is an executive secretary for an aerospace firm as well as a professional vocalist. History has always been of interest to Katherine and is reflected in both her writing and her collection of 300 historically costumed dolls.

SIGNET (0451)

The Timeless Magic of Romance

☐ **DEVIL'S EMBRACE by Catherine Coulter.** For beautiful Cassandra Brougham, the seething city of Genoa seemed a world away from the great 18th-century estate where she was raised. It was here that she met Anthony, and became addicted to a wild and feverish ecstacy that would guide their hearts forever... (141989—$3.95)

☐ **LOVE'S BLAZING ECSTACY by Katherine Kramer.** When she saw the dangerous glitter in the Roman soldier's eyes, Wynne knew she was lost, and as his amber eyes caressed each soft, sensuous curve of her body, she found herself melting into his embrace... his hot, throbbing passion... In one wild, reckless moment of uncontrollable passion, Valerian conquered her body and soul. (133277—$3.95)

☐ **LADY SORCERESS by Patricia Rice.** The warmth of his mouth entrapped her moist lips, and he urged her to complete surrender. Could she deny the blazing desires of this hot-blooded English lord who had once protected her as a child and now sought to conquer her as a woman...? (136101—$3.95)

☐ **IN THIS SWEET LAND, Inga's Story, by Aola Vandergriff.** When blonde, beautiful Inga Johansson escaped from her nightmare marriage, she vowed to make a new life for herself among the ruined dreams and soaring hopes of the post-Civl War South... and as she struggled to rebuild her future, two men ignited her passion and divided her heart. (135849—$3.95)

*Prices slightly higher in Canada

Buy them at your local bookstore or use this convenient coupon for ordering.

NEW AMERICAN LIBRARY
P.O. Box 999, Bergenfield, New Jersey 07621

Please send me the books I have checked above. I am enclosing $________ (please add $1.00 to this order to cover postage and handling). Send check or money order—no cash or C.O.D.'s. Prices and numbers are subject to change without notice.

Name ______________________________

Address ______________________________

City____________ State____________ Zip Code________

Allow 4-6 weeks for delivery.
This offer is subject to withdrawal without notice.